King Daniel

GASPARILLA KING OF THE PIRATES

SUSAN WOLF JOHNSON

BALBOA
PRESS

A DIVISION OF HAY HOUSE

Balboa Press books may be ordered through booksellers or by contacting:

Balboa Press
A Division of Hay House
1663 Liberty Drive
Bloomington, IN 47403
www.balboapress.com
1 (877) 407-4847

Because of the dynamic nature of the Internet, any web addresses or links contained in this book may have changed since publication and may no longer be valid. The views expressed in this work are solely those of the author and do not necessarily reflect the views of the publisher, and the publisher hereby disclaims any responsibility for them.

This is a work of fiction. Names, characters, places, and incidents are the product of the author's imagination or are used fictitiously. Any resemblance to actual events, locals, or persons, living or dead, is coincidental.

Any people depicted in stock imagery provided by Thinkstock are models, and such images are being used for illustrative purposes only. Certain stock imagery © Thinkstock.

ISBN: 978-1-5043-5987-0 (sc)
ISBN: 978-1-5043-5986-3 (hc)
ISBN: 978-1-5043-5985-6 (e)

Library of Congress Control Number: 2016910151

Printed in the United States.

Balboa Press rev. date: 8/12/2016

In token of my appreciation and affection,
this book is dedicated

to

Thomas E. Johnson

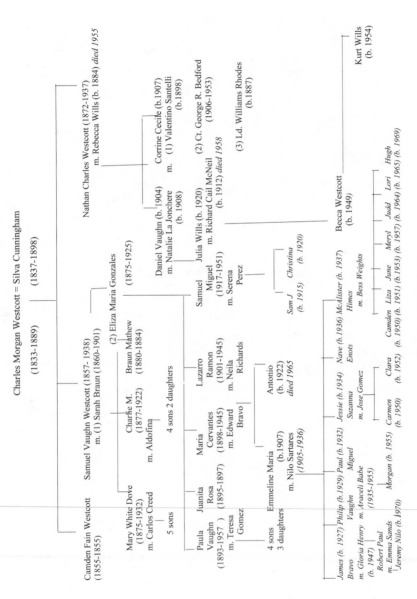

Westcott Family Tree

Look! High above a glittering calm
Of sea and sky and kingly sun,
She shines and smiles, and waves a palm—
And now we wish, thy will be done!

—Sidney Lanier

Contents

Acknowledgments

K_ING DANIEL_ IS DEDICATED TO my husband, Thomas E. Johnson, without whom this book would never have come into being. I also want to thank Lucinda Dixon Sullivan, Karen Brown, and Jean Kouwe for reading every draft of this novel. Their valuable insights and support have sustained me and the creation of this novel.

Heartfelt gratitude goes out to my nephew, Bryon Wolf, for his nautical expertise and valuable contribution to the water chapters of this book. For their intuitive gifts and guidance throughout this project, I thank Christel Hughes and Beth Hardin. In loving memory of Dennis Velasco, gratitude is given for his helpful knowledge concerning the drug-smuggling piracy on the Caribbean in the 1970's.

Special appreciation is extended to the following people who read the novel and offered their excitement and encouragement prior to publication: Lisa McCarthy, Barbara Casey, Susan Leavitt, Richard Kouwe, Louise Prairie, Laurin Farrior, Kathy Whitney, Lillian Joyce, and Jan Witte. Deep gratitude is offered to my editor, Dana Pierson, whose expertise and dedication to excellence overawes me. A warm thank you is offered to Bill Carson for the photos on the back cover of the dust jacket.

Grateful acknowledgement is made to the following 19th Century poets and song writers for excerpts from the following:

"A Seashore Grave To MJL" and "Stirrup Cup" by poet Sidney Lanier (1842-1881).

"When you and I Were Young, Maggie" written in 1864 by George Johnson.

"Child and Mother" by poet Eugene Field (1850-1895).

"Do Lord" Black Spiritual workday slave song (circa 1800).

Seminole chant—Song to bring a child into the world. Author anonymous.

Appreciation is extended to © Storybook Music (BMI) for the use of "I'm Your Captain" w&m by Mark Farner.

CHAPTER 1 ✳ The Queen's Party

To UNDERSTAND HOW THE DISAPPEARANCE of Daniel Westcott bewildered the people of Tampa Bay, you would have to know that the city was much smaller then. More like a sleepy town, Tampa sprawled out and yawned along the edge of the Hillsborough River. In 1972, the largest shipping port on the Sun Coast had yet to attract a major cruise line or an NFL team. Some historians claimed the town's slow growth and propensity to "keep to itself" could be traced back to the early 1930s and the failure of the Tampa Bay Hotel. Before that, beneath the hotel's soaring minarets, cupolas, and horseshoe arches, the palatial palace on the river had attracted well-heeled families who escaped northern winters to play golf and shoot quail on the verdant grounds that surrounded the hotel. After sumptuous meals, they strolled along the rambling verandahs. Once the Great Depression hit, the hotel was abandoned, even ghostlike. Some people claimed the town turned inward then.

In the summer of '72, before anyone knew Daniel Westcott was missing, Tampa's summer routines ran along in the usual ways. Picnics were prepared and packed to shell the beaches of Treasure Island or fish along the causeway. Days lengthened, stretched out by heat. In town, the hot, bright sun of early June sent children to play in sprinklers, while adults lingered in the shade of granddaddy oaks, sipping lemonade and anticipating the summer's one social highlight—the Gasparilla Queen's Party. This annual ball, hosted by the new queen's family, was the most exclusive event in the long line of Gasparilla festivities. It's important to note that it was the patrician families of Tampa who had dreamed up these amusements and scattered them across the calendar year. Their intent was to enhance the town's prosperity and to create a posh social niche for the founding members of the Gaspar Krewe and their families.

The grand town holiday, Gasparilla Day, was seeded in the glory years of the ill-fated hotel and was rooted deeply within the locals' imaginations. It came to full flower through the decades. Based on a mythical pirate and fashioned after New Orleans's Mardi Gras, Gasparilla thrilled the townspeople with an annual pirate fest that paraded down Bayshore Boulevard. Before Tampa hosted Super Bowl XVIII, the celebration was held on the first Monday of February. Banks closed, schools shut down, and businesses locked their doors for the day. Even the mail was held so everyone could enjoy the parade. From convertibles at the head of the motorcade, local celebrities waved as high school bands marched and played John Philip Sousa. Elaborate floats glided in the procession were identified as TECO, GTE, or Freedom Federal. But the most thrilling float—the one the townspeople most heartily cheered—was the royal float. Two thrones centered the moving pageantry and carried the king and queen of Gasparilla, who waved graciously to their loyal subjects. On that day, painted Gaspar pirates walked the parade route. They threw beads, fired blank ammunition from .38-caliber revolvers, and kept pace with the day's main event—heavy drinking. Everyone, young, old, and infirm, embraced the merry event. But the Queen's Party was held for krewe members only.

On the eve of June 10, Gaspar pirates escorted their ladies through the double doors of the Tampa Yacht Club. They could hear the orchestra playing, "Days of Wine and Roses," as the much-anticipated gala began. Women in elaborate gowns graced the ballroom. They toasted one another with grasshoppers and tequila sunrises, drinks as brightly colored as the gems around their necks and wrists. Costumed in plumed pirate hats, the men smoked cigars and downed Harvey Wallbangers. The french doors were open. Couples glided from the ballroom to the verandah outside to dance beneath the waning crescent moon. They waited patiently for their king. Attuned to his big-hearted laugh, they knew it would announce his arrival. At six foot three, Daniel stood above every crowd. With an impressive shock of black hair and a pair of curly eyebrows to match, he wouldn't be missed as he kissed his way across the ballroom or threw an arm across a pirate's shoulders. Despite his sixty-eight years, Daniel would dominate the dance floor in a light-footed foxtrot or a sassy swing. The Krewe of Gaspar drank, danced, and chatted, while the night ticked on. They danced until the moon disappeared behind the live oaks and until the band played its last song.

But King Daniel did not arrive.

Because Daniel was not found for almost a month, stories from that summer had taken on a curious twist. Passed on in ways that are difficult to trace, the details of what actually happened remain debatable, although the outcome was hard fact. A couple of pirates later swore that Daniel was headed for trouble in the worst way. Others said they never saw it coming. What everyone agreed was how the town rallied to help the Westcott family. After all, with Daniel missing, his wife, Natalie, was all but alone in that big house. She had an elderly family retainer there, but now the roles were reversed. Natalie had become Eula's caretaker. Eula's daughter, Niobe, worked there too, but her duties were focused on Natalie's daughter, Julia, whom most agreed was more than a little "touched" in the head.

At the time, Julia was in her late forties—and everyone knew that. At age twenty-two, she'd worn the queen's crown and ridden the float. She'd then married a man named Richard McNeil, who worked for Tampa Electric. He was, of course, a pirate in the krewe. Around the time their first child started school. Julia took to her bed. Some called it migraines. But wait—for the sake of clarity, we must return to the night of the Queen's Party and what happened then.

After the gala ended, pirates and ladies alike speculated about why Daniel would fail to attend his own Queen's Party. Perhaps he or Natalie or Julia was ill. Maybe something had happened to one of the grandchildren, who were mostly grown now. When phone calls to their home went unanswered, a few people drove by the Westcott Mansion on the Bayshore.

Their grand estate, one of the first to be built on the boulevard, had recently fallen into disrepair. Embarrassing as that may seem, in certain circles, the look was coveted. Much of the town's old wealth was dwindling; those in that circumstance took pride in the quiet beauty of a home's chipped and weathered features. They went so far as to scoff at the nouveau riche with their freshly painted soffits and shutters. The custom had become so widespread that pristine houses amid the lot of rundown homes created a checkerboard effect throughout the town. Outsiders puzzled by the phenomenon rightly concluded the neglect varied from a lack of resources, laziness, or at the time, grief. The war in Vietnam raged, and the town had lost more than its fair share of sons. The protest song by Country Joe and the Fish played on jukeboxes in local bars, the lyrics haunting: "Be the first one on your block to have your boy come home in a box." Washington was in upheaval—secrets prevailed. Within days, Nixon would break into the Watergate Hotel. By July, the "amnesty, abortion, and acid" presidential hopeful, George McGovern, would win the Democratic Party's nomination on his promise to end the combat.

But that night, the one we begin with, was peaceful in the West Florida town. Those who drove down the Bayshore, car windows open and night breezes rustling their hair, would say the Westcott Mansion looked lovely nestled on its sprawling lawns, aglow in starlight. The clean, architectural lines of the house created a symmetry that pleased the eye. The white pillars, black shutters, rose-covered trellises, and its side-yard fountain whispered privilege. Here was a home that shielded it residents from ordinary strife. Once the passersby saw the goodness of the house, any doubts concerning Daniel were dismissed. Only a few noticed the light in an upstairs window. No one thought about Julia, but leaning against the window frame, watching headlights glide down the Bayshore, she thought about them.

"Julia! Julia! Julia!"

That's what she heard. Their voices rushed in three or four at a time, the sounds tuneless and harsh. She covered her ears and looked out the window to the Hillsborough Bay, where the water was smooth and unruffled and glistening in the starlight. Had anyone expected Julia would attend the Queen's Party tonight? Earlier, she'd listened for her father's footfall on the stairs and for her mother to follow him into her bedroom.

"Come!" she was sure they would beg. They would insist it was her duty now that her father was king. Julia had thought about it for a moment. If going would stop the clamoring in her head, she would do it—but her parents did not come to her room and ask the question.

Julia touched the sleeve of her silk blouse and for a moment was startled. When had she dressed? After Niobe brought up her dinner tray? Or was it before? She backed away from the window and twisted the button on her sleeve until it wound up taut, snapped, and rolled across the polished oak floor. It disappeared under the bed, hidden, like a pearl. Julia laughed. *Of course!* She remembered now. There was a tray on the bed with a half-eaten omelet. The window was open to the hot evening, and Niobe was at the door.

"Let me get that," Niobe had said, hooking the back of Julia's skirt. "And this." She pulled a fuchsia scarf from the top drawer of the dresser and tied it around Julia's waist. Niobe urged her to the full-length mirror. "Ain't no one prettier than you tonight," she'd said.

Julia sat in the Queen Anne chair that looked out over the water toward Davis Island and downtown Tampa. The slightest sliver of a balsamic moon rose across the bay while the wind kicked up. The water churned the color of India ink. It was quiet now, quiet enough to hear her heart beat. She wondered if it was unusual to hear the soft-pedaled thump of one's own heart, buried as it was in muscle and bone. She realized that hers was connected directly to her brain, where it pulsed like the measured beat of a metronome. She leaned back in the chair and hummed.

> I walked to the hill today, Dear Maggie
> To watch the scene below;
> The creek and the creaking old mill, my Maggie,
> As we used to long ago.

Suddenly she sat up. With the rhythm in her brain, she counted back the nights. One or two? Only one. Yes, she was sure. Julia pressed her hands to her knees, felt them hard and round beneath the satin skirt. The night before last, she'd been sleeping. She had been in bed when she heard her father tramp down the stairs and her mother shout. She'd climbed slowly from the bed and then edged to the door and cracked it open.

"You'll not go out tonight!" her mother had cried. (Or was it a seagull?) And then the first shot wheeled through the house. She'd stepped down the corridor. She had not yet reached the stairs when she heard the second blast. She stopped and waited. Half-expecting the final shot that came with a blur of smoke, she leaned into the stairwell to see her father stagger down the steps and stumble out the front door while her mother stood in the foyer holding the pistol.

Julia fell back in the chair and hummed the tune again. No one saw her on the stairs that night. No one ever sees her. *Clever girl.* She realized, of course, the whole thing could've been a dream. God knows she'd had worse. Still, the fact remained that Daniel was missing. She swept a hand over her hair, which was coarse and dry, now threaded with gray. She tugged the ends. Julia hadn't dared to ask what had happened to him, and no one had told her—not Eula, Niobe, or her mother. She switched the light off next to her chair and sat in the dark. But what if her mother had killed him? Julia twisted a lock of hair around her forefinger. Who thought she was good at keeping secrets? Julia laughed. Not a team of twenty horses could drag it from her. But what would she do if her father was gone?

She folded her hands to ponder the question. First she would separate the chatter in her head, listening closely for the voices of her children.

But where were they?

"Where?" She said it out loud. She didn't always recognize them, especially when they bombarded her at once. But she could guess. She thought the low, whispery voice belonged to the child she never knew, while the abandoned one howled and wailed like a small animal caught in a thicket. She thought of the one who called her sweetly *Mama*, the daughter who used to crawl onto her lap and press gummy lips against her ear, whispering, *"I love you, I love you!"* To this child she struggled to answer, "It is not as it seems."

Julia stretched her hands wide. Her long fingers slipped over the arms of the Queen Anne chair. If her father was gone, she didn't have to wait anymore. She could call *them*. Each of her children. The first one, the second, and third. In sequence, like those shots fired up the staircase. She called them home—the one she did not know, the one she'd shunned, and the one she sacrificed her life for.

CHAPTER 2 ❋ A Wild Goose Chase

Nobody knew Becca McNeil was coming into town, and that's just the way she wanted it. At twenty-one, she'd left Georgetown University to pursue a career on Broadway. That was two years ago, and so far, it hadn't worked out. The night after the Queen's Party, she'd been seen running down the Bayshore, barely recognizable with her hair wild behind her. Rumor had it she'd come home because Daniel was missing, but that was not the case. She came home for one reason: to get money. Becca was Julia and Richard's firstborn, a lively, round-faced cherub with auburn ringlets and a splash of freckles across her nose. At the time, they lived with Daniel and Natalie in the Westcott Mansion. Why the young family didn't move into a house of their own remained a puzzle, but when Julia took to her bed and Richard died shortly after the birth of their son, everyone thought it best the children were settled under the Westcott roof. When Becca started stuttering (a shameful defect in those days), the parents at Gorrie Elementary scolded their children for mimicking her (even while they, the grown-ups, gossiped about Julia's absence at PTA meetings). In spite of Natalie's efforts, Becca grew up sullen and unable to look anyone in the eye. But on Sundays when she belted out, "The Old Rugged Cross," from the church choir, no one could deny she possessed a voice as rich and buoyant as any heard in those parts.

The evening following the Queen's Party, only a few cars passed down Bayshore Boulevard. To Becca, who pulled up in a cab, the Westcott Mansion looked dismal. The eaves were so burdened with soggy magnolia leaves, live oak buds, and twigs that they sagged in places. Standing on the front porch, she sucked in the muggy air and held it for a moment. She knew she would have to explain (yet again) why she had missed her grandfather's coronation in February. Becca had an answer for that. She'd committed to a war protest. But the sooner she could get her granddad alone to ask for the money, the easier she would sleep. He wouldn't ask questions like Nattie, who would interrogate her. She couldn't take that chance, not now. A girl in trouble, she halted on the stairs and pushed her chin out. The resolve she'd felt in New York to end the baby's life felt shaky as she faced the front door of her childhood home. She knocked. When no one answered, she tried the latch; it was unlocked. That should've been her first clue.

"Nattie!" Becca called. She dragged her suitcase over the threshold and into the foyer. The dank odor of the house hit her with its foul breath. She hadn't remembered that. Instead of closing the door, she wedged the ceramic doorstop flat against the bottom to hold it open. The gamy smell of the bay was better than the mustiness inside the house. She called up the stairs. "Granddad, I'm home!" Then she scanned the living room with its arrangement of empty chairs, the family portraits decorating the walls.

She set her suitcase at the bottom step and walked down the dark corridor just past the elevator. From the kitchen, she heard her grandmother's voice talking high and fast. "How're you going to explain this?" her grandmother was shouting.

Becca pushed the door open. Inside the sinks were polished white, and the counters were cleared except for a half piece of banana cake lying on a paper napkin next to the coffeepot. She hurried past the kitchen table, around the captain's chairs, to the counter, where her grandmother sat propped on a stool. Her silver hair fell in wisps from a disheveled bun that hung lopsided at the back of her head. Becca peered around the kitchen. "Who're you talking to?"

Natalie's eyes gazed up, watery and blank. "What? What?"

Becca picked up her grandmother's hand. The palm was damp, sticky as warm dough. "Where's Granddad?" When Natalie didn't answer, didn't squeeze Becca's hand, or acknowledge her presence, she gripped her grandmother's shoulders and shook her a little.

Natalie blinked a few times. Then, as if seeing her granddaughter for the first time, she drew Becca into her arms. "You're home?" she asked.

"I wanted to surprise you."

"You did. Is something wrong?" She took Becca's hands into her own and frowned. "You're too thin. And your hair's dry." She pinched a lock between her fingers. "You're not eating." Natalie's usual drawl, sweet and thick as honey, sounded raspy.

Becca eyed her grandmother, whose face was drawn and pale. Immediately Becca worried about her mother. "Is Mother well?" she asked.

"She's fine," Natalie said and stood up to put the kettle on the stove. "Eula's up with her now. Niobe has the day off." Becca followed her, relieved her grandmother's attention had been diverted away from her. She unhooked two teacups from the shelf. "Go up and see her," Natalie said. "She'll be pleased."

"I will. But where's Granddad?"

"Not here." Natalie's hand trembled as she filled the kettle with water. "He walked out," Natalie said and pressed her fingers to her mouth. "Two nights ago."

Becca had not expected that. She set the cups on the counter. Her grandfather had probably jumped on one those gambling junkets. He could be gone for days. "You haven't heard from him?"

Natalie shook her head. "We missed the Queen's Party last night." It came out a whisper.

Becca opened her mouth and then shut it again. For many years, her grandfather had served the Krewe of Gaspar. He chaired the hospital guild, the Cutthroat Chorus, and once he had the crown stripped from him before the coronation, but he'd never missed a Queen's Party. Certainly he would *never* miss his own. "He would never," Becca said. Natalie gazed down at the floor, wringing her hands like an old dish rag. "Have you called the police?" Becca asked. She swept a piece of hair from her grandmother's forehead. "He could be in trouble."

Natalie glanced up, her eyes wide. "We can't call the police and have reporters coming around here. He's king now."

Becca studied Nattie and knew her grandmother was thinking about the Yorketown scandal and how that had almost ruined Daniel's chance of ever being crowned king. "Let me call," she said.

The teakettle whistled on the stove, and Becca hurried to turn off the heat. She poured water into a porcelain pot, keeping one eye on Natalie, who picked bits of lint off her skirt. From the vacant gaze on her grandmother's face, Becca knew not only would she have to deal with the police, she also knew if her grandfather didn't show up by tomorrow, she wouldn't get the money in time. Becca guessed Nattie didn't have cash on hand, plus she didn't dare ask. As desperate as she felt, Becca worried she might slip and tell Nattie the truth. Besides, her grandmother had a way of seeing right through her. *Family X-ray*, Becca thought. Nattie had already figured out she didn't feel well. Next her grandmother would see the truth.

Becca carried the teapot to the counter and filled Natalie's cup. "The police will want to know what time Granddad left. Where he was going?"

Natalie twisted her hands together again. "I can't remember."

Becca gave her grandmother's shoulders a heartening squeeze. "All right. Have your tea." Becca headed toward the door but stopped before opening it. "Does Mother know?"

Natalie added sugar and swirled the spoon in her cup. "Only Eula."

In the foyer, dusk had fallen in a gray mist. As Becca rounded the corner of the east hall, she knew that either the tide had come in or the wind had shifted. The breeze off the bay was sweet, heavy with the scent of confederate jasmine. She waded through it, the air moist against her skin. Once in the living room, she picked up the phone. She tried to remember the name of the police chief who had let Daniel out on bail after Yorketown had him arrested for allegedly inflating the company's profits. She knew the name was Spanish—Santos, Soto? No—Salazar. She waited for the operator to dial the number. When a woman answered, she asked for him.

When Feo Salazar happened to be at the precinct on a Sunday evening, it might have been luck or fate. This year, for the first time, Spanish Americans had been given a spot in the Gasparilla Parade. Salazar was the founder of the new krewe—the Krewe of SantY'ago. He had worked closely with the Gaspar Krewe to coordinate the first annual Knight's Parade in Ybor City. A historic Tampa neighborhood, Ybor was located just northeast of downtown. Founded in the 1880s by cigar manufacturers, it was populated by hundreds of immigrants, mainly from Cuba, Spain, and Italy. The quaint town was known for its ethnic clubs, elaborate brick buildings, and hand-rolled cigars.

In short order, Salazar told Becca he already knew Daniel had missed his Queen's Party. Then he questioned her. "Your grandfather walked out two nights ago?"

Becca told him they were worried.

"Rightly so," he answered. Had it not been for the ball, Salazar—knowing Daniel's reputation—would have chuckled and asked Becca to sit tight for a couple of days. Instead he felt the urgency and promised to get right on it.

Becca hung up the phone and sank into the yellow armchair. If Granddad didn't come home tonight, she'd just squandered the last of her money on a wild goose chase home. She struggled to come up with another option. Becca didn't hear Natalie shuffle into the foyer. Her grandmother now stood at the edge of the living room, peering in. "You look sick, child," she said with a scrutiny that sent shivers up Becca's neck. She studied her own hands. She didn't dare meet her grandmother's eyes.

From the top of the stairs, Eula called down to the living room. "Miss Natalie? Julia's asking for you."

Becca jumped up, eager to get away. "I'll go," she said. "You rest." She helped Natalie into the chair, fluffing the pillows behind her. Then she turned toward the stairs, leaving her grandmother shadowed in gray light.

Becca gripped the banister and climbed the steps slowly. The runner beneath her feet felt worn, even thinner than she remembered. She noticed the faded walls, the dull sheen of the banister. After so many months away, the house felt different, more dark than luxurious with its brocade draperies and Oriental rugs. Becca ran her hand along the railing. The quality of its air, the sense of tone and texture had changed. As she rounded the first landing, Becca carried herself as carefully as a cup of liquid.

"Miss Becca?" Eula called. "Is that you, honey?" She flipped on the hall light.

Becca raced up the last few steps and almost toppled into Eula's arms. For a moment, while Eula asked about her "singing business" and why she'd come home, Becca clung to the old woman and the musky scent of her skin. Her hair had turned white, and it was wound in a thick braid across her head. Her unusually large hands cupped Becca's face.

"Mr. Dan?" Eula squinted down the hall and then turned back to Becca. The old woman's pupils were clouded, murky white. "I wouldn't say a thing to your Nattie, but don't you know he's up to no good." Eula puffed her cheeks out like she did when she was nervous. "And him Gasparilla King now. I'd give my little pinky to know what he's up to." She pinched the end of Becca's chin. "But don't go fretting about it. Old tomcats ain't rid of easy. And it's burden enough 'round here with Miss Natalie moping and your brother calling every other hour."

"Kurt's calling?" she asked.

Eula's eyes rolled. "Out of the blue!" she said. "Looking for Mr. Dan. Just like you coming home. This whole household turned topsy-turvy, except your mama up here."

"Does Kurt know?"

"No, ma'am," Eula said. "Miss Natalie keeps telling him his granddad's out." She crossed her big hands over her chest. "And I'm praying Mr. Dan's home soon. Lordy knows we're all too wearied-out for anymore of his mischief."

Becca peered down the hall. "And Mother?"

Sadness shadowed Eula's face. "Like a butterfly in a web." She squeezed Becca's arm. "But you go on up. She'll be surprised to see you, child."

Julia sat in her chair overlooking the bay, her hands folded in her lap as her eyes stared out over the water.

"Mother?"

Julia quivered, turned quickly toward the door, and then blinked as if to clear her vision.

"It's me, Mama."

Julia looked up with her beautiful, ruined face and hypnotic eyes dulled by the pills on her bedside table. "You're here?"

Becca knelt beside her chair. "I came to visit." She touched her mother's arm. Julia flinched. She drew her silk robe tighter around her body, eyes focused beyond the window, to the lights flashing across the bay. "Stars," she whispered, "three in a row." Then talking to the space beneath the window, she said, "This is my daughter. Isn't she beautiful? Isn't she just as I said she would be?"

"Mother, listen." Becca pulled an ottoman close to her mother's chair. In slow, careful sentences, she told her about the apartment in SoHo, how she grew sunflowers on the miniature balcony in the summer and strung white lights in winter.

"And you're home?" her mother asked.

"For a while."

Julia gripped the sides of her chair. "Only for a short time? Not to stay?"

"No."

"Do you think that's all right?" Julia asked, staring at the space beneath the window. "It might be, but then—"

"Mother, look at me. It's all right."

"Do you think it's safe?"

Becca stood up, dizzy with her mother's maddening questions. "I don't know," she said and gripped the back of the chair. She realized since she'd been in New York, she felt safer walking the Village after midnight, riding the subway alone, or inviting a stranger home than she did now, standing next to her mother. She was afraid to touch her, to feel her body cringe, or listen as she talked to the space beneath the window. Becca inched backward toward the door. She fumbled for the glass knob, turned it noiselessly, and then eased herself out of the room.

The light down the hall cast Becca's shadow. She moved toward the gigantic version of herself, watching as it crept up the wall and onto the ceiling. The closer she came to the staircase, the more her breath quickened as if her lungs too had begun to contract. She took the steps methodically. When she reached the second landing, she saw Natalie asleep in the yellow armchair. At the bottom of the stairs, Becca hurried across the foyer to the front door and stepped onto the porch. She darted down the steps and crossed the walkway to the Bayshore.

The street was deserted on a Sunday evening. The moonless night cast no shadows over the bay; a lone pelican swept across the water. White balustrades aglow in the streetlights lined the boulevard. Becca looked up and down the sidewalk, which was empty except for a couple of joggers headed downtown. The muggy darkness felt eerie around her, but she took a deep breath and started walking toward Howard Avenue. If her grandfather didn't show up soon, she would have to sublet her apartment, and this would be her home once again. At least for a while.

Becca peered out over the water. When she picked up her pace, her ballet flats clicked along the concrete. A sweat broke over her body as she began to sprint. The thought of returning to the Westcott Mansion scared her more than having an abortion. When she'd left three years ago, she vowed never to return (except for brief visits). Now the town felt alien to her, sinister with the Spanish moss swaying like cobwebs from the live oaks. She pushed her legs to run harder, and her skirt ripped at the seam. The faster she ran, the more the lights on Ballast Point swirled like kaleidoscopes in the distance. While her feet pounded the sidewalk and her arms pumped the air, her heart took off flapping like a captive bird. She couldn't stop, not while her body pressed forward and her chest burned. In that moment, she was determined to outrun her past. She ran until the pounding of her heart drowned out all noises, until all sense of guilt disappeared into the moonless night. She ran until a sharp jerk on her arm spun her to a halt.

A toothless man with matted hair and dirty hands grabbed her. "Heh! What's the hurry!"

She squinted against the glare of the streetlight, shoved her hand into her skirt pocket, and pulled out a subway token. The movement distracted him, and Becca yanked free. She took off running across the northbound lanes of traffic, dodging a car that swerved and honked. Once on the median, she slipped behind a sable palm and dropped the token back into her pocket. Still panting, Becca felt the adrenaline rush. From behind the tree, she could see the bum on the sidewalk grinning, one hand raised above his eyes to block the lamplight overhead. She turned to cross the southbound lanes of the Bayshore when she was stopped by a dark-haired man who had blocked her path with his car.

"Becca? Becca McNeil?"

She stepped back.

"I didn't mean to frighten you." He pointed across the street to her assailant. "He grabbed you."

Becca laid one hand against the palm tree, in case she needed it to propel her into a run. "Who are you?"

"Victor Ramirez," he said. "You went to Plant."

For a moment Becca felt disoriented, caught between the threat of the bum and this man who claimed to know her from high school. She glanced over her shoulder at the sidewalk where the toothless man had vanished. Victor offered her a ride. A bus barreled past them, headed toward downtown. She didn't want to go home. "I'm meeting someone on Kennedy," she lied.

"Good," Victor said. "My car's right here." He pointed to the Camaro, parked alongside the walkway. "You shouldn't be out here alone at night. People have gotten hurt." He ushered her toward the car and opened the passenger door. "I'll take you there."

Once in the car, Becca noticed his double-breasted suit and paisley tie. Self-consciously, she wiped the sweat from her face with the bottom edge of her blouse. Then she twisted her hair, which had clumped in wet strings, into a knot behind her head.

"You sure you're all right?" Victor asked.

She nodded, but tears welled in her eyes, threatening to spill. Not because she'd almost been mugged, but rather, riding in this stranger's car, she felt exposed. The protective mask she'd been hiding behind had started to crack.

When Victor crossed the Kennedy Bridge, Becca asked him to pull over.

"You can't get out here," he said.

She pointed to the Falk Theater. "I'm meeting someone over there."

"I don't see anyone. I'll wait."

When he stopped, Becca reached for the door handle and jumped out.

The neon lights on Kennedy illuminated the boulevard in reds, blues, and purples. Becca kept her pace even and walked along the street edge. She avoided the empty shops where winos slept in doorways. She'd held back the tears as long as she could, but the tears streamed down her face. After passing the blood bank and the Falk Theater, Becca was about to enter the Porpoise Lounge, when she spotted Victor's silver Camaro parked across the street. She kept walking until she came upon a group of teenagers who were standing outside a tattoo parlor. She read the neon sign flashing in the window: The Screaming Blue Eagle. Beneath that she read the advertisement hand-painted in gold acrylic across the top: *We Do It Right the First Time*. The words stung Becca. She hadn't done it right yet. She wiped her eyes with the back of her hand. The fear that swept through her on the Bayshore had somehow dismantled her defenses. With her senses heightened, she kept her eyes peeled on the passersby. She was wary now. When she turned around and saw the Camaro still waiting, she stepped into the entrance of the shop.

The brass doorknob felt slick beneath her hand. Becca pushed the door open, and glass bells jingled melodiously through the darkened shop. She walked inside. The parlor walls were painted crimson, and a myriad of sheer drapes fell onto an elaborately carved table. It looked like a pagan altar. Perched on top was a statue of a blue eagle, curiously hooded in a brown flannel cape. The shop smelled of incense and smoke and vaguely of rotting fish.

Becca shoved her hands into her pockets and wandered through the shop, up to a counter-height table. There she leafed through a design book filled with butterflies, wolves' heads, peace symbols, and swastikas. The drawings reminded her of her brother's collection of tattoo designs that he'd kept hidden in the bottom desk drawer next to his bed. Just the thought of Kurt made her stomach squirm. The old guilt wormed its way through her middle, where it mixed with nausea. Becca knew it wasn't her fault that their mother had refused to love him, refused to look at him, but she couldn't help but feel responsible.

Before Granddad sent him away to rehab in Idaho, Kurt had threatened to tattoo his arms and back and the space beneath his chin. Her first Christmas home from Georgetown, he'd shown Becca his notebook of tattoos, and she'd studied each one. She'd traced the round, silent mouth on Munch's "The Scream" with her index finger, imagined the skull and crossbones etched onto her brother's cheek, and puzzled over the muted post-horn he'd copied from a Thomas Pynchon novel. Of all the designs, the post-horn intrigued her the most. Sitting on Kurt's bed, the notebook open across her lap, she'd asked him what the symbol meant.

"Inamorati Anonymous," he'd said. "It's a club that denounces love." He pointed to the inside of his left wrist. "I'm going to have it tattooed right here."

Becca leaned against the counter. When she heard a rustle behind her, she whirled around. A man draped in a similar brown cape as the one shrouding the eagle limped into the room, leaning heavily on a black cane. She held out her hand. "I'm Becca."

The man didn't accept her hand but bowed instead—a deep, humble bow that made her uneasy. "Eliot," he said. He motioned for her to sit on the stool next to the counter. Then, hobbling in circles around her, he pointed at her with a blackened index finger tattooed to look like the wing of a bird, like all his other fingers, except the thumb, which was the beak. He stared at her. His face had no tattoos, which Becca believed must be the only ink-free flesh left on his body.

She picked up a pen lying on the counter. She couldn't remember exactly what the muted post-horn looked like, but she did her best and drew the symbol onto a piece of scratch paper. Then she handed it to Eliot.

"Are you sure you want this?" he questioned her not politely or as a matter of fact, his words designed to sear into her. He scanned her face, as if he knew she was incapable of making a decision as permanent as a tattoo.

Before Becca could defend her choice, Eliot raised his hand to silence her. "It's enough you've picked it." With the cape still draped over his shoulders, he tottered across the room to a cabinet, where he drew out a covered tray. "Something to drink?"

Becca shook her head. He didn't even look up when she blurted out that the post-horn had many meanings for her, more than she could tell him.

"Good, good," he said. He set the wooden tray on the counter and flipped off the top. The cars buzzed down Kennedy Boulevard, causing the needles to tremble. He pulled up a stool next to her and told her it would hurt some.

She sat close and watched him roll up his shirt sleeves with his birdlike hands. His arms were covered with the tails of animals: rat tails, horse tails, and those of a squirrel, a dog, a rabbit, a fox, and a cat. It startled her to see, in the middle of his right forearm, a snake with ruby eyes, its mouth open and swallowing its tail so it connected in a circle.

Becca laid her arm on the table and told the tattoo artist she was not afraid. Not of needles. "Or pain," she said. Years ago, she had given up certain fears, consciously and in stages. As a child, she'd lie in bed determined not to tremble when Granddad came home late, howling drunk and crawling up the stairs; she vowed never to run and hide when she stuttered, the words stuck like taffy against her teeth; and after her father died, she refused to cry when awakened by her mother screaming in the night. Instead Becca closed her eyes and slipped off to an imaginary world of wood fairies and leprechauns. Now she realized how well her past had served her. Last week in New York, when she walked up to the women's clinic lined with protestors who spit on her and called her a whore, she put her head down and pushed through their threats of hell and damnation as easily as if she were strolling through a grassy knoll.

"Where would you like the tattoo?" Eliot asked. He chose a pen from the tray. Becca flipped her arm over and pointed to the inside of her left wrist. He picked up a needle. With a slow, steady hand, he began burnishing the post-horn into her arm. As Eliot slowly drew the bell of the small bugle onto her flesh, the ruby eyes of the snake glittered in the midst of the blue-black tails on his forearm. The buzzing needles set off an eerie melody in her head, and the snake's eyes seemed to dance and sing, *Decorate your body. It's your body. It's your body.* The rhythm of the chanting, together with the snake's eyes and the piercing of her flesh dizzied her. She must have looked sick, for the tattooist stopped his work and waved a smoking stick of incense above her head.

"You all right?"

She nodded, but a thick nausea rose from her gut, pulsed up through her middle, and lodged in her throat. She imagined the baby growing inside of her, Adam oblivious. He was too involved with his new girlfriend to care about what was happening to her. Still she refused to tell him or to go crawling back. Becca gazed down at her wrist. She would be like the post-horn—muted. Adam would never know the baby existed.

When Eliot realized she'd regained her balance, he repositioned the needle. This time he moved quickly. Becca watched his forearm pulse, and the snake's eyes began again to dance. She heard the snake hum *It's your body, it's your body, it's your body* in a slow, all-pervading voice. As comforting as the voice felt, Becca realized this was not the world she'd escaped to in her childhood. Here she was afraid.

In that moment, a luminous energy filled her. This brilliance shimmered, welled up in the darkness to permeate her entire being. She was all but paralyzed by her desire to be still, to allow the energy to race through her body undisturbed. By the time Eliot finished, she had accepted the snake's voice as both real (because she'd heard it) and unreal (because somehow the voice had communicated without words).

Becca gazed down at her wrist on the table. The post-horn with its muted bell was burnished into her flesh, an inch long, a half inch wide, and not bluish like the tattooist's animal tails, but a distinct black.

"It may fade," Eliot said to her as she searched her pockets for cash, "but it won't disintegrate."

Outside the shop, Becca touched Eliot's work. The tattoo burned with a cottony numbness. She wondered why he'd not objected to the ridiculous pay. He just took the subway token and waved her out the door. Walking back toward the bridge, she spotted the Camaro parked on the corner of Kennedy and Hyde Park. When Victor saw her, he called to her. Becca couldn't believe he'd waited for her. It must have been an hour or more. She peered down Kennedy toward the Bayshore. She took a few steps but then turned around and walked back toward the car, knowing she was in the part of town where you took whatever you could get.

CHAPTER 3 ❋ Child of Mine

JULIA HAD AWAKENED BEFORE THE sun. She'd lain in bed and hummed
the poem she'd set to music years ago. "A Mama's Song," she'd called it.
To the child she never knew. She turned over and flung the pillow over
her head. *Years have passed by now,* she thought. But that's not too long to
wait, not for a child. Beneath the pillow, she sang the song again. Softly,
muffled.

> O Mother-my-Love, if you give me your hand,
> And go where I ask you to wander,
> I will lead you away to a beautiful land,
> The dreamland that's waiting out yonder.

"Get up now, Miss Julia!" Niobe burst through the door. "You know
you supposed to get out of that bed and dress yourself every day."

Julia peeked out from under the pillow and pulled the coverlet up
under her chin. She watched Niobe open the curtains with a sweep of her
hand. "Looky here," Niobe said. "All sunshine and blue sky." She turned
back toward the bed and pressed her hands against her hips. "And you
giving me fits. Don't you know I got things to do?" She picked up Julia's
robe from the Queen Anne chair and shook it twice. "Miss Natalie thinks
I got ten hands, while God gave everyone else two. 'Sweep the pantry,' she
says. 'Just a speck of flour will bring the bugs.' Then she tells me to wipe
down the fridge, inside and out. 'And if it don't look like rain, Niobe, hang

those sheets out to dry, 'cause fresh air keeps them germs away.'" She folded Julia's robe over her arm. "And that's only the beginning. By afternoon, she'll want the front porch scrubbed, an—"

"Where is she?" Julia asked.

Niobe looked up. "Your mama's downstairs."

"No. Where's Becca?"

"Ah, huh! So that's what's rattling you this morning." Niobe walked across the room to hang up the robe. "Well, you can roll out of that bed right now, 'cause Miss Becca's in New York City getting things settled. And then she's coming back."

Julia sat up in bed. "To stay?"

Niobe knitted her eyebrows. "Well, I don't know about that singing job up there. And Lordy knows she's got big dreams. But Miss Natalie said to get her room ready 'cause she's coming home for a while."

Julia leaned back against the pillows. "But why?"

Niobe laughed. "Now that's some question. She's your girl! Ain't you happy about that?" She pulled back Julia's coverlet. "I know you are. So get up."

Julia swung her legs over the side of the bed while Niobe hurried to the closet to pick out the day's clothes. Julia peered down at her bare feet, pearl white against the oak floor. She squeezed her hands together. *The first one,* she thought. Becca was the first child to come home.

CHAPTER 4 ✳ New York City

Wᴴɪʟᴇ ᴀ ʜᴀɴᴅꜰᴜʟ ᴏꜰ Tᴀᴍᴘᴀ businessmen flew to New York regularly, most people in town knew precious little about the Big Apple, and they didn't care. What they loved to hear were jokes about the Yankee town and the quirky laws there—a fine of $25 can be levied for flirting, slippers are not to be worn after 10:00 p.m., and the penalty for jumping off a building is death. They also liked to imagine what would happen if everyone flushed their toilets at the same time. But having lived in the city for two years, Becca took it seriously. Besides her night gig at the Club 100, she'd joined a feminist group that published a weekly pamphlet calling for reproductive freedom and equal pay for women. She'd become fascinated with Gloria Steinem when she learned Steinem's mother had suffered a nervous breakdown when Gloria was only three. Like Julia, Gloria's mother never recovered. When Becca had learned she was pregnant, she confided to a friend in the group, who told her that Steinem had also conceived a child out of wedlock and had an abortion in London. It was then Becca decided she had a new role model and would follow her into a new world. All she needed was the money.

On the second floor of the Club 100, Becca sat outside Pug Kismet's dingy office, waiting for him to finish up with the Smirnoff distributer. Even through the closed door, she could hear his nasally voice dickering with the seller to lower his price. "This club ticks on alcohol," he raved. "I guarantee you twenty cases a week. Isn't that worth something?" Becca chewed what was left of her thumbnail, biting it to the quick until she tasted the metallic tang of blood on her tongue. Outside, an ambulance roared down Twenty-Third Street toward Bellevue. She folded her hands across her stomach, worried she might get sick again. When the siren faded, the door opened. Kismet walked out with the rep and slapped the middle of his back. "With any luck, we'll need twenty-five cases next month." He glared down at Becca, eyed her as the salesman disappeared through the elevator door. "Miss McNeil," he said. "Did you forget something?"

Becca shook her head. "I've got a proposition for you."

Kismet's eyes grew wide in his pockmarked face. "You'd better come in."

Becca followed him into the office and closed the door behind her. Kismet sat down behind his desk and knocked back the last of the scotch in his glass. "So, get to the point."

The room was stuffy, riddled with the stench of soured liquor and stale cigar smoke. A queasiness rose in her stomach. She sat down in the fold-out chair across from him. "I need money."

He pulled out a bottle of Dewar's from his bottom drawer and refilled his glass. "I don't have any work for you." He raised the drink to his mouth and wet his lips. "That's why I fired you."

She leaned forward in her chair. "But I'd work for half."

Kismet folded his hands and rested them on the desk. "You don't look like a beggar," he said. "What's up?"

Becca stared down at her lap. "I've got debts."

"No family?"

She took a deep breath. "My family's in trouble. In fact, I have to go home in a couple of days. But if you could lend me the money, when I get back, I'll work it off for half or even less."

Kismet leaned back in the chair, balancing on the hind legs. A sudden smirk edged the corners of his mouth. "How much do you need?"

Becca blurted out, "Eight hundred."

Kismet lurched forward, and the chair's front legs crashed to the floor. "That's a helluva lot of singing!" He ran a yellowed hand, stained from smoking, through a mat of brown hair that screamed dyed. "Do I look dumb? You want eight hundred bucks so you can run home?" He shook his head and glared at her. "Who d'you think I am, your fairy fucking godfather?"

Becca smiled at the irony of that. If her grandfather hadn't disappeared, she wouldn't be sitting across from this greasy-haired slimeball begging for money. "I'll be back," she insisted. "My life's here now."

Kismet leaned forward over his desk. "Listen, I can't give you a job singing. We're slapping on a new face here—hiring dancers with G-strings and pasties." He reached for his scotch. "Do you dance?"

"Not like that."

Kismet tapped the rim of his glass with his forefinger and scrutinized her. "Look, I'd like to help you. Maybe we can work something out." He reached across the desk for her hand. When she gave it to him, he said, "Maybe you could tend bar. I could give you half now, and when you come back, we'll work on the rest."

Becca calculated her expenses. She wouldn't have any left, but her biggest worries would be over. She smiled. "All right."

He squeezed her hand. "Good, because I like you. You're actually very pretty, and you've got a great voice." He stood up and smiled back at her. "You know, there are other things you can do for me." He patted the front of his pants with his other hand. "We'd make a good team."

Becca froze. She was too stunned to pull her hand back, to grab her purse from the chair and bolt.

"It could be your choice," he said and grinned at her. "Your fingers on my flute, your lips on my reed—you call the shots."

The room was suddenly hot, putrid with his breath that hung between them as he moved closer to her around the desk. She watched his hand lower the zipper on his pants and fumble with the jockey shorts to expose himself. "You're gonna like this," he said. "Like candy."

She winked at him and withdrew her hand slowly from his grip. She needed to make it to the door before he could bar it with his weight and force her to her knees. She flirted with him. "If you'd like a happy ending, I've got some protection in my purse." She bent down for her handbag, but before she could grab it, he snatched a clump of her hair, wound it tightly around his yellowed fingers, and pulled her cheek to his lips.

"I wouldn't touch your nasty cunt with ten rubbers," he sneered. "But your pretty mouth will do just fine." He pressed her face down toward his groin, toward his shriveled-up old duper that was white and wrinkled like a raw chicken leg. The sight of it sent her stomach reeling. She closed her eyes while he rubbed the tip of it across her lips. "Come on, open up," he cooed. Becca heard his singsong voice in her ears. "Come on, baby. This'll get you your money."

Becca kept her mouth shut and felt the tugging at her lips. His crotch smelled like sweat and peanut butter. Suddenly the sickness rose in her stomach with such vehemence, she gasped desperately for air. Kismet grabbed that opportunity to shove himself fully into her mouth. She felt her tongue against him, felt him grow hard. When he pushed himself deeper within her, the force triggered her gag reflex and she clamped down, sinking her teeth into him to stop the rising sickness in her gut.

Kismet jerked and then howled, "You fucking bitch!" He released her hair and whipped his cock from her mouth. He hopped from one foot to another, yowling and clutching himself.

In a mad scramble for her purse, Becca saw him ready to leap at her, his eyes red with fury. She crouched low, pretending to cower, until he was within arm's reach. Then with one swift kick, she sent the wastepaper basket flying into his shins. When he reeled backward, she lunged for the door and yanked it open. She ran down the hall toward the stairwell. Halfway down, she heard Kismet's screech.

At the bottom of the stairs, she raced around the club tables, past the piano bar, and headed straight for the ladies' room. The door was propped open as a janitor mopped the floor. He warned her it was wet, but she pushed past him, locked herself in a stall, and retched into the toilet. She leaned over the dirty commode, careful not to touch anything. She wondered how the baby could still be alive, since she puked half the day and had had nothing to eat but crackers for more than two months.

When she staggered out, she noticed the janitor by the bathroom door, wiping his forehead with a red bandanna. He hung his head, abashed to look at her. For a moment, she was startled—she thought she knew him from somewhere. But as he sloshed the mop across the tiles, the recognition faded. She pulled down a bunch of paper towels and soaked them in cold water. Holding them to her face to calm the redness, she was grateful that the janitor was standing watch, allowing her to wash her face and hands and swish water around her mouth. She rifled through her purse for some lipstick, a piece of gum, a perfume sample. She tried to run a comb through her tangled hair. When she'd finished, she thanked him and handed him two dollars to escort her through the building. The janitor's face flushed crimson, but he nodded and led her out.

By the time Becca reached Broadway, the wind had kicked up. The earlier clouds had moved out, making the day glaringly clear. At Madison Square Park, she sat down on a bench to think. She should have known Pug Kismet was a lecher. Or maybe now that she was "knocked up," she gave off a vibe that invited him. Maybe it was her fault. She covered her mouth with both hands and rocked back and forth. In the last few months, she'd made one mistake after another. The biggest one, the pregnancy, had led to all the rest. It had to end. She grabbed her purse and rummaged through it, realizing there was only one way she could get the money now. She searched her wallet for a key.

Adam's apartment was only three blocks away. With any luck, he'd be off with his new protégé, a Cal Berkeley transplant who'd joined the May

Day tribe and launched thousands of helium balloons tethered by cables large enough to snare the helicopter's rotors at the Vietnam protests in Washington, DC, last year. Becca had been there too, singing and playing backup for Wicked Lester. "She's like me," Adam had said about Louise. "But grittier, more angry."

They'd met at the Club 100. In jest, Adam had told Becca he was ready to plant bombs, take over the government if it refused to end the war. Louise encouraged him. Suddenly he'd stopped studying for the LSAT. He practiced mixing ammonium nitrate with fuel oil in the kitchen sink. Louise researched the speed of shockwaves needed to set off the bomb. They became the team while Becca trudged off to her day job at Belly's Diner. Three months ago, she'd given back the diamond sweetheart ring that Adam had hidden in a cereal box for her to find when she poured Raisin Bran into her bowl. He'd refused to take it back, saying she'd always be his girl. Becca had eyed him suspiciously; behind that sheepish grin, she knew he and Louise had been mixing more than fuel and nitrates together. She'd let the charade go on for a while, trying to defend her turf, and that's when it happened. She'd missed a couple of pills, needed a new prescription, and boom—her period stopped.

Becca found the key tucked between her New York driver's license and voter-registration card. She clutched it in her hand and started walking down Twenty-Third Street toward Adam's apartment. Breezy for June, the wind tousled her hair, cooling the back of her neck. She stopped at a grocery to buy a Coke. Passing through the outside market laden with fresh fruits and flowers, she grabbed a bunch of daisies. If they were home, she'd give them the flowers and ask them if they knew anyone who wanted to sublet her apartment. Then she'd ask to use the bathroom.

When she did finally end it with Adam, she had given him back the ring, but he'd slipped it into her coat pocket when she wasn't looking. In a search for her gloves, Becca found it later. The last time she'd gone to his apartment to pick up a few books, a scarf, and some jeans, she'd left the ring on the top shelf of the medicine cabinet, pushed all the way to the back. She didn't need it then. She'd planned to wait a few months, until the last sparks had died, and then write him a letter telling him where to find it.

Adam lived on the top floor of an eight-story walk-up. There was no doorman, so Becca hit the buzzer next to Adam's mailbox. When he didn't answer, she slipped into the stairwell and began the trek up the 182 steps that she'd climbed more times than she could remember. At the top, she stopped to catch her breath and hike up her jeans that had fallen loose around her hips. She needed a belt now that she'd lost more than fifteen pounds. She struggled to roll the jeans at the top and then pulled her T-shirt down to hide the mess. God, she hoped no one was home! She just wanted to grab the ring and go. She still needed to pawn it in time to make her one o'clock appointment at the East Women's Center.

At the door, Becca hit the buzzer and knocked. She waited and knocked again. Convinced the apartment was empty, she slipped in the key. Once inside, she shut the door and turned the deadlock. She set the Coke and flowers down on the small dining table and scanned the living room. On the wall over the couch hung a poster of the Rolling Stone's *Tumbling Dice* that Becca had given Adam for his twenty-fourth birthday. She leaned against a chair, her knees weak from the climb.

They'd met at Georgetown while Becca was in her sophomore year, Adam, a sixth-year senior, spent more time organizing war protests on the National Mall than attending classes. Adam was beautifully made. His smooth skin and muscled body had attracted her initially. But after she'd come to know him, she'd been captivated by his brazen disdain of capitalism, which struck her as odd; his family were orthodox Jews who owned a lucrative textile mill in Manhattan. They manufactured wool, cotton, and silk in their overseas factory. A political science major, Adam had adopted Marxism as *the* strategy to abolish social and economic inequality between the classes—specifically the non-owning workers and nonworking owners. He wrote long, complicated essays that he distilled for Becca in one sentence: "If everyone's got the same stuff, there's no reason to kill." It wasn't so much his political views that attracted her. He had unbridled passion. He was animated. It was his energy that ignited the spark within her.

As the only student from Plant High to be admitted to Georgetown, Becca's grandparents had beamed with pride. But as that second year dragged on, Becca felt numb, like she was living someone else's life. She confided to Adam her dream to sing on Broadway. By graduation, he had persuaded her to quit school, go to New York, and give that desire a fighting chance. "I'll become the attorney," he said. He'd need the education and the law behind him to battle for social change. Becca stared up at the poster, at the lucky seven mocking her. Not one thing had turned out the way she'd planned. She'd rolled the dice and lost.

On the side table next to the couch, Becca spotted two framed photos, one of her and one of Adam and Louise. She walked over, picked up hers—and was startled. The fresh-faced girl in the frame appeared happy, peaceful in a way Becca never knew she felt until now. She stared at the photo. *It could've worked.* But now she was sneaking in like a thief. She picked up the other photo, the one of Louise sitting on Adam's lap. Tears gathered in her eyes, but even through the blur, she could see it on Louise's right hand—*her* sweetheart ring. She dropped the picture and ran into the bathroom. She flung open the medicine chest, slid her hand along the back of the top shelf. In the exact corner where she'd hidden it, her index finger found the ring. She laughed a little, thinking only Adam would buy Louise the same one! She slipped the ring into her jeans pocket and hurried to the dining table to gather her things. Becca threw her purse over her shoulder and prepared to leave. Then she heard voices outside the door. Adam was talking to Edna Freidman, the neighbor. For a moment, she panicked. She would have to confess, tell him the whole sordid story until she remembered the fire escape outside the bedroom window. She stepped silently toward the bedroom.

Once inside, Becca raised the window and crawled out onto the steel grate. The wind whipped furiously, picking up the ends of her hair so it whirled around her head. She peered down at the street, at the people bustling like miniature wind-up toys along the sidewalk. She gripped the rail, suddenly paralyzed from the dizzying height and the wind that threatened to blow her off the platform. But the balcony felt sturdy, so she inched her way along, toward the flower boxes teeming with geraniums. At the stairs, she forced one foot down and then the next, her palms sweaty from clutching the rail. When she reached the first landing, she crawled across the platform, huddled against the brick wall. She had seven more stories to go, and she couldn't even breathe. Her heart heaved. She'd never make her appointment. For a moment, she thought she'd just go home, confess to Nattie her horrible mistake, and beg forgiveness. Then she pictured her grandmother's face, beet-red with words she'd try to suppress. "You reckless fool!"

The wind thrashed her, and Becca buried her face against her knees. If her father were alive, she'd tell him. She covered her ears to drown out the street noise. Suddenly she felt the luminous energy rise within her. But instead of succumbing to the warm glow that communicated without words, she kept her face pressed to her knees and shook her head. No, she couldn't trust it. As loving as the voice felt, it was probably a trick. Perhaps it was exactly that voice that had lured her mother into the crazy world where no one could reach her. After all, Becca had seen her talk to the space beneath the window. Who the hell was she talking to?

A rattling noise behind Becca startled her. When she turned around, an old woman with black-and-yellow teeth leaned out the window. "You gonna jump?"

Becca's legs wobbled as she leaned against the brick wall to stand up. "I'm resting," she said. But the thought had crossed her mind. Just three steps and whoosh—off the balcony, and all her troubles would be over. Now she knew why so many women in her position had done exactly that. But today was a new world, and she was lucky to be in New York, where abortions were legal. No, she had a chance. She needed to undo what had been done.

The woman hugged a shawl around her shoulders and squinted her eyes at Becca. "These stairs are for emergencies." She waved her hand as if clearing crumbs from a counter. "You'd better move along, or I'll call the police."

Becca headed for the stairs. This time she did not look down. She kept her eyes riveted on the step in front of her and lowered her feet methodically. When she reached the landing, she moved quickly across the balcony to the next staircase and climbed down. In that way, she kept moving. Finally she hit the second floor, found the release handle, and lowered the remaining flight of stairs to the street.

Becca left the pawn shop with only a half hour to spare. When she turned the corner onto Thirtieth Street, she saw the picketers lined up and marching in front of the women's center. Their signs bounced in the air, *Repent, Baby Killers, Protect the Embryo.* Some carried pictures of a fetus's crushed and bloodied skull. Protestors called out, "Jesus saves!" Becca covered her ears and noticed a young woman on the other side of the street watching the protesters' parade. She waited for the stoplight and then crossed the avenue and approached the woman. She pointed to the clinic. "Are you going in there?"

"I need to," the woman said. She hugged a shopping bag in front of her stomach to hide the bulge. "But a friend of mine died last week. They perforated her uterus."

Aghast, Becca studied the woman and realized by the lines on her forehead she was not a young woman. "I thought they were safe now," she said. "They're legal."

The woman stared across the street as a man shouted "Murderer!" into a girl's face. "Legal, yes," she said, "but who'd you think are wielding the knives?" She reached into her bag and pulled out a cigarette. She offered one to Becca, who waved it away. The woman chuckled a little and then scowled. "The same bloody bastards who did them two years ago, along with some seedy wannabes." The woman lit up and threw the match on the street. "You just hope they get it right and you don't end up dead."

Becca took a deep breath. She believed what the woman said was true. She thought of the five hundred dollars the pawn shop had given her for the ring and how she'd bargained for that. But it was enough to get the abortion now. She could try to find a backstreet butcher at home. Her choice. Ha! In the last six hours, she'd become a tramp, a beggar, a thief, and a fugitive. Why not a murderer? She glanced down at her wrist at the muted post-horn. Her head throbbed. She just wanted it over, wanted a chance to get her life back. She watched the picketers wave their crosses in the air, and she struggled to believe in a loving God, one who knew what was in her heart and womb. She wanted him to save her. But when she stepped off the curb and jaywalked toward the clinic, it was her mother's face she saw. "Forgive me, Mama," she said over and over, realizing her crime was against her mother, against all mothers who waited expectantly for their unborn children. She sprinted across the street to avoid being hit by a taxi and then walked straight into the clinic, knowingly into the mouths of wolves waiting to devour both her and her child.

CHAPTER 5 ✳ Stealthy as a Cat

In the New York apartment, Becca tossed fitfully on her futon, trying to erase the images of gown-clad women lined up and waiting. Back in Tampa, Nattie was readying the Westcott Mansion for Becca's return.

Dust flew into the air as Natalie beat an old rug that had been flung over the back-porch railing. When she finished, she leaned the broom against the rail and turned to go back into the house. With her hand on the glass knob, she was halted by an old Irish tune lilting from the open window of the upstairs library. The voice was as clear as trickling water.

"It's Julia," she whispered, and not a dream as she first thought when she heard the voice drifting the dawn just days ago. Silvery and keen, the unadulterated timbre quivered in waves, rising and falling. Natalie thought it was beautiful, graceful like the curve of fluted crystal or the twist of a silver bracelet. She stood rigid as if her movement could frighten the singer like a songbird abruptly shaken, flitting off to another yard.

"It's Julia," she said again, but this time louder. She searched the backyard for Daniel. She'd seen him earlier this morning dressed in green overalls, a faded red bandanna tied around his neck. He was in the back flower garden pulling up weeds. Was it really Daniel—her Daniel—in the clothes of a gardener, a field hand? She'd blinked, rubbed her eyes, but yes, it was him bending over the impatiens, gently pushing back the purple flowers to pull up the weeds underneath. She'd flung open the sash and leaned out their bedroom window upstairs. "Daniel, what're you doing out there?" she'd called. And the way he'd looked at her, frowning, his eyebrows knitted, implied intrusion, as if she were an interloper, and he was surprised that she could see him there in the garden in workman's clothes and not a silk suit with a hand-tailored shirt, smart tie, and a monogrammed handkerchief folded neatly in the jacket's top pocket.

"Daniel!" she'd called again. As stealthily as a cat, he moved silently without rustling the grass. Natalie closed the window and shivered.

Julia stopped singing, breaking off in the middle of a phrase. Natalie hummed the tune, not loudly but coaxingly, as if Julia could hear her and needed the urging of a mother to finish the song. Julia began the melody again, just as Niobe called from the kitchen.

"A Mr. Ramirez is in the front hall. He's wanting to know if he can pick up Miss Becca from the airport this afternoon."

Natalie stumbled over the threshold, sweeping up wisps of stray hair that had fallen around her neck. The screen door slammed behind her. Ever since the night Daniel had not shown up at his Queen's Party, members from the Krewe of Gaspar had been stopping by the house. The pirates' wives brought fresh peach pies, tomatoes, or cucumbers. Eula or Niobe stood in the doorway to accept the bounty, but when the guests asked for Natalie, they all heard the same thing: "Mrs. Westcott does not want to be disturbed." Sometimes Natalie could hear the men's voices as she sat in the living room. "You tell Ms. Natalie that Daniel is just out fishing silver kings. He'll turn up in a flash." Then she'd sink further into the yellow armchair and worry about the gun she'd buried under the Hermes scarf in her underwear drawer.

As Natalie stood in the hall, she thought to call Niobe and tell her to send Victor away, but—who was to pick up Becca this afternoon? The thought was as worrisome as her daughter's voice fading in the darkness of the back hall. *Hush, Julia, hush.* Who could calm Julia now that Daniel was gone? Not her. And how could she have forgotten to make arrangements for Becca? Natalie had asked her not to go back to New York. "Have your clothes shipped home," she'd begged. But Becca insisted she had affairs to settle concerning her job and subletting her apartment. And those were things, she explained, she had to do for herself. Passing the utility room, Natalie fretted that these were the unexpected particulars, the details that Daniel, Richard, or even her mother-in-law had seen to. Now all this fell to her, not logically or in a timely manner. Instead, it rushed toward her frantically like the electrical fire that burst from the worn-out socket in the library. A small fire, yes, and thank God, but a fire just the same, with voluminous smoke that oozed into the draperies, the red leather chairs, and the bindings of books, yellowing the pages. And now today, Natalie knew Becca was coming home—and there was no one to pick her up.

Natalie rushed down the back hall, past the kitchen where Eula sat at the round oak table snapping beans. She spoke in a low voice to Niobe, who was at the sink washing dishes. Natalie couldn't hear the words, muffled as they were and clipped at the ends to make the dialect run smooth. But she knew they were the confidences of a mother and daughter, mixed with laughter and respect, for soon Niobe would guide her mother through the house into the dining room and give her a piece of silver and a soft cloth to rub a shine. Natalie worried how she would pay them this week, since Daniel had always managed the household expenses, including the help. Her own monthly allowance, substantial in years past, had dwindled to the point that in March she'd had to ask Daniel to pay for her coronation gown. Natalie winced, remembering the embarrassment. She'd not squandered the money as he accused but in fact had been setting aside as much as could be spared for a surgery on Eula's eyes. A thick, milky film had been invading her pupils for months now. Natalie suspected cataracts. She knew the procedure was simple in the hands of a competent surgeon. "I've had mine done," she told Eula, who had puffed her cheeks out in disbelief. She told Natalie under no circumstances would anyone take a knife to her eyes.

Natalie hurried past the pantry and broom closet, past the broken elevator that was now stuck halfway between the floors. Her thoughts skipped, tumbled one over another on her way to the foyer. *What would she say to this Ramirez fellow? What about Becca?* In the midst of her worry, she was suddenly grateful that her legs were sturdy enough to carry her up and down the stairs, now that the elevator was stuck like a bullet in the shaft of a gun.

When she rounded the corner, she saw a reflection of Mr. Ramirez in the beveled mirror that adorned the foyer. He was not in the hall. He had let himself into the living room and then walked beyond the piano and loveseats to the west wall, where the Westcott family portraits hung in a framed procession. Ramirez stood straight. He was almost six feet and looked dignified in a pair of white slacks and a seersucker jacket. As he studied the portraits, he cocked his dark head to gain a clearer view. Natalie watched him there, not directly, but his reflection in the mirror. She had the urge to rush up the stairs, to brush her hair, change her blouse, and wash her hands. Her fingers burned, dry with dust. Instead she stepped slowly across the marble floor toward the staircase when he turned and startled her.

"Mrs. Westcott," he said. "A good morning to you." When she offered her hand, he clasped it, his fingers warm and deeply tanned against her skin. "Have you any news?"

Natalie examined his high forehead and sharp nose. "Nothing," she said. She didn't dare tell him that she'd just seen Daniel pulling up weeds in the back garden.

Victor shook his head. "I'm sorry." He told her he knew Becca was coming home later and wanted to save Natalie a trip by picking her up.

Natalie peered at the young man's dark eyes that were both bright and colorless at once. She puzzled how he could've heard Becca was coming home that afternoon. No doubt, Tampa was a small city or a big town (depending on which way one wanted to view it). But still it unnerved her that this young man had discovered (perhaps even *ferreted out*) information on Becca, in spite of the fact that Natalie herself had done her own homework after she saw Becca scurrying out of his car that first night home. Natalie dropped her gaze from Mr. Ramirez's face. Just yesterday, she'd confirmed it with Sophie Myers (the mayor's wife) that Carlos Mendoza (Victor's uncle) headed up the most-respected Spanish family in Tampa. But still, should Victor be allowed to pick up Becca from the airport?

"How kind of you to offer," she said, "but I would never impose."

Victor made a noble gesture with his head, not unlike a bow. "But I'll be in Westshore anyway. And knowing you must be worried sick—" He stared at Natalie. "I just want to help." He stood close to her, his eyes searching her face until she felt uncomfortable, exposed there in the front hall where the sun shone through the second-story windows.

Niobe brushed past them to bring coffee and the morning's fresh pastries arranged on a silver platter. "I'll set these in here," she said and strolled into the living room.

Natalie followed her and motioned for Mr. Ramirez to sit on the loveseat. "It's unusually hot for June, isn't it?"

"Very," Victor answered.

Natalie settled in the canary-yellow armchair adjacent to her guest and poured the coffee. Taking the first sip, she noticed Daniel across the room, sitting on the edge of the piano bench. Still shirtless and dressed in the green overalls that were soiled at the knees, he mopped his forehead with the bandanna. It wasn't his presence in the room or the way he sat hunched over, elbows resting on his knees that surprised her, but if he was dead—wasn't there someplace he should be? She wanted to set the coffee cup down, walk over to the piano and ask him what he was doing here. *But what if nobody is sitting there?* she thought. *What if I am the only one who sees him?* And then it hit her, just as Mr. Ramirez was telling her that he had begun renovation on the Centurion Building in Hyde Park, that Daniel could be angry with her.

With one eye on the piano bench, she asked the young man out of curiosity, "Isn't that the old Maynard Mansion?"

"It is," Victor said. He sat straighter on the loveseat. "I've purchased it with Overstreet and Powell. They're going to use it for their law offices."

Natalie scrutinized Victor. "But it's so—"

Victor laughed. "Dilapidated?" He set his cup on the coffee table. "You're right.

And they were going to tear it down, but I brought them a plan. Not only to revive the building, but to preserve its architectural origins."

Natalie pressed her fingertips together. For an instant, she was mesmerized with the young man's energy and his desire to preserve a failing old building. Then she glanced across the room to Daniel, who was still sitting on the piano bench. He winked at her, a quick, half-cocky flick of his eye. The oddly familiar gesture aroused in her the same old feelings—*not tonight, Daniel. And does it always have to be when you're drunk?* She remembered his laugh, the weight of his arm pulling her close, and his whisper-singing in her ear. "My love, my sweet, sweet love." Natalie supposed (as she wanted to suppose with that wink) that Daniel was no longer angry. And well he shouldn't be. After she'd grabbed the pistol from the gun cabinet, hadn't he dared her to pull the trigger? She stared at him across the room. They were blanks, right? Left over from the Gasparilla parade, surely. The shots had thundered through the staircase, but Daniel kept skipping down the steps, laughing as he ran out the front door. Later, when he didn't come home, she'd checked for blood.

Natalie turned to Victor who had asked about Nathan Westcott. "Wasn't it Nathan who built the house?" he asked.

"It was," she said.

Victor's eyes followed the carved mantelpiece of the fireplace upward to the crown molding that adorned the ceiling. "It's stunning," he said. "In structure and design, it's the most exquisite home on the Bayshore."

"You think so?" Natalie asked. She sipped her coffee. She had always admired the clean, classical lines of her father-in-law's architecture, especially in his residential work. What a shame he'd died at sixty-five.

Natalie reached across the table to pour more coffee.

"Allow me," Victor said. He leaned over to grip the coffeepot. "I've studied Mr. Westcott's designs, and I plan to use much of what I've learned in my own buildings." Victor filled her cup. The scent of fresh coffee was warm in the room, and Natalie felt her head go light. How lovely to be sitting here with this charming young man who was not only concerned with Becca's welfare but believed, just as she did, that her father-in-law was an architectural genius. "And you're from Tampa, Mr. Ramirez?"

He smiled a yes. "Please," he said, "call me Victor." But the smile and control of his voice could not hide the lowering of his eyes and the desire to conceal something.

"And your family?"

"Just north of here," he said and fidgeted on the loveseat.

Natalie caught herself staring again at his black hair, honeyed skin, and raven eyes. She realized he had no inkling of what she already knew about him. But what did she care that his grandfather rolled cigars in an Ybor factory, when she'd been born fatherless—and Catholic, no less! But what intrigued Natalie more than Victor's climb up society's ladder or his foothold in the business world was the childhood story Sophie had told her that kept creeping into the back of her mind.

"Victor was only six years old," Sophie had said. "Well, not a day over seven, I am sure, when the Ramirez family piled into their small pickup truck for a boat outing off the Howard Franklin causeway. They had an eighteen-foot fishing boat tied to a trailer behind the truck, and the boys—Santo, a good four years older than Victor—had crawled into the truck bed while his father drove and his mother made sandwiches in the cab. They had taken a back road and were heading down West Columbus when his father heard the front of the metal boat trailer scrape the asphalt.

He slammed the brakes. When he glanced into the rearview mirror, he saw the bow of the boat hurtling headlong into the truck bed. Little Victor saw it too, and when he pushed his brother aside, the bow of the boat plunged into his chest, splitting it wide open like a watermelon. Somehow the pin that secured the trailer hitch to the truck had snapped, releasing the boat and trailer. When Victor's father hit the brakes, the momentum of the boat barreled into the truck bed and into Victor's chest."

Natalie eyed Victor's starched white shirt and smooth buttons that probably followed the vertical line of his scar. She imagined it had grown with Victor and now stretched wide and long like a chalk mark separating the right side of his body from his left. "It was a miracle he lived," Sophie had told her, "a sheer act of God."

Natalie sipped her coffee. That Victor had survived amazed her, but not as much as the fact that at only six years old, he'd saved his brother's life without a single thought for his own. What kind of a child was that? What kind of a man now?

"You're in the new Krewe of SantY'ago?" Natalie asked.

Victor glanced up, startled. "I am," he said. "My uncle was crowned the first El Rey this year."

"And Daniel was crowned Gasparilla King," she said. "What a coincidence."

"Or *destino*, like my uncle says." Victor set his cup on the coffee table. "He says Daniel is Gasparilla's oldest king while he's the newest."

Natalie smiled. She hadn't thought of that. But now it made perfect sense that Carlos Mendoza had sent over a bouquet of flowers attached with a note offering to help in any way.

Natalie set her cup on the coffee table. "You were out with Becca the other night?"

"I saw her walking," Victor said. He fidgeted, edging himself toward the end of the loveseat. "It was late. I asked her if she wanted a ride home."

Natalie pressed an index finger to her mouth to hide the twitching in her lower lip. "And she went with you?"

"She did."

Natalie gripped the arms of the yellow chair and gazed down at her lap. Ever since Becca quit school and headed for New York to sing on Broadway, Natalie had felt her drifting away from them, floating off like a party balloon that had accidentally slipped their fingers. She imagined smoky nightclubs jammed with beatniks, hippies, and rockers who had flocked to the city to express free love by burning the American flag, crosses, and brassieres. She folded her hands, squeezed them tight, and wondered how Becca, a level-headed child, had ended up like Little Tommy Tucker singing for his supper. She blamed the Jewish boy, not because she was anti-Semitic, but because he'd lured Becca away from her studies, and introduced her to a fantasy world that Natalie never professed to know anything about—except the fact that when the boy tired of her, Natalie knew he would drop her faster than any potato because *his* family would never allow a *shiksa* into their lives.

Natalie gazed up at Victor. "Maybe you should get Becca this afternoon." Instead of the expected smile, he knitted his brow and nodded. Their eyes met openly, and for a moment that Natalie would remember until her death, she knew Victor was just as shaken as she was by the young woman who'd appeared out of nowhere with her painfully thin body, unkempt hair, and pinched expression. Natalie winked at him to test the alliance between them, but Victor's gaze was steadfast, unyielding as the summer heat. "That would be such a help," she said, and this time he smiled and winked back at her.

Natalie searched the room for Daniel, but the piano bench was empty, slipped tidily under the baby grand as if it had never been moved. She was about to call Niobe to escort Victor to the door, when she noticed his hand smooth the faded chintz on the loveseat. It was not the movement that disturbed her but imagining what that hand felt—the worn fibers of fabric gone dull with age. And not only what it felt but knew and what his eyes knew as they scanned the room and saw the ragged brocade curtains, a cracked window overlooking the lawn, and the faded walls that hid the elevator that was stuck halfway between the floors. Natalie refolded her hands in her lap. No, she would not think about the house now or that Victor had walked into their lives, not only interested in Becca but bearing full coffers. Beyond the piano, she caught a glimpse of Rebecca's portrait hanging on the wall. Her heart thumped wildly against her chest. She covered her mouth to stifle a chuckle, the ludicrous irony that she—the undesired daughter-in-law—had become the matriarch, the fated judge of a young man with Spanish ancestry who had come seeking entrance into Tampa's gentility by offering what? His heart?

Natalie pushed out of her chair and smoothed the creases from her skirt.

Victor stood up after her. "The coffee was delightful," he said, "like our visit." Together they smiled, as if they had been intimate friends for years.

Natalie escorted Victor to the foyer. "You'll bring her straight home?"

"Of course," he said.

She watched him skip down the front steps, waiting until he opened the door of his shiny car stretched out on the driveway.

"I'll see you then," she called.

As the car disappeared down the Bayshore, Natalie leaned over the railing and let the wind play havoc with her hair. Smoky clouds gathered in the east, black and threatening above the bay. Natalie gripped the porch rail while a north wind zipped across the water, ruffling it, so it resembled the white layers of a petticoat. She called softly for Daniel. While she searched for the sea-foam green of his overalls, she thought about Victor, about his bravery in saving his brother and his determination to preserve the old, deteriorating buildings in town. Natalie squinted in the wind. But even more important was their unspoken understanding. To what? To protect Becca? Yes, to keep her safe.

Natalie stopped before entering the house. The air had grown heavy, thick with the coming of rain, and the smell was virile like the turning of fresh earth. She thought of the flowers Carlos Mendoza had sent to the house yesterday and imagined what Daniel would have said had he been home. *Who are those from, Nat? And what does he want?* But now that it had been decreed that Daniel must watch in his overalls, at his place at the piano, through a cracked door or an open window, Natalie alone called the shots. For what if Becca came home to stay and Victor courted her? The whole house could be turned upside down, shaken loose of dust, cleaned up and repaired, and in light of all that had passed, Becca's return and the rejuvenation of their home was at least something real, something tangible that Natalie could possess—if only for the shortest time.

CHAPTER 6 ❋ The *Sea Booty* Adrift

ON THE MORNING OF JUNE 16, while Becca slept upstairs in the Westcott home, newspapers hit the porches of Ybor City. They were tossed onto red-bricked driveways in Ballast Point and carried up walkways to the Bayshore mansions. By nine o'clock, the entire town was abuzz with the whereabouts of Daniel Westcott. The *Tribune* quoted the dock master at the Tampa Yacht Club saying, "Danny set out early that Thursday [the day he disappeared] with a young feller, a hairy sort, all mustache and mutton chops. I'd never seen the likes of him before." Then he said the two of them had rigged up Daniel's thirty-six-foot Hatteras with seven-foot ugly-stick rods and thirty-pound test monofilament. They filled the bait wells with live shrimp, pinfish, and mullet and headed south to track silver king tarpon. They returned that afternoon empty handed, having thrown back a couple of barracudas. Sometime in the wee hours of the next day, the dock master claimed the *Sea Booty* must have taken off again, because when he came into work at 5:00 a.m., the boat was gone.

At the yacht club, the news was not surprising. Everyone knew Daniel was hell bent on breaking the tarpon record. At breakfast that morning, a few of his cronies scoffed at the headline: Westcott's *Sea Booty* Adrift.

"Adrift my ass!" one of them said. They'd bet their bottom dollar that Daniel and his fish whisperer had slipped out that night and were living on the boat. They'd be throwing out lines just as the moon popped the horizon, when the waters were moving and the tidal feeders were quick to act. As fishermen themselves, they understood. They poured a little whiskey into their morning coffee and toasted their king. Let the old king hunt silvers! The peak migration had already passed, schools were thinning, but they knew what Daniel knew—the biggest daddies held out through June.

Not everyone in town was as confident about Daniel's situation as his krewe mates. In Ybor City, Victor Ramirez ordered *café con leche* while his uncle clipped the end of a hand-rolled Butera and brushed the tip onto the floor. Carmine's buzzed. Patrons stood clutching newspapers, smoking and waiting for tables to clear. Victor slid his chair in close.

"He's gone too long," Carlos said. "Without sending word, I mean." He tugged sharply on his beard as if to pull answers from the snowy whiskers. He talked on in a Spanish/English mix about Daniel being caught in the Gulf Stream, swept away by the river within a sea. "El Triangulo Diablo," he said. His eyes grew wide, and he licked the end of his cigar. "Or it could be *piratas*."

Victor held the steaming mug to his lips. The piracy on the Caribbean, rampant in the last few years, was a secret to no one. Led by gun-slinging pot smugglers, the sea thieves would cruise the night in rusted old dinghies, searching for a powerboat to hijack so they could pick up their stash in Colombia. They would gut the yachts for maximum capacity and then paint water lines on the hulls to give the illusion they weren't riding low even when laden with marijuana. Afterward, they would sink the boats.

Victor was not the only one to imagine Daniel Westcott trolling the midnight waters, the lights on the *Sea Booty* bringing in tarpon. His uncle said surely Daniel would carry a pistol and spot the thieves riding too close. He would fire his gun into the night to ward off attacks. But what if the scoundrels kept coming? The *Sea Booty* would make a dazzling prize for their illicit affairs.

Carlos pounded his fist on the table. "We can sit no longer." He struck a match on the bottom of his shoe and lit the cigar. "We must launch a search." Then he told Victor to go the Westcott home, to tell the family of his intentions, while he would convince Feo Salazar there was not a minute to lose.

By ten o'clock that morning, everyone had read the newspaper—except Becca, who had lain awake most of the night trying to figure out her next step. She had fallen into a restless sleep at dawn and was awakened by the front-door chimes. She dragged herself out of bed. Through the upstairs window, she could see the next-door neighbor, Ruby Taylor, on the front porch. She handed Natalie a pear pie and asked her if Daniel had come home in the night. Dressed in a cornflower-blue suit, Mrs. Taylor craned her neck trying to get a glimpse inside the house while Natalie stood on the threshold and blocked her view.

"I heard gunshots the other night," Mrs. Taylor said.

Becca cracked the window open slightly. That was the first she'd heard about those.

"Just blanks," Natalie said.

"They sounded real."

Natalie stepped onto the porch, barring the door behind her. "Blanks sound real," she said matter-of-factly. "Daniel was cleaning his pistol, and it went off." Then she took the pie, thanked her neighbor, and disappeared into the house.

Mrs. Taylor stopped midway down the stairs and glanced back at the front door. She looked confused. Becca pulled away from the window to avoid being seen. She closed the curtains. In spite of the air conditioner switching on and off, the summer heat seeped through the old windows and rubbed against her. Her skin was drenched with sweat. Last night she'd found a cotton nightie that barely reached her knees, and now she felt displaced, a giant in her childhood room. She'd outgrown the little-girl vanity, the matching dressers, the Madam Alexander dolls with their sweet, pink lips smiling down from the bookshelves. Some of the dolls had chipped paint around their mouths and fingers. Becca had never played with them. Something about them spooked her. They'd belonged to her mother. In fact, the whole bedroom was filled with musty furniture, books with ragged spines, and a pointillist oil of an English wishing well that had been her mother's when *she* was growing up.

Instead of crawling back into bed, Becca pulled out the vanity stool and sat down. She felt burdened with an undeniable weight, a heaviness she tried to sleep off. In the mirror, dark circles underlined her eyes. She blinked a few times and then shuddered. *How could this be happening?* She pinched the skin along her cheekbones, not only to force some color into her face but to awaken from the nightmare that would not end. At the clinic, while she waited her turn to terminate the pregnancy, she'd felt the floaty, out-of-body feeling trying to tempt her again. But right then and there, she realized it was only fear that produced it; she'd whisked it away with a shake of her head.

I am not a child anymore, she reassured herself. She could not live in a fantasy world of frogs turning into princes and sooty girls going to a ball. She gazed up at her favorite childhood books lining the bookshelves: *The Little Princess, The Secret Garden, The Wizard of Qz.*

All innocence, she thought. The real world was full of lechers—selfish, narcissistic men bent on satisfying their basest needs. No, she needed a clear head to navigate what lay in front of her as skillfully as possible.

Just then, the front-door chimes pealed through the house again. Becca got up and drew back the curtains to see her best friend, Margie Nelson, swinging a Maas Brothers bag and chewing bubble gum. Margie sold children's shoes for the largest department store in town. Becca raised the window and called down to her.

Margie waved back, her sun-bleached hair in loose curls over her shoulders. She let herself in the door. Margie had grown up in Hyde Park, the middle of seven children. She'd married her high-school sweetheart one month before he was shipped off to 'Nam. He was one of the boys who'd not returned. Two weeks before his tour ended, his campsite was ambushed, raided in the night by a gang of Viet Cong. He was running through a rice paddy when a grenade hit him. They sent home what they could—a set of dog tags, a Saint Christopher's medal, his wedding ring.

Margie knocked on the door and then slipped into Becca's room. "Was it awful?" she asked, breathless from the stairs.

Becca eased herself onto the bed, and Margie snuggled in next to her. "Actually, once in the door, it was clinical—papers to sign, hospital gowns, and a row of women lined up for the slaughter." Margie grimaced as Becca smiled wryly.

"It's over now; time to forget."

Becca stared down at the comforter across her lap. "It's not over," she said. "I'm still pregnant."

"Huh?"

Becca closed her eyes. "I couldn't do it." She poked a finger through an eyelet on the comforter. "I walked out. I didn't even get my money back." She looked at Margie. Becca couldn't tell her that something surreal, something suspicious was trying to overcome her, make her do things she didn't understand. She stared down at her hands. "I wandered the streets until 4:00 a.m., knowing I should go back, but I didn't. I just came home, and now I can't sleep or think or figure out what I'm supposed to do." She stood up, stepped to the window. "I'm so confused."

Margie followed her and gripped her shoulders. "You need to tell Adam."

Becca crossed her arms and gazed down at the floor. She tried to block out the night Adam was supposed to pick her up from work and didn't show. She knew he was with Louise and had forgotten her, so she accepted a ride home with a guy who'd been listening to her gig all night. She'd been so angry and hurt, she invited him inside for a drink. They'd smoked some pot, and he'd kissed her. On the futon, she'd imagined Adam was watching as the stranger unhooked her bra, nuzzled his face between her breasts, licked her nipples. She'd let him slide her panties down and fondle the softness between her legs. But when he unzipped his jeans, she'd stopped him. Becca felt her heart beating wildly within her chest. She couldn't even remember his name now.

Becca shivered in spite of the heat. She realized if she'd slept with the stranger that night, the baby could be his. But that hadn't happened. No, the baby was Adam's. But still she couldn't tell him. She wanted his love, not obligation. If she told him about the baby, how would she ever know the truth? Becca held up her wrist to distract her friend.

"What's that?" Margie pulled Becca's hand in close. She traced the post horn with her index finger. "A tattoo? Is this the newest Manhattan rage?"

Becca winced at the sarcasm. "It's a symbol for lost love," she said, defending herself. "It helped me get through the … you know." She couldn't even say the word now. "See how the horn's muted?" She eyed Margie carefully. "I don't want anyone to know about the baby. Especially Adam."

"But if you don't have the—you-know-what, the whole town will know soon."

Becca turned toward the window. "If only my father were here. He'd know what to do." Her voice sounded small and far away.

"Look, you'll figure it out. You still have time." She hugged Becca's shoulders.

Becca stared out the window. "If my grandfather weren't missing, I'd just leave." Then she told Margie about the gunshots the neighbor heard. "Nattie said it was blanks from a Gasparilla pistol, but I still worry about those Yorketowne scalawags."

Margie's eyes grew wide. "You haven't seen the paper?"

Becca shook her head.

"The *Sea Booty's* missing." Margie pressed her fingertips together. "They think your grandfather could be on it."

Becca walked back to the bed and sat down.

"It left the yacht club the same night he disappeared." Margie settled on the vanity stool and faced Becca. "Actually, early the next morning."

A flicker of hope shot through Becca. "He could be alive."

"Of course he's alive." Margie pressed her hands against her knees. "Yorketown's long forgotten. And murder? It doesn't make sense." She reached for her purse. "Why do you think he's dead?"

Becca tugged the ends of her ponytail. "Nattie thinks he's someplace he can't leave."

Margie rolled her eyes. "Not until he wants to!" She leaned in close. "Your Nattie's rattled on a good day, and she's probably right about the gunshots." She winked. "Old pirates like to play with their pistols." Then she turned around on the stool, dug through her purse, and pulled out a pot of lip gloss. "Besides, dead bodies turn up fast, especially if they've been shot." Peering at Becca through the mirror, Margie dipped her forefinger into the raspberry shine and spread it across her lips. "Trust me: he's alive. But what he's up to now has the whole town guessing."

Margie set the gloss on the vanity table and rummaged through her shopping bag. She lined up a tube of mascara, blush, and concealer on the table. "Samples for you," she said with a smile. "Oh, and these." She pulled out four tickets to the Hats and Hammers fundraiser Tuesday night. Margie was a member of the Chiselers, a preservation organization committed to saving Henry Plant's faded castle on the river, the old Tampa Bay Hotel. "The junior members are sponsoring it," Margie said. "We're trying to raise enough money to have the dome in the ballroom professionally cleaned."

Margie spread out the tickets like a hand of cards. "I'm collecting the money," she said and grinned. "There'll be tons of paperwork and bills to pay after the party. I'll have some cash for a couple of weeks. We can borrow it and replace it, with no one the wiser."

Becca hugged her knees to her chest. "What if—"

"Shh!" Margie said. "Just make up your mind, and I'll do the rest. Besides, I bet your grandfather shows up, and we won't need this money."

She fanned herself with the tickets. "In the meantime, find out if you can reschedule that appointment."

Becca cringed at the thought of the women's clinic but kept her mouth shut.

Margie handed Becca the tickets. "You should come—and you should bring Nattie."

"How can I?"

"Well, you look a little ragged out, but not pregnant." Margie pointed to the makeup. "That'll help." Then she walked to the door and winked. "Besides, right now your grandfather has center stage."

Determined to dress before noon, Becca rifled through her unpacked suitcase, searching for something to wear in the heat. She flung two pairs of jeans, a stack of T-shirts, and a couple of nightclub dresses onto the floor. Then she headed for her closet, where her debutante dress hung next to the court gown she'd never worn. She'd planned to attend her own coronation two years ago when she was up for queen, but Adam had chastised her. "You're missing the demonstration for what?" In response to the Kent State massacre, Becca and Adam had planned to attend an emergency protest in front of the White House that Saturday. Adam had paced the apartment sermonizing. "We need every warm body, every voice, every sign-carrying, sane human being to stop this senseless murder." He glared at her. "And you're going to be a Sarsaparilla Queen?" *There's no explaining Gasparilla to Adam*, she thought.

Becca would never know if she'd won the crown. When she called to tell Daniel she couldn't make the ball, she'd been disqualified. Granddad had hidden his disappointment like a war wound, but Nattie raged on that Becca had disgraced her legacy, thrown dirt onto her great-grandmother's grave, bruised her mother's already-tenuous reputation, and ruined any chance of her own daughter's reign. "No one has ever dropped out of the court two days before the ball!" Nattie insisted.

At the time, the accusations had rolled off Becca—nothing was more important than the war. But flipping past her debutante dress and the blue sequined gown she'd never worn, she felt a twinge of guilt. She pushed them aside and pulled out a white halter sundress, the hemline edged with yellow daffodils. She slipped off the nightie and stepped into the dress. Nattie could not accuse her of being a hippie while wearing Lily Pulitzer. On the vanity, she found her wristwatch and positioned the crystal carefully over the tattoo. She was relieved when it covered all but the tail end of the horn. She did not want Nattie to see it. Not yet.

In the kitchen, Becca found her grandmother perched on the counter stool, hidden behind the newspaper. As soon as she saw Becca, Natalie spread out the Metro section on the counter, revealing a full-blown picture of Daniel dressed in his king's regalia—an ermine-edged scarlet robe, a jeweled crown, and ebony boots. Four Gasparilla pages trailed behind him, carrying the train of his cape. "His coronation," Natalie said.

Becca pulled up a stool and studied her grandmother carefully. From the flat tone of her voice, Becca couldn't tell if she was disgruntled or pleased.

"Did you know it was a day of *destino*?" Natalie smiled. "Fate."

Becca poured herself a cup of coffee from the thermal pot and watched Natalie run her fingers over the print of Daniel's face. She seemed so enchanted with the picture, so caught up in the memory that Becca sipped her coffee silently while her grandmother chattered on about the ball and how the auditorium was decorated like an English castle. Black-and-white satin streamers cascaded from a centered chandelier that was decorated with twelve-pointed stars. "The balconies were draped in white gauze fringed with silver," Natalie said. "And Daniel's throne was canopied, embossed with the Westcott coat of arms."

Becca chose a banana from the fruit bowl on the counter and ate it in three bites.

"You're hungry," Natalie said and stood up. "I'll make some eggs."

"Not now," Becca said and reached for a clump of grapes. "Tell me about the *Sea Booty*." She would read the article later, but now she wanted to know her grandmother's take on the news.

Natalie picked up the paper. "They don't have much to go on." She brushed a wisp of hair from her forehead. "The dock master thinks the boat took off sometime the morning after Daniel disappeared." She folded the newspaper. "But he can't be sure."

"They radioed it?"

"Couldn't reach it."

"Still, it's a chance."

Natalie shook her head. "It's nonsense." She clicked her fingernails against the counter tiles.

"Right, his Queen's Party." Becca plucked a grape from the bunch and rolled it in her palm. Each year, the new queen was elected by the krewe members. This year, it was Melanie Peebles. She'd just turned twenty-two and was a recent graduate from Florida State University. Becca plopped the grape into her mouth and chewed it thoughtfully. "But what do the police think?" she asked.

Natalie slid off the stool. "Well, Chief Salazar was here first thing this morning." She wobbled to the fridge. "Said he had a few leads to check out."

"Like gunshots?"

Natalie whirled around. "Where'd you hear that?"

Becca pointed to the Taylors' house.

"What does that Yankee Doodle know?" she huffed. "I told her it was blanks." Natalie grabbed a carton of eggs from the fridge and set them on the counter. She cracked two eggs into a bowl, grumbling all along. "Daniel was just cleaning it, for mercy's sake. What's wrong with that?" Then she muttered something under her breath.

"What?"

Natalie looked up, startled. "Scrambled or over easy?"

"Scrambled," Becca said. "I can make them."

"Oh no! Eat your fruit." Natalie whisked the eggs, her face growing redder with every beat. She zeroed in on Becca. "How'd you get so skinny anyway?" she prodded. "You don't have that starving disease, do you? I hear it's epidemic among singers and movie stars."

Becca hugged her bare arms across her middle. *If Nattie only knew.* "I'm not a star," she said. "In fact, I lost my job. I need to borrow some money."

Natalie turned from the stove, her face stricken. She pressed her fingertips to her lips. "The accounts are overdrawn."

Becca stared at her, incredulous. "How could that happen?"

Natalie spooned the eggs onto a plate and added a piece of cornbread. "I don't know," she said, her face suddenly pale. She set the food in front of Becca. "The bank said we owe them."

Natalie reached into her skirt pocket and pulled out a wad of cash.

"Where'd you get that?"

Natalie slid a stool in close to Becca. "I found it two days ago in my lingerie drawer," she whispered. "Two thousand dollars."

Becca dropped her fork. "Don't you see, Nattie!" She gripped her grandmother's arm. "Granddad left this for you. He must be on the boat."

Natalie frowned. "What's he doing? Robbing a Bahamian bank?"

Becca ignored her. "We have to call Chief Salazar."

"And have it blasted all over the newspapers?" Natalie's voice vibrated an octave above normal. She peeled off two twenties and laid them on the counter for Becca. "We won't tell anyone," she sniffed. "I'll not have the likes of Ruby Taylor knowing we're penniless."

"But—"

"But nothing," Natalie interrupted. "This is *my* house," she said fiercely. She shoved the cash back into her pocket. "*My* money." She handed Becca the fork. "As far as I'm concerned, you're a child come home, and I'm gonna watch you eat every bite on that plate."

Stunned by the edge in Nattie's voice, Becca shoveled the eggs into her mouth.

"The money's our secret," Natalie said.

Becca bit off a piece of cornbread. The food tasted buttery rich, but it slid down easily. The sickness was easing. She took a sip of coffee and thought about the missing boat and the money in Nattie's drawer. It made sense to her. Margie was right: her grandfather was alive. And what difference did it make if the police knew? Granddad would be home soon. She peered down at the muted post horn hidden beneath her wristwatch. "Our secret," she said.

Down the hall, Eula hummed a melancholy tune that Becca had not heard since she'd left home. "Miss Julia's feeling mighty punk today," Eula said. She sauntered into the kitchen with Julia's breakfast tray balanced on her shoulder. "She barely ate her toast."

Becca pushed her plate away. "What's this?" she asked pointing to the tray.

"Your mama takes her meals in her room," Eula said.

Becca squeezed Natalie's wrist. "She comes down to play the piano?"

"No, ma'am," Eula said, setting the tray on the counter. "She doesn't come down t'all."

"You told me she was fine, Nattie." Becca frowned, still holding her grandmother's wrist. "That's not fine. She's not seeing anyone or ever leaving her room? How long's this been going on?"

Eula picked up Julia's plate and scraped the uneaten eggs into the garbage. "Since the day you left."

"Eula!" Natalie snapped.

"I'm just truth-telling."

Natalie wiggled out from Becca's grip. "The truth is the doctor said, given your mother's history, it's not uncommon. She feels comfortable there; safe." Natalie carried Becca's plate to the sink. "I even heard her sing a few days ago. It was early morning, and your mother's voice was as clear and lovely as any songbird I've ever heard." Natalie folded the towel and hung it over the dish rack. "It's been years, you know."

Suddenly dizzy, Becca felt the lightness rush through her body. Then she heard the wordless voice call to her. "*Come, come,*" it said. She shook her head to clear it, and a scene flashed in front of her eyes.

It was nighttime; she was little. She'd awakened in her bed to the sound of her granddad thundering down the hall. She sat up in time to see him stumble through the door. "Yo ho, sweetheart!" he howled. Curly black hair sprang from beneath his hat and spilled out over his shoulders. His cheeks were gashed with red and purple wounds, and his front teeth had been knocked out. He smelled dank like a pickle cellar. When he moved toward her bed, she screamed, a yowl of all her strength. She gripped her pillow and kept shrieking until her mother appeared in the doorway and pushed past the pirate to the bed.

"It's only paint," Julia said and hugged her. She turned to Daniel. "You'd better go. She's frightened."

Trembling, Becca buried her face in her mother's neck, while Julia rocked her and sang the tune about Maggie and the old creaking mill. She fell limp against her mother's body, absorbing the rhythm. Then suddenly her mother's face turned white. Her song stopped.

Becca's whole body buzzed with the memory. She remembered how her mother's arms had gone rigid around her, and she sat staring straight ahead. Then she got up and walked out of Becca's room as if in a trance. Her mother had not sung to anyone, at any time, since that night. Becca turned toward her grandmother. "You heard her sing?"

"Clear as rain falling."

Just then the front-door chimes rang through the house, but instead of Eula jumping to answer it, she looked to Natalie. And Becca understood— Eula didn't want to be the bearer of bad news.

"I'll get it," Natalie said.

Becca stopped her. "Let me." She slid off the stool and hurried through the front hall past the elevator and broom closet where she'd played hide-and-go-seek as a child. Once in the foyer, she opened the door, and instead of Chief Salazar or a reporter, she found Victor in a white suit, twirling a Panama hat in his hands.

"I should've called," he said. "But—"

Becca interrupted. "Fleets are stopping by today."

A nervous smile twitched the corners of his mouth. "I bet," he said. "This whole town's abuzz." His dark eyes squinted as the sun hit the quarter mark in the sky. "My uncle's downtown with Salazar. They go back years." Victor crossed his middle finger over his forefinger to imply their friendship. He told Becca how Carlos had taken Salazar under his wing when the chief lost his mother. Salazar was only sixteen at the time, and his dad started drinking heavily after his wife's tragic death—suicide. The families lived next door in West Tampa, and Carlos—who was newly married—started inviting Salazar to dinner every night. "My uncle said he was a hungry kid with no place to go." Victor tapped the hat against his palm. "Carlos kept him off the street."

Becca listened intently while Victor told the story. She had a hard time visualizing Salazar as a frightened teenager. He was so solid now, upright and sturdy.

Victor paused for a moment, held the hat still. "My uncle's anxious to start a search."

Becca gazed down at the threshold. She realized Victor had come to ask permission to launch a search for her grandfather. The way he fidgeted with his hat, she suspected he was cautious after picking her up at the airport, afraid his intentions could be construed as meddlesome, "small-town pushy" as Nattie would say.

Becca stepped onto the porch. A boggy breeze blew in from the bay, soft against her face. "That's kind of your uncle."

Victor stopped twirling his hat. "That's all he wants, to help you and your family." He opened his mouth to say something else but shook his head instead.

Becca felt awkward standing in the doorway with his dark eyes on her, as if he wanted something but expected nothing. She thought it unusual that Victor and his uncle were anxious to find her granddad, while Daniel's yacht club cronies were convinced Daniel had taken off to hunt tarpons. She wondered if they had privilege to some knowledge that no one else had. Becca felt obligated to return his kindness. "There's a fundraiser at Plant Museum Thursday night." She looked down at her bare feet. "Would you?"

"Go?" Victor asked. "Sure, I'll go."

Becca smiled at his eagerness. She walked with him onto the porch. "It's getting hot," she said. "Soon, the rain." She shielded her eyes from the sun and squinted down the walkway to his car parked on the drive.

"Would you like some coffee?" she offered.

Victor glanced at his watch. "Can't, but I'll call you—before Tuesday." He started down the stairs.

Becca watched as he backed out of the driveway and disappeared into the whiz of cars heading south on the Bayshore. She gazed out over the water to the clouds gathering in the east. As the formations twisted with the wind, she still felt haunted by the memory of her granddad barging into her room that Gasparilla night and her mother's attempt to comfort her. She twirled a piece of hair that had fallen loose from her ponytail. Becca realized that night, that event had been the beginning of her mother's descent into a nether world she'd not been able to transcend.

As Becca turned to go into the house, she spotted a box wrapped in brown paper propped up by the front door. Her name was scrawled out in red ink across the top. There was no postage on it, so it must have been dropped off. Hoisting the package into her arms, she slipped through the front door and ran up the stairs. In her room, she sat on the bed and tore through the paper to find an old whiskey container bent at the corners and rippled with water stains. She peeled through the tape and turned back the flaps. Inside were two leather-bound journals wrapped in an ivory damask cloth. When she lifted out the first book, she was struck by the dank scent that emanated from its pages, as if holding it in the warmth of her hands had called forth the gist and sum of its substance; the malodorous stench of a house set in a climate that was too hot and too humid, making it host to the untold number of inevitable molds that thrive in damp, dark crevices. And while the scent was as familiar as certain corners of this house, there in the mix, was a peculiar strain, unacquainted and odd, that made Becca wonder. *Where did these come from?* She turned the diary in her hands and opened the cover.

Never believe freedom is God-given;
It is a struggle, a contest to be won.
And only those who can define it,
exact it within their souls
Can hope to attain it, and soar
ungrudgingly through the world.

RWW
1897–1930

Becca flipped through the pages. As the writing evolved from a girlish hand to a sophisticated script, she realized the diaries had been written by Rebecca Wills Westcott, her great-grandmother. A picture fell onto Becca's lap. Posed beside Gasparilla King IX, Rebecca stood regally adorned in her queen's robe and crown. Her tawny hair was swept up in a Gibson Girl, and the skin on her face was plump and smooth. She'd worn the queen's crown just as Julia had—and Becca, her namesake, had rejected it. Studying the photo, she recognized parts of her own face staring back at her. She examined the page where the writing was beautiful at times, and at others, scribbled and rushed.

Having caught a ride in a hay wagon out of Dothan to the southern edge of Georgia, the lovers started out on foot through the north Florida woods. Close to nightfall, they heard voices, saw torches moving toward them in the dark. "Run!" Charles had hollered. Chasing the lovers through the woods, the posse of slaves that Clive Cunningham had sent on his own horses to bring his daughter home, fired their rifles into the night. In the scuffle, Silva was shot. The bullet embedded just beneath her shoulder blade, above her heart, where one inch lower it would have knocked her to the earth with her first son, Camden, inside her. Charles carried her into a palmetto bush, covering her mouth to muffle her screams until the last of the torches disappeared into the woods. Then he built a shelter around her, laid down moss to soften her sleep, and let her rest the night before he dug the bullet out with a pocket knife and burned the wound to stop the bleeding. He caught possums, picked berries, walked miles for water, covered her body at night with his own to keep her warm, and why? Because she carried his child, a child he knew nothing about? Or was it because his religion dictated a man should protect a woman, love her as he loves himself? Alas, no! As Silva lay there, feeling the quickening in her womb, she knew that a man's first love for a woman was always lust, no matter how it was shrouded in doctrine or hidden with honor, and Charles' hands moved quickly that night to save her because he could envision no life without her.

Becca used her index finger as a bookmark. She felt her chest grow tight. She'd heard the family lore about Silva fleeing her Alabama home with her great-great-grandfather, Charles Westcott. She'd even heard how Silva had rescued an Indian child from deportment to Oklahoma. But she never knew her great-great-grandmother had conceived her first child out of wedlock.

Becca was about to open the diary again when she heard Natalie calling up the stairs for Niobe. Her voice was shivery. Becca wrapped the journals in the ivory damask and hid them under the bed. She ran from her room and down the hall to the stairs, where she saw Natalie in the foyer. Her face was unusually slack, and her mouth gaped open in a brittle O.

"It's Kurt," Natalie said. She gripped the newel post as if to steady herself. "He took off, said he had to go home. His grandfather was missing!"

Becca raced down the stairs. "But who told him?"

Natalie slit her eyes. "It must have been you," she accused, "or Eula."

The news was out. "It could've been any one of his friends," Becca said. She didn't expect an apology, and she didn't get one. Instead she thought of her brother making a break across the grassy plains of Idaho on a trek toward Tampa. The last time she'd seen him, he'd been beaten up by a pusher who'd refused to give Kurt a hit of acid. He'd called the dealer a candy-ass cheapskate and then sucker-punched him in the gut. Hurt people hurt people, and Kurt had ended up broken. Granddad had found him in the front yard. Kurt's right eye had been split open, his nose was broken, and later, they discovered he'd ruptured his spleen.

Becca led Nattie through the foyer toward the living room. She could feel the tension rise in the house like waves on the bay. She settled her grandmother into the yellow armchair. "Everything's going to be okay," she said.

But she didn't believe it—not for a second.

CHAPTER 7 ✳ Tongue of the Ocean

By June 18, Carlos Mendoza had convinced Chief Salazar to launch a search for Daniel and the *Sea Booty*. After nine days had passed with no word, even the most confident krewe members were beginning to scratch their heads and wonder if some misfortune had befallen their king. Eight o'clock Monday morning, Salazar called Captain Craig Mortenson and Victor Ramirez down to the precinct. Mortenson was the town's "old salt," a wiry, no-nonsense bachelor whose heart had been hooked by the sea. For years, he'd chartered fishing expeditions along Florida's west coast, through the Caymans, the Bahamas, and the Virgin Islands. He knew those waters better than his own backyard. He also held the yacht club's longest-running tarpon record, a 221- pound silver king that he'd caught four years ago.

Salazar had called Victor down because he knew Carlos had confided in his nephew about his concerns for Daniel Westcott. As far as he could see, Victor possessed a cool head and was not given to wild imaginings like his uncle Carlos. Plus, he'd seen the kid grow up. He knew all about the accident that should've taken his life. After his father died, the young man had pulled himself up by the bootstraps and started his own business. Salazar respected that. Right now he needed someone like Victor who could manage Carlos and keep the Westcott family calm at the same time.

By the time Victor was led through the police department into Salazar's office, Craig Mortenson was already there. The old angler had pulled off his fishing cap, which revealed a freckled bald spot that crowned the top of his head. He jumped from his seat and thrust out a hand to Victor, who clasped it immediately. "Mortenson," he said, "but call me Captain—everybody else does."

Victor nodded and scanned the police chief's office, his attention captured by a bookcase filled with trophies and Little League photographs with Salazar posed as coach.

Salazar leaned across his desk. "Glad you could join us," he said to Victor. He pointed to a chair.

Mortenson clutched his cap nervously and continued his conversation with Salazar. "If Danny was looking for tarpon, ain't no better place than Tampa Bay, especially the bridges. 'Silver magnets,' I call them." His voice bellowed like a bullfrog's. "Just drifting live sardines in the shadow lines gets you hooked up."

Salazar asked Mortenson to take his seat. The captain backed up slightly and settled on the chair's edge. "So you think Daniel wouldn't have left the bay?" the chief asked.

Mortenson cocked his head, as if trying to shake water from his ear. "I'm saying he didn't have to. He could've gone to Charlotte Harbor or Pine Island, but with schools greyhounding here, it's unlikely."

As Victor watched the exchange between the two men, he realized he had no idea why Salazar wanted him there. He knew nothing about investigations, fishing, or manhunts. He assumed it had something to do with his uncle.

Salazar chewed the tip of his pen and then tapped it on the desk. Victor studied him. He knew the chief needed to account for the missing days; neither Daniel nor the *Sea Booty* had shown up on Tampa Bay. "Couldn't Daniel have gone further?" Salazar asked, running his hand through a thick mass of salt-and-pepper hair.

Mortenson shrugged, the tips of his shoulders poking up like sticks beneath his shirt. "Anything's possible; the *Sea Booty*'s a big girl." He pulled a pack of cigarettes from his top pocket and offered it to the chief and then to Victor.

They both waved it away. Salazar stood up and began to pace. "Where would *you* go?"

Mortenson lit the cigarette and inhaled deeply. "Boca Grande," he said and leaned back in the chair. "But I caught my prize silver off the coast of Andros."

Salazar stopped pacing. "Does Daniel know that?"

Mortenson grinned. "Everybody knows that."

What everyone didn't know was how Mortenson had hired an island native who was savvy with the barrier reef, the mud flats, shallow sand, and the upwelling cool water from the Tongue of the Ocean just a mile off Andros Island. The oceanic trench had a six-thousand-foot drop-off that resulted in a variety of deep-sea life, including the humpback whale Mortenson had traveled 262 nautical miles to watch. One predawn morning on the north edge of the trench, a bleary-eyed Mortenson caught sight of a humpback waving its tail. When he climbed the fly bridge of his twenty-nine-foot Luhrs and spotted the fin through the binoculars, not only did he see the whale, he also marveled at the sight of the slob-sized tarpon that cruised neatly through the water just meters away from the humpback. He called to his island boy, "Rig up the chateaubriand!" As he motored toward the tarpon, the boy baited the line with a blue crab.

Once they were within a couple hundred feet of the silver giant, Mortenson cut the V-8 and zeroed in with a trolling motor. When he saw the tarpon's monster eyes, he took the rig and flung the crab well ahead of the silver king. He watched the bait sink slowly as the giant fish approached. A hit! The rod tipped and bounced while Mortenson cranked the handle in a fury to come tight to the beast. Suddenly a six-foot tarpon flew, its gills rattling as the king danced his tail across the water. Then the giant silver spun a cartwheel in an attempt to throw the hook. But Mortenson cranked and hauled, and eventually he pulled the tarpon into the boat. He had fed that tale to many a hungry ear on his charters, to his yacht-club cronies, but never once had he mentioned his island guide.

Salazar leaned over and placed his hands on the desk. "So, Daniel could've followed your lead—taken off to find his prize." Mortenson opened his mouth to answer, but Salazar rushed on. "And he wasn't alone, at least not that first morning. Word has it he hired some tarpon guru."

Mortenson's eyes grew round. "That kid wouldn't know a silver king from his own a-hole." The captain's hand quivered as he cupped it around the cigarette to catch the ash.

Salazar handed him an ashtray. "You know him?"

"I've seen him. Hanging around the Conch Shell on Pass-A-Grille." Mortenson flicked the ash. "One thing for sure—it ain't tarpon that kid's after."

Victor felt the tension rise in the room. Salazar pressed his fingertips together as Mortenson spouted off about the mutton-chopped twenty-year-old that everyone called Cuda, short for barracuda. He'd come from Puerto Rico with his mother just a couple of years ago. He and a couple of his long-haired buddies scraped barnacles off boat bottoms or polished teakwood for beer money. Mortenson said last summer, after Cuda took off for a while, he came back sporting a gold chain around his neck. In the bar, he bought a round of drinks for everyone and bragged about his ship coming in—literally. He'd just paid cash for a twenty-eight-foot Trojan Sea Breeze.

"He's smuggling," Mortenson said. "Running ganja from Jamaica into Pass-A-Grille." The next question hovered silently in the cigarette smoke between them. Then Mortenson bellowed, "I couldn't tell you why Danny was fishing with him though. It don't make sense."

Salazar sat down at his desk and scribbled out Cuda's name on a legal pad. For the next few minutes, he picked Mortenson's brain about the boy's pals, the kind of car he drove, the last time he'd seen him; that sort of thing. Then he asked the old salt if he'd be willing to lead a search to find Daniel Westcott.

"I'd be much obliged," he answered.

That afternoon, Salazar picked Victor up at his downtown office, a two-story building on the south end of Ashley Drive. Victor had renovated the concrete-block warehouse, stuccoed it, and then added four-foot, wood-framed picture windows and plate-glass doors. His uncle had bought the building for him and even paid for the renovations to help Victor get started. Carlos insisted Victor needed a downtown address to attract the finest architects and the wealthiest banks and to inform the Tampa zoning commissioners that concerning development, Victor was, above all, a serious player.

Victor met Salazar on the corner of Ashley and Brorein Street. The chief had changed into his street clothes, left his squad car in the garage, and borrowed his wife's Pinto wagon to drive across the Howard Franklin to find the boy named Cuda.

"Thanks for coming with me," Salazar said when Victor jumped into the car. Victor rolled up his shirt sleeves and said, "My afternoon was running slow anyway." He sensed the chief was nervous.

"After this morning, I'm not sure where this investigation's headed," Salazar said. "But I need someone I can trust—especially if there's smugglers involved." The chief went on to say he suspected a few of his men at the precinct were involved with pot smuggling in a big way. "It's a clandestine business with far-reaching tentacles. Difficult to track, and lots of money is involved." Then he shook his head. "But let's not jump to conclusions."

As they made their way through downtown, Salazar changed the subject. He started asking personal questions. "So, how'd you get into development?" He glanced over at Victor. "I thought you were a tile setter like your dad."

Victor felt his cheeks go hot. He assumed his uncle had told Salazar the nuts and bolts of his story, but for some reason, the chief wanted to hear it from him. "I grew up laying tiles, that's for sure," Victor said. A certain shyness overcame him any time he was forced to talk about himself.

"I knew your dad," Salazar said, keeping his eyes on the road. "Used to see him at Carmine's drinking *café con leche* with your uncle. He could be a tough guy."

Victor laughed. "Yeah, when I was a kid, he'd grab my ankles and yank me out of bed at five a.m. He figured I wouldn't fall back asleep if I was already on the floor."

The chief chuckled. "Sounds like your dad."

"But my mom was right behind him, putting my socks on." They both laughed at that. Then Victor told Salazar about the art scholarship he'd earned to the University of Alabama.

The chief's eyebrows shot up. "You went to college?"

"Nope," Victor said. "My dad needed me in the business. There was lots of competition at the time, and I was good at mosaics, creating my own designs." His cheeks flared again.

"I'll bet."

"Then my dad died, and Uncle Carlos said, 'Time to get off your knees, boy!'" Salazar turned onto the Howard Franklin Bridge. "I got my contractor's license, and my uncle found me a couple of small projects. My business took off from there."

While the chief weighed the story, Victor gazed out the window at the sun sizzling over Tampa Bay. Sailboats, trawlers, and cruisers darted across the basin, while a couple of skiffs trolled the shadow lines beneath the Gandy Bridge, tarpon hunting. Victor was fascinated with the bright water that teemed with a silent life he knew nothing about. He sensed something mysterious in its vastness, in the small ripples that skittered the surface. After the accident, his father swore off boating, sailing— anything that had to do with the water. Even when Victor begged to go fishing off the causeway, his father would ruffle the curls on his head and challenge him to a game of hoops. As he looked across the bay sparkling like a cool gem, Victor imagined a life on that water like Mortenson's or even Daniel Westcott's—who everyone knew fished like a pro even if he was an amateur.

When Salazar turned down the air conditioner, vaporous clouds spewed through the vents, struggling to keep pace with the day's heat. He pulled a kerchief from his pocket and dabbed at the sweat trickling down his neck. "You know, I wanted to talk to you about your uncle," he said. Salazar coughed a little to clear his throat. "Carlos has some sort of affinity with Daniel Westcott. Something to do with being crowned the first king of SantY'ago, while Daniel is Gasparilla's oldest king."

Victor nodded, eager to divert the attention from himself.

"But Carlos doesn't really *know* Daniel," Salazar said. "Doesn't know anything about him, except what he wants to believe."

Victor aimed an air vent directly on his face. He wasn't quite sure what Salazar was getting at, but he assumed the chief knew a lot more about Daniel Westcott than he was willing to let on. "This kid named Cuda doesn't sound like a fishing guide," he said, throwing out a verbal hook.

Salazar pressed his lips together. "Right, he sounds like a smuggler. Maybe there's a connection here." He shifted uneasily in the seat. "You know Daniel's grandson?"

"Not really," Victor said. "He's younger than me."

Salazar nodded and pulled on his chin. "I might be grasping at straws, but I thought Cuda could be one of the boy's friends. Maybe the fishing outing was a way for Daniel to check on him, offer some guidance." Then he said, "I've heard the grandson's away at rehab right now."

Victor gazed out the window. "I didn't know that," he said. Then he thought about the Little League photos he'd seen in Salazar's office. Victor knew the chief and his wife were childless. Salazar had championed the Boys and Girls Clubs of America, the Head Start programs, and coached Little League in Belmont Heights, where it was tough to get fathers to coach because most of them were in jail.

"You remember the Yorktowne scandal?" Salazar asked. When Victor said he'd been in high school and hadn't paid much attention to it, the chief told him how Daniel had been arrested, handcuffed, and locked up the night of his Becca's debutante ball.

Victor sat straight up in his seat. "His *granddaughter* Becca?"

"That's right," Salazar said and smiled at him. "His *only* granddaughter." Victor wiped the sweat from his brow, embarrassed by his obvious interest. The chief said by the time he'd made it to the cell block to question Daniel, he'd found him on the cot, head in hands, mumbling to himself. "When he saw me, he jumped up and started dancing a little jig." Salazar chuckled. "He sang some ditty as he danced, like he was putting on a one-man show."

"Was he drunk?"

"Stone-cold sober," Salazar said. "I never had any intention of holding him without bail, but I couldn't help watching him play out his act."

"What about the Yorketowne affair?" Victor asked. "Was he guilty?"

Salazar mopped the sweat from his forehead again. "They were all a bunch of rascals in that company. Scamps, every one of them. When we finally untangled the web, the whole dispute was settled by attorneys behind closed doors. Fines were paid, but no one went to jail."

Victor mulled over the story. "So why the song and dance?"

The chief pulled on his chin. "I think our King Daniel is a master of diversion."

Once off the bridge, Salazar turned toward the Pinellas Bayway which would lead them to Pass-A-Grille. "Let's hope we can find this Cuda kid and find out what he was doing on the *Sea Booty* the day Daniel disappeared."

Salazar turned onto Gulf Boulevard. They hadn't gone a half mile when they spotted the Conch Shell's driftwood sign hanging between two palms. The chief pulled into the gravel lot. The bar was nothing but a cedar shack with a thatched roof and a parking lot full of pickup trucks and motorcycles. Salazar parked next to a banana tree. When Victor saw him pat the side pocket of his khakis, he realized he'd hidden a revolver there.

On their way through the lot, Victor noticed peace symbols on bumper stickers and Gasparilla beads hanging from rearview mirrors. He expected a young crowd. When they reached the door, Salazar pushed on it, but it stuck. With a slight thrust of his hip, it popped open, and the two of them stood on the threshold, blinking into darkness. A hush fell over the room.

As Victor's eyes adjusted to the light, he saw gamesters gathering cards and stuffing money into their pockets. Then, like cockroaches, they skittered out the back door. By the time he and Salazar made their way to the bar and pulled out stools, half the tables had emptied. Outside, engines revved and took off.

"What can I get y'all?" The bartender threw down a couple of Budweiser coasters. He set his hands on his hips and eyed Salazar cautiously. The man couldn't have been more than five feet six and was pushing 250 pounds. Sporting a kelly-green T-shirt and an orange beard, he looked like a disgruntled leprechaun who'd just ran out of luck. Salazar asked for two Cokes. The man grabbed two cups from the top of a stack of red plastic tumblers. "You're not from around here, are y'all?" he asked as he filled the cups with ice. When he set the drinks on the bar, Salazar pulled out his wallet badge.

"I'm looking for a twenty-year-old kid named Cuda," he said. "Heard he comes in here a lot."

The bartender threw up his hands. "I just sell drinks," he said, backing away. "I don't know nothing."

Salazar slipped the wallet back into his pocket. "Look, I don't care what goes on here. I'm out of my jurisdiction. I just want to talk to the boy."

The bartender crossed a pair of meaty arms over his belly. "Is he in trouble?"

"He went out fishing with a Tampa man, a Daniel Westcott, the day before he disappeared. Daniel hasn't turned up yet." Salazar stirred the drink with a straw. "Thought the kid might know something."

The bartender waddled in close to Salazar and lowered his voice. "Does the guy have a boat?"

Salazar nodded. "A thirty-six-foot Hatteras. It's missing also."

"Don't know him," the bartender said too fast. He grabbed the towel that hung from his waist and began wiping the bar with a fury. "Lots of fellers come and go."

The leprechaun was lying. Victor knew it, and so did the chief. But Victor also knew Salazar would not pry. Instead he slipped two dollars under the coaster as if to thank the tight-lipped bartender for the most revealing information he could've offered—silence. Victor scanned the bar and considered the furtive glances thrown their way. It might take the chief a few days, but he'd uncover the connection between Daniel Westcott and the kid named Cuda.

Back in the car, as they headed for the bay way, the chief said, "That's not what I wanted to hear." Victor peered out the window at the intercoastal shimmering like a jewel. "I probably shouldn't tell you this," Salazar said, "but I checked Daniel's bank accounts this morning. He's broke."

Victor felt his heart jump in his chest. "Totally?"

Salazar nodded. "He's living on credit." Victor noticed the chief's knuckles blanch white as he gripped the steering wheel. "I don't want your uncle to know that Daniel's flat broke; let him draw his own conclusions about Cuda. Same goes for the family. We need to protect them now. Nothing's been proven yet." When Victor agreed, Salazar added, "But this whole disappearance act is beginning to stink."

CHAPTER 8 ✳ "Ch-Ch-Ch-Changes!"

Thursday evening, the night of the Chiseler's fundraiser at the old Tampa Bay Hotel, a purple van painted with flowers and peace symbols drove into town. The people who saw it called it a hippie van, and watched as it turned onto Brorein Street and crossed the bridge to the Bayshore. Apparently it drove right up under the portico of the Westcott Mansion and parked.

A long-haired young man dressed in bell-bottom jeans jumped down from the driver's seat and sprinted up the steps to the house. A couple of people strolling along the Bayshore that evening thought it might be the Westcotts' grandson home from rehabilitation. But no one knew that it was, in fact, Adam Dicker, who had driven all the way from New York City to talk to Becca.

In the time it took Becca and Victor to stop at his office and sign a contract that had to be postmarked and mailed that night, Adam had already located the old hotel where Natalie said he would find Becca. It didn't look like a hotel now. Years of neglect had taken its toll on the dazzling gem set amid the swamp sand on the Hillsborough River. The Cuban mahogany doors that were once polished to a high sheen had warped in the intense heat. French glass windows were scratched, and clouded venetian mirrors hung haphazardly throughout the building. Priceless artifacts and exotic furnishings had fallen to ruin. After a quick and artless renovation, the city had offered the University of Tampa what was left of the shabby relic. Adam wandered through the lobby, through the mix of students who carried backpacks flung over their shoulders. Members of the Chiselers Club handed out pamphlets that outlined their intentions to restore the hotel to its original beauty. When Adam couldn't find Becca in the crowd, he headed back to the verandah and settled into a rocking chair to wait for her.

The evening had crept up heavy and warm. Cicadas began their high-pitched song that carried out over the river with a quivering force that was palpable in the dusk of night. As they followed the walkway to the hotel, Victor held Becca's arm like a porcelain doll's ready to crack. Or so she thought. Ever since he'd picked her up, Victor had been preoccupied, quieter than Becca had ever seen him. Her attempts to engage him in conversation were met with one-word answers and thin smiles that dissolved into silence. *Something was wrong,* she thought. Halfway up the stairs to the hotel, a gust of wind blew Becca's skirt and puffed out the front. Victor laughed, his first hearty gesture of the night. He asked her if she'd swallowed a watermelon. *Just a seed,* she thought, *right now.*

Becca was smoothing the front of her dress when she noticed a scruffy-faced man cross the verandah. She didn't recognize him. Maybe it was the beard or the way he looked oddly out of place in the context of the old hotel—either one, she'd turned away. But when Adam caught her at the double doors and stepped right out in front of her, Becca gasped.

"Thank God, you're here!" he said. Becca blinked hard in the failing light. The brightness in Adam's eyes frightened her, and she stumbled awkwardly into Victor, who caught her by the waist. Adam eyed Victor's seersucker pants, white jacket, and pink tie. "I called everyone," he said turning back to Becca. "Pug Kismet told me you'd gone home."

Becca winced at the sound of the letch's name. She clutched her pocketbook tighter and stared into Adam's face. "What're you doing here?"

"We need to talk," he pleaded and pointed toward the rocking chairs. Becca tried to introduce the men, but Adam ignored Victor's outstretched hand. He just kept begging. "It won't take long," he promised her.

Becca urged Victor to go inside. When she realized his reluctance, she whispered to him, "Tell Margie I'll be right in."

After Victor disappeared through the double doors, Adam led Becca to the last rocking chair on the north side of the verandah. The night had become suddenly still. Becca sat down, and Adam pulled up a chair to face her. "Look, I know I've been a shit, but everything's changed." He leaned forward and placed his hands on her knees as if gripping a steering wheel. "I've been drafted," he said, his eyes flashing. Becca held her breath as he explained how his low draft number had kicked in after he graduated. Neither his parents' connections nor his failed status as conscientious objector could help him now. He'd been ordered to boot camp in upstate New York. "I've got to report on June 24."

Becca's hand flew to her mouth. "You're going?" she asked through her fingers.

"Hell no!" The cicadas, in full song, accompanied Adam's litany. "They said I could be a cleric or a medic, but I'd still have to carry a gun." He clenched a fist and pounded it lightly on Becca's knee. "Fuck 'em." Becca felt his energy charging every cell in her body. "I've heard of guys who flunked their physical by swallowing tinfoil or starving themselves, but it's hit or miss. I can't take that chance." He wiped the sweat from his brow. "If I don't show up, they'll throw my ass in jail."

Becca gripped the arms on the rocking chair. Lamplight from the walkway cast a glow across Adam's face. "I'm leaving," he said. "Toronto. And I want you to come with me."

A roaring noise started in Becca's ears. She swallowed hard and studied his hands, which still clutched her knees. "What about Louise?"

"That was a mistake."

Becca kept her eyes riveted on Adam's hands, remembering all the nights they'd caressed her. She ached for him. "When are you going?"

He looked up, hopeful. "Tonight. I gotta make the border by midnight Saturday."

Becca leaned back in the rocker. She pictured them skipping down the steps of the old hotel, jumping in his van, and escaping together. They both had something to run from now.

"We could get your things," Adam said.

"I want to." Becca took a breath. Then she told him about her grandfather, how he'd been missing for twelve days. She told him the bank accounts were overdrawn, her grandmother was cracking under the strain, and Victor's uncle was helping the chief of police launch a search for Daniel and the *Sea Booty*.

Adam blinked a few times as if baffled by her family's trouble. He released her knees and folded his hands in his lap. "You're not coming with me?"

"I am! But I have to go in here for a while." She nodded toward the hotel and then covered Adam's hands with her own. "I don't want anyone to know I'm leaving." What she meant was she didn't want anyone to stop her.

Adam pinched the end of her chin between his thumb and forefinger. "You're so thin. I'm worried about you." Becca shrugged. Adam peered up at the wrought-iron railings, the chipped paint on the horseshoe arches, the brick mortar stained with mildew. "What is this creepy place?" he asked.

"Just an old hotel," she said. "The townspeople are trying to clean it up."

"Well, good luck on that." Adam tucked a piece of hair behind his ears. "And you're right. This whole town's weird." When he leaned in close, Becca breathed in the scent of him, a woodsy, outdoor smell like cedar. "You don't belong here," he said. "*We* don't belong here."

Through an open window, Becca could hear the pianist playing McCartney's "Maybe I'm Amazed." She placed a hand on Adam's stubbly cheek. "Meet me at home in two hours. I'll be packed and ready to go."

Adam smiled the big toothy grin she loved. "I'll wait 'til I see you on the front porch," he said. "I don't think your grandma likes me." He reached into his pocket and held up a ring. "I'm serious this time, Becca. I want to marry you." When he slipped the ring on her finger, she realized it was just like the one she'd pawned, the same one she'd seen on Louise's hand in the picture. She tried to interrupt him, but he put his fingers to her lips. "Shhh," he said. "I'll make it all up to you. You won't be sorry." Her head went dizzy when he kissed her. "Hurry up." He nuzzled her neck. "I miss every inch of you."

Just inside the lobby of the old hotel, Becca leaned against the door jamb to catch her breath. She glanced down at the ring on her finger and turned the diamond to the inside of her palm. She would ask Adam about the ring tonight after she told him about the baby. She'd tell him how she had hidden the first one in his medicine cabinet and used it to get the abortion she couldn't go through with. He'd understand, just like she would understand if this was Louise's ring. She didn't care. She just wanted Adam to love her and take her away from this town. *And that's exactly what he's going to do*, she thought.

"Are you okay?" Victor startled her.

Becca clasped her hands behind her back. "Adam's a good friend." She wouldn't tell Victor he was dodging the draft. Somehow she didn't think he'd approve. Instead she smiled at him while his dark eyes examined her. Although the steadfast way he held her in his gaze was undeniable scrutiny, Becca felt oddly comfortable in his presence. There was a sureness about him, an unwavering goodness that was not attached to circumstance. "Let's go in," Becca said.

Victor caught Becca's elbow and led her through the lobby, down the hall lined with Oriental ceramics and potted palms and into the solarium lined with elongated windows and curved walls. The glow from the lamplight filtered in through the chintz sheers and mingled with a round of yellow lights circling above the arches. The blend emitted an amber haze so thick and lush, it settled on the faces of gentlemen dressed in suits and bare-shouldered women flouncing around in summer dresses.

"Something to drink?" Victor asked.

Becca nodded, and Victor disappeared through a throng of bow ties, starched white shirts, and fuchsia, lilac, and azure skirts that dusted the floor. Faces emerged in the crowd: Julie Schaeffer, Gasparilla Maid, 1970; Laura Rhodes of the Rhodes family Trucking Corporation; Patricia Flynn, her father the 1967 Gasparilla King; and Robert (Buddy) Myers, a Gaspar pirate, who had been kicked out of three law schools and was now contemplating medicine. Then there was Major Mike Harris, one of the lucky ones home from 'Nam with three pins holding his right shoulder together. Besty Thompson, Leila Stokes, Kyle Saunders, Benny Glynn, and Randy Waters all moved in the dusty orange light as if it were the Captain's Ball or a queen's party, and not the junior members of the Chiselers gathering for a fundraiser. The scene looked very familiar to Becca and yet surreal too.

From the northwest corner of the room, the pianist tapped out "The Entertainer." In a whirl of perfumed smoke, Becca saw Margie push through the crowd and splash her grasshopper on Kyle Saunders' jacket. "Sorry, sorry," she apologized and wiggled her way toward Becca. "You finally made it. What's up?"

Becca whispered, "Adam's here." Margie's eyes grew wide when Becca showed her the ring on her finger.

"He knows about the baby?"

"Not yet; I'm telling him tonight, before he leaves." Becca leaned in close and told Margie as discreetly as possible that Adam had been drafted and was leaving for Toronto. "He wants me to go with him."

Margie's mouth flew open. "You're going?"

"Not until my granddad shows up." Becca didn't want anyone to know she was leaving tonight. Not even her best friend. Margie's skin left the warm scent of jasmine against Becca's cheek. "But I won't need the money now. We're getting married."

"Wow, Becca. Wow!" Becca hushed her, and Margie lowered her voice. "Any news on your grandfather?"

"Not yet, but Victor says the search will start soon."

Just then, Becca heard her name shoot across the room. A small group followed Buddy Myers through the hazy solarium, in a fussy but directed rustle of skirts and expectant faces. Betsy asked about New York, while Pattie wondered how long Becca had been home. Mike said he was sorry about Becca's grandfather, and everyone agreed how frightful it was Daniel had been missing for two weeks. Randy asked if she was looking for a gig in town.

Becca pressed her hands together. "I'm just visiting." She shifted her weight from side to side, a centerpiece in the half circle. Although it felt odd to be surrounded by her childhood friends, she managed the smiling and the short hugs. She set her shoulders square, and shot back quick, plucky answers to all the questions they fired at her. It was all simpler than she'd imagined. A welcome break, actually, from the nights she'd spent reading the first volume of Rebecca's diary with its tedious lists, dog-eared pages, and the feeling that someone was looking over her shoulder.

Through the crowd, Becca spotted Victor holding up two drinks. He excused himself through the circle and handed Becca a tequila sunrise. The room fell silent. Outside, a freighter sounded a long, low bray. The vibration drifted in the air for some time, a dissipating moan that was more felt than heard. Night had fallen, and the dank scent of the river had moved in, as if the freighter had churned up the bottom and called forth its charge.

"I didn't know the Chiselers had a new member," Buddy said.

"He's my guest," Becca announced and introduced Victor around.

"You're from the Krewe of SantY'ago?" Randy asked, ignoring Victor's outstretched hand. "Wasn't your father crowned king this year?"

"My uncle," Victor said and raised his glass. "To the new El Rey, the counterfeit king." He laughed, and Margie, Leila, and Beth laughed right along with him. But the men wanted to know where Victor went to school, what kind of business he was in, and who he worked for.

"I'm renovating the old Maynard Mansion in Hyde Park." Victor went on to explain the project, but soon the men turned away from him. Their conversation drifted to the rise of downtown, to a possible pro football franchise, and, finally, to the weather. Becca crossed her arms tightly, disappointed by her friends' cold reception of Victor. She felt suddenly protective toward him; she didn't want him to be hurt.

Outside the wind had kicked up and filled the curtains that now billowed in and out like uninvited guests. Across the room, the piano had been rolled away, and in its place, a five-piece band began to warm up. When the band started, a gust of wind burst in through the open doors and blew a plastic cup off one of the tables. It bounced twice and then rolled across the dance floor. Victor asked Becca to dance. She smiled and set her drink down.

If Victor was shaken by her snobby friends, he didn't show it. He took her hand and led her to the dance floor. Then he slipped his arm around her waist and guided her in an easy foxtrot across the floor. The band played Marvin Gaye's "What's Going On," and Becca realized she hadn't ballroom danced like that since Leila Stokes's father was crowned king her senior year of high school. She peered out over his shoulder—and at the faces spinning past her.

"You're quite the enigma," Victor said. He pulled her away just enough to see her face. "The talented, mysterious, and troubled Becca McNeil."

Becca gazed up at his dark eyes. "Troubled?" *How could he know?*

"Well, you're grandfather's missing."

"Right." Outside, thunder rolled, not the distant rumble of heat thunder but a sudden crack, unexpected, and threatening—and close.

Then Victor asked, "How's your mother?"

Becca felt her body tense as he guided her along the edge of the dance floor toward the doors that opened onto the river. She fixed her gaze over his shoulder and ignored the question. No one asked about her mother—except an outsider.

Caught up in the rhythm, Becca thought about the diaries hidden under her bed. She'd finished the first volume last night, and had stayed up until 2:00 a.m. reading about Charles and Silva Westcott fleeing to Florida, straight into the horrors of the Seminole War. She'd learned about the contagious diseases that raged in the pen off Egmont Key where the Seminoles were held while waiting shipment out to New Orleans. She read how an Indian woman had thrust an infant into Silva's arms to save him from deportment and certain death and how Silva had adopted him. She read about Yankee occupation troops, the end of the Civil War, and the gambling entrepreneurs who came into town with their diamond stick pins glittering in the late-afternoon sun. They strolled down Tampa's main streets soliciting mulatto prostitutes who decked themselves out in feathers and wore high-button shoes. She read about the building of the Tampa Bay Hotel, the casino, the state fair, and the first Gasparilla. When she finished, she'd flipped through the second volume. Strewn among Rebecca's holiday guest lists, menus, and an elaborate family tree, Becca saw her mother's name, Julia, Julia, Julia, punctuating the entries.

Victor caught Becca's gaze. "Far away?"

Becca's face flushed. "I was thinking about my great-grandmother. She used to dance in this ballroom when the hotel was in its heyday."

"That is far away." Victor said as she led Becca along the edges of the dance floor. Lightning flared through the elongated windows and illuminated the dancers who swayed to the smoky beat. Near the doors,

Becca felt the dampness of the river, of the night swelling as the first scatter of rain blew in.

"It's the storm before the drought," Victor said.

"But it's not supposed to rain, not tonight."

Victor gripped her tighter. "Well, we'll have to forgive it, won't we?"

Forgive it. The words stunned Becca because they were exactly what her father had said. "Let's forgive it." And then he said there was nothing in a family that could not be forgiven. But at the time, Becca didn't know who should be forgiven. Her mother—for shunning Kurt? And she didn't know why Kurt had been the one her mother had refused to rock or hold or feed. She only knew that after he was born, Natalie had led her to her mother's bed, where Julia stared straight ahead and twisted the linens between her hands.

Becca shivered as they danced past the open windows where the wind gushed in. Did Rebecca know the reason for Julia's madness? Had she recorded it in the second volume? Did she know, as Kurt grew older, why Nattie had said to Becca, "You've only got one job, child. Keep your brother away from your mother."

Becca pressed closer to Victor, to absorb his warmth and the easy flow of his body. "Forgive it," Victor had said. Just like her father had said, "Yes, let's forgive it." But how could Kurt have gotten away from her? He was only three at the time. Becca was already eight, and she had helped to hide the colored eggs in the back garden. Nattie had dressed him in a white suit with short pants, a navy shirt, and polished white shoes. After finding each egg, Kurt ran first to Nattie and Grandpa Dan and then to Eula, who brushed back the curls from his hot face. One moment, he'd been right there, licking the eggs, stuffing them in his pockets, stomping on one and then another in the grass. And then he was gone!

Becca had raced up the stairs; she knew where he would go. She could still smell the sweaty scent of him lingering in the stairwell. When she reached the east hall, she didn't need to knock because the door was wide open. Her mother sat in the Queen Anne chair in front of the window, holding the basket of eggs in her lap. Julia's hair was long then. Dark, chestnut-brown and shiny, it cascaded over her white linen dress. She held a blue speckled egg between her thumb and forefinger. She turned it in the light.

"Purdy," Kurt said.

Becca stepped up behind her brother and caught his shoulders. He flinched.

"Purdy egg," he said. He was trembling. He wiggled away from Becca and edged closer to his mother. Julia let the egg slip into her palm. She cradled it there, covering it with her fingers. Then she let out a small cry like that of a sparrow being squeezed. The egg split. It was a muffled crunch, fast and merciless, that sent the hard-boiled insides squishing around her fingers.

Outside thunder cracked, a jolt that set the dance floor vibrating. Victor spun Becca past the open door of the solarium. The rain spattered in, driven by the wind. The wind whined as it rolled in off the river, as if it were an animal caught in a thicket. He twirled her toward the edge of the dance floor, close to the windows where the lightning flashed in. It was all a bit bizarre—the wind gusting in from the river, the silver-streaked lightning, the rain acting as if invited to be a part of the dance. It came in quicker here, by the doors. It was like a game. Then the music stopped. Becca stepped back to applaud the band, her breathing fast. She turned to Victor to thank him.

"The pleasure was mine, I assure you." As Victor led her toward the tables, Becca felt like she was coming out of a trance. The music, the dancing, and Victor's questions had driven her into the past, into Rebecca's diaries, and what may have been recorded in the second volume. She would take the diaries with her tonight. After all, they'd been sent to her.

When they reached the table, Victor handed Becca her drink. He was smiling. "We tripped the light fandango."

Becca sipped her drink as the band launched into David Bowie's "Changes." Buddy came up to them, his speech slurry from too many beers. "Bowie stole your act," he said to Becca. "Ch-ch-ch-changes." He sang off key.

Becca laughed. Then she stuck her tongue out at him like she did when they were young.

After Buddy wandered off, Victor asked, "What did he mean by that?"

"Oh, I stuttered as a kid," Becca said. "Buddy used to stand next to me in the spelling bee. He'd blurt out the letters when I couldn't. I think it traumatized him." Then she glanced down at her watch. "You know, I need to get home. My grandmother's alone."

"You won't dance with me again?" Victor asked. But Becca could tell he was relieved. He downed his drink in one gulp. "Let's go."

They were headed toward the door when Buddy stopped them. "You can't leave now. You have to sing."

"Another time," Becca promised.

From the bar, Mike Harris, the Vietnam vet, overheard the request and waved his good arm in the air while the damaged one lay pressed against his ribs, bound in a sling. "Sing for me," he called out.

Becca couldn't refuse that.

Buddy led her back toward the stage while Victor lagged behind. "Sing that song you sang at the Captain's Ball," Mike begged. "Right before you took off for Georgetown."

Buddy blurted out the title, "Easy for You."

Becca stepped up on the stage, and the sax player handed her a microphone. "I usually play my own music."

The sax player grinned, his teeth slick against a thick, brown mustache that concealed his upper lip. "Hum a few bars," he said. "We play anything."

The keyboard player nodded at Becca while the drummer tapped his sticks together. She covered the microphone with her hand and hummed the opening measures. After the first three lines, the sax player jumped in and picked up the melody. Then the bass and guitar joined in. Once through the refrain, they stopped. "We got it," the drummer said.

Becca turned to the audience, to the expectant faces lined up in front of her. She cued the sax player, and the drummer rolled out an introductory measure. The music began.

"Don't think I don't see," she sang. Those off-side brushes and stolen looks." The music swelled around her. She heard her voice strong above the instruments. As she listened to the flow of words, to the shift of colors from the sax, the bass, and guitar, she felt outside herself, euphoric. The music was loose and free, like her voice. The effect was as buoyant as a sailing ship. "You just turn and walk out that door," she sang. "But oh darling, we both know how easy this leaving is for you."

The moment the music stopped, Becca heard Victor's praise coming from the crowd.

Buddy turned to him. "Didn't you know?"

"She's the best!" Mike called from the bar.

With the applause still coming in waves, Becca turned to the band and started clapping for them. The musicians bowed in turn. Then Becca took Victor's outstretched hand and stepped down from the stage. The band kicked up a jaunty rendition of "Twist and Shout," and one by one, the crowd moved onto the dance floor.

Victor led Becca through the ballroom. They'd almost reached the solarium when she spotted a shadowy figure hidden halfway behind a pillar. In the dim light, she thought it was Adam. She squinted at the soaking-wet T-shirt, the stringy hair, and tattered jeans hanging on his hips. "Oh God," she said to Victor when she recognized his flame-red hair. "It's my brother."

Kurt's flip-flops were covered in mud, and black muck spattered his jeans. "Nattie told me you were here," he muttered. The smell of rain, stale smoke, and liquor clung to him. He pulled a pack of cigarettes from his back pocket, tapped one out, and lit up. He took a drag, his hand shaking.

"Granddad just vanished into thin air?" he asked through the smoke. "How's that possible?"

"We have some leads," Victor said.

Kurt slit his eyes and staggered up to Victor. "Who're you?"

Becca stepped between them, realizing her brother was out-of-his-mind drunk. "This is Victor," she said. "His uncle and Chief Salazar are launching a search for Granddad."

"That's right," Victor said and held out his hand.

Kurt stepped passed Becca and blew smoke in Victor's face. "I need a drink."

Becca pulled him toward the lobby. "Not here."

Kurt shook her off and squared himself in front of Victor. "You'll get me a drink, won't you?"

Becca could see her brother's anger smoldering. She turned to Victor. "Just get him a beer."

Victor crossed his arms over his chest. "I don't think so," he said. "But I will take him home."

Kurt glared at him. "Who'd you think you are, Mr. Pink Tie?" He threw down his cigarette and took a swing at Victor's face.

Victor blocked it and easily caught Kurt by his wrist. He struggled to free it, but Victor held him fast. Kurt shouted, "Lemme go, you dirty spic." The band stopped.

Becca felt her face flare at the sound of her brother's name-calling. Still she wanted to protect him. "Don't hurt him," she begged.

When Victor released him, Kurt barreled headfirst into Victor's chest, knocking both to the ground. As they rolled and flailed, Buddy and Mike came running over. With Mike's good arm and Buddy's help, they pulled the men apart.

Becca ran to Kurt and helped him to his feet. "Stop it!" she screamed. "We're going home."

Kurt brushed himself off. "I'm not going anywhere with that creep."

Buddy stepped in and took a hold of Kurt's arm. "Hey, you muskrat," he grinned. "I'll take you home."

Kurt laughed. "Okay, Buddy boy. We'll get ourselves a drink."

Becca turned to Victor, who'd pulled off his tie and was holding it in his hand. "I better go with him," she said, apologizing. She wanted to explain her brother's anger to Victor. She wanted to tell him it had nothing to do with him, but there wasn't time. She looked past Victor to the faces staring at her and Kurt. *Couldn't one thing ever be easy?* she thought.

As the three of them walked through the solarium into the lobby, Margie ran up behind Becca and hugged her. "Remember, you won't be long here," she whispered.

Becca heard it as "you don't belong here" *And I don't,* she thought. *And that's why I'm leaving tonight.* She turned to say good-bye to Victor, who appeared unshaken by the calamity, by the guests pointing fingers, and their whispers. She waved to him, believing it would be the last time she ever saw him.

CHAPTER 9 ✳ King-napped

Earlier that afternoon in Salazar's office, Victor and his uncle sat across the desk and listened while the chief told them his undercover agent had found one of Cuda's cohorts, who was willing to talk for free beer. Uncle Carlos chewed the tip of his unlit cigar while Victor studied Salazar's face and pressed the palms of his hands together.

Apparently the agent had hooked up with a kid named Spaceman, a buddy of Cuda's, who had enrolled in a local high school under Cuda's legal name and was earning a GED for him. Over some Bud Lites at the Conch Shell, Spaceman bragged that Cuda paid him in weed, two pounds a month, just to go to night school for him. For the diploma, Spaceman was getting 1 percent of the profits from Cuda's latest drug run to Jamaica. Salazar read from the agent's report. "Cuda's got one big boat this time—a thirty-six-foot Hatteras. He's filling her belly with six thousand pounds of salad, which should clear about a million bucks."

Carlos tapped his cigar on the desk. "That smuggler's kidnapped Daniel and the *Sea Booty*," he sputtered. "We have to find them!"

Salazar leaned back in his chair. "It's not that easy." Victor knew in the last two days that Salazar had done his homework. Cuda and his gang would be hard to track. "There's a lot of moving parts to this," Salazar explained. The chief told them about the skiffs that ran the blocks of weed from the docks to the boat. He told them about the stash houses, and the trucks, drivers, and crews, and the mountain-dwelling king daddies who sold ganja to the white men with boats. "And weather's always a factor."

Salazar warned that a tropical storm could rise out of nowhere and hang up a boat for days. "We can't be sure where Cuda is."

Carlos pulled a lighter from his pocket and examined the flame. "The *Sea Booty*'s got a radio, *si*?" He puffed on the cigar to light it. "We make a story. Tell those king-nappers they go free for Daniel's safe return."

Salazar ran a hand through his salt-and-pepper hair. Victor knew the chief thought Daniel could be party to this drug run, but he didn't want to tell Carlos. Not yet. Salazar talked on. At the Conch Shell, his undercover agent had heard about a snapper fisherman from Naples who regularly drove his *Bait Master*, a sixty-five-foot Cyrus Hull, complete with ice, food, and beer to meet his smuggling crew in Kingston. Victor studied Carlos, who was blowing smoke across the desk. Salazar was right. His uncle had no idea the chief was trying to draw a connection between this fisherman/smuggler and Daniel Westcott. Carlos was convinced of Daniel's innocence.

Salazar leaned across the desk. "What if Daniel's not on the boat?"

Carlos tugged on his snowy beard. "Where else could he be?"

Salazar shrugged. "I'm just saying if he's not, we'd tip off Cuda, and he could stash their load off Andros Island and sink the boat." Salazar picked up a pen and tapped it against the desk. "Then they could motor into Freeport on a skiff, and we'd have nothing but Spaceman's story, which isn't worth peanuts without evidence."

Carlos threw his hands up. "We can't sit and do nothing! This Cuda knows where Daniel is!"

Victor believed that, and from the look on Salazar's face, he knew it too. The chief chewed the tip of his pen. "Spaceman's our key," he said after some thought. "Seems like he can be bought for the right price." Salazar jotted down some notes on a legal pad. "Cuda might tell Spaceman where and when he's planning to make his drop. Then we could head him off."

Carlos jumped up from his chair. "That's it! We'll catch that barracuda and bring Daniel home."

Salazar kept writing as Carlos paced the room. His portly body moved to an internal rhythm. Without taking his eyes off his notepad, the chief told them Captain Mortenson wanted two seafaring vessels to capture the *Sea Booty*. They could take the *Lady Luck,* but they'd need another boat. "The captain's charting out the course right now," Salazar said. "He'll give us all the details in a couple of days." Victor thought about his uncle's sixty-foot Cascade schooner, one of the largest sailboats in town. But that schooner would be worthless on this search mission. They needed sleek motorboats that could maneuver whatever channel Cuda decided to take to unload his stash.

As if Carlos had read Victor's mind, he blurted out, "I can get a twenty-five-foot Sea Craft Angler. It's one of the fastest boats around here."

Salazar set his pen down. Victor knew that was last thing the chief wanted—to risk his best friend's life (or anyone else's, for that matter). But smugglers carried guns and used them when threatened. Victor also knew the Tampa Police Department was not equipped with vessels sophisticated enough to be involved with capturing smugglers. And from what Salazar had confided to him, the department was crawling with corruption. The chief had to hand-pick the men he could trust to join this mission. One slip of the tongue could tip Cuda off and blow the chief's whole sting operation.

Victor felt himself being drawn further into this search for Daniel Westcott. He pressed his palms onto to his knees. "I might be able to help," he offered. "I'm taking Becca to a fundraiser tonight." He leaned forward in his chair. "I could ask around. They're all Gaspar pirates, members of the yacht club." Victor smiled. "I might be able to rustle up a boat."

Salazar's face lit up. "Tell them I'd man the crew, and I'd be responsible for any mishaps."

Victor stood up to shake the chief's hand while Carlos spouted on that this was *his* search, *his* plan to find Daniel Westcott. They couldn't just leave him out! Victor led his uncle through the police station, wondering how he would find a yacht club pirate to lend him a boat this evening. He didn't know then how the night would literally blow up in his face.

CHAPTER 10 ✳ The Clock Struck Ten

AFTER BUDDY DROPPED BECCA AT the Westcott home and took off with Kurt, she ran up the porch steps and slipped quietly in the front door. From the foyer, she spotted Nattie in the living room, asleep in the yellow armchair. Becca tried to get up the stairs without waking her, but her grandmother caught her on the first landing.

"You're home?" Natalie struggled out of the chair. "Where's Kurt?"

Becca turned on the stairs. "He's out with Buddy."

Natalie clutched the newel post. "He's drunk."

Becca wanted to say, "What did she expect?" but instead, she said, "Buddy promised to take care of him. He'll be all right. Go to bed."

Becca started up the stairs again; Natalie called after her. "Hey, did that Adam fellow catch up with you?"

For a moment Becca froze. "He did."

"He's your old beau, right?" Natalie turned on the hall light. "What did he want?"

"He just stopped by on his way to the Keys." Nattie scrunched her face and set her hands on her hips. Becca knew she didn't believe her. Her grandmother scrutinized her. "I'm so tired, Nattie." Becca called down. "I'm going to bed." She ran up the last stairs. "You should too."

Once inside her room, Becca locked the door. She pulled down her suitcase from the top shelf and started throwing in jeans, T-shirts, a couple of sweaters, and her tennis shoes. She slipped off the summer halter and hung it in her closet. She wouldn't need that now. Instead she threw on a pair of khaki shorts and a peasant top. She grabbed a hand mirror, her hairbrush, and the makeup Margie had brought her and tossed it all in the suitcase. When it closed easily, she grabbed the diaries out from under the bed and stuffed them in too. Then she stood by the door and listened. She cracked it open an inch. Down the hall, she could hear Nattie talking to her mother. Damn! She couldn't chance being caught. She glanced down at her watch. She still had half an hour.

Becca sat on the floor, pulled out the second volume of Rebecca's diary, and started to read. She read about Daniel and Natalie's marriage. The reception had been held right here on the grounds of the Westcott home. It was early spring, the azaleas and bougainvillea had been in full bloom, and Japanese lanterns hung from the live oaks. The wedding had made front-page news of the Metro section. The clipping fell out. Becca examined the photo of the newlyweds. Barely twenty, Natalie looked like a child. But as young as Daniel was, he still had a certain swagger about him. *Big grin, cocky,* Becca thought. She slipped the clipping back into the journal.

About halfway through the diary, Becca noticed a page that had been dog-eared. It had been read so many times, the folded corner had turned a dirty yellow. She turned to it immediately.

> *... and there in the hall was a terrible racket of crying and fighting going on. I rushed from my room to see Natalie's wild arms and fists flailing at Daniel's chest while he tried to calm her.*
>
> *"Could have been!" Natalie screamed. "She's in there curled up and bleeding. And you say, 'Could have been!'" Natalie kept beating at him. "She said the filthy pirate climbed the trellis to her bedroom and then he defiled her! Go find him and string him up!"*
>
> *It was just past midnight on Gasparilla, and the pistols could still be heard firing in the streets. When Natalie spotted*

me in the hall she dropped her hands to her side. "It's Julia,"
she said. And I nodded because I'd heard.

Then Daniel said, "The streets are crawling with pirates.
How am I supposed to find the one?" Natalie wound up again
and started grabbing at Daniel's beard.

"You find him," she said. "And we'll drag him through
those streets and hang him!"

I gripped Natalie's shoulders as tightly as I could because
she was trembling and frightened. I told her to go to Julia.
Go and sit with her. And that struck her right, gave her a
purpose.

She said, "Yes, I'll go sit with Julia."

Then I said I would call the doctor. Instantly, Natalie's
eyes fixed on me, and we both knew in that moment the
horror of this night may have just begun.

Becca's stomach tightened. She checked the date of the journal entry and counted back the years. Her mother had been sixteen. A familiar sickness rose in Becca's throat. The wretched pirate had climbed the trellis to Julia's room and raped her. Becca remembered Parade Day when she was a child. She remembered the throngs of people and pirates who would stumble up the walkway drunk. They'd pound on the front door, looking for a place to pee. She always wondered why Nattie locked the doors—now she knew.

Becca closed her eyes and felt the lightness rise in her body. She heard the wordless call somewhere above her head. *"Come, come,"* it said. She willed the impulse away, but even as she did, she heard a commotion outside. Pistols fired through the air, and headlights from cars and trucks streamed into her room as if it were Gasparilla Night. Pirates trudged through the front yard on their way downtown to the U Club. She could hear them howling and singing their bawdy songs as if they were right outside her window. Becca covered her ears and glared at the bed that was aglow with the flickering light. It was then she saw the girl curled up and crying beneath the sheets. Becca blinked, and the room went dark.

She clutched the diary that rested on her lap, and the room lit up again. This time, while the pirates hooted outside, Becca knew the girl in her bed had been raped by one of them. She *knew* that girl was her mother. She shut her eyes tightly and wondered how she could be seeing this. It was too clear for imagination, too real for a dream. Was she hallucinating? Had someone slipped something in her drink at the fundraiser? She shook her head; the room went dark again.

Becca sat next to her bedroom door, clutching the diary, until the lights and sounds faded completely. She glanced at her watch and then heard the grandfather clock down the hall strike ten. She tucked the diary back into her suitcase and listened at the door. She couldn't wait any longer. She slipped out of her room and tiptoed toward the stairs. Just before rounding the east hall, she heard footsteps behind her.

"Becca?"

She stopped and whirled around. She saw her mother coming toward her in a flowing, white nightie. Her hair was teased out wild around her face, and her eyes squinted in the dim light. Seeing her mother like that, Becca pictured her as that sixteen-year-old girl, struggling in bed with the Gasparilla pirate hovering above her. *But why didn't she scream?* Becca imagined the pirate had gagged her with his own foul handkerchief and pinned her legs beneath his. He must have held her arms above her head with one hand, while he managed the zipper of his pants with the other. When he finished, he'd slipped off the bed, back out the window, and down the trellis of the house—probably the same way he entered.

"Where're you going?" Julia asked.

Becca tried to hide the suitcase behind her. "Nowhere, Mother."

"You're leaving, aren't you?"

"No, I'm not."

Her mother inched closer. "But you should leave," she said and squeezed Becca's arm. "It's safer that way. Take your suitcase and go."

Bewildered, Becca kissed her mother on the cheek. The old childhood guilt wormed its way to the surface. Unexpected tears sprang to Becca's eyes. But what had she done? Stuttered? Not kept her brother away? But then the same worn-out question taunted her—*Why was she allowed to see her mother while Kurt was not? What had he done?*

Becca nodded to her mother, knowing she wouldn't get the answers tonight. "Go back to bed now," she said. Her mother smiled, and like a child, tottered down the hall and disappeared into her room.

Becca raced down the stairs and out the front door. Once on the porch, she cursed the coach lights that glared down on her like spotlights. *I can't stay there,* she thought. Scanning the yard, she noticed an old garden chair sitting under the live oak. That would be a good place to wait for Adam. She hurried down the front steps, brushed the dried leaves from the chair, and sat down. The moment she settled, all the energy that had propelled her through the evening drained from her body. An intense weariness set in, like she'd been running an endless marathon her whole life. She leaned back in the chair and closed her eyes.

Becca didn't know how long she'd been waiting, but at some point, she'd opened the suitcase and pulled out the second volume of Rebecca's diary. The floodlight, positioned to illuminate the live oak, shone on the journal while Becca remained hidden within the remaining darkness under the tree. A light breeze rustled the leaves and set the moss swinging lazily overhead. Cicadas hummed in the air that had been washed clean with the rain. Becca opened the diary and easily found the dog-eared section that she read again. She puzzled over the events of that Gasparilla Night, hopeful that the following pages would explain what had happened to her mother. Even if she'd been raped at sixteen, that wouldn't account for her mother's refusal to love Kurt or her fear that even now, Becca was not safe in the house. Something that began that Gasparilla Night had been perpetuated throughout the years and had permeated every thought, every cell of her mother's being.

Becca turned the page. But instead of an explanation, there in the middle of her mother's nightmare was a hand-rendered family registry. Becca ran her fingers over the names—Charles Morgan Westcott and Silva Cunningham—her great-great-grandparents. She followed the descendent lines down to Camden Fain Westcott, Silva's first son, who died the same day he was born. Born blue, with the cord wrapped around his neck, he never had a chance. Silva had wept bitterly when she lost him.

Becca remembered the story that Rebecca had recorded in the diaries. The day the Indian woman thrust the infant into her great-great grandmother's arms, Silva didn't think twice. She'd taken the child and hidden him. After the war, she'd christened him Samuel Vaugh, and together, she and Charles raised him as their own. Rebecca had added his name to the Westcott family tree. Becca examined the right side of the registry and noticed Daniel's sister, Corrine, and a list of her marriages. She'd only heard snippets about her great aunt, how she was feisty, beyond control. She and Kurt shared the same flame-red hair, apparently inherited from their patriarch, Charles Westcott. When Corrine left for Europe and didn't return, Rebecca disowned her.

There in the floodlight under the live oak, Becca traced Samuel Vaughn's familial line down through his first wife, Sarah, their three children, then over to his second wife. She wondered why if Samuel had become a Westcott son (so much so that Rebecca had included him in the registry), why hadn't Becca ever heard of him? She followed the line down through Samuel's second wife and discovered the handwriting changed next to Emmeline's brother, Antonio. Directly under his birth date was the addition: "Died 1965." But how could Rebecca have recorded that after having died herself in 1955? Becca gripped the ends of the diary and pulled it closer. Down the page, through the births of Emmeline Bravo's children, she realized the names were all penned with a strange hand.

Becca's eyes shot across the page to her own lineage, where she spotted her great-grandmother's name. There Rebecca's death had been recorded in the same thin scrawl. Whoever had the diaries not only knew Samuel Vaughn's family but Charles Westcott's as well. Becca stared at the family tree. *Who was this person?*

A pair of headlights flashed onto the driveway. Becca saw Adam's purple van pull in and park under the portico. Instead of jumping up and grabbing her suitcase, she leaned back into the darkness and drew the diary close to her chest. Beneath the portico lights, Becca could see Adam rap his fingers on the steering wheel to the beat of Hendrix's "Cross Town Traffic." She clutched the diary and sensed a strange vibration pulsing from the journal into her hands. She couldn't move. Something had riveted her to the chair. She was held captive in its force. She even tried to call to Adam as he jumped down from the van and ran up the steps to slip a piece of paper beneath the front doormat. But not a sound passed her lips. It wasn't until he climbed back into the driver's seat and started to leave that something snapped inside her.

"No! Wait for me!"

But the words came out a whimper, barely audible, and Adam disappeared down the Bayshore.

Becca sat frozen in the chair as panic began to rise within her. *"No, no,"* said the voice above her head. *"Come now."* And this time, she couldn't fight it, will it away, or shake it free.

The part of her that had struggled to maintain control let go and surrendered. She felt suddenly free and expansive at once. It was like she'd slipped into another world and was somehow tuned into a different frequency. She knew she was sitting beneath the live oak in her own yard, but what she saw and heard was different, as if someone had switched the channel and she was watching a new show.

The cicadas were still humming, but the night was *younger* somehow. The sun had not yet set, and was glowing like a hot, orange ball in the western sky. From where Becca sat, she could see a cactus that had gone wild and flared out on a weeded lawn that was now more sand than grass. A small house stood beyond it. On the front porch, an old woman sat wrapped in an afghan, while a young girl pushed herself back and forth on a double swing that hung from chains that were bolted into the porch's ceiling. Becca blinked a few times to clear the vision, but it remained intact. Later she would say the scene had been prophetic and had come to warn her. But tonight she knew only that it had something to do with Rebecca's diary that she held close to her chest.

CHAPTER 11 ✳ Sins of the Father

Beyond the wild cactus that had outgrown the front yard and reached its spiny arms toward the road, the July sun seethed orange in the western sky. Too big to swallow at once, it hovered mean on the horizon and flushed the sky with shades of fevered pink. Emmeline pulled the ends of the afghan tight around her shoulders. She wondered how many hours the two of them would have to sit on this porch going over the same tired questions while they waited for Becca to show up on the driveway.

They sat—Emmeline on a flat-bottomed chair that she'd leveled herself, sawed off the curves that once rounded into half-moons and rocked with the touch of a finger but were now sanded flat. After five babies, eleven grandbabies, and one great-grand, Emmeline said she'd done all the rocking she could bear in a lifetime. Morgan, Emmeline's seventh grandchild, sprawled out across the double swing with one foot hanging down, pushing the wooden planks to keep the swing moving. The two of them could see the wild cactus splayed out half on their property, half on the Farraguts', with its mesh of needled arms, circular, almost in motion, and the center arm jutting straight up and barbarous, having grown seven inches in the last two weeks.

At least they thought—spiny and green as it was—that it was a cactus (but then no one knew for sure). Neither Emmeline nor Morgan nor the Farraguts. In fact, no one knew exactly how it got there. But Emmeline was sure it did not exist fifty-two years ago when she moved into the three-bedroom bungalow on the corner of Powhatan and Seminole, north of downtown Tampa in the Heights. She said the cactus sprang from the earth one day somewhere between the births of Jessie and McAlister. It must have started small, a mere snub of a thing, growing between the yards, unnoticed by anyone until it was of some breadth and shape. Its prickly exterior defied removal.

Morgan, the girl, looked out onto the yard at the cactus. She pondered the shadow it cast on the ragged lawn that was strewn with rusted tricycles, bald tires, and miniature dandelions popping up amid the rubbish. She wore a long, gauzy dress of sheer cotton with straps as fine as embroidery threads that draped her shoulders. Her bare foot kept the porch swing swaying on rusted chains. "You think Julia knows?" she asked Emmeline.

Emmeline leaned back. She kept her legs tucked tight, close to the flattened bottom of the chair and hidden under a burgundy skirt edged with black lace. She worked her slack lips without a sound as if they were attached to the answers in her mind, rummaging one over the other, carefully before she spoke.

"She knows," Emmeline said again. She watched her granddaughter's face, the features wistful, as if they had not yet settled into the proper proportion, undecided on which curve to take or where the fullness should be. Morgan had already turned seventeen but was so slight that she appeared no older than a twelve-year-old child. Her pale hair and skin looked as if it had withstood years of harsh washing in lye. Her complexion was parched, as if it had been skipped by youth. It had somehow just forgotten to round out her body and make her lips full and her cheeks lush.

"Julia knows," Emmeline said. "But not like knowing the day of the week. More like rain coming and no clouds—by smell." Emmeline paused for her granddaughter to stop the swing, momentarily and as she always did when contemplating Emmeline's responses.

"If Julia knows," Morgan pondered, "why wouldn't she say? Why would she just let it smolder until it made her crazy?"

Emmeline hugged an old afghan around her shoulders. She knew by the sun setting orange in the west that she shouldn't be cold. She should not feel the chills that flared up from the base of her spine through the middle of her back and clutched her neck. But seeing Morgan cradled there in the swing, curled and swaying, she understood that this was the child she'd sawed off the legs of her rocking chair for. This was the child whose youth had been skipped as she was somehow ironically gripped in a perpetual childhood. She was both too young and too old, trapped in a bind, doomed to wither not by age or disease but by some defect of her soul. And yet Emmeline firmly believed this failure to thrive was not anything permanent. Morgan just needed to end her obsession with the Westcott family—and their diaries—to claim her own life.

"And who should Julia tell?" Emmeline asked. "Natalie?"

Morgan dropped her leg. Her bare foot pushed the splintered pine of the porch to set the swing in motion. "She could have told Rebecca," she said, "before she died."

Emmeline drew the afghan tighter, crossing the ends over her chest. Her mind flitted over answers for this child, ones she'd given before, ones that had hushed Morgan, satisfied her, or caused her to ponder. Whichever the reaction, any approach stopped the inquisition. Now as she searched again, the words that kept repeating in her head were about how the father's sins would be visited upon the children, generation after generation. She had never believed, not once, that the Bible was the Word of God. These were but words of men, strung prettily together; they were not without wisdom, she conceded, but words from the mouths of men just the same. And now in her old age, she wondered if God maybe did say those words and that she was being shown how it was true.

"She couldn't tell Rebecca," Emmeline said, "because it was Rebecca who brought the baby here to me, hungry and crying. She asked me to care for him and to give him a home—and to never say where he came from."

"And they paid you so you wouldn't tell," Morgan said.

Emmeline didn't look at her granddaughter but out beyond the porch to the cactus with its center shooting straight to the sky. "It wasn't just that," Emmeline said. "They promised to pay for the child, for his clothes and food. They wanted him to be educated right; they felt they owed him that."

"And they reminded you of how you owed them: your life," Morgan said. "Because without them, or Silva Westcott rather, you never would have been born."

Emmeline nodded, wondering if she had told Morgan that before or if her granddaughter had deduced it from the diaries that Emmeline began reading to her when she was just a child. The diaries had been the start (and if not the start, surely they were the impetus that set the curse of the fathers, their sons, and the generations to come into motion). For without the diaries, the complications might have died. They might have drifted into a murky past that was changed by faulty memories, numbed by alcohol, and lost in a crazed mind. But Rebecca appeared one day on the front porch of the bungalow, half carried by her only son, Daniel, who had driven her out to the Heights to the small house on Powhatan and Seminole where she'd left the baby years ago. Rebecca did not ask about the child; he had become a man and had been sent away to school. Nor did she set foot in the house. Instead she shivered on the porch, wrapped as she was in a mink stole because the day was dreary and cold. Rebecca stood there leaning on her son, about as close to death as Emmeline had ever seen a body out of bed. She'd thrust two large books, bound in navy leather and wrapped in an ivory damask tablecloth, into Emmeline's arms.

"Keep these," Rebecca had told Emmeline, her eyes squinting under fatty lids. "Don't let anything happen to them. In time, give them to Becca."

That was all she said. With that she hobbled down the stairs on Daniel's arm. Emmeline had called after her. "In what time? How in time? How will I know?" Rebecca had turned just before Daniel helped her into the car.

"You'll know," she called to Emmeline. "You'll *feel* when it's safe to send them."

So Emmeline stuffed the leather-bound books swaddled in fine linen under her bed. She forgot all about them—until Morgan found them and cut her front tooth on the corner of the first volume. It was then Emmeline began to read them, rocking Morgan in the same chair she sat in now, before she'd sawed off the legs and sanded them flat. She'd read the diaries to Morgan as if from a storybook. Morgan would drag the books to her and climb up on her lap in the old rocker to hear how Charles and Silva had settled near Fort Brooke, a wooden encampment built at the mouth of the Hillsborough River and Tampa Bay. It was there Silva gave birth to their stillborn son.

Barren through the next seven years while the Seminole Wars raged on, Silva often passed the pen where the Indians were held like cattle waiting deportment to Egmont Key. From there, they were shipped to New Orleans and finally taken to Oklahoma, where most of them starved to death their first winter. As Silva passed the pen one summer day, a Seminole mother thrust her infant son into Silva's arms. She ran with him through the rain. She hid him until he was two, until the wars were over, when she hoped she could raise the child as her own.

Morgan sat straight up on the swing, her cotton dress billowy around her. Her hands rested quietly on either side of her body. "You owed them," she said, as if weighing the story again. "I suppose we all owe those Westcotts our lives."

Emmeline knitted the fingers of her hands together. They were worn, knotted, and dark purple around the knuckles.

"You couldn't turn Julia's child away," Morgan said. "You had to accept him and not tell him who his mother was to return the debt to the Westcott family."

Emmeline studied Morgan's face, aglow in the orange haze. She knew, in spite of the allure of the summer night that beckoned a young woman to seek her own life, there was not one thing on her granddaughter's mind except how Silva's rescue of the Indian child had prompted Rebecca to bring Julia's baby to Emmeline. She knew exactly why Morgan had become obsessed with the two acts of the women she did not know. Ever since Morgan had found the diaries under the bed and crawled onto Emmeline's lap to hear the stories, her granddaughter had fallen into the world of pirate ships, parades, and Gasparilla balls with queens wearing blue satin dresses, fur-trimmed capes, and jeweled crowns, and kings wielding mighty scepters. Her fall was not gradual. It was not one that Emmeline could've seen coming; rather, it was swift, inevitable, and complete. So when Morgan's budding womanhood sought expression in her body and was blighted, it was not a conscious refusal but a practiced inattention to the call of her own life. Emmeline imagined that if she could hear the sound of her granddaughter's soul, it would be a low, searching moan, calling as if in a dream: *Morgan, Morgan, Morgan.*

Emmeline felt her skin creep in the breathless heat. She was grateful she'd sawed the rounded legs off her chair and had ceased the rocking, for that's what it would take to stop Morgan from crawling onto on her lap, even now. What was she now but an old child come to hear the stories? But when the rocker stopped flat, Morgan took to the swing, cradled herself there, and kept it moving by the twitch of her foot. As if the stories were somehow connected to the movement, Morgan took over the telling.

Not that she told them to anyone except Emmeline; disclosure was not the purpose of the telling. Rather it was a means to hear them again and again, as if a rhythm had been set early on in her life—the *blub-blub, blub-blub* of the rocker and the stories together, being told from the leather-bound diaries. And Morgan did not just tell them; she ruminated and pondered on them. She asked Emmeline questions. "Does Julia know?" Emmeline would answer truthfully what she believed in the deepest part of herself—that Julia did know, even though she never once mentioned to Rebecca or Natalie that she thought or even felt that the child she had conceived at sixteen was not only alive but living just miles from her.

Morgan slumped down, her head leaning against the arm of the swing. She looked like a rag doll lying there cradled, her cheeks flushed. "Becca should have read them by now," she said. "Don't you think?"

Emmeline tugged the ends of her afghan and nodded. "She probably has."

Beyond the cactus, hidden cicadas chirped noisily while the night crept up heavy and warm. Emmeline did not rise to turn on the porch light; she welcomed the dark that would dim her granddaughter's face and shroud it in a veil from her view. Beneath its flushed exterior, Emmeline sensed a pallid grief. Not for the loss of youth—as one would expect of a young woman the years had betrayed—but instead for the loss of the diaries that Morgan had found under the bed and dragged through the house. And there in the dark, Emmeline mulled over the fact that Morgan's grief was not for the diaries themselves but for what existed in them—a world that Morgan felt belonged to her and yet was at once lost.

Emmeline turned away from the cactus that appeared shadowy in the dark. From where she sat motionless in her chair, she could see the sloping curve of her granddaughter's chin as it caught a glint from the distant streetlight that had just flicked on. There in the half dark, Emmeline saw the pallor return to Morgan's cheeks and a settling fall across her face. She was waiting; it was as simple as that.

From the afternoon of the third Friday in June—the day she and Morgan had read in the newspaper that Daniel Westcott had disappeared, and Emmeline decided it was time to rewrap the diaries in the ivory damask tablecloth, pack them into a cardboard box, and have them driven to the Westcott Mansion—Morgan had been *waiting*. Emmeline counted back the days. She imagined Becca had received the diaries that Friday afternoon (unless they had fallen into Natalie's hands—or God forbid,

Julia's). Emmeline shivered. But no, she wouldn't think of that now, not after all the nights she and Morgan had spent on this porch believing that Becca was reading the diaries, and when she'd finished them, would seek out the other Westcott family. Although Morgan never once said that Becca would search them out, Emmeline *knew* when she'd read in the paper three days ago that they'd found Daniel. She'd watched Morgan drag through the house, sleep until noon, lie in the swing, and pace up and down the splintered slats of the porch, just like she would pace them tonight. Emmeline knew Morgan was waiting for Becca to show up on the front steps of the bungalow.

Emmeline stretched her legs in a wide V, out from under the burgundy skirt edged in lace. They were swollen from the knees down. Spider veins gathered in blackish clumps at the ankles and flared up a bright purple through the calves. Her feet were sandaled, bound in leather straps across the toes, and pulled taut behind her heels. She tapped her feet against the porch. *What if Becca did show up? What if she walked across the gravel driveway, past the weedy lawn and wild cactus, having read the diaries and searched the family out?* What would Morgan say to her? Emmeline watched her granddaughter gazing through the wooden slats of the porch swing, her pale head bent, almost ashine in the dim light. She would not say a thing. Instead she would stand before Becca, her body a bleak question in itself. Her response would resonate from her as if part of the rhythm, part of the blub-blub, blub-blub of the rocking and stories from the diaries. It would be a silent mien that pleaded, *Look at me, look at me.*

CHAPTER 12 ❋ A Time Bomb

Downstairs, the teakettle had been whistling for a good ten minutes while Eula was in the garden house searching for a jar of pickled watermelon to serve at dinner tonight. Natalie rolled her stockings over her knees. *Let the kettle burst! Let it spit all over the kitchen!* she thought defiantly. *I will not go downstairs with my stockings bagged at the ankles like an old woman.* She smoothed her hair, which was already pinned up and damp around her temples. Then she remembered: the air conditioner had clicked off in the night. She'd heard it—one tight clap, like the snapping of a rubber band. She'd sat straight up in bed, hoping it was not true. *Not with guests coming for dinner tonight.*

Yesterday, Chief Salazar called and said the *Sea Booty* had been hijacked by a gang of smugglers, and there was a chance Daniel was on the boat. *Kidnapped.* Natalie had pressed the phone to her ear to steady her hand. The way Salazar chose his words, she knew he was trying to downplay the danger. She let him talk on. He'd just received confirmation that the *Sea Booty* was anchored at St. Ann's Bay, Jamaica. They didn't know exactly when the boat would head out and return to Tampa. But Salazar said he and Carlos Mendoza were putting a crew together to head off the smugglers before they reached the desolate spit of land on Egmont Key. When he stopped talking, an awkward pause followed. Natalie's mind raced. She thought to thank him, to apologize for the inconvenience. Nothing seemed right. So she invited him—and Carlos Mendoza—to dinner Sunday evening.

Natalie gazed out the window at the sun climbing fast. Last night after the air conditioner had clicked off, she'd gotten up to open the windows first in Julia's room, Kurt's room, and then Becca's. She would not have them smothered by morning. And she was right to do so. Her efforts were rewarded by a soothing breeze that wafted in from the bay. It drifted through the house, heavy with the scent of confederate jasmine. But the windows would have to be shut by ten and the blinds drawn until the last of the heat settled with the sun. She sat on the edge of the bed to lace up her sturdiest shoes for the work to be done today. When she headed out the door, she tripped as the heel of her shoe caught on the edge of a hall runner. She worried now that the rugs would swell, soak up moisture, and ripple with barely perceptible waves that would transform them into treacherous, insidious traps. *Pick up your feet, old girl!* She stepped gingerly down the hall and licked her lips, which were cracked and dry and tasted of salt that had blown in with the night air.

When she was halfway down the stairs, the teakettle stopped whistling. It couldn't have been Niobe who had taken it off the burner; Natalie had just heard her low, raspy voice coaxing Julia out of bed. Perhaps it was Eula, who had found the pickled fruit easily and hurried back to the house to catch the kettle. But when Natalie reached the kitchen, she discovered her grandson perched on the stepstool, leaning over the counter, his hands cupping a can of Coke. Flame-red hair rippled over his shoulders and hung loosely down his bare back and arms, giving him a delicate, feminine demeanor. He'd turned eighteen this past winter, but his body was still like a fragile twig with a freckled torso and overlong arms. It pained Natalie to look at him.

"Sitting in the dark?" Natalie asked as she brushed by him to the cupboard.

Kurt squinted his eyes at her. "It's hot in here."

Natalie unhooked a hand-painted cup hanging from the low shelf. She grabbed the kettle and poured the water. The kitchen was dim, shaded by the back porch beyond. It felt cool to her with the sun on the front of the house.

"You'll get used to it," she said. She pulled up a stool next to him and squeezed his skinny arm. Three nights ago, when he'd showed up drunk and asking about Daniel, Natalie had tried to calm him. "How'd you get here?" she'd asked.

"Hitchhiked," he'd said, "from Minidoka, Idaho, through Wyoming, Nebraska, and Missouri." He'd caught a freight train in Tennessee and rode it to the border of Alabama and Florida, where he'd started out on foot again—until a trucker with a load of tomatoes and a couple of bottles of Jack picked him up and drove him all the way to Tampa. When he tore out of the house looking for Becca, Natalie had called Prairie Pines and talked to his counselor. "Try to keep him talking," the woman had said. "He's in crisis."

Natalie dragged the teabag back and forth through the cup of hot water, struggling for something to say. She looked up at Kurt. "I remember when you used to run down by the river all day. You'd come in all sweaty, your skin heat prickly."

Kurt tapped his foot against the counter. He kept his head bent.

"You wouldn't sit a minute," she went on. "Not even for a lemonade."

"I was fishing."

"Or chasing gators." Natalie laughed. "Once you came home swinging an otter in your net. Wanted to put him in the bathtub."

A tight smile twitched the side of Kurt's mouth.

"You loved the heat," Natalie said, sipping her tea. "You used to lie in the grass in the thick of summer. Short britches and no shirt, your ear to the ground. You used to say you could hear the center of the earth rumbling."

Kurt shifted uneasily on the stool. "I was a kid."

Was a kid? Natalie watched the sulky way her grandson bent his head and sat slumped, his shoulders rounded, and his foot banging the counter in a tedious *thump, thump, thump.* The same small boy was there, with a set of creases sketched in like pencil lines just beneath his eyes that gave him a mournful, hangdog expression even when he was smiling.

"Right," Natalie said. "You'd come in rolling your tongue, thrumming it against the back of your teeth. 'It sounds like this,' you'd say. 'Like this.' Then we'd hear the twelve o'clock train whistle, and you'd run back outside. You never did connect that whistle with the thundering beneath your feet."

Natalie thought to leave him alone. He looked worn-out and bedraggled. His hair was uncombed. Sweat beaded on his nose. He'd not had time to settle or adjust to the peculiar quiet of the house that used to ring with his grandfather's booming voice or the constant rustle of newspapers that were fanned out and hiding Daniel's face while cigar smoke rose like signals above his head. Neither had the boy acclimated to the heat, to the dank scent of the house and boggy air. *It was positively fetid this morning,* she thought, *thanks to the sulfur rolling in from the bay.* But what did Natalie know about the Idaho plains or the sheep farm where Daniel had sent the boy a year ago? The rigorous life—sleeping in tents and eating out of tin cans—would "give the boy perspective," Daniel had said. "Teach him something besides how to find the best street corner to buy dope."

Daniel had made the final decision to send Kurt away the night he was found in the front yard, beaten to within an inch of his life. At least that's what Natalie thought. *The way his eyes were all busted up, his spleen crushed, and an arm broken in three places.* She shuddered as the gruesome images flooded her imagination again. *Some friends, those pushers.*

"He's a troubled boy," Daniel had said.

Natalie agreed. *But shouldn't he be?*

Natalie studied her grandson. Yes, the same small boy was there, barred at his mother's bedroom door, kicking frantically to be let in. She, his Nattie, had to drag him away.

She couldn't love him enough. Neither could Rebecca or Daniel, Richard, or even Becca, because his mother had refused to.

Natalie slid off the stool and headed toward the stove. "You'll be a help today, with the guests coming this evening." She unhooked an apron from the pantry door and tied it around her waist.

"I'm not going to be here," Kurt said. "I've got things to do."

Natalie poured hot water into the teapot and watched the steam fog the window above the sink. "You'll come to dinner, then? I expect that much of you."

"Why should I?"

"Respect," Natalie said, not turning to face him. "These men are risking their lives for your grandfather."

"The chief isn't coming." Kurt clinked a spoon against his mug. "Only that spic and his uncle."

Natalie spun around. "You need your mouth washed out with soap?" She picked up a spatula and waved it at him. "No more name calling! Victor was the first one to help us, and without his uncle, there wouldn't be a search."

Kurt rolled his eyes. "I don't like them weaseling 'round here. They've got their own krewe. Why don't they just stick to it?"

Natalie was about to tell him to tell him to zip it when she noticed Daniel, clad in his pirate hat, slip by the window. *What was he up to now?* She banged the spatula against the window. "Hey!" she called out.

"Who's that?" Kurt asked.

Natalie's hand flew to her mouth. No, she wouldn't tell her grandson that Daniel was in the backyard, any more than she would tell him that the air conditioner had snapped off in the middle of the night. Instead she hurried to the back door and stepped onto the porch in time to see Daniel disappear around the side of the house. She wanted to ask him about the boy named Cuda and his gang of smugglers. She also wanted to tell him she was tired of his silly game, slinking around like a ghost. If he was dead, why not let everyone know? Certainly other people should not be risking their lives in a dead man's hunt.

Natalie leaned over the porch railing. She refused to chase Daniel through the yard and around the house. She would wait until he returned. She shoved her hand into the pocket of her dress and touched the note Adam had left under the front doormat for Becca. Natalie squeezed the paper between her fingers. She'd almost given it to Becca when she saw her on the front porch at 4:00 a.m. She was in the wicker chair, sleeping. But how could she? She knew that Adam wanted Becca to follow him. "Someplace peaceful," he'd said. *Where was that?* she wondered. *The Keys?*

What a muddle, Natalie thought as she turned to go back in the house. How silly of her to think it could happen easily—that Victor and Becca would slide into an untroubled romance. For there was some enchantment about Becca, a moth-musk allure that had the power to draw the rebellious Adam Dicker all the way from New York and captivate Victor Ramirez so much that first night he drove her home. Natalie shuffled through the back hall and pondered the possible outcomes. Even before she reached the kitchen and found Becca leaning against the counter in a cotton nightie, her hair tussled and her eyes red-rimmed and puffy, Natalie knew her granddaughter hadn't the slightest notion of the spell she'd cast upon the men. It was the tilt of her head, the way her lips turned a pout, the touch of her hand, and her voice. *Yes, it was her voice,* Natalie thought, listening to her tell Kurt that Carlos Mendoza would not be coming for dinner.

"Good," Kurt said. "Now we can cancel it."

Becca sighed and rested her chin in her hands. "Victor said he'd bring his architect. He's joining them in the search."

"Oh?" Natalie said and sat down at the counter. She was deeply disappointed that Carlos had canceled the dinner and hadn't even bothered to call her.

Kurt jumped off the stool. "Let me get this straight: the plan was to entertain Chief Salazar and Uncle Wiggly, and now we're stuck with Victor and his sidekick?" He tucked his hair behind his ears and glared at Natalie. *At least he didn't use the S-word for Victor,* she thought.

Becca shrugged. Natalie knew after the note she herself had found under the doormat last night, her granddaughter didn't give a fig who was coming to dinner. She stepped back to examine these two young adults. She remembered as children how dearly they'd loved their grandfather. Becca was always the "challenge," so Daniel had said, the one who would defy him and run off and hide when she should've been practicing her music. But that was her way. For in school, didn't she always make the ceramic ashtrays with Daniel's initials scrawled along the edge? And poor child—she'd had such a painful transition after her father died. But Kurt was barely a year old when Richard passed in the night; naturally, the boy gravitated toward Daniel.

Natalie examined Kurt. How Daniel adored him—the chubby, red-haired toddler who crawled up on his grandfather's lap and pulled his chest hairs. But what Natalie couldn't understand was that as much as Daniel expected perfection from Becca, he indulged Kurt. He took him fishing when he should've been in school. And when Natalie warned Daniel that Kurt showed no interest in his studies, no interest in anything except a fishing pole, Daniel looked blankly at Natalie and said, "Somebody needs to love him."

Kurt pounded the Coke can on the counter and then crushed it in his hand. "Well, count me out," he said fiercely. "I'm not coming to dinner." His hair fell over his shoulders and parted at the bony protrusions that stuck out like wings on either side of his freckled back. He turned around and eyed Natalie with a wry smile. "Besides, no one's asked me to join the search."

Natalie's breath caught in her throat. Here was Kurt being left out again, but the thought of him on one of the rescue boats sent a shiver through her body.

Becca caught her brother's hand as he passed her. She pulled him close. "Mother's coming down for dinner," she said. "I told her you'd be here."

Kurt stood stunned. Natalie knew that was the bait that could bring the boy home tonight. She watched his shoulders slump as she imagined the last time Kurt could have seen his mother, perhaps peering at him through the upstairs window while he tossed a ball in the front yard. But Natalie sensed his excitement that Julia would actually come down! That she might sit across from him or next to him in the dining room, through a whole dinner where he could watch her and maybe even touch her. Kurt slipped out the door without a word, but Natalie knew he would show up tonight.

Natalie poured Becca a cup of tea. "This architect fellow, where's he from?"

"I don't know," she said as she listlessly stirred in a bit of sugar. "You can ask him tonight." Becca tapped the spoon against her cup and let out a sigh. "His name's Evan."

Natalie headed toward the fridge. "How about a swiss-cheese omelet?" she asked. "Your favorite."

"I'm not hungry."

Natalie stopped and set her hands on her hips. She couldn't take another second of Becca's misery. Besides, she would need her granddaughter's help entertaining the young men tonight, especially if Kurt showed up. *Anything could happen.* She reached into her pocket and pulled out the note. "Look what I found."

Becca glanced up. "From Adam?"

Natalie nodded. Becca didn't even reach for the note; she just kept tapping her spoon against the teacup. "I don't know how it slipped my mind," Natalie said and rattled off some excuse. Becca ignored her. When Natalie went to stuff the note back in her pocket, Becca plucked it from Natalie's hand and buried her face in it.

Dear B,

Waited as long as I could. But now, I think it's best that I leave without you tonight. How can I take you away from your family with your grandfather missing? I'll send for you when I get settled. Hopefully your granddad will come home soon. Then we'll start a new life, a peaceful life. One without wars and guns and drafts. Remember my promise.

I love you. A

Becca held the letter to her chest. She glared at Natalie. "You hid this from me?"

Natalie wiped her hands on the apron. She was about to make up another excuse when she noticed Becca's pinched face. She saw that her granddaughter was ready to break into tears. Natalie slid onto a counter stool next to her. "I couldn't bear for you to leave now."

Becca eyed her grandmother. "I'm not leaving *now*. Didn't you read this?"

Natalie folded her hands in her lap and squeezed them tight. "But you were going to."

Becca squirmed, placed her fingers over her mouth, and turned away.

"I know you love him," Natalie said, her voice soothing. "But this peaceful place—'no guns, no war'—where is it?"

Becca was quiet.

Natalie waited. She could wait all day. She'd cancel the dinner tonight for a chance to break through her granddaughter's carefully constructed plan.

Becca stared down at her teacup. "Toronto," she whispered.

Natalie's head went dizzy. These days everyone knew why young men took off to Canada. "He's—" Natalie started, but Becca finished.

"Dodging the draft," she blurted out. Then she spilled the whole story. "Adam can't kill anyone," she defended him. "It's against ever fiber in his being." Becca rattled on about the travesty of the Vietnam War, the evil politics, the greed behind it, and how it was nothing like World War II. "Adam's a visionary, nothing like—" Then Becca stopped.

Natalie studied her granddaughter. She knew what Becca was going to say "nothing like the people in this town." Natalie shivered in spite of the heat. She understood Adam was a rabble-rousing dissident, but she never thought he'd dodge the draft. *He was a fugitive now, a criminal, and he wanted Becca to join him as soon as he got settled?* Natalie caught her thumbs twiddling like an old woman's. *What to do now?*

Becca leaned in close to her grandmother. "He's a good guy, Nattie. We're going to be married."

Natalie glanced across the kitchen at the clock hanging on the wall. She was speechless. If Becca married Adam, she'd never come home again. Natalie pressed her thumbs together to still them. How long would it be before Adam sent for her? She was sitting on a time bomb. Every second mattered now. She couldn't put her finger on it, but she didn't trust Adam Dicker. True, he'd just skipped the country to avoid the draft, but it was more than that. Natalie watched her granddaughter, the way she curled the letter into a cone. Then she came to another realization: Becca didn't trust him either.

Natalie got up and set her teacup in the sink. She took a deep breath. For now, she'd do the only thing she could: divert Becca's attention and hope for a miracle. "So, your mother's coming down for dinner tonight?"

Becca folded the letter into a small square. "I invited her."

"And Kurt?"

"I didn't tell her about Kurt, but she knows he's home." Becca sipped her tea. "She must know he'll be here."

"She won't," Natalie said and felt her chest go tight. There was a muffled banging on the screen door. Natalie hurried down the back hall, thinking it could be Daniel unable to open it. *But shouldn't he glide through doors? And freely like rainwater seeping through walls?* Then Natalie saw Eula behind the screen, her arms loaded with jelly jars of sweet pickles, jams, and chutney.

"I couldn't find the one, so I brought them all," Eula said, squeezing through the door and releasing some of the jars into Natalie's hands. "Oowee! It's heating up out there."

Natalie led Eula past the utility room toward the kitchen, knowing full well by the colors of the jars that Eula had brought every preserve except the pickled watermelon. Now Natalie would have to go out to the garden house later and bring it in herself.

After she guided Eula into the kitchen, Natalie set the jars on the counter next to Becca. "Put them here," Natalie said. But Eula stood motionless, her milky eyes squinting. In that instant, Natalie knew it was not the dark hall or the labels she couldn't read, but Eula's last sight had drained finally from her eyes. All rooms, all days would be dark for her now.

Becca jumped off the stool and took the remaining jars. She led Eula to the counter and asked if she would, for the dinner tonight, braid her hair in one thick plait down the back of her head.

If extinguished eyes could shine, Eula's were brighter than any sun. Her face lit up, and her hands stretched out to stroke Becca's thick, uncombed hair. She weaved the locks around her fingers as if remembering some code, some fine and secret season. Natalie marveled at the energy in Eula's hands. Yes, she could still braid hair!

A light breeze drifted in from the backyard, and Natalie remembered the open windows upstairs ready to draw in heat. "Don't worry about your mother," she told Becca. "I'll tell her about Kurt."

Halfway up the steps, the grandfather clock chimed the ten strokes of morning. The sound echoed through the staircase and stopped Natalie on the second landing. The house was uncommonly tranquil with the noise of the kitchen remote and the upstairs hushed and darkened before her.

She climbed the last steps and headed down the hall toward Becca's room. The door was wide open. Inside, a mild breeze ruffled the lace curtains. Natalie was just in time; the sun had hit the quarter mark in the sky and streamed through the window in one long beam across the wooden floor. She pulled down the sash and then the shade. When she turned to leave, she tripped on something sticking out from under the bed. She would break a leg yet! If not climbing the stairs or catching the edge of a swollen rug, then by stumbling on hidden traps lurking beneath her feet. She bent over to shove the object further under the bed when she was struck by the buttery texture of worn leather. *Of what? A briefcase?*

A book!

She pulled it into the dim light and examined the cover, the navy-blue leather and frayed corner. She sat down on the unmade bed and opened it.

The beginning of the book was written in a bold, coarse hand— chunky letters in black ink that look like a youngster's. As Natalie thumbed through it, the penmanship became smaller and more sophisticated. She turned the pages faster, and yes, as the writing progressed, it was undeniably the finer, sweeping hand of Rebecca. Natalie stopped a quarter of the way through the book and read:

> *Silva said she passed the Port of Tampa daily, saw the wretchedness of the Indians in the pen. How lucky Osceola had died. He had been spared to witness his people rounded up and corralled into the army-built stockade where they waited for shipment out. Silva said it was always from Tampa Bay—the deportment to Egmont Key where the Indians would be held until they could be transferred first to New Orleans then to Oklahoma. Silva winced, remembering the Seminole cries that hovered over the dusty town—the bitter wailings of a people half-starved, the old, the women with infants, the weak, all rounded up from the fringes of the river—driven in like cattle.*

And then down some:

> *… weighing it and saying, yes, she would do it all again. First for the mother in that pen whose gaze had captured Silva's and beckoned her close that August day before the sky burst open, and then for the infant laid in her arms, wrapped in deerskin, his hair a black sunburst around his head, and his lips pressed tight as if having tasted life's venom. Silva fled with the child, ran home with him under her coat, her head a rattle, but her heart aimed straight through the squalling wind and needled rain.*

Natalie rested the diary on her knees. This was Silva's story, as told by Rebecca, that Natalie had heard in snippets from Nathan when he was alive. She turned the page. The details of Charles and Silva's lives had been recorded here in black ink and a bold hand. Natalie sniffed the air, which had suddenly gone stale. *But where'd the diary come from? And why did Becca have it?* She flipped through the pages again and saw the names fly by—Daniel, Eula, Nathan, and her name, Natalie, again and again. She stopped near the end of the diary where she spotted an odd entry, a list of ballroom gowns and events to which they were worn:

> *Tampa Bay Hotel Opening Ball, February 5, 1891*

> *Crimson red velveteen, cut in a deep V front and back with a long, narrow skirt and a wide velvet sash draping the back.*
>   *Jewels: Flowered garnet stud earrings and a matching garnet necklace with twenty-four stones (Nathan)*

The Ladies Auxiliary Annual Ball, August, 1892

Layered yellow chiffon flounces to the floor beaded just along the edges. Bodice cut low and flat across, cinched waist, gathered in back.

Wide garden hat with yellow, white, and purple ostrich plumes.

Jewels: Ivory cameo necklace (Silva Westcott's) on woven strands of gold.

Ivory and gold earrings (Silva's)

2-carat diamond solitaire engagement ring (Nathan)

The Museum Guild Extravaganza, September 1893

Bright gold satin with an empire Chantilly lace bodice, tucked cleverly to hide the fullness of a four-month pregnancy, full satin bow in back; pearled cuffs.

Jewels: Diamond cluster earrings, laced diamond necklace with matching bracelet (Nathan)

Natalie examined the next page, where the events and detailed descriptions of the gowns continued. Interspersed between the annual auxiliary and museum balls were the opening Casino Night, the New York Opera, assorted magicians, tricksters, and clowns, and halfway down the page, Natalie spotted the first Gasparilla Coronation!

The Gasparilla Coronation Ball, February 1914

Fuchsia organdy flecked with silver and gold threads, and stays sewn into the middle, pulled taut at the waist, tapered skirt with tulip bottom, edged in embroidered fuchsia lace. (Needed: one heavy corset)

> *Jewels: Emerald-and-gold drop earrings with matching*
> *ring*
> > *Emerald, gold, and pearl necklace*

Natalie was about to turn the page when she heard footsteps on the stairs. She closed the diary, and when she shoved it back under the bed, she struck something hard. She got down on her knees and peeked under the eyelet dust ruffle. Another diary! The footsteps on the stairs grew louder. She pushed both volumes deep under the bed, and after smoothing the dust ruffle, she struggled to her feet. Her legs had cramped; she limped across the room. When she leaned against the door to catch her breath, she heard Eula's whiny voice singing in the stairwell.

> I got a house in Glory Land that outshines the sun, O
> Lordy!
> > When I leave this world of dust behind, I'm rising to
> that land, O Lordy!
> > > I got a house in Glory Land that outshines the sun—
> > Look away beyond the blue!

Natalie waited until Eula had passed, and then she slipped down the hall to Julia's room.

Julia sat facing the bay, dressed in a white linen skirt and a crocheted top. Niobe had pulled her hair back in a french twist. For an instant, with Julia sitting just so, her hands peaceful in her lap and her head turned toward the water, Natalie imagined her a girl again, with her whole life stretched out before her. Oh the dreams she'd had for Julia! Her music, her marriage and children, and travel—there was so much Natalie wanted to show her. And simple things—like how to arrange flowers on a dessert buffet, the way to turn china cups to show off the fine painting, how white vinegar puts a shine on anything (even a child's nose), and how pictures are mounted to last forever.

Julia turned in the chair. "Morning, Mama."

"You're lovely this morning, darling."

Natalie hurried to the window to lower the sash and draw the blinds. "Why the shade?"

"It's so hot today. And we want to keep the house cool for the company tonight."

"Yes, Becca's friends." Julia's eyes brightened. "I'd like to meet them." Natalie drew up a chair next to her daughter. Julia squinted and touched her cheek. "I look okay?"

"Lovely," Natalie said. She averted her eyes from the deep lines that creased Julia's forehead and cheeks. She was no longer a young woman. Although she seemed calm this morning, Natalie knew she could erupt in a flash. She would not ruin this night for Julia or make it any harder than she knew it would be—but for the boy. How could Kurt continue to pay for a crime he never committed?

"Julia," Natalie took her daughter's hand. "Someone's coming tonight. Someone who wants to see you very much."

Julia gazed toward the window as if she could see the water through the blinds. Her eyes were wide and round and still the vibrant green of her youth.

Natalie squeezed her hand. "It's Kurt, darling. He's home. He'll be at dinner tonight."

"Who?"

"Kurt, your son."

Julia pulled her hand back. Her eyes blinked once and then narrowed into fine slits. She turned away.

Natalie knew better than to push her. The same terror that glazed Julia's eyes the night they'd found her, curled and bloodied in bed, transfixed her even now. Natalie sank back in the chair. The old hate burned within her and made her hands itch to do what she should have done that night—found the pirate herself, ripped the beads from his waist, looped them around his neck, and strangled him. She could've done it, and she should've, when Daniel was too drunk to fathom the damage.

Natalie edged out of the chair, her legs wobbly beneath her. She wanted to tell Daniel there was honor in retribution, that it was not just revenge (as he tried to convince her), but a responsible, noble act. If Julia could've been told they'd found the filthy pirate, punished him (or had even tried), then maybe, just maybe, Julia would have tried too. But having failed her so miserably, how could Natalie ask any more of her? She squeezed Julia's shoulder. "Think about it."

Natalie stepped into the hall and thought of the shrimp that needed to be thawed and cleaned for dinner. She thought of salad greens that needed to be crisped, of tomatoes that needed to be picked, of the cream that had to be whipped—and of the pickled watermelon that still needed to be brought in from the garden house. She hurried to Kurt's room to close the windows, even though she knew it was too late. The house had already taken on heat.

CHAPTER 13 ❋ "Buzz Quoth the Blue Fly"

Run! Close the door—and lock it. Even though Natalie had told her to never, never lock the door. Julia flipped the latch. She pressed her hand to her chest and felt her heart tremble. Kurt did not see her. She stood beyond the corner of the east hall while he came out of the library carrying a pile of books in his arms. How tall he was! And that hair? Flame red.

Julia stepped across her bedroom to the Queen Anne chair and gripped the back of it. Outside, the day blistered. Even with the blinds closed, the air had grown heavy and thick with the smell of sulfur from the bay. "Heavy as a hog's breath," her father used to say. Julia walked around the chair and sat down. She wondered if she'd imagined Kurt, her third child, lugging books down the corridor of the east wing. She was capable of that, of wanting him home so much that she actually saw him—a lanky pup with big hands and feet. The beginnings of a man.

But how do you talk to a child you've abandoned?

"Why? Why?" he would ask her.

The thought that she'd seen him frightened her, but not as much as the possibility that he might, in fact, be home. He had rolled across the country like a tumbleweed to get here.

While Becca flew home. But why? To nest?

Julia leaned back in the chair and squinted against the heat. She shuddered.

One. Two.

Hadn't she called them home? Her children.

But what kind of voice, what kind of power could carry the wish between her heart and theirs? What could propel it like gunshots up a staircase.

She ran her hands over the arms of the chair. She knew her father was missing. She knew the whole town was searching for him. After that night—when she'd heard the gunshots and watched him stagger down the stairs—she didn't know where he was. *If he wanted to,* she wondered, *could he walk freely into the house like Becca and Kurt did?* And if he could, what would stop her first child—the one she'd conceived at sixteen but never knew—from showing up, too? She hummed "The Mama Song" song softly to herself.

> There'll be no little tired-out boy to undress,
> No questions or cares to perplex you,
> There'll be no little bruises or bumps to caress,
> Nor patching of stockings to vex you;
> For I'll rock you away on a silver-dew stream
> And sing you asleep when you're weary,
> And no one shall know of our beautiful dream
> But you and your own little dearie.

A light knock rattled the bedroom door. "Mother?" he said. "It's Kurt." Julia stiffened. She heard a hand on the doorknob, trying to get in. "Are you sleeping?" he asked.

She closed her eyes. *Yes, I am.*

Julia didn't know how long she'd dozed or when the pounding on her bedroom door had stopped. But she'd dreamt about the "Tailor of Gloucester," the poor, wizened man who'd become so sick on Christmas Eve he couldn't finish the cherry-colored coat for the mayor who was to be married in the morning. The little mice who lived in the tailor's shop snipped and cut and sewed the beautiful silk coat and embroidered it with pansies and roses while the tailor's cat meowed at the shop door to be let in. Did the mice let the kitty in? Oh no! They chanted something mysterious that sounded like—

"Buzz, quoth the blue fly; hum, quoth the bee;
Buzz and hum they cry and so do we!"

Julia leaned back in chair and let the chant spin through her head. Kurt was coming to dinner tonight. He expected to see her. Well, maybe she could go down, but she wouldn't let him in when he knocked at her door. Who would do something silly like that? Not the mice.

"Three little mice sat down to spin.
Pussy passed by, and he peeped in.
What are you at, my fine little men?
Making coats for gentlemen.
Shall I come in and cut off your threads?
Oh, no, Mr. Pussy, you'd bite off our heads!"

Julia laughed. She loved that tale by Beatrix Potter. Wise woman, that one! She closed her eyes and dozed off again.

CHAPTER 14 ❋ Working on a
Big Catch

On Mortenson's boat at the yacht club, Victor, Salazar, and the captain pored over the nautical chart that would guide them to Cuda and the *Sea Booty*. The morning's milky haze hung over the water now but would burn off by ten, leaving the sun to sear through their cotton Ts. When Victor stepped onto the twenty-nine-foot Luhrs, Mortenson threw him a charter T-shirt that pictured a sailfish bursting from the water. The caption below read "Fish Your Wish." Victor had shed his starched shirt and donned the gift. In spite of its light weight and the tidal breeze that blew in from the bay, sweat was already collecting on his neck. He welcomed the odd break in the weather—no rain in sight. That meant a clear ride home for Cuda and his gang.

Victor leaned over the map that was spread out across the bait wells. A fishy odor, mixed with the scent of gasoline and strong coffee, rose up near the three men. Victor accepted a Styrofoam cup filled with the black brew. The coffee tasted thick and bitter on his tongue. As the captain explained the chart, Victor marveled how the pieces of the case had shifted into place as if by some divine plan. Salazar's agent, posing undercover as Benny Fine, a strip-joint owner from Clearwater, had gone back to the Conch Shell with $50,000 in cash and asked Spaceman if he could get in on Cuda's drug run. The agent, dressed for the part in a pair of khakis and a sport coat, told Spaceman there was a thousand bucks in it for him. Spaceman bit. "The deal might be locked up," Spaceman had warned, "but there'll be another one."

Spaceman radioed Cuda and got the thumbs-up—he'd make room for the new money man. Cuda said they'd trucked out over six thousand pounds of weed from Murray Mountain and had started loading the boat at the St. Ann's buoy marker. They planned to shove off in two days. Spaceman said Cuda would land on Egmont Key. The island had a stash house and a long stretch of secluded beaches to unload the skiffs.

Mortenson ran a bony finger along the chart from St. Ann's Bay, around the southwest tip of Cuba to Inagua Island. A cigarette flopped between his lips. "My guess is Cuda will refuel here first, then he'll head up to Andros." He tapped his finger on the Bahamian island. "She's nearly secluded." The captain plucked the cigarette from his mouth and held it between his thumb and forefinger. "It's easy to top off the tanks here and move out fast."

Victor cocked his head to dodge the smoke that Mortenson exhaled through his nose like a dragon.

"Then what?" Salazar asked.

The captain shrugged. "Cuda will want to land after midnight. Want the early hours to unload." Mortenson's gravelly voice vibrated through the fog. "No one's running then except pirates and smugglers."

Ripples slapped up against the boat in a rhythmic swish that kept Victor slightly off balance. He noticed the sweat starting to bead on the chief's forehead. "How long will it take?" Victor asked.

Mortenson smoothed the chart that curled at the edges. "My guess is anywhere from twenty-five to thirty-five hours, depending on the seas, how many knots they're running, how many times they stop." He peered up at Victor and Salazar. "We can't know for sure."

Salazar studied the map. "We can't wait ten hours. We need Spaceman to radio the *Sea Booty* as Cuda comes closer to land."

Mortenson agreed.

Then Salazar pointed to Egmont Key. "So he's landing here. Where should we stake him out?"

Mortenson pointed to the northern tip of Anna Maria Island. "If we anchor here, we should be able to spot him coming in."

The open water around Egmont appeared massive to Victor. "What if we miss him?"

The captain took a last drag from his cigarette and dropped the butt into his empty cup. "We won't; it's a common passage. We'll stake one boat here on the northern end, while the other one can follow the tender down once it's spotted the *Sea Booty*." Mortenson picked up a pen and drew a couple of arrows on the chart. "That way, whether Cuda comes up the east side of the island or the west, we'll catch him here." He drew a circle around Passage Key. "This'll work as long as Cuda doesn't get wind we're on his tail."

Salazar pulled a handkerchief from his pocket and mopped the sweat that dripped down his face. He told Victor and the captain that he'd held off the *Tribune* reporters by telling them that Daniel had gotten lost on a fishing trip to Freeport. A search was being launched to find him. If Cuda happened upon the news, he'd laugh, believing his drug run was in the clear. At least that was the hope. "Not even the men in my precinct know the real dope behind this search," the chief said. "The few officers I can trust will either be with us that night or covering the department while we're gone." Salazar shook his head. "It's the only way I know to protect this sting."

While the chief leaned against the bait wells, Victor thrust his hands into his pants pockets. Salazar said he'd studied the reports on Cuda, trying to figure out what kind of character they were up against. He'd learned that the kid had started smuggling weed at sixteen when he still lived in Puerto Rico. His dad was in jail, so his mother moved them to Florida to get Cuda away from his wayward friends. Cuda managed to stay clean until his mother was diagnosed with lung cancer and couldn't afford treatment. The summer before his senior year, Cuda and his buddy took off in a Pontiac Bandit, seeking the great fields of hemp the government had planted throughout Kansas, Iowa, and Nebraska during World War II. At the time, the stalks were used to make rope for parachutes. But since then, the fields had grown wild. Just outside Omaha, Nebraska, Cuda and his cohort found roadsides, riverbanks, and open fields laden with what looked like marijuana. They lopped off the tops, long buds of hemp, bagged it, dried it, blocked it, and sold it at Woodstock, where everyone was already too stoned to realize the "funk pot" didn't contain THC. That trip put five thousand bucks in Cuda's pocket and paid for the drugs to keep his mother alive.

Victor watched Mortenson roll up the chart. Salazar said, "I'm not surprised that Cuda had been lured into a smuggler's life—I've seen plenty of good kids go down, but Cuda's not a punk." In fact, he'd become a local idol, a demigod of sorts that patrons at the Conch Shell worshiped with devilish glee. He also had a bar named after him in Puerto Rico—Barracuda's.

Salazar's agent said two kids in their early twenties had pulled up chairs and sat down at the table while he and Spaceman were cutting the deal. They listened for a while and then joined in. They'd bragged to the agent how Cuda had hooked up with Jinx, the biggest King Daddy of Jamaican ganja. Together, Cuda and Jinx were filling the pockets of the poor with cash. Weed farmers, truck drivers, and harvesters were all getting rich while Cuda's friends back home were given all the weed they could smoke. The boys slapped Spaceman on the back, proud of the fact he was earning their hero a GED. "Cuda didn't have time for school," they said. "He operated on karma—*instant karma* like the Beatles' song."

Among the islanders, Cuda was legendary for stealing crabs and then stuffing the pots with fifty-dollar bills. When the fishermen found the soggy bills, they'd whoop and holler like kids who'd been visited by the tooth fairy.

Victor pulled a handkerchief from his back pocket and wiped the sweat that rolled down his face into his ears. "So what do you think Cuda will do when he realizes we're tailing him?"

Mortenson tapped out the last cigarette in the pack. "He'll run," he said. "And when we catch him, he'll fight." The captain crushed the empty package in his hand and stuffed it into the Styrofoam cup. "He packs heat, and he'll use it." Mortenson lit the cigarette and told Victor and the chief how Cuda had been ripped off a couple of times early in the game. Once he'd delivered a hundred pounds of pot to a house on Gulf Boulevard and was greeted by a shotgun. He came up empty-handed that time—he swore it'd be his last.

Victor watched Mortenson blow smoke rings that dissolved immediately in the tidal breeze. "You think Daniel's on the boat?" Victor had waited to ask this question. He knew Mortenson and the chief understood the implication, the one his uncle refused to entertain.

The captain lowered his sunglasses and peered over the top. "I don't think he's been king-napped, if that's what you mean." Mortenson leaned in close and lowered his husky voice. "Danny's in the red, you know." He almost whispered.

Along the docks, fishermen and day riders were starting to load their boats with ice, beer, and bait. The old salt whirled around to see if anyone was within earshot. "I heard some pirates talking in the card room," he went on. "Daniel hasn't paid his bill in months."

Salazar's eyebrows shot up. "Where'd the money go?"

"Gambling."

"All of it?" Victor asked.

Mortenson took a deep hit on the cigarette. "When it comes to gambling, Daniel's no featherweight." Smoke slithered from the captain's mouth. "I've seen him upside down in poker, up to his ears in markers, and whatever cash he's got left on the table, he shoves to the middle. Winner takes all." Mortenson flicked his ash overboard. "The hell of it is he usually wins those jackpots."

He went on to say how Daniel could magnetize a crowd around a craps table. Once he got the dice rolling, everyone in the game started to win. Daniel's favorite bet was the hard ten. After a few passes, the whole table would be hooting and hollering, raking in the dough. Soon there'd be people, five rows deep, surrounding the gamblers trying to get a glimpse of the action. "I've never seen anything like it." The captain pulled off his fishing cap, bent over and wiped his bald head with edge of his T-shirt. "Plus, he's always at the dogs, jai alai, Tampa Downs, anyplace he can win cash."

Salazar leaned against the bait well, staring at Mortenson. "How'd you know that?"

The captain's face flushed, and the freckles on his head popped a dark brown. He smoothed the fiberglass along the side of his boat. "See this *Lady*, she's all I got. Makes for some lonely nights, Chief." Mortenson plopped his cap back on his head and then took another drag of the cigarette. "I've seen Danny lose a fortune in one night."

A groan escaped Salazar's lips. "Okay, fellas, let's keep a lid on this show."

Mortenson shrugged. "The gambling's not a secret, and Danny always seems to win it back." For a moment, the men's eyes locked, and Victor knew Salazar had helped the captain connect the dots. Daniel needed money. He could be party to this drug run. Mortenson crushed the butt into his Styrofoam cup.

"But that's not the whole picture." Victor leaned in as the captain started to defend his friend. "I've seen Danny give a bum the shirt off his back, seen him stuff a hundred bucks into a waiter's pocket. Daniel never discriminated. Rich, poor, white, black, smart, dumb … makes no never mind to Danny," he said. "Everyone's equal in his eyes." The captain spread his arms out. "He's got a heart the size of Montana." Mortenson started to roll up the nautical chart, visibly embarrassed by his outburst.

Salazar pulled on his chin and nodded at Victor. "Yep," he said, as if suddenly convinced of his plan. "This search is on the total Q. T."

Victor wiped his palms on the sides of his pants. He knew the chief wanted to get to the bottom of this scheme, but he also understood that Daniel, despite his shenanigans, was a loved man, a family man, and an integral part of this community. Victor stood up a little straighter. Whatever doubts he'd had concerning this search/sting evaporated with the morning mist. He felt honored to be part of the mission to help Salazar protect Daniel, his name, and family until the truth behind his disappearance could be uncovered.

Captain Mortenson was about to slip a rubber band around the nautical chart when the three of them heard a boat horn wailing through the fog. Victor leaned over starboard and squinted toward the bay. A Sea Craft motored into the marina. Victor could see a man at the helm, but he couldn't make out his face; the center console had been enclosed by an aluminum frame lined with heavy plastic. The rig looked like a makeshift tent. When the Sea Craft glided within fifty feet of the main dock, Victor's uncle pulled back the plastic and waved his hand in the air.

Victor and the chief climbed off the *Lady Luck* and hurried down the dock to meet the boat. "What's this?" Salazar asked, pointing to the Sea Craft. He caught the line Carlos had thrown him and tied it around the mooring.

Carlos grinned. "My *very* fast boat." He wore a Tilley hat with nymphs, streamers, and wet flies attached to it. The lures glinted like ornaments in the sun. "See these?" Carlos pointed to the twin Johnson outboards. "Fifty miles an hour at full throttle."

"But this isn't a cabin," Salazar said, referring to the plastic tent. "Good for rain, but that's it." Victor knew the chief was thinking about bullets.

Salazar shook his head and crossed his arms over his chest. "We can't take this boat," he said. "We'd be sitting ducks in this dinghy."

Captain Mortenson joined them on the dock with a friend in tow. He introduced them to Hank Poppy, a stout Dutchman with a thick head of blond hair and a reddish mustache. Poppy thrust out a burly hand that was shaggy as a paw. "You need a boat, Chief?" He shook Salazar's hand and then squeezed Victor's so hard his fingers crunched.

Poppy turned to Salazar. "The captain tells me you're headed for Freeport, looking for ol' Danny Boy. I got a Bertram 46 right over there." He pointed to a slip twenty yards away. "She's brand spanking new. You can use her if you want." Poppy grinned. His capped teeth clicked in the sun, as shiny as a row of Chiclets. "I'd go with you, but I'm leaving for Atlanta tomorrow. Family wedding."

Salazar held a hand to his forehead to block the sun. "I think we've got a boat, right Victor?"

Victor shook his head. "Sorry, Chief, I couldn't get one." He didn't want to tell Salazar how the Gaspar Krewe members had basically ignored him Thursday night. He realized they didn't intend any harm; they just had no interest in him, in his business, or the new krewe that had crowned his uncle the first king of SantY'ago. Still, a wave of embarrassment washed over him.

He couldn't figure out why he was so drawn to Becca. Ever since that first night he'd seen her running down the Bayshore, her skirt torn, he felt as if he'd been called by some higher force to protect her. And yet he knew, just like her friends, she had no interest in him at all. She was only being polite, asking him to the fundraiser and dinner that evening—grateful that he was helping with her grandfather's search. After all, she had another life, and he'd seen it. Two long-haired hippies, one her brother and one her boyfriend. As soon as her grandfather was found, she'd head back to New York and to her career on Broadway. From what he could see, there was no room in her life for a guy who was working his ass off to make a name for himself in this town.

Victor shielded his eyes from the sun and peered down the dock at Hank Poppy's sleek fishing yacht rocking in its cradle. Its deep v-hull and fly bridge gleamed in the day's fresh light. The cabin probably slept six. She was a fisherman's dream. Victor felt his throat catch. "She's a beauty."

Salazar touched the tips of his fingers together and turned to Poppy. "That's generous of you, but she's more than we can handle."

Mortenson stepped between the men. "I can captain her, Chief." Before Salazar could object, Mortenson turned to Victor. "You can take the *Lady*," he said. "She just about drives herself."

Poppy slapped Mortenson on the back. "Now that's a plan, Captain." He peered down at Carlos on the Sea Craft. "You're the new king, right? From the Krewe of SantY'ago?" Poppy had to repeat the question, louder the second time, because Carlos couldn't hear above the revving engines and the fisherman loading ice.

"*Si, si.*" Carlos grinned and puffed out his chest. "I'm going to bring *your* king home."

Poppy threw his head back and laughed. "You do that! And I'll bet you'll be more comfortable on the Bertram than that beat-up ol' rig you found."

Carlos leaned over port side to get a glimpse of Poppy's swanky boat. Victor felt the coffee churn in his stomach. He wracked his brain for a reason to leave his uncle behind. *God help him,* he thought. *Uncle Carlos is just too hot-headed, too much of a risk.* Victor could never forgive himself if something happened to him on this manhunt.

Poppy pointed to a rifle leaning against the plastic tent. "That's for pirates, eh?" Carlos stepped in front of the gun, as if to hide it. "Well, don't use it on our Gasparilla King!" Poppy chortled. "My bet's the fishing got slow, and Danny got hooked on the blackjack tables. Wouldn't be the first time."

Poppy turned to the chief and gripped his arm. "The dock master will take care of everything," he said. "She'll be fueled and stocked with food and beer." He pulled on his mustache. "You want some live shrimp, a few squid?"

Salazar's hand shot up like a traffic cop's. "Oh, no. We're not fishing."

"As you wish," Poppy said, and started down the dock. He laughed long and hard. And then his voice carried out over the water. "Bring our Danny home, fellas! I bet his old lady's mighty pissed off by now."

Once Poppy disappeared into the club, Salazar turned to Mortenson. "We can't take that boat."

"We need her, Chief." The captain kicked the remains of a crab carcass into the water, somebody's leftover bait. "Poppy's a good man, and he loves Daniel like a brother." Mortenson shoved his hands into his cargo shorts. "When Danny was flush, he bailed Poppy out more than once, kept him from going bankrupt." Victor glanced down the dock at the *Blew Bayou*. She was as shiny as a new toy.

"Now Poppy's in the chips," Mortenson said. He searched his pockets for a cigarette and cocked his head toward the yacht club. "Come on, Chief. He knows we're working on a big catch. Take his boat."

Victor sucked in a deep breath. The air was heavy and hot. What choice did they have? They needed a boat, and they needed it now.

Salazar wiped the sweat from his forehead. "You'll probably need some help throwing lines, right?" he said to Mortenson. "Besides my man."

"That I will." Mortenson had found a crumpled cigarette in his back pocket and smoothed it between his fingers. He caught Salazar's eye, and they both looked at Carlos.

Before Carlos could answer, Victor swung a protective arm across his uncle. "I know someone," he said. "My architect. He'll help you, Captain."

Salazar pressed his lips together. "He's someone we can trust?"

"Absolutely, and he knows boats."

Carlos grumbled and stomped his foot like an angry child, but Victor calmed him. "You're my first mate, Uncle. We've got the *Lady* to navigate." The more Victor talked, the more Carlos relaxed.

When Mortenson headed back to his boat to prepare for a late-morning charter, Salazar leaned against the mooring, as if waiting for Victor to finish with his uncle. Finally, Carlos conceded and announced he would take the Sea Craft back, since they'd decided to use Hank Poppy's Bertram for the search. Salazar untied the rope while Victor pushed the boat off. Once Carlos passed through the marina, Salazar slapped an arm around Victor's shoulders. "I've got an idea," he said.

Victor noticed a slight twinkle flash impishly in the chief's eye. "Your uncle wants a lead part in this search, right?" Victor nodded while Salazar grinned. "Let's give it to him," he said. The chief proposed that Carlos could use the Sea Craft, dock right here at the yacht club, and receive radio reports from the *Lady Luck*. That way he could relay the search's progress to the Westcotts while they waited. "It's going to take hours." The chief tugged on his chin. "Someone will need to inform them."

Relief flooded Victor's body. "That's good, Chief. I don't want my uncle out there."

Salazar planted a firm hand on Victor's back. "Me neither, my friend." They started down the dock, toward the yacht club. "I hear you're joining your uncle at the Westcotts' for dinner tonight."

"He canceled," Victor said.

Salazar frowned. "Why?"

"He's got some silly notion that it would be inappropriate for him, a widower, to attend Mrs. Westcott's dinner party while Daniel's missing. Something about being a lone wolf and my aunt flipping over in her grave."

Victor and Salazar shared a hearty laugh, and then Victor asked, "Why did *you* cancel?"

Salazar let out a deep sigh. "They'd ask too many questions I wouldn't be able to answer truthfully." He kept his gaze straight ahead as they walked. "As it is, I borrowed your uncle's take and told Natalie Westcott that Daniel may have been kidnapped by the smugglers."

"Probably not, right?"

"Right," Salazar said. "I had to tell the family something, and it's a good cover for now." They stopped on the dock just before Mortenson's boat. "I also told Mrs. Westcott about the bogus search to the Bahamas. She knows our mission is secret." Salazar set his hands on his hips and then turned to Victor. "Are you going alone tonight?"

"Nope," Victor said, pulling off the captain's T-shirt. "I'm bringing my architect, Evan Stone. He's the one who'll help us on the search." Victor folded the T-shirt in half. "He can man the *Lady Luck* with me as long as my uncle agrees to your plan."

Salazar was staring at Victor's chest.

"Oh sorry," Victor said, and held up the T-shirt to hide his scar. "I don't think about it much."

"No, no," Salazar said, waving his hand in the air. "I just didn't realize —"

"It's really big, right?" Victor laughed. "Well, it just about killed me." Victor knew his uncle had told Salazar about the accident.

"I heard you saved your brother's life."

Victor laughed. "I was a kid. I loved my brother. It's no big deal." Victor noticed how Salazar's body visibly relaxed.

"You're a good boy," Salazar said and he laughed. "All these years, I thought your uncle was just bragging on you." He placed a firm hand on Victor's bare back. "You're a rare bird, my boy, and I'm happy to have you on my team."

The men shared a handshake, and Victor climbed on board the *Lady Luck* to retrieve his dress shirt. He had some work to finish before the dinner party tonight.

CHAPTER 15 ※ Moonlight Sonata

Upstairs, while tepid water filled the bathtub, Natalie spread a chemise blouse and a long silk skirt across the bed. *Made in Paris*, the label read. She smoothed the fineness of the silk between her fingers and admired the bright colors that swirled together like a fancy modern painting. Daniel called this her peacock skirt. She sighed, gathered her robe and hairbrush from the vanity, and stepped into the bathroom. The day's heat had risen to the second floor and been trapped there. While her housedress fell easily to the floor, Natalie's underclothes clung to her like scotch tape. She peeled them off and climbed into the tub. After she finished her toilette, she would open the windows and hope for a cooling breeze to drift in off the bay.

Natalie pressed her back against the porcelain and relished in the feel of the tub against her skin. She was about to close her eyes when she saw Daniel in the mirrored bathroom door, sitting on the edge of their bed. Instinctively she sat up and covered her breasts with the flats of her hands. Wouldn't you know he'd show up now—and be dressed in a pinstriped suit so wrinkled and loose it hung on him as if he'd slept in it all night. She eyed him through the mirror and thought of her friend, Sophie Meyers, who claimed she'd seen ghosts in the old Ashley house when they first moved in some twenty-odd years ago. The historic home, three blocks down from the Westcotts', had sat abandoned for almost a decade. In that time, it had collected cobwebs, black mold, and mice. Ridding the house of vermin was the easy part, Sophie had said. Late at night, she shared, diaphanous creatures decked out in Victorian frippery supposedly glided down the twin staircases and made merry around the dining room table. Sometimes they fought. "All silently, of course," Sophie said. But the malevolent energy they emanated as their contorted faces and fists flying in mock air fights was said to be palpable. "It rattled the house like thunder," she said.

Natalie soaped her underarms. She watched Daniel through the mirror. He was hunched over on the stool. As he folded and unfolded his hands, she sensed something unnatural about him, far beyond the mischief in his eyes. His once-plump face appeared slack, paler than an onion. Skin hung from his lower jaw as if he were losing weight. *How was that possible?* Natalie splashed water over her shoulders. Since no one else had seen him, Natalie assumed he'd come seeking her alone, especially now in the privacy of their bedroom. She shivered and added a bit of warmth to the bath. Maybe Daniel was still angry about the gunshots. Well, hadn't he dared her to pull the trigger? And besides, this disappearance act had worn out its welcome. She'd seen it all before—his gambling junkets to the Bahamas, his all-night binges. She'd even found photos of those island women who draped silk scarves over their naked shoulders. "Havana hussies," she called them.

Natalie pressed her palm to her chest. A rage started to build inside her. It festered like it had on the night Daniel had come home at five a.m. after Georgia Meeker called earlier that evening. With the sharpest whine of a long-toothed cat in her voice, she asked Natalie which cousin ("Or was it a niece?") Daniel was seen dancing with at Malios. But whatever the madness, she thought back to the way she'd reached for his eyes with her fingernails that predawn morning, thinking if he couldn't see, he couldn't betray her. Or the night she'd heard his footsteps as he flew down the stairs and she raced to his gun cabinet to grab the revolver from the rack—and why? Because he was going out and leaving Natalie alone in the living room again? Yes, it was exactly *that* madness—that helium buzz, the giddy, high-pitched hissing that pulsed her brain with fiery reds and then spread black and blue like spilled ink until it was black all over and exploded into a smoking pistol—that drove her to shoot him, not once, not twice, but three times, all tripped by the eagerness of a twitching finger.

Did she want to kill him? Probably no more than she'd wanted to claw his eyes out the morning he admitted seeing Georgia Meeker at Malio's and introduced the blonde woman on the dance floor as one of "Natalie's French cousins."

Did Natalie know the pistol was filled with blanks? *Yes*, she reassured herself now, *that must be it.* She must have known they were blanks. When she'd reached for the gun, she could not remember anything except the black whir in her brain, the cool weight of steel against her palm, and Daniel standing on the stairs, his face a riddle, peering down at her as she pointed the pistol at his heart.

Natalie climbed from the tub and slipped into her robe. When she stepped over the threshold into the bedroom, the doorbell screeched up the stairs and down the east hall. The sound split her ears. She imagined a baby squirrel, a lizard, or God forbid, a rat, had crawled into the chime cabinet and gotten stuck there. The creature had probably died and compressed the bells into one clamorous shriek. Once the noise subsided, she realized Daniel had left the bed. She dashed across the room and batted the heavy brocade curtains that were drawn to shield the sun. "Come out!" she shouted. Then she peered into the closet and behind the loveseat, but Daniel had vanished again.

Natalie sat down at the vanity and opened the mirror top. She picked up the Ivory Rose foundation and smoothed it beneath her eyes and over her cheeks in quick, sweeping motions. One of the guests had arrived and had been greeted by the clanging bell. *How embarrassing,* she thought. Natalie knew the young men were coming to comfort her, to assure her that even if Daniel was not on the *Sea Booty*, the smugglers would know where to find him. She glanced around the room, hoping Daniel would show up again. She wanted to tell him the buzzing in her brain had stopped. It had flown off like a wild bird spirited into night. She also wanted to tell him about the diaries.

Natalie set the makeup bottle down. A chill crept up the back of her neck. She'd been so pleased this morning to stumble upon Rebecca's diary. But what was in that second journal? Not Silva's story but probably Daniel's and hers. And Julia's. Natalie quickly powdered her face and brushed a bit of color onto her cheeks. She'd never told Becca about Julia's rape. How could she? No, she'd wanted to protect Becca from the horror of that night and preserve Julia's integrity. Natalie gripped the sides of her chair. *What an old fool!* she thought. If Becca had read the diaries, the only person Natalie had succeeded in protecting was that filthy pirate.

Natalie stood up and shuffled over to her lingerie drawer. She rummaged through the underclothes looking for the pistol she'd wrapped in a Hermes scarf. The scarf was folded into a neat square. The gun was gone. She flung the drawer open and searched under every bra, panty, girdle, and slip. Then, with an odd tightness in her chest, she spun around, expecting to find Daniel standing behind her pointing the pistol at *her* heart, but the room was empty.

Sunlight leaked through the crevice between the curtains, casting a warm glow across the wood floor. For a moment, standing in the silence of the room, she had a clear sense that Daniel had taken the pistol. For what, she could only speculate. Then as if he could hear her, Natalie made him a deal. "Keep the gun," she said out loud. "And bring me the diaries under Becca's bed." She didn't wait for an answer. Instead she dressed quickly. Before she left the room to greet her guests, she opened the windows to catch whatever breeze the bay had to offer.

Halfway down the hall, Natalie heard Beethoven's "Moonlight Sonata" rising up through the stairwell. On the first landing, she stopped to listen. The music started low and then bloomed like an enormous flower. For a moment, she thought Daniel was playing the piano. She hurried down the last steps. In the living room, she saw Becca bent over the baby grand, ready to turn the page for a gentleman who was seated at the bench. He was dressed in a white dinner jacket. Becca wore a black halter that shimmered with flecks of silver rhinestones. Natalie reckoned the dress was a costume she'd worn on stage in New York. Still, her granddaughter looked lovely tonight. Her hair was pulled back in one thick braid and soft curls wisped around her forehead, making her face appear almost full. Natalie watched as Becca flipped the score, and the gentleman's hands floated across the keyboard. He held his wrists high and steady while his fingers moved with a power she'd rarely seen. The house vibrated with music. When he finished, Natalie stood dumbfounded.

"He's a natural, Nattie," Becca said and introduced her to Evan Stone. "He's only had a few lessons from an old auntie who used to let him bang on her spinet piano."

Natalie extended her hand. "Surely you've been trained, Mr. Stone. No one plays with that kind of technique or expression without years of study."

The young man pulled on his chin and laughed. "Nope," he assured her, "I've never had a formal lesson."

Natalie took a step back. Something in his laugh and in the way he tugged at his chin struck her as familiar. She studied his deep-set eyes and full lips. She asked about his family.

"I grew up in Seminole Heights, one of a half-dozen kids." He mopped the sweat from his brow with a hanky he'd pulled from his back pocket. "My dad died the year I was born."

Becca slid the bench back beneath the piano. "Evan's Victor's architect. He's joining the search for Granddad."

Natalie gripped the sides of her skirt. She didn't know what was queerer, Mr. Stone's first name pronounced with a long E or a total stranger risking his life for Daniel. "However did that happen?" The question popped out harshly.

Becca pressed her stubby nails into the flesh on Natalie's arm. She tried to pull away, but Becca held her fast. "Captain Mortenson needs help on his boat, so Evan volunteered." Becca smiled at him. "We're grateful, aren't we, Nattie?" When Natalie didn't answer, Becca reminded her that no one knew about Cuda and the *Sea Booty*. "Everyone thinks the search is headed for Freeport."

While Becca rattled on about the importance of keeping the smugglers a secret, Natalie felt like she was getting a tongue lashing. She was about to defend herself when she was drawn to the deep V on Becca's bodice. She eyed her granddaughter's breasts, which appeared suddenly lush, pressed taut against the flimsy top. She blinked a couple of times. When had *that* happened? And how could she have missed it?

"It's broiling in here," Becca said, fanning her face.

"Indeed," Natalie said. She noticed the sweat gathering on the lovely cleavage between her granddaughter's breasts. "Shall we have drinks on the porch?"

Becca frowned. "I'm not sure it's any cooler out there. That's why we stepped inside."

"Nonsense." Natalie turned toward the foyer. "With the sun going down and the breeze off the bay, it should be quite pleasant out there by now." At the staircase, she stopped and called Niobe to take drink orders.

On the porch, the evening was steamy, heavy with the scent of confederate jasmine that hung thick from the trellis next to the porch. Natalie swept a piece of hair from her forehead. Not a breath of air blew in off the bay. She thought to fetch a couple of electric fans from the pantry when Victor's Camaro shot into the driveway like a silver bullet. He jumped from the car and bounded up the stairs carrying a bottle of wine.

"A gift from my uncle," he said, handing the bottle to Natalie. "It's a dry Riesling. Wonderful with dessert."

"Hardly a replacement for his company," Natalie said. The disappointment in her voice startled her. "Thank you," she added.

"He sends his regrets," Victor said. "He's with the chief." Then Victor turned to face them all. "The search begins tomorrow!"

A small gasp escaped Becca's lips. She covered her mouth.

Victor rushed on to explain that the *Sea Booty* had left Jamaica at noon and was expected to hit Egmont Key around midnight tomorrow.

Natalie felt the wine bottle go heavy in her hands. She'd never expected the search to take place. She figured Daniel would turn up dead or alive before it was launched.

Becca gripped Victor's forearm. "My grandfather—he's on the boat?"

Victor covered Becca's hand with his own. "We can't be sure." He gazed down at her, cool in his seersucker jacket and navy pants. The heat hadn't hit him—yet. What had hit him was the sight of Becca, her braided hair, the glittering bodice, and the dewy moisture between her breasts. He took a half step back as if to regain his balance. Natalie sighed. She wasn't the only one who had recognized the change in Becca. She excused herself to put the wine on ice.

In the kitchen, she found Niobe finishing a platter of melon slices wrapped with prosciutto. Natalie eyed the canapés curiously. Something was amiss. "Are those drinks ready yet?"

"Yes'm," Niobe said. "I'm going now."

Natalie held the door for Niobe, who clutched the silver platter like a treasure chest. She had managed to add the canapés to the drink tray, but the whole assembly looked shaky. Natalie followed her down the dark hall to be sure she didn't trip on a swollen rug; then she headed back to the kitchen to find an ice bucket to chill the wine.

In the pantry, Natalie scanned the shelves for Daniel's black leather bucket but spotted two small fans instead. She pulled them down and dusted them off with an apron that hung over the stepstool. Then she sat on the stool to collect her thoughts. Her heart had been racing for days. With so much trouble running amok in her brain, the sight of Becca in her sparkly dress thrilled her. She was certain Victor had seen it too. His eyes drank Becca in, and his yearning for her was clear. Natalie clutched her hands in her lap. She needed to tell him to hurry, but to what? To kiss her? Yes! Just like Daniel had kissed Natalie underneath the bleachers at the homecoming game. Of all the girls, Daniel had chosen her, Natalie La Jonchere, a Catholic girl with no Gasparilla lineage, no hope to be a maid, let alone a queen! She was a girl with no father.

Natalie squirmed on the stool and remembered the day Rebecca had called her into the living room to chat with her behind closed doors. It was three days after Daniel had announced their engagement. Her mother-in-law-to-be paced the room, smoothing her hair, which was wound high in a massive chignon. Rebecca talked about commitment, family, and hard-earned loyalties. Her eyes were steely, but her velvet voice lilted with a soothing, hypnotic rhythm.

"In a marriage," Rebecca started, "there are certain social and religious values that must be shared." She moved closer to Natalie, who sat in the yellow armchair. "Do you understand?"

Natalie didn't, but she nodded anyway.

"Good, then you must realize how this union could damage Daniel." Rebecca gripped the back of the armchair and leaned in close to Natalie. "Don't get me wrong—you're a lovely girl. But because of your unfortunate beginning, this marriage could greatly threaten Daniel's business ventures." Natalie felt Rebecca's breath hot on her neck. "Not to mention how it could ruin his chances of becoming Gasparilla King." Then Rebecca dropped a check into Natalie's lap. Natalie didn't count the zeros or even touch the check. She stood up, feeling dirty. The check fell to the floor, and Natalie fled the living room.

"It's a furnace out there," Niobe said, bursting into the kitchen. "I'm fetching more ice."

Natalie jumped to her feet, grabbed the wine bottle, and slipped it into the fridge. She set the fans on the counter. "Bring these when you come."

Natalie hurried down the back hall and through the foyer. When she stepped onto the porch, she felt her cheeks flush at the first glimpse of Victor squinting and mopping perspiration that streamed into his eyes faster than he could catch it. And poor Mr. Stone, the underarms of his snow-white jacket were ringed with sweat.

Victor mopped his brow with a wet cocktail napkin. He was finishing a conversation with Becca about Daniel's search. Natalie squeezed between the two of them, realizing she'd missed something important. She started to ask a question when Niobe ran onto the porch.

"Here's the fans, Miss Natalie." She set them down alongside the porcelain bowl she'd filled with ice.

Evan started to laugh. He picked up one the fans and held it against the mound of ice. "Old-fashioned air conditioning."

Becca giggled, and Victor reached for an ice cube to cool his forehead. Becca turned to Natalie. "Perhaps they should take their coats off," she suggested.

"Of course," Natalie answered. "And please loosen your ties."

The men stood up and began to peel the jackets from their steamy bodies. Natalie turned away, embarrassed by the indelicate grunts and moans, especially from Mr. Stone, who couldn't quite shake off the white jacket because it had seemingly melted onto his body. *Such feverish creatures!* Natalie thought. Only Becca looked unruffled. The heat had produced a most natural glint to her cheeks. Sleek in her black gown flecked with silver, she shimmered like a cool, extraordinary gem.

When the men settled back into their chairs, Natalie realized their shirts were soggy. All the cocktail napkins had been crumpled and soaked with perspiration. She didn't think the evening could've gotten off to worse start until the next door neighbor, Ruby Taylor, skipped up the front steps like she owned the place. At the top of the stairs, she handed Natalie a loaf of banana-nut bread.

"I thought I heard you out here," Ruby said. "Are you having a party?"

Natalie eyed her next-door neighbor, who was sassy in a Lily Pulitzer frock the color of frosted raspberries. She accepted the bread and made introductions. By now the men had rolled up their sleeves, removed their ties, and unbuttoned their shirts. They resembled a pair of rednecks—wiping sweaty palms on their pants before they shook Ruby Taylor's hand. Natalie shuddered, dreading the words that could fly from her neighbor's mouth. *What were those gunshots she'd heard?* Or *Why in God's name were they outside on such a fretful evening?*

Ruby stared right into Natalie's face. "Daniel's search starts tomorrow, right?"

A silence, as thick and sticky as the air, hung between them. Evan reached for his beer, while Victor rolled his shirt sleeves up another inch. Becca chewed a thumbnail. Natalie reached for the back of the wicker chair to steady herself. *How could Ruby know about the search?* She must have hidden behind the trellis and heard every word before she climbed the steps to the porch. Now this nosy neighbor knew more about the search than she did!

Ruby scanned each face and finally settled on Natalie's. "Has it been called off?" When no one answered, she asked, "Did they find him in the Bahamas?"

Natalie may have imagined it, but she thought she felt the first breath of air rise from the bay. "Not yet," she said and sighed with relief, "but we're hopeful."

Victor chimed in. "We leave for Freeport tomorrow."

Evan nodded heartily while Becca jumped up and offered Mrs. Taylor a melon canapé.

Ruby hesitated and then touched the rim of the platter. "My pie plate," she said and turned to Natalie. "To think, you used it for hors d'oeuvres."

Natalie imagined falling between the porch slats and slithering away like the creature that had climbed into the chime cabinet and died there. She made a quick apology and excused herself to check on dinner. Once inside the door, she saw Eula coming down the stairs, clutching the baluster and sliding her feet cautiously from one step to the next. Her silvery hair was braided in a thin coil around her head, and her white dress hung like a crisp A on her wiry frame. Natalie waited for her to reach the bottom. "You can't be climbing these stairs alone," she scolded.

Eula jumped and clutched her big hands to her chest. "Oh, me! Miss Natalie, you scared the bejesus out of me."

Niobe had heard the racket and came running down the hall. Natalie was about to clout her for using Ruby Taylor's pie plate for the canapés when she realized it must have been Eula who found the dish and mistook it for a porcelain platter. She handed the banana bread to Niobe. "Now take your mama to the kitchen." Then she mouthed the words—*and watch her.*

Niobe pretzeled her arm around Eula's. As they headed off toward the kitchen, Natalie called after them. "Is the cake frosted? The berries cooling?"

"Yes'm," they chimed together.

Then Natalie remembered the pickled watermelon that had not yet been brought in from the garden shed. She told Niobe to fetch it.

"But there's one out there," Niobe said. "Right on the counter."

Natalie shook her head. "There's everything but."

"But I saw it. Yellowish, pink on the inside. Black letters on the jar, W A T—"

"All right, but check—and put it on ice before you serve it."

As Niobe turned to leave, Natalie squeezed her arm. "Do your best with Julia?"

Niobe grinned. "I always do."

Before Natalie returned to her guests, she peeked through the side window that framed the front door. Ruby had left. Natalie took a deep breath and stepped onto the porch. Dusk had fallen, and the expected breeze had finally blown in and cooled her face. Evan had settled into the wicker rocker and appeared almost comfortable in his damp shirt. Victor sat next to Becca on the porch swing.

"My AC man will be here by eight," Victor said. He kept the swing moving with a stroke of his foot.

"Wonderful," Becca said. "We can't go through another day like this."

Natalie sat down in the wicker rocker next to Evan. "Like what?"

"In this heat." Becca fanned herself with a limp napkin. Then she lifted her glass to propose a toast. "To the gentlemen. They're sending their air-conditioner man over in the morning." She turned to Natalie. "It's broken, you know."

Natalie glared at Becca. *And how are they to pay for that?* her eyes demanded.

Victor must have seen her concern because he immediately assured her. "It's the least we can do." He leaned over to touch Becca's glass to his own. "Consider it a thank-you for dinner this evening." Their glasses met. The crystal connection sent out a ring that caught the breeze and spun it upward and out toward the water until it dissipated like a distant wind chime. Natalie followed the sound, admiring the brightness and harmony of it. *If only that could last.*

Just then a thud sounded in the doorway, and Eula stumbled onto the porch. "Dinner is served," she announced, clutching the sides of her skirt. Her milky eyes gazed out toward the water, and she curtsied to the live oaks just beyond the front steps.

Natalie pushed out of her chair and caught Eula by the arm. Once inside the door, she hissed, "Where's Niobe?"

"Upstairs with Julia. She told me to get everyone 'round the table."

"I'll do that." Natalie guided Eula down the back hall into the kitchen. "You stay put." When Natalie returned to the porch, night had fallen. The scent of jasmine wafted in,

heavy and sweet, and Natalie squinted, trying to make out the faces that had all but disappeared in the dark. She called them to dinner.

Victor stood up and offered Becca his hand. He led her to the front door while Evan followed behind. "The night's cooling off," Victor said.

Natalie smiled. "And so it is." Victor guided Becca through the foyer, his hand steady on her elbow. If Natalie could will a spark to fly between them, to set Becca's heart on fire as wildly as Victor's, she would gladly give her life in return. Then she could die peacefully knowing that under their reign, the house would be restored, Julia would be cared for—and perhaps even Kurt would be saved.

In the dining room, the windows had been raised, and a light breeze ruffled the lace curtains. Candles flickered on the table, six of them, each set within a spray of marigolds, oriental poppies, and sweet violets. Two larger candles lit up the buffet.

Natalie instructed Victor to sit at the head of the table, flanked by Becca and Evan. She settled in on the other end. Although the empty seats created an awkward distance between them, Natalie welcomed the chance to sit down. She'd been on her feet all day, and her old legs ached. Across the table, Becca shot her a quizzical glance, and Natalie understood it— *How long could she hold dinner? What if neither Julia nor Kurt showed up?* To buy time, she asked Victor about the plans for tomorrow's search. She thought it was safe to talk about it now in the privacy of the dining room without that big-eared Ruby Taylor lurking behind the trellis.

Victor cleared his throat. "My uncle has agreed to stay behind and receive radio messages from Hank Poppy's boat. He'll call you from the yacht club." Victor unfolded his napkin and laid it in his lap. "It could be a long night, but at least this way, you'll know when we've spotted the *Sea Booty*." They all understood Carlos would tell them whether or not Daniel was on the boat.

A gust of wind stirred the lace curtains, and Natalie tapped her foot. Perhaps it was best if her unseen guests didn't show. She lifted the crystal bell to call for dinner when Niobe appeared in the doorway with Julia.

Natalie blinked in the candlelight. For an instant, as her daughter stood in the doorway wearing a long, gauzy dress of white silk, Julia looked just like the young woman Natalie remembered waltzing with her king at their coronation ball. Julia's hair had been swept into a high french twist and was secured with a jeweled comb. The shimmering stones caught the light and set the walls aglitter.

"Mother!" Becca jumped up and led Julia into the dining room. Awkward in their rumpled shirts, Victor and Evan stood and nodded politely as Becca introduced them.

Natalie beckoned to Niobe, who flitted from one foot to another, captivated by the guests' excitement and her own fine handiwork she'd accomplished with Julia. "Come here." Natalie grabbed the edge of Niobe's skirt and pulled her in close to whisper, "Start the dinner."

"But Mr. Kurt—"

She squeezed Niobe's hand. "I said begin it."

With that, Niobe hurried off to toss the greens and warm the rolls. Natalie scanned the table at her guests settling back into their chairs. After all these years, wasn't it enough that Julia had come down to dinner and was dressed to the nines! How could Natalie expect more?

She turned to Evan. "Becca tells me you're an architect. Are you working on the Centurion Building with Victor?" Natalie leaned back in her chair. She knew how to get men to talk about themselves. After dinner, she would propose a toast to thank them for their part in Daniel's search, but for now she listened to their banter about the revival of Hyde Park and the plans for a performing-arts theater.

Julia's eyes lit up. "It'll be like the old Tampa Bay Hotel, with dancers like Anna Pavlova. She danced there, you know."

"Even better," Evan promised. "It'll survive."

Becca laughed. "I'd like to see a theater in this town attract more attention than a fishing tournament."

Julia started to fidget and stared at the empty seat. She turned to Natalie. "Where's Daddy tonight?" Her voice had turned brooding. The men stopped talking. They waited for Natalie to answer. She clutched the napkin in her lap.

"He's not coming," Becca said.

Just then Niobe entered the room carrying a chilled crystal bowl mounded with red leaf lettuce, tomato wedges, and sliced mushrooms. Directly behind her, Eula balanced a basket of dinner rolls in one hand and the plate of pickled watermelon in the other. She had piled the slices too high into a towering pyramid, and the top tier wobbled perilously. Natalie took the plate, but before she could set it down, three pieces toppled off. They made a loud splat on the tablecloth. The room fell silent, but then Julia broke into peals of laughter so infectious that the men howled right along with her.

"This is Becca's great-great-grandmother's recipe," Natalie said, giddy with relief. The commotion had completely diverted Julia's attention. She passed the watermelon to Julia, who spooned a slice onto her plate and then passed it onto Evan. Nervous sweat glistened on poor Mr. Stone's face, but Natalie felt bolstered by the blunder. If only Kurt stayed away, the dinner would proceed peacefully.

Once the conversation reverted to talk of an NFL franchise, Natalie picked up a roll and buttered the inside. She had begun to relax when she saw Daniel across the room, leaning against the china cabinet. He'd changed out of his wrinkled suit, and he now sported navy pants with a white dinner jacket exactly like Evan's. His hair was combed straight back, and he grinned like an old hound on his last hunt. He flashed a quick, surly wink at her. Then it hit her—Daniel had brought in the pickled watermelon! Natalie flushed. She tingled with the same schoolgirl thrill, as memories of their courtship—that first kiss they shared, the daisies he'd gathered from the garden, and the English lavender soaps he bought for her bath. She eyed him across the room and nodded with gratitude. But she made it clear with an expedient, no-nonsense glare, there was no way she would bed with a ghost.

As soon as the salad plates were cleared, the smell of roasted garlic tinged with lemon filled the room. Niobe entered with an oblong platter tossed with tricolor pasta, orange puffs of gulf shrimp, and broccoli florets. Julia clapped excitedly as Niobe set the dish on the buffet.

Victor raised his glass to toast the chef, when they heard the front door fling open. A gust of wind swirled through the room, and Natalie turned to see Kurt staggering in from the hall. His hair hung in strings, hiding his face, and he rocked back and forth on his heels like a frenzied animal.

"You couldn't wait?" His words scattered the room in a drunken slur.

Becca jumped up from the table. "We've just begun." She clutched his arm. "There's a place for you."

He yanked his arm free. "Don't touch me."

Two large candles on the buffet cast a spotlight on Becca and Kurt. Becca leaned in close to her brother and pointed across the room to the table.

Julia's face glowed eerily in the candlelight. Natalie searched the room for Daniel, but in the strange light, she saw no one—not Eula, Niobe, Evan, or even Victor. Everyone had vanished except Julia, Becca, and Kurt.

"Look, Kurt, it's Mother," Becca said.

Natalie's eyes were riveted on Julia. She felt suspended in an ephemeral passing, a netherworld between time and motion where she dared not speak, move, or breathe.

"No," Kurt said, covering his eyes with his hands. "She doesn't know me." He shook visibly with a terrible, violent trembling. "Do you?"

If Julia didn't answer, Natalie was afraid Kurt would go wild in the room, shatter the crystal, and send the plates, the silver, and the burning candles crashing to the floor. But in the faint light, Julia pushed back from the table. She stood up and looked directly at her son. She didn't flinch or betray a retreat. She merely said, "Yes, you are Kurt."

CHAPTER 16 ✷ War Games

Victor's A/C man arrived at seven sharp. Becca heard the front-door chimes screech through the house, an annoying scrape like nails on a chalkboard. She was about to throw on her robe and answer the door, knowing the man would want to conquer the attic before the sun did, but Nattie had beaten her to it. Becca heard her grandmother offering him coffee before he could cross the threshold into the house. Becca fell back on the pillows and pulled the covers over her head. Chief Salazar and the search team were headed out to Egmont Key this evening with Captain Mortenson's boat and Hank Poppy's new Bertram.

Becca had stayed up late last night explaining to Nattie how Victor had ended up on Daniel's search instead of his yacht-club cronies. "Salazar trusts Carlos Mendoza," she said. "They're like brothers, and Victor's the son Carlos never had." In order to secure the hunt, the chief needed to involve the fewest amount of searchers possible. "We don't know what's going to happen out there, Nattie," Becca said. "It's best the Gaspar Krewe knows only about the bogus search to Freeport, for now." Becca suspected there was more to the cover-up that they wouldn't let on to anyone, but that was okay. She ran her hand over her belly, which was beginning to round. She, for one, understood secrets.

When the grandfather clock chimed eight, Becca crawled out of bed and threw on a pair of shorts and a sleeveless blouse. A slight breeze rustled the curtains. The air felt boggy again today, fusty once more with smell of sulfur rising from the bay. Becca untangled last night's braid from her hair and brushed out the knots. She thought about Adam. If he'd crossed the border Saturday night as planned, he'd probably found a place to stay. He'd be calling her soon. If her grandfather turned up tonight, she'd be free to leave. Whatever had bound her to the lawn chair the night Adam had come to fetch her would have to release its hold. She told herself it was duty that compelled her to stay. She had to be here for her family. Once Grandpa Dan came home, she could run to Adam. Becca smoothed her hair and gathered it in a ponytail behind her head. She wanted to make sandwiches for the men, maybe even an apple cake to help them pass the hours waiting for the *Sea Booty*, but she had no idea how much food was in the house. She would need to take inventory and get to the store.

In the kitchen, Becca was surprised to find Kurt up already, sitting at the counter, a mug of coffee cupped between his hands as if he were cold. Nattie bustled around like a flustered hen, gathering carrots and zucchini to make a salad. "Ask your sister," she said to Kurt. "I've nothing to do with it."

Kurt turned to Becca. "Why can't I go on the search?" A strand of red hair swung in front of his face, which was swollen from last night's binge. "I'm the grandson."

Becca poured herself a cup of coffee. "You weren't supposed to be here." She spooned a little sugar into her cup.

"So?" Kurt said. "They just asked Evan yesterday."

Becca knew where this chatter was headed. "Nattie needs us here, Kurt. It's going to be a long night."

Kurt eyed her suspiciously. "You think I can't handle going with the men." His voice rose. "You think I'm not good enough."

"What do you think?" Becca fired back. "They need a drunk on board?" Even as she said it, she regretted every word.

"Shut your hole," he sputtered. "You have no idea who I am!" Spit flew from his mouth.

Nattie chopped the carrots with a furious energy. "Stop it!" she said and waved the knife like a samurai warrior.

"She started it!" Kurt raged and turned to Becca. "You think I'm a drunk and a junkie. But you're a whore! A slut! A bitch in heat lapping up attention from any ol' mutt that comes around here!"

Becca flew at her brother. She slapped his arms, his face, anything she could grab. He dodged her, laughing. Then he caught her by the wrist and twisted her arm behind her. "Lemme go!" she screamed and spun herself around to face him. That's when he saw the tattoo.

Kurt held her wrist to the light. "What's this?" Becca struggled to pull free, but her skinny brother strong-armed her. "It's the muted post-horn," he said in awe. "It doesn't look exactly like this but it's close enough."

Natalie had dropped the knife and was trying to wedge herself between them. "What is it?" she spluttered.

"A tattoo." All the anger drained from Kurt's voice. "*My* tattoo from Pynchon's novel, *The Crying of Lot 49*."

Natalie stared at Becca's wrist, her mouth agape. "Whatever possessed you, child?"

Becca yanked her hand free and rubbed her wrist, which burned bright pink. "It's a symbol for lost love," she said, avoiding her grandmother's glare. "I got it after Adam and I split."

Natalie's face turned the color of ripe tomatoes. "How foolish," she said coolly, "now that he wants to marry you."

"You're getting married?" Kurt glanced from Nattie to Becca and then back again.

"Not until she joins the draft dodger in Canada," Natalie said, unable to hide the smirk on her face.

Kurt plopped down on the stool, his eyes as wide as a kitten's. "You're marrying a draft dodger? In Canada?" He flipped the hair from his face. "Geez, and I thought *I* had problems."

"Right," Natalie said smugly. "Becca's fiancé is a criminal. Get a good look at your sister; once Granddad's found, we'll never see her again."

In that moment, Becca hated her grandmother. Nattie knew exactly what she was doing, trying to shame Becca into staying. Becca turned her head to hide the tears that sprang to her eyes. God help her, since it was all out anyway, Becca wanted to tell them about the baby—and she may have if Kurt hadn't already called her a whore. Instead she bit her lip and glared down at the post-horn.

Kurt sighed heavily and pointed to the tattoo. "That takes guts," he said. "More than I've got." He stared down into his mug. "And Canada."

For a moment, the three of them slipped into an eerie silence. Then Natalie went back to chopping the carrots. Kurt gazed up at Becca. "Where'd you get it?" Becca told him about the Screaming Blue Eagle on Kennedy. Kurt nodded and ran his fingers over his left cheek. "I'm gonna have a skull and crossbones tattooed right here."

Natalie dropped the knife again. "Over my dead body."

Kurt laughed, and even Becca had to smile. Kurt downed his coffee and stood up. "First the tattoo, then the recruiting office. I'm going to 'Nam," he announced. He shuffled his feet to a little dance. "Uncle Sam wants you!" he chortled and pointed to his chest. "They'll even take me."

Becca gasped, and her grandmother swooned. Nattie fanned herself with a kitchen towel so vigorously she stumbled over her feet and finally plopped down on a counter stool.

"You don't want that war, Kurt," Becca said. "It's evil."

Kurt smiled. "Oh, but I do, sister." He kissed her on the cheek, more like a betrayal than a good-bye. "It can't be any more evil than this family." He laughed. "At least there, I'll know who my enemy is." He headed toward the door.

"What about Granddad?" Becca asked.

Kurt shrugged. "When he gets back, he'll just throw my ass in rehab." He stood on the threshold. "I'm making it easy on him, on all of you." With that, he pushed through the door and disappeared.

Natalie leaned over the counter, holding her head and rocking. "No … no … no …" she said. Becca couldn't help but think her grandmother's ploy to shame her had backfired. Now Nattie was losing both of them. Still Becca felt sorry for her.

"Don't worry, Nattie," she said. "Kurt's run away before." But even as she said the words, she knew something had changed. She'd felt the resolve in her brother, like a missing piece had slipped into place. For the first time in her life, she envied him. Whatever freedom he'd found to propel him out the door, she wanted.

When Nattie had calmed down, Becca rummaged through the fridge and made mental notes on what she would need to make sandwiches for the men. "I'm going to the store, Nattie."

"You need money, child?"

"Nope," Becca said. "I haven't spent a penny of the forty bucks you gave me." She bent over and hugged her grandmother, knowing they were all suffering in their own ways. "It'll be more than enough."

Becca climbed the stairs, two at a time. When she reached the top landing, she wondered if Nattie had brought her mother's breakfast tray up this morning since both Eula and Niobe had the day off. Becca thought to check on her. As she passed Kurt's room and the library, she heard the phone ring down the hall. She stopped. *It could be Adam.* She turned and ran back toward the staircase, where the phone sat on a small desk. She wanted to answer it before her grandmother.

"Hello?" Becca said and pressed the receiver to her ear. She heard someone breathing and then a click like someone had picked up. She placed her hand over the mouthpiece and called down the stairs. "I've got it, Nattie!"

When she was convinced her grandmother had hung up, Becca asked, "Adam? Is that you?" She heard a woman's voice, soft and breathy. It was Louise. Becca felt her stomach drop. "Has something happened to Adam? Is he okay?" What she heard next was unconscionable. Louise told her that when Adam left Tampa, instead of heading straight to Canada, he'd gone back to New York. He'd made a mistake. He and Louise had gotten married at the courthouse before they left for Toronto. "We just want you to send the ring back. After all, it was mine to begin with, right?"

Becca listened to all of it and wrote down the address, a PO box. When Louise finished, Becca tore the note off the pad and stuffed the address in her shorts pocket. Then she slammed the receiver into its cradle and ran back to her room.

Once inside, Becca slid down the door and pressed her back against the wood for stability. For a moment, she couldn't think or breathe. The sun glared in through the window with an intensity that made the room pulse. She blinked to clear the dizziness that passed in waves before her eyes. The room felt liquid. She imagined Adam standing in front of her. He looked down at her, his eyes comforting, but detached. "How could you?" she asked him. "How could you leave me now?"

He stared down at her. "I had to," he said. "Otherwise, I might … go mad."

"You?" Becca asked. She felt her arms go limp in her lap. She had no defense against madness, never did.

Adam reached out a hand to help her up, but she waved him away. She slipped her hand into her pocket and pulled out the address Louise had given her. She stared at the numbers a long time. Then bit by bit, she tore the paper into tiny fragments. For a moment, she clutched the scraps in her hand. With one defiant toss, she flung them into the air. The pieces caught the sunlight and fell confettilike through the room. As they settled on her lap, she felt a calmness ease through her body. It was over: Becca and Adam. *Finished.*

The day's heat beamed in through the window and shone on the edge of a diary that was sticking out from under her bed. Becca picked herself up from the floor. She brushed the pieces of paper from her shorts and headed for the second volume of Rebecca's journal. Once it was in her hands, she flipped through the pages that dealt with events directly following her mother's rape and the Westcott family registry. When she found the spot, she sat down on the vanity seat and read.

> *Just before the library, I heard Daniel in a rage. I stopped short of the door to listen. "What! What do you mean Julia's pregnant? She's just a child," he ranted. "That can't be possible!"*
>
> *Next I heard the crack of Natalie's hand as she smacked Daniel across the face. "A child?" Natalie screamed. "Are you crazy? She's a young woman! And now she's carrying that filthy pirate's baby!"*
>
> *Then Natalie started to cry. I peeked into the library. And there Daniel had his arms around her, trying to comfort her as best he could. I let them be for the moment. This was no time to make arrangements.*

Becca closed the journal on her finger to save the place. So that's it! Her mother had conceived a child on the night the pirate raped her. That could be the reason she'd gone mad. Becca reopened the diary and felt its strange energy vibrating in her hands. She read on.

CHAPTER 17 ✳ A Last Act of Redemption

From the porch swing, Emmeline saw her granddaughter's face light up first like a small moon and then flick off into darkness. Beyond the wild cactus that had outgrown the front yard and reached its spiny arms toward the road, the streetlight sputtered on and off, signaling the newly fallen night.

Morgan had settled into the swing with her back leaning against the wooden arm. Beneath the gauzy cotton dress, one leg was flung out across the seat while the other hung down. With a bare foot, she pushed off the splintered slats of the porch to keep the swing moving. "Rebecca brought the child here so you could repay the debt," Morgan said.

Emmeline gripped the arms of the rocker. Here it was again—the same old edict that sounded more like a judgment than a statement of fact, as if those words and the words "Does Julia know?" were scorched onto her granddaughter's brain. Emmeline leaned back in the rocker. She knew by the weird tone of her granddaughter's voice that the coming night would not quell her or stop the torment that circled her mind. She realized now that the day Morgan had crawled under the bed and cut her front tooth on the corner of the first volume, Emmeline should have locked the diaries in the cedar chest. But how could she have known that the fair-headed child who dragged the books through the house and crawled up on Emmeline's lap would somehow become lost in those handwritten pages?

"It was a gift," Morgan said. "Samuel's mother asked Silva to care for him, and it made no difference to Silva he was an Indian child." Morgan stopped the swing. "Without her, he would have died."

Emmeline had slipped into the rhythm of the story, into the singsong way Morgan repeated it, and she agreed—the baby would have died. If not on the boat to New Orleans, then surely by the time the weary tribe reached Oklahoma. For it was the winter following the end of the Seminole War, and there were no shelters (or tools to build them). There were no guns to shoot the squirrels that romped the snowy reservation. But Silva had saved the baby that late August day and had run with him through the streets and needling rain. Once at home, she unwrapped the deerskin and showed him to Charles. They named him Samuel Vaughn Westcott.

"You didn't know him, did you?" Morgan said.

"Some," Emmeline said. The streetlight had flicked on but was still wavering, pulsing like a heart. She knew Morgan was goading her, trying to get her to say that she knew Samuel Westcott well, had sat at his feet as a young girl, and listened as he talked about Silva Westcott, his white-skinned mother. He wore a silver locket around his neck that held her picture. Every so often, as he would sit rocking, he would tell the story how his white mother and father had christened him in the Episcopal church downtown. He would squeeze the locket in the palm of his hand, and then he would close his eyes as if seeing her in his mind and say, "But I had to leave her."

Emmeline remembered how she and her cousins would scramble around his feet and clamor for answers."Because," he would answer, "she was a fine woman with a fine family, but that family was not mine." Then he would tug on his woolly hair that he kept long and braided in two thick plaits. "They wanted to make me a pirate." He'd laugh and throw his head back. But Emmeline believed Samuel Westcott left simply because it was the men of that town who had shipped out his real mother and killed her in the first place.

Morgan tapped the porch with her bare foot. "You did know him then."

Emmeline said, "Yes, I certainly did." She looked out over the lawn, where the streetlight cast an elongated shadow of the cactus and its spiny arms that stretched almost to the porch. She would have to answer Morgan soon; the way her foot tapped the splintered slats, there would be no calming her now.

About the time Morgan was born, Emmeline had made peace with herself. Knowing how Silva Westcott had saved her grandfather's life, how could she refuse Rebecca and Daniel when they showed up on the front porch with the baby, crying and hungry and in need of a mother? She'd stood in the doorway as Rebecca stepped past her and over the threshold with the infant bundled in a crocheted blanket. She rocked him so fast, his cries filled the tiny rooms of the house.

Instinctively Emmeline had reached for him. She loosened the blanket and pressed her hands gently at his back and neck to let him know he was secure. Her own children, James, Philip, and Paul, clung to her legs. She reached into the pocket of her housedress, pulled out a caramel for each of them, and told them to go out back and play.

"Do you know who we are?" Rebecca had asked as she followed Emmeline into the front room.

Emmeline nodded. She had seen Nathan's picture in the business section of the newspaper, lauded for his unique, architecturally styled homes. Rebecca had always been a constant on the society page. But seeing her in the front parlor with the March sun on her face, Emmeline was astonished at how young Rebecca looked. Her tawny hair was swept into a french twist, and her skin was still smooth, even though Emmeline estimated her to be well over fifty. She had, after all, this grown son, Daniel, who had a daughter of his own—Miss Julia Westcott, who was soon to make her debutante ball.

"Then you know Samuel was the adopted son of Charles and Silva Westcott," Rebecca said.

"Yes, I know." Emmeline pressed the infant to her bosom. He'd stopped crying and now gazed up at her with gray eyes.

"Good," Rebecca said. She lowered herself to the sofa. "This should be easier then."

Daniel sat down next to his mother. From what Emmeline could see, Daniel was a perfect cross between Rebecca and Nathan Westcott. His hair was the color of his mother's but wavy like Nathan's. His nose was straight, like all the Westcott men's, except for the crisp turn at the end, which was identical to his mother's. He was dressed in a pair of white linen pants and a cotton jersey pullover. He looked as if he just stepped off a yacht. "The baby needs a home," Rebecca said. "We're hoping you'll take him."

Emmeline eased herself and the infant into the armchair. She thought of her three young sons playing on the rusted swing set in the backyard, her baby girl asleep in the crib, and the possibility of another seed growing within her. "I couldn't," she said.

"I know it's a lot." Rebecca got up from the sofa. She pressed her hand on Emmeline's shoulder. "But we'd pay you. We'd pay you enough to help your family."

Emmeline peered out past the weeded lawn and saw a flash of heat lightning shimmer in the sky. How many times had she remembered that day and wondered if it was a needed blessing or a hopeless curse? For what were the odds that her husband would have his body blown to bits in a trucking accident just two months after the baby was brought to her?

Emmeline figured years ago that it was either the untimely presence of the child that brought the calamity, or the misfortune was already brewing well before any tangible signs were visible. And that providence, in its need to restore, had brought the baby and his secured wealth to salvage the family. For how would Emmeline, pregnant then with her fifth child, have been able to care for them all? Although she'd made peace with her decision, she knew if she had it to do over again, she would turn the baby away, not to defy providence, not because she didn't love the child she thought of as her own son, but because she so sorely missed Nilo and his wire-thin body wrapped around hers like a strong reed, she would do anything to prevent him from leaving her. When Rebecca offered to pay for the child, Emmeline should have handed the crocheted bundle back and said no.

But instead she asked, "Who is he?"

"He's one of ours," Rebecca said. "We can't keep him, and we can't bear to adopt him out to strangers where we'd never know what happened to him."

Emmeline shifted her gaze from Rebecca to Daniel and watched him shuffle his feet along the worn hook rug. Daniel's wife? But no. There'd be no reason for that. And in that instant Emmeline knew: *the child belonged to Julia.* She was sixteen or seventeen by now and must have gotten into trouble, borne the child, and now Rebecca and Daniel had come to hide it.

Still on the sofa, Rebecca had leaned into the room as if to diminish the distance between them. Her almond-shaped eyes narrowed, and she pressed her lips together before she spoke. "But you must raise him as your own," she said. "You must never tell him where he came from."

The baby had fallen asleep. Emmeline smoothed the wrinkled frown from his forehead with her fingertips. "What's his name?" she asked.

Rebecca glanced at Daniel, who lifted his broad shoulders to his ears and then let them fall. "You name him," she said.

So Emmeline named him "Evan" (with a long E for the debt that had been repaid the Westcotts), and "Stone" because his eyes were slate gray, threaded with flecks of silver, like granite.

Morgan set the porch swing moving again. The rusted chains squeaked, high-pitched and ornery like a peeved child. Emmeline thought to reverse the course of the night and ask Morgan the question that had bewildered Emmeline ever since Rebecca returned seventeen years ago and stood shivering on the front porch with the leather-bound diaries wrapped in ivory damask. After Rebecca had warned her never to tell Evan Stone his true lineage, why did she come back that dreary day and thrust the diaries into Emmeline's arms and tell her to send them to Becca?

Emmeline wove the fingers of her thick hands together to combat the cold that stiffened them despite the heat. "Why?" she asked Morgan. "After all the years, why would she want Becca to know?"

Morgan stopped the swing with a final thud of her foot. She sat bolt up, drew her knees to her chest, and tugged the cotton dress over them. "To free herself," Morgan said. And she said it decisively, as if she'd exhausted the question before and had come to the same single conclusion. "She couldn't die without passing the story on. It's like a legacy."

Emmeline folded her hands together. She imagined the stories rising up like river gas trapped beneath the mud, bubbling and fuming, defiling the air.

"But Rebecca was clever," Morgan said. She lowered her legs and stretched her bare feet onto the porch. "She never mentioned Evan's name." Morgan pushed the swing back and held it taut with both feet. "A part of her still wanted to hide it."

"Maybe," Emmeline said, "but the birth certificate was sent to me by private courier. I filled it out and mailed it myself. Rebecca never knew his name."

Morgan released her feet, and the swing flew out over the porch. The rusted chains ripped into a high squeal that pricked the back of Emmeline's neck and spun gooseflesh down her arms. "She didn't want to know the name," Morgan said, gripping the sides of the swing as it swept out toward Emmeline and then back, banging the porch rail.

"So why would Rebecca drag herself out of bed just days before she died to deliver the diaries to me? And why would she tell me to send them to Becca, when she knew the diary was incomplete?"

The rusted chains slowed to a muted creak. In the pulsing light that shone from the street, Emmeline saw her granddaughter's face contort. Morgan never knew that Evan's name was a secret to Rebecca.

"She didn't want Evan to know," Morgan said, staring out toward the street. "Only Becca. And then only that the child existed." Morgan stopped the swing and waved her hand as if to dismiss the issue. "But it was to free her," she said, her voice rising. "Don't you see? Then Rebecca could die peacefully, thinking she had settled the score between the families."

Yes, Emmeline thought, *the score had been settled, and they had paid—Nilo, Evan, herself, and Morgan perhaps most of all.* "But that's no reason to tell Becca," Emmeline said.

Morgan turned her small face toward Emmeline, but Emmeline turned away. She looked out past the yard, to the east, and at the gibbous moon that was just beginning to rise. An orange haze hovered around the moon, making it appear whiter and larger as it began its ascent through the sky.

"Then it was for Julia's sake," Morgan said.

And it could be for Julia, Emmeline thought, looking out at the wild cactus. A last act of redemption for a scourge that was never her fault. Just then, the streetlight sputtered off. The two of them sat bathed in orange light. Emmeline gazed down at her swollen feet, which were bound in her sandals' leather straps across the toes and tied taut behind her heels. She bent over to undo the straps, knowing how long the night was going to be. *Already,* she thought, *my feet have fallen asleep.*

CHAPTER 18 ✳ The Stakeout

A T NINE O'CLOCK MONDAY NIGHT, Victor and Evan followed the *Blew Bayou* out of the marina at the yacht club into Hillsborough Bay. Even though the sun had set over half an hour ago, the evening came on heavy as a hog's breath. The night weighed in at ninety degrees. Victor sat bolt upright in the captain's chair, his senses firing at top speed. Earlier that afternoon, Captain Mortenson had shown him how to navigate the *Lady Luck.* While it proved to be much like driving a car, the captain had suspected immediately that Victor had little boating experience.

"After the accident, right," the captain had said. "Your dad destroyed the boat." Victor had been so young, he didn't realize at the time how guilt had slowly sucked the life from his father, initially leaving him crippled, and then killed him off at forty-six. "Lucky for you, your uncle took over the reins," Mortenson said. "You grew up good."

Victor trailed two boat lengths behind the *Blew Bayou* as they headed south toward MacDill Air Force Base. Evan sat next to him on the fly bridge, on a separate, cushioned bench.

The captain had given him a charter T-shirt that he'd tucked into his cargo shorts. Evan gazed out over fly bridge into the water. "We've had extreme tides lately," he said.

"Why's that?" Victor kept his eyes riveted in front of him.

"The super moon." Evan pointed to the glowing ball, three times its normal size and the color of wild salmon. Victor couldn't help but ogle it. Mortenson had said Cuda would wait for a full moon to unload his stash on Egmont Key. Moonlight made it easier to navigate the waters and to spot pirates. Now that Cuda controlled the *Sea Booty*, he had to watch out for smugglers who would cruise the night in old tenders, searching for a powerboat to hijack. Victor mused, if pirates plundered the *Sea Booty* tonight, they'd find her belly already stuffed with six thousand pounds of weed. He gripped the helm. He understood the sea thieves would also be eyeing the *Lady Luck*. But the most dazzling prize would be the *Blew Bayou*. Forty-two feet of prime smuggling vessel. Yachts like these didn't roam open waters at midnight. But the chief had assured them he'd taken every precaution to ward off pirates. Both boats carried armed men solely for that purpose. Salazar had introduced them this afternoon.

One of Salazar's men, Tiger, would be on board the *Lady Luck*, and Slick would be riding with Mortenson and the chief. Tiger sat on the deck below Victor and Evan. He'd stretched his lanky legs in a V across the bait wells, which were filled with ice, sodas, and sandwiches that Becca had brought over this afternoon. He wore black pants, a long-sleeved black shirt, and slicked-back hair that hugged his head like a skullcap. He moved with deliberate strides, as if every action was calculated. Victor had called him Panther by mistake when they were loading the boat.

"Low tides make it hard to get on the flats," Evan said. "And high tides push the fish tight into the mangrove tree line."

Victor studied his architect. "You fish a lot?"

"Some."

Evan had been raised in a small house in the Heights, one of half a dozen children. Victor wasn't even sure he'd had a father growing up. Yet somehow he'd ended up at Rice University and graduated summa cum laude. Evan was one of the brightest, most innovative architects Victor had ever known, maybe a genius. "I thought all you did was work," Victor said.

Evan laughed and slid his fingers through a hedge of sandy hair. "Redfishing's good this time of year. Most of them are over slot, but they're great fun on light tackle."

Victor mopped the sweat from his face with the edge of his shirt. He'd thrown on a white sleeveless T with wide-cut armholes. The air breezed right through it. "You grew up on the water?" he asked Evan.

"Sort of. I used to help out on charter boats like this one. Baiting hooks, cleaning fish." Evan leaned back on the bench. "I got to pilot some big boats, though. Good summer job."

Victor realized then that Evan should be the one navigating the *Lady Luck*, but he didn't want to give up his chance. Plus, if anything happened, Evan could be his fallback.

"Mostly I fish with a small skiff and a pole." Evan laughed. "But honestly, that's the best way to catch redfish. They're jumpy gamesters, usually found in knee-deep water or less. You need a stealth approach."

Victor kept his eyes peeled on the Bertram, and Evan kept talking. He said the flats were covered with scaled sardines, so the redfish had plenty to eat right now. "The trick was to throw something different at them, like cut bait. But not in the middle—that spooks 'em. Better to cast ahead of the school. Redfishing also requires patience, polling your skiff, looking for channels or potholes. Nervous water."

While he talked on, Victor wondered how they were going to catch Cuda. He knew they were going to stake out on the north end of the island near the lighthouse and wait until eleven to send Tiger and Slick out in the thirteen-foot Boston Whaler they towed behind the *Lady Luck*. The men would head toward the ruins on the south end of Egmont Key where Cuda was supposed to unload his stash. There the smugglers would pile the bales of weed onto a couple of skiffs that would be waiting for the transfer. That's where Salazar wanted to catch Cuda—red-handed with the reefer and the *Sea Booty*. If they missed them there, Salazar would be forced to chase the smugglers through Tampa Bay to Hurricane Hole on Tierre Verde. Salazar never said, but Victor knew the chief suspected Daniel would be the one to motor the *Sea Booty*, clean as a whistle, back to the yacht club. The perfect crime.

As they passed MacDill, the boats were still motoring slowly enough for Victor to see Mortenson's cigarette smoke rising into a cloudless sky. There hadn't been any rain in three days, since the night of the fundraiser at the old hotel. The result was a thick haze that hung over the town and made everything look bleary. The super moon only enhanced the effect, a red-orange glow that spread feverishly across the horizon. From where Victor sat, he could see Captain Mortenson on the fly bridge of the Bertram, talking into the short-wave radio. Salazar and his gunman had gathered on the deck below, leaving Mortenson alone on top. Victor realized he didn't know much about boating or smuggling or extreme tides, but he knew this sting/rescue mission had too many Xs in the equation. Salazar had said from the beginning—there were too many moving parts. One breakdown in communication could blow this operation to smithereens.

Just ahead, Mortenson had slowed the *Blew Bayou* to an idle and was waving Victor to catch up. Once they were within earshot, the captain hollered, "We're kicking up the knots." He motioned to Salazar and the men to take a seat. "We just got news Cuda's moving faster than expected. We don't want to miss him at Egmont." Mortenson flicked his cigarette butt into the water. "The *Lady* can't go full out towing that tender, so we'll run ahead of you. With any luck we'll make it." Then he quickly mapped out the channel using his right hand as a pointer. Pinellas Point to the west, Cockroach Bay to the east, and beyond that they would pass under the Skyway Bridge. Then it was a straight shot through open water to Egmont Key. "It's right at the mouth of Tampa Bay," he told Victor. "You can't miss it." Mortenson started revving his engines. "When you get close enough, you'll see the lighthouse. Just follow her in."

Mortensen hit the throttle, and the *Blew Bayou* shot through the water like a steam engine. Victor nodded first to Tiger and then told Evan to hang tight. He took off behind Mortenson. But within ten minutes, Hank Poppy's Bertram had peeled way ahead. The *Lady* followed as best she could with the tender bouncing behind her like a toy on a string.

By the time they passed Pinellas and Cockroach Bay, Victor could no longer see the Bertram. Lights from the coasts were beginning to fade. What stretched ahead was ink-black, except for the Skyway and the moonlit path shimmering on the water. In spite of losing sight of the captain, Victor felt exhilarated. He loved the feel of the water beneath the boat, the powerful engines propelling them, the balmy night licking his face like a warm tongue. Since he'd started Ramirez Properties, his only dream had been to renovate the old historical buildings of Tampa. But flying across the open water, feeling as free as a sea bird, he knew this mariner's world was something he'd longed for and had missed his whole life. He didn't want the solitary existence of Captain Mortenson but the life he'd missed as a child.

Racing under the Skyway Bridge with only the moon to light the way now, a spark ignited within him. He could have this life and a partner to share it. An unexpected ache tugged at his gut. *Becca.* After tonight she'd disappear from his life, as suddenly as she'd burst into it running down the Bayshore weeks ago. And then what? She'd go back to New York to pursue her career, her relationship with the long-haired Adam. Victor let out a sigh. He'd move on, find someone else. He knew, even though they'd been born and raised in the same town, he and Becca remained worlds apart. Even their krewes were delineated by race, a concrete hierarchy that Victor had no chance of cracking. Just after the *Lady Luck* passed Tierre Verde, Victor could see a flash from the lighthouse at Egmont Key. He kept the throttle at full speed. With any luck they'd be there in ten minutes.

CHAPTER 19 ❋ Ghosts on the Wall

ONCE VICTOR'S AC MAN CHANGED out the compressor, the atmosphere in the house changed dramatically. The air turned chill. Becca thought it had a sweeping quality that crept into corners and closets and made them as crisp as the centers of rooms, where the vents spewed cold air. She'd left the house that afternoon in a pair of shorts and a T-shirt that clung to the sweat on her back. Now in her bedroom, she slipped off the wet clothes and searched her drawers for a pair of jeans, maybe a sweater. As she passed the vanity, she caught a sideways glimpse of her naked body in the mirror. She stopped. When had that happened? Becca touched her belly, which protruded like a mushroom cap that had popped up overnight. And good God, those nipples! They stood at attention from a pair of breasts that poked out, swollen and veiny. How would she hide them? She grabbed her jeans, tugged them over her hips, and struggled to button them at the waist. Then she threw on a baggy sweater. That would work for now. She told herself—*just get through the night*. Once they found her grandfather, she would get out of town; fly back to New York, start over again. Becca had hidden the diamond ring in her vanity drawer. She had no intention of mailing it to Canada. Instead she would pawn it just like the last one and get the abortion she should've had weeks ago.

Before Becca went downstairs, she peeked into her mother's room. Julia had fallen asleep, her head lolled over like a rag doll's against the side of the Queen Anne chair. Becca eased the door shut and then slipped down the west hall, past the library and Kurt's bedroom. Nattie said he hadn't come home all day. Becca hoped he'd stopped in a bar to show off the skull and crossbones tattooed on his cheek, hoped he'd get drunk enough to forget about enlisting. She was halfway down the stairs when she saw Natalie sitting in the yellow armchair, hugging the phone to her ear. Becca stepped into the room and pulled up a chair to face her grandmother.

"Early?" Natalie said, her voice aquiver. Becca knew she was talking to Carlos Mendoza. She clasped her hands over her belly and waited. The air conditioner clicked on with a whirring noise, like the old vacuum that droned through the house so loudly that when Niobe turned it off, the house became still, somber as a deserted church. Becca didn't know which was worse, the eerie silence or this new arrival. She shivered.

Natalie twisted the fringe on a silk shawl that she'd draped over her shoulders. She thanked Carlos and set the receiver back in its cradle. "Cuda's ahead of schedule," she said. A stray hair sprang from her bun and bounced wildly as she talked. "They *had* plenty of time, but now they don't. They're racing to catch the *Sea Booty* at Egmont." Natalie wrung her hands. "They could miss it."

"They won't miss it," Becca said.

"They could."

Becca leaned forward and rested her elbows on her knees. They might miss Cuda, but they couldn't lose the *Sea Booty*. Victor had told her this afternoon how Cuda had planned to pile the bales of reefer onto skiffs and motor them to Tierra Verde. "And leave the *Sea Booty*?" she'd asked. Victor said someone would drive the boat home. "My granddad?" It'd all clicked into place then. Becca knew Salazar suspected her grandfather was involved with the smugglers. She chewed the nail on her little finger while Natalie fretted, too worried to tell Becca to stop. She eyed Nattie. "You think Granddad's on the boat?"

Natalie shrugged. "Carlos says he's been king-napped."

"But what do *you* think?"

"I don't know." Natalie's voice rose an octave. "Should I know?"

Becca leaned back in the chair. She'd quit asking questions after Victor told her Salazar's men wanted to get to the ruins on the south end of the island to hide out and wait for Cuda. She couldn't help but picture Fort Dade, the old military outpost on Egmont Key. The relic from the Spanish-American War had been described in the first volume of Rebecca's diary. The Seminole Indians had been interned there before they were shipped out to reservations in Oklahoma. Victor said the island was like a ghost town now. Some of the original houses and barracks were intact enough to walk through, but in some cases all that remained were piles of brick and bits of concrete.

The grandfather clock chimed eleven. They hadn't heard a word from Carlos in over an hour. Becca started pacing, but Nattie told her to sit down. She was driving her crazy. Natalie had lit a candle and placed it on the piano. A vigil for Daniel, she'd said. The wax had burned to nil, and Becca wondered how they would manage the hours ahead. She studied the family portraits that hung in a framed procession on the back wall. The oldest one dated back to Charles and Silva Westcott. Becca leaned forward and rested her elbows on her knees. She tried to guess the ages of Nathan and Rebecca, poised as they were, Nathan in a gray suit and Rebecca in a plaid blouse trimmed with a white, ruffled collar. The collar rose high and stiff around her neck. Her great-grandparents' faces were serious but not somber. Like all the photos taken in that time period, nobody smiled. Becca estimated that they would have been in their late sixties.

The air conditioner whirred overhead, spewing out cold air. Becca clutched her knees and scrutinized the portrait of her parents, Julia and Richard. They were smiling. Radiantly. The photograph must have been taken shortly after they were married. Her mother had been so beautiful in that picture. Then Becca scanned the childhood portrait of Julia, and on the other side of her parents' photo, she settled on the portrait of Daniel as a young man. She squinted in the dim light. There was an innocence about him that intrigued her. As hard as she tried, she could not visualize this fresh-faced young man as her grandfather. All Becca remembered of Daniel now was his ruddy face, big ears, and slightly bulging eyes.

Becca fell back in the chair and willed the night to go faster. Then it struck her: she would get the diaries and show them to Nattie. After all, her grandmother had lived through much of that time, and Becca had some questions to ask her.

"Where're you going?" Natalie asked as Becca bounded up the stairs. Her grandmother's voice had grown thick. *From fatigue,* Becca thought.

"I'll be right back."

When Becca returned with the journals, Natalie sat bolt upright in her chair. "What do you got there, child?"

"Diaries," she said and settled in next to Nattie.

"But where'd they come from?"

"They're Rebecca's diaries." Becca peered at her great-grandmother's portrait. The air conditioner clicked off. In the eerie silence that settled over them, Becca felt her ancestors watching her—and listening.

Natalie frowned and touched the leather. "Where did you find them?" Her eyes scrutinized the diaries.

"On the front porch about ten days ago." Becca opened the first journal. "They came in a box, addressed to me."

Natalie leaned in close while Becca flipped through the pages. She started reading just before Silva Westcott found the Indian child.

> "Silva said she passed the Port of Tampa daily, saw the wretchedness of the Indians in the pen. How lucky Osceola had died and been spared to witness the stockade where his people were herded for shipment out. Always from Tampa Bay—the deportment to Egmont Key where they would wait for ships to transfer them first to New Orleans then to Oklahoma. The Seminole cries loomed over the dusty town—the bitter wailings of a people half-starved, the old, the women with infants, the weak, rounded up from the fringes of the river—penned in like cattle."

Becca stopped. "Egmont Key," she said. "That's where the men are now. The same place they imprisoned the Seminoles years ago. And from there the soldiers shipped them to reservations." Becca gripped her grandmother's hand. "They died there. Did you know that? It was winter. They had no food, no clothes, no shelter, no tools, *no nothing* to help them. The soldiers just dropped them off and let them die."

Natalie leaned over and touched the page. Becca felt her tremble.

"That's why Silva took the baby," Becca said. "For the mother first." She pointed to the next sentence and read on. *"And then for the infant laid in her arms, wrapped in deerskin, his hair a black sunburst around his head."* The air clicked on and droned through the house. "Silva fled with the child," Becca said, raising her voice to compete with the noise that whizzed through the overhead vents. "She hid him under her coat and ran with him because the soldiers would've killed him." Becca studied her grandmother. "Did you know that, Nattie? Did you know about the baby?"

Natalie sunk back in the armchair and pursed her lips. "Maybe," she said under her breath. "Maybe Rebecca told me."

Becca nodded and eyed Nattie. She wondered how much information her grandmother actually knew and had been hiding from her all these years. "Well, Rebecca could've told you. Because Silva told *her* everything. And then Rebecca wrote it down."

Natalie's eyes grew wide. She pointed to the other diary on Becca's lap. "What's in *that* volume?"

"Lots of Auxiliary Balls, captain's parties, Gasparilla festivities," Becca said. "Clothes and things."

Nattie twisted the fringe on her shawl. "Is that all?"

Becca took a deep breath. She didn't have much time left to find out what had happened to her mother. She figured it was now or never. "No," she blurted out. "She wrote about my mother's rape."

Natalie gasped. Her hands flew to her mouth, and she rocked back and forth. "Show me," she said through her fingers.

Becca opened to the dog-eared page that had turned dirty with use. She read to Nattie.

"And there in the hall was a terrible racket of crying and fighting going on. I rushed from my room to see Natalie's wild arms and fists flailing at Daniel's chest while he tried to calm her. 'Could have been!' Natalie screamed. 'She's in there curled up and bleeding. And you say could have been!' Natalie kept beating at him. 'Go find him then,' she said. 'Go find that filthy pirate and string him up!'"

Natalie held up her hand to stop. "We should've," she said, "found that pirate and hung him." She started rocking again and staring straight ahead as if she were reliving that Gasparilla night. The stray hair bobbed from her bun. "I was just going to say good night to Julia, and I found her curled up and whimpering in bed. When I went to comfort her, I saw the blood." Becca leaned forward and clasped her grandmother's hands to calm her. "That's when she told me the pirate had climbed the trellis to her room and hurt her." Nattie squeezed Becca's hands until they burned. Then she searched Becca's face. "What about Julia's baby?" Nattie asked. "Did Rebecca say what happened to him?"

Becca flipped through the pages of the diary. "They planned to adopt him out," she said. The grandfather clock chimed half past the eleventh hour, and Becca felt time dissolving into the fogginess of a dream—Louise's call this morning, Adam's final betrayal, and the diaries revealing hidden information. How could any of this be real? Becca shook her head to clear the haziness clouding her mind. She opened the diary to the pages she'd just read this morning. And there, scribbled on the top was an address.

Mr. and Mrs. Donald Ferretti
802 Bloomsberry Road
Hamden, Connecticut

Becca read the journal entry that was written by Rebecca and dated November 7, 1936:

> "Julia is home, and looks well, in spite of the difficult birth that Dr. Philips said was arduous and painful. But a deep melancholia has beset her. She drags herself through the house in night robes, refusing to dress, and Natalie hovers over her like a frantic hen. If she doesn't improve, Dr. Michaels will have to be called. I don't think she is sleeping well."

Natalie kept her head down and rocked back and forth in the yellow armchair. "I sat by Julia's bed," she said, "and sponged her poor, sweaty body." Nattie hugged the silk scarf tight across her chest. "The doctor said it was weakness, like a new kitten. But she would get well. He promised."

Becca ran her finger down the page and quickly read the next two entries.

November 9

> "The Ferrettis contacted Daniel at his office. Well, of course they're upset, but at least they hadn't brought the baby home yet. Daniel talked to Sister Cecilia and told her under no circumstances should the child leave St. Agnes' until a decision has been made concerning his welfare. Julia worsens. I tried to talk to her about the baby, but she turned away, pretended I wasn't in the room. If she doesn't get better we may need to bring the baby home. But that could ruin her life too. Not to mention how it would tarnish the Westcott name. Dr. Michaels prescribed a sleeping draught."

November 13

> "The baby cannot be adopted out yet. Julia's mental health hinges precariously. She refuses to come out of her room, refuses friends. She will not even see her father. I asked her

if it's the baby she misses, but she sneered at me, turned away. She looks harried now—her hair is dull and her skin's pasty yellow. Sister Cecilia says they can't keep the baby much longer."

Natalie twisted the fringe around her fingers. "They shouldn't have taken the baby away from Julia! Couldn't they see that?" She glared at Becca. "I told Daniel to bring the baby home. We would raise him!"

Becca patted her grandmother's knee to calm her. "They wouldn't do that?" she asked.

"No!" Natalie said. "You read it! Rebecca said it would tarnish the Westcott name. But Daniel worried what the town would think too. 'No wagging tongues about this family,' he'd said." Natalie stared past Becca toward the piano.

"Listen to this, Nattie," Becca said. "Rebecca had a dream, three days later." She read the next entry.

November 16

"Last night I dreamt Silva sat across from me at the dining room table and told me to write about the Indian child she had saved from deportment, about the mother who had thrust the infant into her arms. When I finished, she repeated the story, and I wrote it again. When I completed it the second time, she started it over at the beginning, and I stopped her. Why the same story again and again? And she said I needed to hear it.

At five a.m. I called Daniel into my room and showed him the diary, how I had begun it in 1895, at Silva's request, to record the stories she could no longer write because her eyes had grown dim. I told him about the dream. After he read about the Indian child, he looked up at me and said—If the family is still in Tampa, I will find them."

"There's more," Becca said. But Natalie didn't answer, didn't budge. Becca shook her a little. Then she glanced across the room. The candle that had almost burned down hours ago was still flickering. Its light cast an eerie glow over the piano keys. "What is it?" Becca asked. "What do you see?"

Natalie shivered.

"The candle?"

Natalie pointed toward the piano. "It's Daniel," she whispered.

Becca spun around in her chair and scanned the room. "Where?"

"Sitting on the piano bench."

Becca squinted in the half dark. She knew better than to say her grandfather wasn't there. After all, she'd seen her share of phantoms lately. "What's he look like?"

"Strange. Like a gardener. Dressed in overalls. But he's holding a pirate hat on his lap."

"What's he saying?" Becca asked.

Natalie's eyes were riveted on the piano bench. "He doesn't."

"Doesn't what?"

"Talk," Natalie whispered. "He just shakes his head like he's sorry."

"For what?"

"Everything." Nattie wrung her hands.

"For getting involved with smugglers?" Becca asked.

"Maybe for not finding the pirate. For not trying." Natalie's voiced trailed off. "Maybe for some other things." Nattie stared at the piano bench for a long time. Then she reached for the second volume of Rebecca's diaries. "May I see this?"

Becca passed it to her. Her grandmother flipped through the pages as if looking for something specific. The air conditioner clicked on and blew out the last of the candle. They sat in silence. When the telephone rang, they both jumped. Natalie refused to pick it up, so Becca answered. She knew it was Carlos Mendoza with news of Daniel.

Family Portraits

CHAPTER 20 ✳ "I'm Your Captain"

A<small>S THE</small> *L<small>ADY</small> L<small>UCK</small>* <small>APPROACHED</small> Egmont Key, whenever the lighthouse beam flashed across the water, Victor could see Captain Mortenson on the Bertram's fly bridge, wagging a cigarette at them. Once within earshot, Mortenson told them to throw the anchor. Evan scrambled down the ladder to follow the captain's bid. A southeasterly breeze had kicked up with enough gust to dry the sweat from Victor's T-shirt and ruffle his hair. But in spite of the wind, the water gleamed as smooth and reflective as God's own mirror.

"Just let her drift up here," Mortenson said, waving them in. He'd thrown out boat fenders alongside the *Blew Bayou* to protect her. When the *Lady* floated in close enough, Mortenson clasped hold of her like a runaway child. He pulled her up next to the Bertram and tied some lines to keep her tethered.

When he'd finished, Mortensen set his hands on his hips. Before Victor knew what was happening, the chief and Slick had jumped in the Whaler and taken off. "Riding the shoals," the captain said. "But we can't go any further in this boat. The tide's too low. We'll run her aground." A cigarette dangled from his mouth. "They think Cuda's on the south end, unloading. But we can't be sure."

The lighthouse flashed on, and Mortenson pointed toward the northern tip of the island. "Tiger and I are taking the *Lady* around now. Her draft's low enough to make it." Then he held out a hand to hoist Evan onto the Bertram and then a hand for Victor. Once on board they stood across from the captain while the lighthouse flashed every thirty seconds. There were out far enough in the channel that the lighthouse beam hit the Bertram dead on. Mortenson took a long drag on his cigarette. He said they'd stopped using the radio; they had an inkling Cuda may have been tipped off. That's why he'd changed his plans and headed out early. Then the captain grabbed his windbreaker, his fishing cap, and a fresh pack of cigarettes. "If Cuda hits Tierra Verde and unloads his stash, all we got is an empty *Booty*."

Victor wanted to ask about Daniel, but the way Mortenson's eyes darted from the *Lady Luck* to the lighthouse to the channel, Victor understood all plans had been scrapped. They were winging it.

"Just stay put for now," Mortenson said, jumping onto his boat. "You're anchored in tight." The captain climbed the fly bridge while Victor and Evan untied the lines. "We'll either radio you or send someone back to get you." Mortenson started the engines, and Tiger pushed off. Victor and Evan watched the *Lady* peel away into darkness. Thirty seconds later the boat appeared in the lighthouse beam, and then the scene went black again. It was like watching a film clip in slow motion. Within minutes the *Lady* had disappeared around the north end of the island.

"This spotlight reminds me of a prison camp," Evan said, shielding his eyes from the glare. "*Hogan's Heroes*."

Victor nodded. "It's better than pitch."

Evan shrugged. "Moonlight's better. It's steady, not so bright." He plunged his hands into the pockets of his cargo shorts. "After the beam, you're blinded. A lot can happen in a few seconds."

Suddenly Victor realized Salazar had left them unprotected. He immediately started searching the bait wells, the pockets alongside the boat, for a weapon. He'd grope around in the dark, grab hold of something, and then examine it when the lighthouse flashed on. He found a fishing gaff, some lines, a net, and a set of boning knives. When he opened the leather box, the knives were lined up by length. He pulled out the two shortest ones and handed one to Evan.

"What am I supposed to do with this?" The lighthouse flashed on, and the knife looked smaller than a box cutter in Evan's hand. "This would barely scale a redfish."

Victor's first impulse was to laugh, but the breeze off the water had shifted. He sniffed. The air carried an electrical charge that buzzed around and through his body. It smelled like fear. "Why don't you check the cabin," Victor said. He started up the ladder to the fly bridge. "There's got to be a pistol on this boat somewhere."

The bridge on the Bertram was twice the size of the *Lady Luck*'s and three times as complicated. When the lighthouse flashed on, Victor gawked at the navigational gauges that spread out fifteen strong across the dash panel. He could pick out the depth finder, the fuel gauges, and the clock, but the rest boggled his mind. A black ball compass bobbed at the panel's center, and the helm rivaled the size of the steering wheel in Victor's car. He gripped the wheel's slick chrome. How he'd like to pilot this beauty! The bow of the boat pointed toward the open waters of the Gulf of Mexico, while the stern provided a perfect view of the Skyway Bridge. Victor imagined flying this yacht across the sleek waters of Tampa Bay.

"Hey!" Victor heard Evan calling from the deck below. "I found a pistol."

Victor headed for the ladder and was halfway down when the lighthouse beam lit up the deck. In that flash, Victor saw a skinny kid with his hair stuffed beneath a baseball cap. He was pointing a gun at Evan's back. The light flicked off, and Victor froze.

"Keep on coming!" the kid said. When Victor heard the voice, he knew it was Kurt's. Victor took the steps slowly. He'd almost reached the bottom and smack! The beam hit them again. A maniacal grin spilled across the boy's face. "Join my krewe, matey!" He pulled off his cap, and the wind wrestled his hair. The ends swirled around his head, fire-engine red. Medusa. "Come on, come on," Kurt said and waved the revolver at Victor. "Stand next to your buddy here."

In the darkness, Victor sidled next to Evan. He knew Kurt was flying on something, but he didn't seem drunk. The Bertram rocked gently on the water, just enough to keep them unbalanced. "Take your shirt off," Kurt said to Victor. "I wanna see your fancy scar." Victor pulled his shirt over his head. He knew he could get the gun from the boy, but he needed Kurt to calm down; he didn't want him to do anything crazy.

When the lighthouse cast its beam, Kurt ran the gun barrel down the length of Victor's chest. "Impressive," he mocked. "Some kind of hero, right?" The kid frowned, crammed his nose into Victor's. "You're vermin." He pressed the revolver hard into Victor's breastbone. "In 'Nam, I could kill you, and they'd call *me* a hero. You know why?" He wheedled the gun in deeper. "You're the enemy."

For a moment Victor held his breath. He knew Kurt had singled him out, turned him into an adversary the kid could see while the real enemy lurked deep inside the boy, dragged him into the gutter, and beat him up.

Kurt turned to Evan. "What happened to Salazar and the captain?" When Evan told him, the kid howled with laughter. "I jumped this boat thinking I'd be chasing the *Sea Booty*, and I end up with two losers." Victor was about grab Kurt's wrist and wrench the gun from his hand when he spotted a skiff in the water behind the Bertram. He waited for the lighthouse beam. And sure enough, the figure looked like Tiger, dressed all in black, guiding the skiff alongside the stern of the *Blew Bayou*.

Victor would bide his time for now and wait for help. He figured Tiger must have caught whiff of Kurt's threats, because he'd cut the motor upstream and was gliding silently through the strong incoming tidal currents toward the transom of the boat. The next time they were plunged into darkness, Victor nudged Evan and nodded toward the back of the Bertram, hoping he would see the skiff when the lighthouse flashed on. But Evan missed it, checking out Victor instead.

"Guess what, mates," Kurt ranted. "We're goin' to the south end. To find my granddad." Then he started to sing. "I'm your captain, I'm your captain. . . ." He pranced out in front of them, his back to the stern and the gun still aimed at Victor's heart.

Victor listened to the song and felt his stomach churn. Suddenly Kurt stopped dancing and glared at them. "Whose gonna drive this mother?" He waved the revolver at Evan. "You, Mister Evan Steven. You drive, so I can keep an eye on our hero." Kurt pointed to the ladder. "Get going."

Evan hadn't reached the second rung when Victor saw a leg hike over the port side of the Bertram. The lighthouse flashed off, and Victor blinked in the pitch that followed. He felt adrenaline pulse through his veins. The man climbing onto the boat was wearing a ski mask. He was not Tiger. Victor knew he had about twenty seconds to get the revolver from Kurt, and the quicker the better—before anyone's eyes had a chance to adjust. Victor took two steps toward Kurt, and then he dove for the gun. He grabbed the boy's wrist, but Kurt flinched, and the revolver flew up between them and slid across the deck toward the stern.

The lighthouse beam flashed on, and the masked man crouched low on the deck, his limbs crawling spiderlike. The revolver had landed within a foot of him. He lunged at it, sweeping it into his hand before Victor or Kurt could stop him. In an instant, the man sprang to his feet. He held his own pistol in his right hand and stuffed Kurt's gun into the back pocket of his black jeans. "Nice boat you got here," he said, waving Evan down from the ladder. "How about I borrow it for a while." Victor could see his eyes shining through the mask holes. There were two small slits for his nose, but the rest of his face was covered. Victor estimated him to be in his mid-twenties. Still, he was no rookie. Victor knew his plan was to seize the *Blew Bayou* for his own smuggling deal.

The thief pointed his pistol at Victor, then at Evan, and finally at Kurt. He patted the kid's gun in his back pocket and cocked his head nervously.

"Why don't you guys just mosey off this boat and take my skiff to shore. No one needs to get hurt here."

Victor retrieved his T-shirt and held it to his chest. "We're waiting on a load from Jamaica," he said, thinking fast. "Six thousand pounds of weed's coming in on the south side of this island."

The thief threw a hearty laugh. "What are you guys? A bunch of fucking narcs?"

"I'm part of Cuda's crew," Kurt said, dead serious. Victor watched the thief's eyes narrow in on the boy.

Kurt wound his hair in a knot and plopped the fishing cap back on his head. He motioned to Victor and Evan. "These guys own the boat, but I was taking it over when you showed up." Then Kurt spouted off about Cuda, how he'd talked Daniel Westcott into using the *Sea Booty* to pick up the stash in Jamaica. "You've heard about it, man," he said. "It's all over the Conch Shell. Everyone's waiting for this load to come in. Cuda's biggest run yet."

"Wait a minute," the thief said, tugging on his mask. "I know you. You're the Squirrel. The red-headed kid from Tampa, always hanging around the bar waiting for someone to throw you a lude or a hit of acid."

"I'm Daniel Westcott's grandson," Kurt said, setting his hands on his hips. "And you're the Spider, right?"

When the thief didn't deny his identity, Victor thought he'd never seen a nickname so aptly given. The kid looked like a spider.

"I wanna get down to the south end of this island and help Cuda get his stash to Tierra Verde," Kurt said.

The Spider's shiny eyes riveted on Victor and Evan. "So these guys are narcs?"

"They're a couple of pansies," Kurt said. "They've been left here to stake out the *Sea Booty*. It's got to come through the channel at some point." He shuffled his bare feet on the deck. "Chief Salazar took off in a tender to nail Cuda at the ruins. He's unloading there."

"Holy shit!" the Spider said. "Cuda's cooked?"

"Maybe," Kurt said. "But if we get these bozos out of here, so they can't radio the chief, we might be able to help Cuda. There's a million bucks riding on those skiffs."

Even behind the mask, Victor could see the wheels turning inside the Spider's head. Cuda was the smuggler's guru, the Robin Hood of Passe-A-Grille, and any chance to help him would gain Spider instant fame at the Conch Shell. Victor glanced at Evan, who shrugged. If Spider took this bait, it was any man's guess what could happen now.

The Spider scratched his head. "I don't know, man. It sounds kinda risky."

"It's risky," Kurt agreed. "But if you don't wanna help, just beat it."

The Spider flinched. "Listen, Squirrel, I ain't no pansy. But what's in it for me?"

Kurt grinned. "Seriously?" he asked. "The reefer business is exploding. There's a lot more players in the game now. Boats, drivers, stash houses, trucks, investors—you name it." Kurt leaned against the pedestaled fishing chair. "A two-bit punk hijacking yachts on his own doesn't stand a chance."

Victor eyed the Spider. Kurt was playing his game, luring him into a tantalizing web. "So you're saying there'll be a gig for me?" the Spider asked.

"If you help Cuda bring this load home, you could probably name your gig." Victor watched Kurt tap his foot on deck, as calm as the glistening water beneath the boat.

"So what's the plan?" the Spider asked. He was still wielding his gun at them, but Victor knew the thief was sucked in.

"We're headed to the south end, near the ruins," Kurt said, pointing toward the northern tip of the island. "The *Sea Booty's* probably unloading now." Then he turned to Evan. "What about the tides?"

Evan peered out over the water. "We should be able to make it. The water's rising fast."

"Wait," Spider said. "How about we leave these monkeys here?"

"Nope," Kurt said. "Hostages might come in handy. Something to trade." Kurt smiled and then asked for his gun back.

The Spider reached for his back pocket and then stopped. "How about I hold it for now?"

"Suit yourself," Kurt said. "Why don't you tie up your skiff. We'll use her to help Cuda run the load into Tierra Verde." Kurt motioned to Evan to climb the fly bridge.

Evan was already at the helm, revving the engines when Spider said he'd take the pedestaled fishing chair. "I'll pick off any two-bit pirate who blinks at this boat." He kept his mask on.

Kurt shrugged and told Victor to pull the anchor. Then he hollered to Evan. "When you think it's safe, run this bitch full out!"

As Victor engaged the windlass and wound the anchor line, he thought how quickly the events had shifted. Despite losing his gun, Kurt had managed to land in the captain's seat once again. Still, Victor didn't trust him; didn't think for a second there was any camaraderie between them. He and Evan were just a pair of hostages to Kurt. They'd wanted a gun; now they had two. Plus they'd managed to acquire their own gunman. It worked for now.

Victor eyed Kurt as he leaned over the boat, squinting into the darkness. There was something desperate about him, some reckless spirit driving him. Then it hit Victor: the kid had no fear because he had nothing to lose—or so he thought.

Within minutes the *Blew Bayou* was gliding south toward the deep channel. They needed to get across the northern shoal of the island without hitting ground. Now the lighthouse beam lit up the port side of the boat markers that would guide them to the water that surrounded the island. Spider sat on the fishing throne keeping watch. As they motored toward the west side, the moon rose to twelve o'clock high and cast its light across Egmont Channel. Victor hiked a knee onto the seat next to the cabin door, so he could face the hull, while Kurt held on to the ladder. He told Evan to punch it.

The Bertram trudged out across the outer shallows of Egmont Key, trailing the skiff behind it. From here Victor could see that the island was small, maybe four hundred acres tops. But this east side, away from the lighthouse, was cast into darkness. The running lights on the boat lit up the water directly in front of them, but the coast was nearly invisible. Now Victor understood why Cuda had chosen the dark end of this island and had waited for the full moon to transfer his load.

When they spotted the ruins, Kurt told them to cut the engines and the lights. They would motor slowly toward the partially submerged relics, remnants of the Spanish-American War fortifications. Some of the ruins were large enough to hide a boat that didn't want to be found, especially if the seekers were coming from the north. The silhouettes of the ruins and an unlit moored vessel would appear virtually indifferent. But it would be far easier for Cuda to spy the forty-six-foot Bertram motoring toward them. Evan inched the Bertram along the coast, as close as it could get without running aground.

They'd just passed the first ruin when a spotlight shot out from nowhere. "Shit!" Kurt said and hit the deck. "It's a fishing spot!" Victor followed Kurt's lead and fell to his hands and knees. But Spider, true to his word, gripped the pistol with two and hands and spun around, trying to figure out where the light was coming from. He took cover beneath the throne and then fired a shot into the air to scare off the intruders. What followed was a shower of bullets aimed right at Spider. He plunged to the deck and landed face down just beneath the fishing chair. Evan flicked on the running lights.

"It's the *Sea Booty*!" Kurt hollered. The boat was less than forty feet away from them. "They got my grandfather!" He scuttled out across the deck and found his revolver in Spider's back pocket. He then jumped up and started firing at the boat. This round of bullets spawned another storm that pummeled the Bertram. Victor dove headfirst into the kid, taking them both down. But it was too late. Kurt had been shot. Evan trumpeted the boat horn, five short blasts. He waited a few seconds and then fired five more. The shooting stopped.

Evan raced down the ladder to check on Spider. He almost tripped over Victor, who knelt next to Kurt. The boy writhed on the deck, hugging his chest. "Lemme look at you," Victor said.

Kurt's eyes screamed with pain, but he hissed through clenched teeth, "Don't touch me, you spic."

Victor grabbed him anyway to steady him. Then he ran his hands over the boy's body. He found a wound in Kurt's chest. He pulled off his own shirt and wrapped it as tight he could around the boy's torso.

"What's happening?" Kurt asked, looking down and seeing blood. His voice quivered low.

Victor knew the kid was going into shock fast. But his wound was almost bloodless. Most of what covered the deck in a thick, purplish gore oozed from beneath the pedestal fishing chair.

A few seconds later, Evan joined Victor. They both kneeled over Kurt. Victor cocked his head toward Spider. "How's he doing?"

Evan shook his head and whispered, "He took a bullet to his brain."

A roaring started in Victor's ears. If they didn't get Kurt help soon, he'd be gone too.

Victor told Evan to take off his shirt. "Tear it in strips and wrap his head. We're swimming in this." Victor's knees and the edges of his shorts were seeped in blood.

While Evan tended to Spider, they heard footsteps on the swim platform coming up the stern. This time it was Tiger. He'd swung the *Sea Booty* up close enough to jump on Spider's skiff, and then he'd reeled himself to the stern of the Bertram.

"Jesus Christ," Tiger said when he climbed on board. He was still holding the pistol that had caused the carnage. Victor watched as he scanned the blood-soaked deck. "What the hell happened?"

Victor told him as calmly as he could. But Tiger kept interrupting, saying when he saw the masked man, he assumed big trouble. "But the shots kept coming," Tiger said, stuffing the gun in the pocket of his black jeans. "Why'd they keep coming?"

Victor crouched next to Kurt, watching the color drain from his face. Victor peered down on the boy. "This is one troubled kid. In a fight for his life now."

Evan was on the fly bridge radioing Bradenton emergency when Tiger called up to him. "Take him to Manatee Memorial. Tell 'em to meet you at the docks on Waterfront Park." Then he told Victor that Salazar and the captain had taken off in the *Lady* in hopes of catching Cuda before he could unload the skiffs at Tierra Verde.

Victor kept slight pressure on Kurt's wound. With his free hand he felt for the boy's pulse. It was slowing down. Then he glanced up at Tiger. "What about Daniel?"

"We found the *Sea Booty* empty." Tiger ran a hand through his slicked-back hair. "Salazar said Cuda wouldn't take him on the skiffs. No reason for dead weight. He would've left him on the *Booty*." Tiger stood up and headed toward the stern. "We don't know where the hell Daniel is."

"You going after Cuda?" Victor asked.

"Yep," Tiger said. Hiking one leg over the stern, he told Victor not to let the kid lose consciousness. "Do anything to keep him talking."

Victor would try, but he knew he was the last person Kurt wanted to talk to.

CHAPTER 21 ❋ King Daniel

Daniel cracked the door of the garden house and peeked outside to see if anyone was around. The sun had already burst forth and was inching its way up the horizon. He'd wanted to get out earlier this morning to water the grass before Natalie could see him. But when Becca received the call about Kurt late last night, he'd immediately fled to the hospital, to the operating room where the boy's life hung in the wings.

Now Daniel tiptoed through the backyard, toward the garden hose that was coiled like a snake and lying in the grass next to the house. Once he'd found the end, he dragged the hose through the yard toward the spigot to hook it up. He sang quietly, under his breath.

> I'll south with the sun and keep my clime,
> Yo-ho! Yo-hoo! Yo-ho! Yo-hoo!
> My wing is king of the summertime,
> Yo-ho! Yo-hoo!

In green overalls and a plumed pirate hat (creased and dusty from the attic, but with a certain aplomb still, elegant and wide-brimmed to shield him from the menacing sun) Daniel attached the hose to the water spigot, gone orange with rust. He pulled a wrench from his back pocket and banged it on the water handle to loosen its corroded hold.

Spit on it, old man; you don't have the strength you used to.

Then he hooked an end of the wrench into an open hole and leaned on it with all his weight until it gave up, sputtering, and hot water shot through the rubber hose. The tubing jumped in the withered grass and gyrated there, and Daniel stepped on it, feeling it alive and moving beneath his bare feet. When he reached the end, he leaned over, grabbed the nozzle, and directed the water to flow in an arc, a shimmering, clear rainbow onto the sun-parched lawn.

For a moment, in the cool light that was still morning, still serene, but moving quickly to that high place where it would send out its edict like a bright eye, suddenly Daniel was a boy of five, watching the arc flow from the pink tip of his penis while his mother called to him from the library window upstairs. "Button up your trousers, young man. And finish your business inside." But the arc was beautiful in its shape, sloping and strong, and moving at his command. He couldn't stop it if he'd willed it, couldn't cut the flow in midstream, for his mind was bound to the release, to the arc itself, sweeping up in a rounded curve, against the blue morning and the fragrant white jasmine, and falling eventually into the young grass that was yet above his ankles.

Now Daniel squeezed the water that coursed through the nozzle with the tip of his thumb. The arc shattered into a fine spray. He stepped lightly across the lawn that was brittle and split like shards of glass pricking his feet. From the position of the sun rising above the twin oaks, he estimated the time to be around ten o'clock. Here, this morning, in his overalls and pirate hat, he would water the grass until the ground pooled, saturated, and bubbled, until he could see a sprig of green popping up amid the withered turf. He sang.

> My breast to the sun his torch shall hold,
> Yo-ho! Yo-hoo! Yo-ho!
> And I'll call down through the green and gold,
> Yo-ho! Yo-hoo! Yo-ho!

He fancied himself a vivifier, a savior.

Daniel settled his body, gone lank this last month from roaming, no sleep, no food, just an odd wakefulness as if between time, juxtaposed between the heavens where the sun's heat was not weighted against the skin but remote and veiled as music playing in a dream. And cool was unimaginable, for nothing was quenched or sated, but drawn out hard and moving endlessly toward an unknown. He settled himself into a metal lawn chair. From where the water hit the seared lawn, no longer a spray but a constant stream, worms floated to the surface. Daniel saw them wiggle in the dead grass, the small, common angleworm that he could easily gather and take to the river's edge to fish. He could take the worms down and show the boy, Quinn, who sat on a plastic bucket with his cane pole baited and his line flung into the Hillsborough River, waiting for a bite.

"Give me one of your worms," Daniel said. He was ten now, hefty for his age, and it was springtime, the river spilling over with new life. "I'll trade you five of mine for one of them."

The boy flashed an impish grin that was sportive and gleaming white within his black face. He stuck his hand into the bucket and pulled out a sooty gray worm the size of a skink lizard. "This one's slick and mighty," Quinn said. "Gonna fetch me the biggest bass this river ever give up."

"Trade you ten for one," Daniel said, digging his heels into the muddy soil along the river's edge.

"Ain't trading," Quinn said, reeling in his line. "These here's magic crawlers, and there ain't no mo' where they come from." Quinn hooked the giant worm through its middle. It revved and squirmed, flared up mean, and Quinn jumped. "They's vicious too," Quinn said, shaking his hand. "They bites."

Daniel stepped closer to Quinn. The boy was naked except for a pair of tan cotton shorts hanging low on his hips and torn at the pockets. His skin appeared oiled and hardy, more protective than clothing, and his eyes were squinty in the sunlight. His hands were swollen past the wrist.

"You're all blown up," Daniel said, watching Quinn cast his line into the river.

Quinn squeezed his hands shut; they didn't close completely because the fingers were three times their normal size. "They's achy too," Quinn said.

Daniel stared at the hands and then at the shiny worms in Quinn's bucket. "Worms don't have teeth," he said.

Daniel leaned back in the lawn chair, still watering the grass and watching the angleworms float and wrap their bodies around the hay-colored sprigs sticking up from the lawn.

Worms don't have teeth.

Daniel ran home and told his father about Quinn's magic crawlers, how he was catching the biggest bass in the river, how the worms were so mighty they were biting him, and his hands were blown up like balloons.

"Worms don't bite," his father said. And Daniel knew that before his father sent the gardener down to the river to check on the boy, and he stomped on those baby rattlers, killed every one of those snakes left in Quinn's bucket, and they all died before Quinn, smashed beneath the gardener's boot, and the boy was taken to the hospital kicking and screaming, and swollen clear up his arms and into his neck.

> Time take thy scythe, reap bliss for me,
> Yo-ho! Yo-hoo! Yo-ho! Yo-hoo!
> Bestir me under the orange tree.

Daniel stood up and brushed smooth the creases in his overalls. His arms had grown hard and thin, and his belly had wasted, worn clean away. He was rugged and lean, a slide back to youth, and he imagined this time between death and burial as an ecumenical passage, a time of shedding past sins. It was so clear now, what was not at all discernible in his life, and if he had to define it, he could, for the sense of what he felt this morning, watering the dead lawn and watching the worms slither up from the earth, was an adage, an apothegm that he could identify in one word: separate. And it was all so simple, the fallen leaves of an oak tree, squirrels rushing acorns to their nests, the lap of waves on Old Tampa Bay, a cardinal's song, the gusting wind, and sun, and heat, ice, flame, red and blue, and separate, and not as he viewed the world when he lived within its rainy arms. For he had been born believing that all was his for the taking and not that he should hurt anyone in claiming what belonged to him, but rather, like the storm cloud moving across the sky, he absorbed everything in his path, growing more fearsome and powerful for the bulk.

Daniel shook the hose, shattering the water into a hundred glasslike droplets that sparkled in the sunlight. A handsome, powerful buffoon, that's what he was in his life. And hadn't he learned the part early? Growing up the only son of Nathan and Rebecca Westcott, a Gasparilla page at age six, a pirate at twenty-one, and a king at sixty-eight.

Hadn't he died a king?

King Daniel. Gasparilla King of the pirates.

And on the eve of his crowning, as with many of the memorable events in his life, he thought of Quinn, the river boy, who, through his pride and selfishness had saved Daniel's life, for Daniel would have bartered all of his night crawlers, his pocketknife, and his father's gold watch for just one of Quinn's worms. In the weeks that followed the boy's death, Daniel formulated a theorem, a philosophy that would take him beyond his youth, beyond the country club card games of Palma Ceia into the gambling dens of South Tampa, and out of Natalie's bed into the arms of more women than Daniel could remember.

"Hush, Danny, hush," the girl would say after he lay drunken and snoring, sprawled out on damp satin sheets. Daniel would snore all the louder, believing in Quinn and his selfishness, for had the boy been generous and shared the magic crawlers, Daniel would have pricked the thickish body of the baby rattler with his hook and been bitten just like Quinn. He would have lain beside the boy on the riverbank or in the hospital, with the rattler's venom racing through his veins to stop his heart, because he didn't know those crawlers were snakes any more than Quinn did. The two of them would have fished side by side, enduring the bites, waiting to hook a prize bass. But what disturbed Daniel the most was the menacing thought that he could have been the one to find the rattlers' nest, gathered the snakes in his own bucket, and if Quinn had asked him for one of the crawlers, would he have given the boy one?

Could he be blamed for things he didn't know? Like the separateness of being or the women's souls he'd left behind that now weighed as heavy as stones inside him, while the sun, settled above the twin oaks, overhead and burning, felt fleeting on his skin?

Daniel waded through the muddied lawn, toward the house to turn off the water. He tipped the edge of his pirate hat and pulled it down on his brow. He wouldn't miss these late-summer days, desiccated drudgeries, of waiting for the relief of cloud cover, thunder, and then the rain that crashed in torrents to the earth, bouncing on the streets like grease spattering in a hot skillet, and steam rising up thick from the ground as if sent straight from hell.

> Then, time, let not a drop be spilt;
> Yo-ho! Yo-hoo! Yo-ho! Yo-hoo!
> Hand me the cup when'er thou wilt.

What Daniel will miss is this house, the wood siding slick with fresh white paint, the shutters spanking black around the windows, the generous porches stretching out onto the lawns lush with leafy oaks, azaleas, and impatiens, red tea roses, yellow jasmine, winding bougainvillea, all in bloom together, as if that could happen, once in a special season.

A season of love.

In the backyard of the Westcott mansion, this yard that Daniel had baptized with his own arc as a child, now a young man of twenty-four, leading his bride along the stone path, through the crowd, past the gardens lit with torches, to the dance floor just below the gazebo where the five-piece orchestra played the Tales from the Vienna Woods, Daniel spun Natalie in a graceful waltz. Beautiful Natalie. Smooth black hair to her waist, floating behind her as they danced, and silken skin that made Daniel's fingertips tingle with just a touch. His queen. And he had not betrayed her, not as she thought, for in his heart she would always be his queen; but his body, aah, his body, not want to, but have to, have to, couldn't stop it if he'd willed it, for his mind was bound to the release.

Dear Daniel, whatever were you hoping to find between those shiny sheets? And isn't that your mother calling you to button up those trousers and finish your business inside?

In the garden that night, the Krewe of Gaspar congratulated Daniel on his new bride, who stood beside him like a prize, leaning against his body.

Daniel's body. Daniel's first death.

Wiping his muddied feet on the mat just inside the back door that led to the kitchen, Daniel heard the old grandfather clock in the living room chiming the hour. *Babong, bong, bong*, he counted out the low toll as it vibrated through the house, the twelve strokes of noon, like the twelve of midnight, equal in timbre, in resonance, as if it could be the night, the last night that he turned on the stairs to Julia's room to find Natalie standing on the lower landing, pointing a revolver at his chest.

"You'll not go up there tonight," she'd said.

And what did she think he would do? Other than sit with his daughter, hold her hand, and maybe sing a tune to his mad, mad Julia. Seeing Natalie on the landing, her gray hair gone wild, skin wizened, and her crooked fingers holding taut the Francotte revolver from his gun cabinet, he wondered where the Natalie of the garden had disappeared. He hadn't realized then that plucked by his own hand, she had dried up and withered. The Natalie flower.

He'd laughed at her, the old woman with the gun, not out of scorn or hatred but jovial disbelief that she would pull the trigger, that she *could* pull it and spatter Daniel's heart all over the stairs, for he was a good man, despite the failings of his body, the body that God himself had created, not endowed with normal appetites but seething with desire. A monster, she had called him. But could he be blamed for things he could not control? No, at least not then, not that night when he started down the stairs, and the revolver exploded, tripped by Natalie's finger. When Daniel saw Natalie in the foyer, circled in smoke, it was not that she still aimed the gun at his chest or fired two more shots, but rather, it was the utter astonishment shone bright across her face that he was still standing, his hand resting gently on the banister, that made him feel as near to death as he had peering at the snakes crushed on the stones by the riverbed.

He'd walked out that night, down the stairs and past Natalie with the gun still smoking from the fired blanks. He stumbled out the front door, crossed the street, and headed down the Bayshore abuzz with fluorescent streetlights. Maybe he'd been swaggering, the gin causing his feet to drag, or the stunned expression on his face made him an easy target, for two stocking-faced thugs jumped from a beat-up GTO, grabbed him on the sidewalk, and knifed him in the belly. One of the men opened the trunk and pulled out a cement block tied with a long rope. Together, they shackled his ankle and threw his body into the bay.

> Tis thy rich stirrup-cup to me;
> Yo-ho! Yo-hoo! Yo-ho! Yo-hoo!
> I'll drink it down right smilingly.

Daniel stole down the back hall, past the kitchen and the elevator door, into the front foyer, where he discovered Natalie in the living room, asleep in the yellow armchair. She stirred and sat up straight, blinking to catch a glimpse of what she saw moving in the foyer: a rustle, the quick step of a cat, the clap of the air conditioning switching on, billowing the draperies, but whatever she saw, she settled back into the armchair and closed her eyes. Daniel was invisible.

And fading, so he felt, climbing the stairs to Julia's room. His step was so light, he could hardly feel the wood against his bare feet. But Natalie couldn't stop him now, couldn't see him as he mounted the second flight, reached the top landing, and swerved off quickly down the east hall to Julia's bedroom.

Julia sat by the open window, wrapped in a fire of Japanese silk, a kimono of deep reds, yellows, and burnt orange. Her dark hair was finely threaded with silver and was bound in a royal-blue ribbon at the nape of her neck. Daniel leaned against the door jamb, watching his daughter before he entered.

Julia, O my Julia, is that you with your eyes so round and placid that they have come to mirror the drowsy calm of the midsummer water? Is that you, grown old in this room as life has passed by out there on the sidewalk, down the streets, and along the bay? And where is your song? Sweet Julia, the one you used to sing about Maggie and the old creaking mill?

Daniel slipped into the room. He moved silently across the polished oak floor to the bed, where he took off his pirate hat and eased his body down on the edge closest to Julia. He wanted to caress her face, but his hand would feel like the splash of cool wind against her cheek and would startle her, set her searching the room, so he let his hands go limp in his lap.

"Julia," he whispered, "I've come to say good-bye."

She shuddered and clutched the silk kimono to her body. And beyond all reason, beyond all that he knew within him now or before, he asked her forgiveness. For whatever he'd done or not done or should've done, he told her, folding his hands in his lap, he meant only to love her. And how could she accuse him so? Not that he came into her bedroom that Gasparilla night, his painted face a mass of scars and glass beads swinging from his belt, for on Gasparilla he always surprised her in her room, waking her from sleep when she was very young, catching her on the phone as a teenager, tickling her, and hollering yo-ho-ho, and she saying, "Oh, Daddy, you are such a rogue."

But did he ever lie beside her? Hold her too tight or lift her nightie and let his hand slide along the inside of her thighs? Did he ever slip his trousers down, feel the throbbing between his own legs, and force her under his weight?

Oh, God, no, and no and no. The pirate's rape was in her mind; that's what he'd told the doctor. But the child she carried was real. Something must have happened there, that night in her room, not want to, but have to, have to, but no, no, that was not right. That never happened. Daniel spread his hands over his knees and squeezed them until the knuckles turned white. But at one point didn't she invite him? Told him to leave the penny beneath her dinner plate. Didn't she love him dearly?

Sweet Julia. Daniel still loves you.

And Daniel would have sat on that bed and watched Julia as she stared numbly out the window on the southeast corner of the Westcott home. Watched her until the sun slumped over the roof and the room settled into dusky shade, thick and still and so laden with damp heat that the desk and chairs, curtains, chests, mirrors, and rugs all seemed blurred, veiled in mist. He would have watched her, waiting a move from her hands or lips, a tilt of her head, a word that he could interpret as a pardon that would release him, set him free as a wild bird headed straight for the heavens. But a trumpet sounded in the foyer, echoing Beethoven's "Ode to Joy." It bounded up the stairs and down the east hall, calling Daniel to his feet. And knowing the summon was for him (for who else was waiting for the invocation?) Daniel shuffled out of Julia's bedroom. He grabbed his hat but did not turn back to catch a last glimpse of his daughter, for what did it matter now?

At the top of the stairs, Daniel halted and rubbed his eyes, for the sun was blazing in through the second-story windows, gleaming on a boy who was dressed all in white like a Gasparilla page: white shorts, a white ruffled shirt, white socks and shoes. He stood on the bottom step, leaning against the banister with a full-grown rattler coiled around his neck.

"Quinn?" Daniel asked.

The boy just grinned and beckoned Daniel down the steps. Once in the foyer, Quinn opened the front door, and Daniel slipped out, following the boy's lead.

"What're you doing here?" Daniel asked. The walkway was hot beneath his bare feet.

"I been sent to fetch you," the boy said. "Seems you got away and been lost 'til now." Quinn reached for Daniel's hand. "I'm to bring you back."

Along the Bayshore, Daniel had to skip to keep up with the boy. The sky was cloudless and so blue that the water appeared murky and sullen beneath it. The bay was empty except for a ship heading out from Ballast Point, and Daniel squinted in the glaring light to glimpse the ship's bounded sails and the streamers coursing from the masts.

"Look!" Daniel said. "It's the *Jose Gasparilla*." He stopped and leaned over the iron railing to flag the ship. "Hey ya, mateys!" he called out. "What's your business?"

"You, Danny, you!" the pirates howled from the deck, shooting their pistols into the air and hoisting bottles of rum to their lips. "We've come to see you off, old man. Come to watch your last parade."

Daniel flung his right leg over the railing and waved his hat above his head. "Come on now and pick me up." Daniel could already taste the acrid sweetness of the dark rum burning his throat. He could feel the sharp crystals of salt collecting on his face and the tilt of the ship as he hung from the main mast. "Yo-ho! Mateys!" he called. "Come get your king!"

King Daniel. Gasparilla King of the pirates.

Daniel would have swung his other leg over, sat propped there on the railing, and would have swum to the ship, even while it was fading from sight if it hadn't been for the boy's hand clutching his shoulder. And when Daniel turned to Quinn, it wasn't the excellence of his white clothes that shimmered ethereally in the brisk of day, or the determined set of his face, but rather it was the snake coiled around Quinn's neck, rattling its tail and poised to strike that stopped Daniel. He climbed down from the railing and followed Quinn, who walked in front of him now while the snake jeered over the boy's shoulder, its emerald eyes lidless and calculating.

"How far?" Daniel asked.

"You been drifting," Quinn said, continuing his lead. "Jus' washed up on shore this morning. We gettin' there."

Daniel felt light—not airy or gay, but the lightness that comes from the lack of substance, the absence of density that gravity cannot control. He could not turn back, could not slip away from the snake's eyes that kept him tethered, floating in midair like a kite on a string.

And Daniel could not go home.

He must face his body unforgiven, unclean, ripped at the belly, the clothes worn away, the flesh bloated, disintegrated, and stinking. It was past fear, what he felt now, just a few feet from the shore, from where the gray moldered body awaited his return. It was past judgment, past hatred or love or jealousy or joy; past any emotion he'd ever felt, now or before, and knowing the separateness of being: that those emotions were a part of him but not him, just as his acts on earth were committed by him but not of him, and knowing that, just that, he could rise into the air, circle his body, and feel peace.

CHAPTER 22　❊　A Spotted Blowfish

Bᴇᴄᴄᴀ ᴡᴀs ᴀᴛ Mᴀɴᴀᴛᴇᴇ Mᴇᴍᴏʀɪᴀʟ Hospital in Kurt's room when Natalie called and said they'd found a man's body in Hillsborough Bay. She glanced at her watch. It was 10:15 Tuesday morning. Still in yesterday's clothes, Becca tugged on the cable-knit sweater, pulled it down over her tummy that pushed out the top of her jeans. She'd been up all night. "Do they think it's Granddad's?" she'd asked.

Natalie whispered—it couldn't be Daniel. She'd seen him last night. "Don't you remember?" Nattie's voice quaked. "But they want us to go down and see for sure."

"Just sit tight," she told her grandmother. She'd be home in an hour or so. Then Natalie asked about Kurt. Becca reached across the bed and placed her hand over her brother's. He looked so peaceful with his eyes closed, his hair flared out on the pillow like a halo. "He's resting now," she said. "But they saved him, Nattie. Victor, Evan, and the doctors—they all saved his life."

Becca heard her grandmother let out a deep sigh. "Glory be," she said and breathed heavily into the phone. Becca could see Victor sitting across the room with his head leaning against the wall. They'd given him a hospital gown that he'd thrown over his bloodstained shorts. His eyes were closed.

Just then the doctor walked into the room. Becca and Victor jumped up at the same time. Becca told Natalie she'd be home soon and hung up the phone.

"Dr. Bridges," she said, thrusting her hand out to greet him. "I'm Kurt's sister, and this is Victor Ramirez." The doctor was still in his surgical scrubs, a shower cap gathered around his head. Becca thanked him for saving her brother's life.

The doctor scanned the monitors above Kurt's bed. "This is one lucky young man," he said and turned to Victor. "So you're the one who bound the wound?"

Victor nodded.

"I couldn't have saved him without you." Dr. Bridges went on to say the bullet in Kurt's chest just barely missed his heart. "Somehow you managed to keep his lung from collapsing."

Victor stood with his arms crossed over his chest. He said it was Evan who managed the channels, guided the Bertram through the canals to get to the docks at Waterfront Park, where the ambulance was waiting. "The tides were high. We got lucky."

"That's how it goes sometimes," Dr. Bridges said, jotting notes on his chart. He gazed up at Victor. "But the other one," he said, shaking his head, "was awfully young to die."

Then the doctor turned to Becca. "Your brother can go home in a couple of days as long as he remains stable." Then he walked out, leaving her alone with Victor.

Becca tugged on her sweater again. "I need to go home," she said. "A body's been found in the bay. My Nattie said we're supposed to check it out."

Victor put his hands on her shoulders. "Do you want me to go with you?"

The offer brought tears to her eyes. She covered her face to hide them. "No," she said, shaking her head. "I was just so sure my granddad was on the *Sea Booty*. Maybe they've arrested him." She hiccupped a little. "And they don't want to tell us."

Victor clasped her hands. "Look, I don't know anything about the smugglers, but your grandfather was not on that boat."

Becca gazed up at his dark eyes, searching hers.

"I talked to Salazar's man." Victor said. "If Daniel had been on that drug run, Cuda would've left him on the *Sea Booty*. And he wasn't there."

Becca dropped her gaze to the linoleum floor, shiny beneath her feet. "But you can't be sure." As she said this, she felt a vibration coming through Victor's hands, some sort of energy pulsing from his fingers into hers. She sensed an innocence about him that she was drawn to, something whole and pure.

"I'm sure," he said. "Now, do you want me to come with you?"

Becca stared at his face, ragged with fatigue. She did want him to come with her. She wanted to be wrapped within that warm wholeness that rose from him and beckoned her to merge with it. But he looked so exhausted, utterly wrung out. "No, go home and rest," she said. She released his hands and grabbed her purse. "I've got to get Nattie." Becca started to leave, and Victor sat down in the chair next to Kurt's bed.

She stopped at the door. "You're not leaving?" she asked.

Victor pressed his hands together and leaned over to rest his elbows on his knees. "Someone's gotta be here when Kurt wakes up."

The sun beat relentlessly on Daniel's old Cadillac as Becca sped down I-75 to get back to Tampa. She could see waves of heat rising from the pavement, and a blistering wind pummeled her face as it blasted in from the open windows. The air conditioner was broken, but that was the least of her worries. She glanced in the rearview mirror. Black smoke spewed from the exhaust in one thick trail. She hadn't seen it last night at two a.m. Now the soot billowed out behind her, a smoggy, dark cloud that would compel any patrolman to pull her over. Becca couldn't imagine the last time the car was serviced; it would never have passed inspection. She kept her eyes peeled for a cop and then pressed the accelerator to the floor. What difference did it make if she was speeding when she'd be stopped anyway?

By the time Becca drove under the portico of the Westcott mansion, her clothes were drenched with sweat. She parked the car and ran inside. The chill of the house met her in the foyer. When Becca didn't see her grandmother, she called up the stairs. "Nattie!"

Niobe came running from the kitchen. "Your Nattie ain't here," she said, drying her hands on her apron. "She took off with Miss Taylor."

Becca stared at Niobe incredulously. "The next-door neighbor?"

"Yup," Niobe said and shifted her weight from side to side. "She brought over some banana pie and asked 'bout Mr. Dan. Your Nattie said she needed to go down to the morgue and straighten things out." Niobe's eyes widened. "And Miss Taylor said she'd drive her."

"And Nattie went?"

"She did," Niobe said. "That's a neighborly thing to do. Don't you think, Miss Becca?"

Becca shivered as the sweat on her back went icy. "It is," she said, but an alarm sounded in her brain. Nattie would never go anywhere with Ruby Taylor unless she'd become totally unhinged.

Becca was headed out the door when something propelled her to turn back to the living room. As she searched the room, she found the photo of Rebecca, adorned in her queen's robe and crown, lying on the cushion of the yellow armchair. She stopped. The picture had fallen from the diaries. "Niobe, did you see a set of books here?"

"No'm, I ain't seen nothin'."

Becca picked up the photo and puzzled a moment. After Victor called last night, Becca had fled the house, leaving the diaries with Natalie. Perhaps her grandmother had found something in them that had pushed her over the edge. But still, where were they? She turned to Niobe. "There's two big books," Becca said, making the shape of the diaries. "Will you look for them, please? Start in Nattie's room." Niobe nodded, and Becca opened the front door. When she stepped outside, the heat sucked the breath right out of her. She braced herself, managed the stairs, and jumped in the Cadillac.

At the morgue, a giant policeman greeted Becca from behind his desk. "Are you Miss McNeil?" he asked. He flashed a shy smile, but his eyes bulged with a fury, liked they'd seen too much. "I'm sorry," he said, looking down on her. Then he whirled around to catch a glimpse of Natalie, who was seated next to Ruby Taylor in a row of folding chairs just beyond the front desk. "She didn't need to come here," he whispered about Nattie. "We matched the dental records. We know it's Daniel Westcott."

Becca gasped. Her hands flew to her mouth.

"I'm so sorry," the policeman said, nodding like he understood. "Your grandmother showed up before we could call her."

Becca watched as Natalie shuffled down the hall toward her. Her grandmother had wrapped herself in the fringed scarf she'd worn last night. The silk appeared ratty under the fluorescent lights. When Nattie reached the desk, Becca could see a purple flush spilling across her forehead and cheeks. Her eyes darted from Becca and then back to the policeman who stood over six foot six. "You tell him," Natalie said, pointing to the policeman. "It's not your grandfather in there."

"I'm sorry," the gentle giant kept saying. "So sorry."

Natalie stood behind Becca and tugged on her sweater like a frantic child. "You tell him," she whispered. "It's not Daniel."

"I'll take care of it," Becca said and led her grandmother back to the chair. When Becca settled her down, she thanked Ruby Taylor. "You can go home now."

Ruby peered curiously at Becca. "Shouldn't I sit with your grandma?" she asked. "While you talk to the man?"

Becca thought of Victor waiting at the hospital for Kurt to wake up. "Sure," she said. "Why not."

When Becca returned to the desk, she asked the policeman if she could see Daniel.

"Oh no," the policeman said, wringing his massive hands. "You don't have to. We know it's him."

"But my grandmother," Becca said. "If I see him, I can tell her. Otherwise she won't believe it."

The policeman guided Becca just beyond the desk where Natalie couldn't see them.

He wore a thick belt that sported a polished silver buckle in the shape of a horse saddle. Becca couldn't help but stare at the stirrups and decorative spurs that studded the corners. The belt looked curiously out of place in this sterile setting. "You don't understand," the policeman said. "Your grandfather was pulled from the bay this morning." Large drops of sweat gathered on his forehead. "If you would have been there, maybe. But once out of water, the flesh decomposes so fast. You won't recognize him. It would be worthless now."

"Not worthless," Becca said. "If I see him, I can tell her it's him. She'll believe me."

The officer took Becca's hands into his own. "You don't want to see him," he begged. "You don't want to remember him like this. It isn't him."

"No," Becca said, and pulled her hands back. "You don't understand." She tried to keep her voice down. "My grandmother talks to him. Sees him sitting at the piano." She whispered. "If he's dead, she needs to know."

The policeman stepped back and wiped his forehead with the back of his hand. He drew a deep breath. "Isn't there anyone else?" he asked. "A friend?"

Becca thought of Chief Salazar and Captain Mortenson still tangled in Cuda's drug run. "There's no one," she said.

The man finally relented. He hung his head, and Becca followed him past the front desk, through the hall, where she stopped and told Natalie she was going to see if it was Daniel or not. Then the policeman led her down a second hall that was lined with closed doors. "I wish you wouldn't," he said. His silver buckle flashed in the fluorescent light. He stopped in front of a steel door.

Before they entered, he handed Becca a surgical mask. "I'm so sorry," he said again. He tied a mask over his own nose and mouth.

They entered a dimly lit room. In the center stood a long table, humped with the shape of a body that was covered with a sheet. "It's freezing in here," Becca said, following the policeman.

"Wait," he said and held up his hand. Becca watched as he pulled back the sheet and began unzipping a clouded plastic bag. The room filled with a rank odor of mold and rotten flesh so caustic that Becca began to choke. "You all right?" the policeman asked. Becca nodded, and the officer moved deftly around the room, setting up a light over the corpse.

The eyes were gone. Washed-out sockets gaped in an otherwise swollen head. The nose was only intact at the bridge, as if the rest had been scraped off, having been slapped up against a break wall for untold hours. Brownish-blue spots splotched the lips and cheeks, which were bloated to three times their normal size. The face resembled a speckled blowfish thrown from the water.

"The light," Becca said to the policeman. "I can't see." She felt the officer's massive hands grip her arms as the light fluttered off and then grew bright around her. She tried to run toward the door, but a bird with a thumb for a beak, like the one on the tattooist's hand, flew at her face and squawked—*decorate his body, it's his body, it's his body.* Becca lashed at the bird and caught something sharp against her palm. As she felt her body being lifted, she realized the bird had bitten her.

"Miss! You all right?" The officer had lain her on the terrazzo floor just outside the room. He waved some smelling salts beneath her nose. She sat up, coughing. Blood dripped down her hand, onto her sweater. The policeman's pasty face flared red. "You hit my belt." He apologized and wiped Becca's hand with his shirt tail.

Becca leaned back on the wall and pressed her neck against the cool cement. "That can't be my granddad."

The policeman nodded, his bulging eyes moist. "It's not," he said. "Your granddad's gone. It's just a rotten suit of clothes in there now."

Becca closed her eyes. "What can I tell my Nattie?"

With that the policeman stood up and disappeared behind the steel door. Minutes later he slipped out. He told Becca he would be right back. When he returned he carried a first aid kit and a small envelope. After he cleaned and bandaged Becca's hand, he handed her the envelope. When she opened it, her grandfather's gold wedding band spilled into her hand. She read the inscription inside: 4-7-1928.

Becca gazed up at the policeman. "Why didn't you give me this before?"

The officer stared down at his feet. "I didn't see it until you were already in the room. Somehow we missed it." He shook his head. "I'm so sorry."

Becca slipped the ring back into the envelope. After seeing her grandfather's body, she understood how easily they could overlook that ring. In fact, she was grateful it hadn't been lost, since she'd noticed Daniel was missing a few fingers.

By the time Becca returned to the waiting room, she'd already signed the papers, releasing Daniel's body to a funeral home to be cremated. She tucked the gold wedding ring into her jeans pocket.

When Natalie saw her coming, she popped up and shuffled toward Becca. "You told him, right? You told him it wasn't Daniel."

When they left the morgue, Ruby Taylor on the right side of Natalie, holding her arms, and Becca on the left, the afternoon sun blinded them on the steps, and Nattie tripped. They caught her just before her knee hit the cement.

"Whoa!" Becca said, grateful for Ruby Taylor's help now. Together they guided Natalie down the remaining stairs and through the parking lot. Once Becca settled Nattie in the front seat of the Cadillac, she turned to Ruby and thanked her. Ruby gleamed. "Come to the funeral if you want," Becca said. "And then to the house. We'll be receiving guests there." The words flowed from Becca's mouth like she knew exactly how to plan a funeral. But she didn't. She'd only been nine when her father died, and Nattie had made all the decisions. Still Becca could see the church, the flowers, the casket, the guests, the minister giving the eulogy. The whole scene was as vivid in her mind as if it were happening right now.

Black soot still spewed from the old Cadillac when Becca turned onto the Bayshore and headed toward home. Nattie had not said a word the whole time. Becca slipped her good hand into her jeans pocket and handed her grandmother the wedding band. For five blocks Natalie stared at the ring. She turned it in her hand like an odd gem between her fingers. Then just past Rome Avenue, a peculiar whine began to emerge from her grandmother. The cry was high and mournful, but Nattie's lips remained closed. Her eyes never blinked, never wavered from their hold on the ring. Becca thought she'd slipped into a trance.

CHAPTER 23　❋　Sucking Chest Wound

CHIEF SALAZAR CALLED VICTOR DOWN to the precinct Friday morning, three days after he'd caught Cuda and his toadies in their skiffs headed for Tierra Verde. From the fly bridge, Captain Mortenson had spotted them on Tampa Bay, but Salazar waited for Tiger to catch up in the *Sea Booty* to help the *Lady Luck* surround the smugglers. The gang was a stone's throw away from Hurricane Hole when the yachts captured them on the water. Once Cuda realized they were outnumbered and overpowered, he followed the Luhrs to Fort Desoto, while the *Sea Booty* took up the rear. A smugglers' parade, Captain Mortensen had called it later. As soon as they reached the docks, Salazar arrested the whole gang.

Outside the chief's office, Victor knocked twice before letting himself in. Salazar glanced up from a pile of paperwork on his desk and told Victor to take a seat. Dark smudges ringed the chief's eyes, and his face sported a full day's stubble. Victor knew he hadn't slept in days. Salazar set his pen down and folded his hands on the desk. "How's Kurt?"

"Going home today," Victor said and pressed his palms into his knees.

Salazar rubbed the stubble on his chin. "Tiger's real torn up about the shooting. He's thinking of quitting the force."

Victor shook his head. "It wasn't his fault."

"I know, but the whole scene spooked him." Salazar leaned back in his chair. "He can't believe he read it wrong—the masked man, the gunshots aimed at the *Sea Booty*. Plus, he didn't know how many thieves had captured the Bertram. Didn't know you and Evan were still on the boat, let alone the kid."

Victor had replayed the scenario over again in his head. Each time he'd imagine Kurt had been found in the belly of the Bertram, or he'd been party to the search from the get-go, or the kid didn't stow away in the first place. Victor had even blamed himself—he should've known the masked thief was not Tiger. "It could've played out a thousand ways," he said.

"That's always the case. But the aftermath's the reality." Salazar pushed back in his chair, balancing on the hind legs. "How's the family holding up?" he asked.

Victor rubbed his hands on his pants. His palms were beginning to sweat. "I haven't talked to them since they found Daniel's body," he said.

Salazar's eyebrows shot up. The chief said he wished he had more information for them, some conclusive evidence on the cause of Daniel's death. "We've considered everything from foul play to suicide."

Then Victor asked about Cuda.

"Tight-lipped," Salazar said. "Claims Daniel gave him the *Sea Booty*. Swears he didn't hijack it." The chief leaned forward and the chair fell onto all fours. "In Cuda's case, grand larceny would tack on another five years to his prison sentence." Salazar spun around and grabbed a plastic bag from the credenza behind his desk. "Turns out Daniel's death is convenient for Cuda. Maybe too convenient," he said. "We're waiting on the coroner's report for more conclusive evidence."

Victor mulled over the information. He wanted to ask more about the cement block that was tied to Daniel's ankle when Salazar passed the baggie to him.

"Take a look at this," the chief said.

Victor turned the weighty object in his hands and then examined the gun close up.

"Look familiar?" Salazar asked. "It's a Francotte revolver. A hand cannon from the 1930s. We found it on the Bertram."

"Kurt's?" Victor asked and held the revolver to the light.

"Probably from Daniel's collection," the chief said. "Nobody but a wealthy pirate would own a revolver like that." Salazar pointed to right side of the barrel. "See this—A LIEGE, 502. It's authentic."

"Is it loaded?"

"Nope, but it could've been," Salazar said.

"We heard it go off. A couple of times."

"It could've been blanks." The chief reached for the revolver. "A lot of pirates carry the antique guns, fill 'em with blanks, and shoot 'em off on Gasparilla Day. Most of them are toys compared to this one." Salazar set the revolver back on the credenza. "We're hanging on to it for now." Then he turned to Victor. "That's driving Tiger crazy too. That the kid could've been shooting blanks." The chief went on to say that the man they called Spider had been booked a few times on petty theft, assault and battery, and driving without a license. "He was headed for trouble for sure, but chances are he didn't calculate on losing his life that night."

A knock on the door interrupted them. This time Salazar jumped up to answer it. He kept his voice low as he talked to his deputy. "I'll be right back," he said to Victor, and shut the door behind him.

Victor rolled up his shirt sleeves. His own desk was piled with appraisals, subcontractors' estimates, and bills, but he had no juice for work. When he'd left his office this morning, Evan was hunched over his drafting table, deep into plans for a Sun Coast Bank building downtown. That contract would push Ramirez Properties over the top monetarily, not to mention the prestige the company would gain. This deal was the brass ring he'd been waiting for. But now, so close to success, he felt a nagging emptiness tug at his chest.

Victor pushed out of his chair and started pacing the room. When the ambulance had met them at the docks and the paramedics jumped on board the Bertram, Victor overheard the men clattering on about Kurt's sucking chest wound. He'd watched them cut the makeshift bandage from the boy's chest and seal the bullet hole with plastic from the gauze package. One of the medics gave Victor a thumb's-up for lying Kurt on his left side. "You let his good lung breathe," he said. "He's still alive."

Victor stopped pacing and studied the photo of Salazar grinning alongside his Little League team from Belmont Heights. The chief appeared out of place surrounded by a sea of small black faces, but he looked happy. Victor's chest tightened again. He knew he'd have to swing by the Westcott Mansion later and tell Becca he was sorry about her grandfather. And then what, good-bye? He felt the strangest sensation of being stretched in two directions.

Victor gazed down at the credenza, at the revolver wrapped in plastic. He'd waited in Kurt's room until the boy's fingers started to twitch and a deep moan escaped his chest. Finally his eyes opened. Victor had braced himself for the insults the kid would assuredly fling at him. But when Kurt woke up, the oddest smile spread across his lips. The grin, so foreign on Kurt's face, frightened Victor. He pressed the nurse's call button. Surely the blood loss had caused some brain damage.

After Kurt scanned the room, he gazed at Victor. "I'm still here," he said, a little surprised. "I wasn't, you know."

Victor stood by the bed, still wearing the blood-stained shorts. His body hummed with a waning tension winding down like a coiled spring. "Right, you were on the boat. You got shot."

Kurt winced. "Oh, yeah," he said. "But after the gunshot, before I came back, I was …" He stopped, examined the room again. "Maybe it was a dream," he said. "But it felt nice, like heaven."

"Angels?" Victor asked. He couldn't help himself.

"No, it was a light beam, like a flashlight checking me out." Kurt reached up with his left hand and squeezed the bed rail like he was testing its soundness.

"Your chest wound?"

Kurt squinted. "No, it was searching for something else; something I didn't even know I had." He peered at Victor. "The light brushed away everything I thought was important—like being cool or having money. Or even getting high." Kurt laughed. "Not only was it not important, it wasn't even real." Then his face grew grave. "But the feelings were real. All the sadness, the loneliness."

"Did the beam find what it was looking for?"

"Well, the searching stopped. Right about here," Kurt said and pointed to the center of his chest. "And the light filled me up with a feeling of—I don't know," he said, embarrassed. "Maybe love, but pure. Like nothing I've ever felt before. And it filled a place deep inside me where everything else goes silent."

Victor felt a little numb on his feet. He wished the nurse would come. He worried something had come unhinged within the boy's mind.

"The light gave me a choice," Kurt went on. "I could follow it, or I could come back to Earth." He let go of the bed rail and folded his hands across his middle.

"It talked to you?" Victor asked, leaning against the wall.

"Not with words. I just felt it, knew it in my mind." Kurt gazed down at his hands. "I said I didn't want to come back."

Victor eyed the boy. "Then what're you doing here?"

Kurt smiled sheepishly. "My granddad showed up. He was standing off in the distance, wearing a pair of green overalls and a red bandanna tied around his neck. He looked like a janitor. In fact, he was carrying a broom, like he was sweeping up a mess." Then Kurt gazed up at Victor, his face in utter awe. "My granddad told me I had to come back. My mother needed me."

Victor heard the door swing open, and the nurse walked in. "Well, well," she said and poured some water into Kurt's Styrofoam cup. "Welcome to the land of the living."

Or maybe the half-dead, Victor thought as he stepped outside the room to catch some air.

Victor saw Daniel's revolver, lying inert on the chief's credenza. The gun appeared innocent, stuffed in its baggie; nothing more than a collector's item. Victor picked up the revolver and turned it in his hand. He hadn't known in the hospital that it was Daniel's body they'd found in the bay. He wondered how Kurt had taken the news or if they'd even told him by now. He hoped the boy's tenuous grip on reality wasn't further dismantled by his grandfather's death. Victor examined the gun through the clear plastic. Salazar had called it a hand cannon. The cylinder actually looked like a perfect replica of a miniature cannon. The revolver was exactly the kind of gun a pirate like Daniel Westcott would carry.

Just then Salazar returned. The chief's bloodshot eyes spewed an anger Victor had never seen before. "God damn it!" he spat and kicked the legs of the folding chair. "That no-good varmint knows exactly what happened to Daniel. It's written all over his face." Salazar was talking about Cuda. "We just can't confirm anything."

"Did you get the coroner's report?" Victor asked.

Salazar slipped four fingers through his wiry hair, tugging on it a bit. "Appears there was damage to his gut, but the coroner can't be sure what caused it. Could be knife wounds, but they can't rule out gunshot."

"They found bullets?" Victor clutched the revolver that was still in his hand.

"Nope," the chief said. "But the wound's gaping and so decomposed, a bullet could've lodged free." Salazar plopped down in the folding chair. "And the cement block apparently slipped off his ankle when they pulled his body from the bay, so they can't be sure how it was tied." Salazar pressed his hands together. "There's an outside chance it was suicide, but most signs point to foul play."

Victor set the revolver back on the credenza. He recalled the afternoon they'd left the Conch Shell, and Salazar told him Daniel's disappearance act was beginning to stink. "Looks like our pirate king's still a master of diversion," Victor offered. "Even in death."

The chief smiled, the first break in his mood all day. "You're right," he said and laughed a little. "I don't know why I'm surprised."

As Victor headed toward the door to leave, he told Salazar he was going to the Westcott home to pay his respects.

The chief jumped up to shake Victor's hand. Then he grabbed Victor and held him in a bear hug for few seconds. "Thank God you didn't get hit." When Salazar let go, he told Victor that they'd get to the bottom of this yet. Now that they had the coroner's report, the next plan was to offer Cuda's gang a reduced sentence for information on Daniel's death. "They might cave," Salazar said. "When they realize they're just a couple of punks, headed for three squares and a bunk."

By the time Victor pulled under the portico of the Westcott home, thunderclouds had gathered over the bay. The air churned heavy and wet, ready for the cloudburst to spill the much-needed rain on the parched town. Victor trudged up the front steps. The ache in his chest spread wide and long and followed the scar that split his middle. He rang the front door chimes. While he waited, the wind kicked up and set the wicker rocker moving all on its own. The movement so distracted him, he didn't hear Niobe open the door.

"Good day to you, Mr. Ramirez," she said and curtsied. She invited him into the foyer that was laden with fresh flower arrangements, funeral sprays, and potted plants. Niobe picked up an orchid with spiraling blooms that extended just above her head. "The church's already plum full of flowers," she said. "Florists are sending the rest here." She smiled and hugged the lady slipper to her chest. "We're having guests tomorrow after the funeral."

"If everyone's busy, I can come back," Victor said.

"Well, Miss Natalie's up with Kurt, and Miss Becca's in the backyard settin' up chairs." Niobe's dark eyes flashed invitingly. "We're run off our feet today."

No sooner had Victor offered to help than Niobe was ushering him through the back hall toward the kitchen. "The chairs been delivered this morning," she said. "A hundred of them." She glanced back at Victor, as if to be sure he was still following her. "Not everyone will get a seat." Niobe pushed through the swinging door. "Cause it's gonna be big, big, big!"

When Victor entered the kitchen, he saw Eula stacking boxes of cookies, plates of finger sandwiches, and trays of brownies on top of one another because the counters were full. Whole clove-studded hams, apple pies, banana cakes, bottles of wine, a pork crown roast, bowls of coleslaw, potato salad, and more lined the counters. Victor had never seen so much food. As overcome as he was with the show of generosity, the unsound practicality astounded him. *Didn't some of it need to be refrigerated?*

"Where are you going to put all this food?" he asked Niobe.

She just shrugged and found a place to settle the orchid. "Miss Natalie will know. She always does." Eula nodded in compliance. Then Niobe led him to the back door. "Miss Becca will be happy to see you," she said and gave him a little shove onto the back porch.

For a moment Victor stood behind the railing and watched while Becca bent over a white, wooden folding chair. As she struggled to open it, he noticed her cutoff jeans, blousy top, and bare feet. She'd wrapped a blue bandanna around her head to keep her hair from falling in her face. Her profile caught the gray light from the sky, and once again he was stunned by her beauty. A certain calmness, a mysterious repose seemed to be growing within her at a time when he thought she'd be falling apart. His chest ached, and he realized something within him wanted Becca to need him.

"Hey," he called to her, "need some help?"

Becca had finally peeled the chair open and set it on the withered lawn. "I'm not so good at this," she said with a smile.

Victor skipped down the steps, grabbed a chair from the stack, and flung it open with one quick jerk.

Becca blinked a couple of times. "I guess that's the way it's done."

As they worked together in a race against the storm threatening from the east, Victor told her how sorry he was about her grandfather's death. He explained how Salazar was trying to figure out exactly how Daniel had been lassoed by a cement block and ended up in the bay. While Becca appeared to listen, Victor knew she was distracted by something more perplexing than her granddad's demise. "Are you leaving after the funeral?" he asked.

Becca stopped fumbling with the chair and twirled a lock of hair around her index finger. "Not right away. I want to be sure Kurt's well." A dreamy expression swept across her face. "And there's talk about a flotilla, a ceremony of sorts, to throw Granddad's ashes into the Hillsborough Bay."

"His final sail?" Victor offered.

"Something like that." Becca picked up a chair to arrange it with some others in a semicircle under the live oak. The tree's limbs spread out like arms stretching across the backyard. A pair of jenny wrens hopped along the branches, squawking intensely at them. "They've been scolding me all day." Just as Becca said the words, the male swooped down and pecked the scarf off her head.

"They're dive-bombing you," Victor said, amused with the bird's antics.

Becca shooed the wren away. "They're building a nest." She peered up at the tree. "We're standing too close. They don't trust us."

The sky had grown a deep purple above them, and a gust of wind blew through the yard with a fury. Becca said they should head inside when a thunderbolt split the sky and lit up the backyard like a theater. Victor grabbed Becca's hand to run to the porch, but she pulled him in the other direction. "This is closer," she called above the wind and pointed toward the garden house that was just beyond the live oak. They ran around the chairs, through the yard, and burst through the open doors of the small wooden house. Once they were inside, the clouds let loose. Rain crashed down on the tin roof, pelting it with gigantic drops that had been stored in the heavens way too long. The torrents pummeled the miniature house until it shook, teetering on the blocks that held it above ground.

Victor and Becca stood panting just inside the doorway. They wiggled in deeper to shield themselves from the rain, but the garden house was stuffed with lawn mowers, weed eaters, and shelves filled with everything from jarred preserves to odd cushions and rusted paint cans. Victor sucked in his chest to give Becca more room. With her body wedged against his, he breathed in of the scent of her, a heady duo of fresh roses and sweat. Her head was bent just beneath him, but he could feel the beat of her heart in sync with his own. This melding of flesh, of muscle to muscle, bone against bone stirred an impulse, a desire buried deep within him that urged him beyond the restraints of class or race or even time. He raised a hand to Becca's chin and lifted her face to meet his. While he gazed at her and absorbed the warmth of her eyes, the heat of her breath enveloped him. He kissed her.

CHAPTER 24 ✳ A Closed Casket

On Friday, July 1, the day of Daniel Westcott's funeral, the townspeople bustled through their morning chores in an attempt to accomplish a full day's work. Afternoon appointments were canceled, shops closed, and after lunch the children who were attending the funeral were picked up. By now, everyone had heard that Daniel's body had been found in the bay, but precious few had an inkling how he'd become entangled with the marijuana smugglers who were captured near Hurricane Hole. A couple of Daniel's cronies had been privy to the information—or misinformation— when they happened to see Evan Stone pull into the yacht club with the *Blew Bayou* early Tuesday morning. Tongues wagged when they realized the deck of Poppy's Bertram had been drenched with blood. Who was this fella, Evan Stone? Apparently he didn't stick around for questioning.

Someone called Chief Salazar at the police department to tell him a stranger had just motored into the marina with Hank Poppy's yacht. But Salazar could not be found. Two officers sped down to the club to check out the boat. Immediately they ordered it to be cleaned up. A dictate from the chief, they said. Daniel's cronies stood on the dock and watched as a detailer sprayed down the yacht. As the water in the slip turned pink and headed out toward the Hillsborough Bay, they wondered if it could be Daniel's blood being washed away. Even after the newspaper reported Daniel's body was found floating up against the seawall near Howard Avenue, a growing suspicion loomed among the old king's cronies. Distrust burned within them. A few of them were hell bent on smoking out the dirt on Evan Stone.

By midmorning, while many people were still buying flowers and sympathy cards to take to the Episcopal church downtown, Becca and Natalie scurried around the kitchen at the Westcott home, arranging platters of food to be served to the guests that afternoon. Becca had not bothered to dress this morning; she'd just thrown a robe over her nightie and raced downstairs to finish the preparations. She and Nattie had stayed up past midnight, slicing hams; assembling dessert trays, cheese platters, and fruit bowls; and gathering up bottles of wine, Coke, and beer to be iced in coolers. Yesterday afternoon when the food kept arriving, Victor called his uncle to pick up the overflow and store it at his friend's delicatessen. Uncle Carlos promised to deliver it promptly after the funeral—in time for the guests' arrival.

Becca piled the last of the brownies and date bars onto a large ceramic plate. "Nattie, why don't you get dressed," she said and wiped her hands on a kitchen towel. "Eula can finish up here." She peered through the window that overlooked the backyard, where Eula was wiping rain from the chairs. "Where's Niobe?" she asked.

Natalie stood at the sink, peeling shrimp. Her hair swung from a disheveled half-bun that bounced haphazardly when her chin periodically dipped, as if she were falling asleep. "She's up with your mama," she said groggily, "trying to persuade her to go to the funeral."

Becca marched over to her grandmother and turned off the faucet. "Well, we won't force her. It might be too much, especially with all the company coming today." Becca spun Nattie around, untied her apron, and pulled it over her head. "Get going now. It's getting late." Becca led her grandmother to the door. "I'll be up soon," she said, "to check on you. And Kurt."

While Becca hurried through the kitchen to call Eula, she worried how Nattie would make it through the day. At least she'd stopped seeing

Daniel and had, for the moment, quit talking to him. Considering the turmoil of the last seventy-two hours, Becca supposed that was progress. But then there was Kurt, lying upstairs, knocked out on painkillers. The doctor said it could be a week or so, but he'd come through this unscathed. Becca opened the back door and stepped onto the porch. The air smelled fresh, rinsed clean by the thunderstorm. A cool breeze rustled the grass, where new shoots were already beginning to sprout. As she watched Eula bend over the chairs, wiping one and then another, she spotted the doors on the garden house that were still flung open, inviting. Becca's fingers flew to her lips.

She remembered the question Victor had whispered in her ear after he'd kissed her. "If I'm not made for you, why does my heart tell me I am?" She'd not answered him. Instead, she'd returned his embrace that invited her to meld into his flesh, to merge with the wholeness of his being. With Victor she felt safe, yet tingly alive. The sensation was so different from what she'd experienced with Adam, who'd made her blood boil.

As she leaned against the porch railing, the jenny wrens flitted through the backyard, chattering and gathering bits of moss for their nest. Now and then, the male would swoop down and peck the braid that crowned Eula's head. Becca rubbed her tummy that had grown round and hard. But how would Victor feel if he knew about the baby? He wouldn't want any part of her. What man would? She let out a deep sigh. After the flotilla, she just would leave, fly back to New York, where she could disappear into the crowd once more. She called to Eula to finish the dessert trays and then headed inside to dress.

Upstairs, after she'd tried on every possible outfit in her closet, Becca raced down the east hall, straight toward her mother's room. She met Niobe standing outside the bathroom door, knocking. "Wash up quick now," she called to Julia. "Everyone's 'specting you at your daddy's funeral today."

Becca brushed by Niobe. "I need to borrow a dress," she said. "Nothing I have suits." The truth was nothing fit.

Niobe fumbled with the doorknob. "She's gone and done it again," she sputtered. "I told your mama—never, never lock the door!"

Becca took the opportunity to slip into her mother's room and search the closet. She started at the left end, where the older clothes were hung, thinking they'd be closer to her size. She was flipping through the St. John's knits, Gasparilla gowns, and Lily Pulitzer skirts when she found a flowy A-line dress with a gathered empire waistline. That would give her the room she needed. And it was black. At first she worried it looked like a bathing suit cover-up, but with the right jewelry, she could pull it off. Becca wiggled out of the bathrobe and let it fall to the floor. She was about to step into the dress when her grandmother burst through the door.

"Niobe, are you in ..." Nattie stopped cold in the doorway. She gazed at Becca, who fumbled with the dress, struggling to pull it over her bra and panties.

Becca felt the heat of her grandmother's eyes burrow into her skin, even as she pulled the black jersey over her telltale tummy.

Nattie shuffled into the room and shut the door behind her. "You're pregnant?"

For a moment, Becca thought she could lie. Her grandmother looked so exhausted, her hair in strings around her face, and the black suit harsh against her pasty skin. If there was any hope Nattie would believe her, Becca would have spared her the truth. She slipped her arm through her grandmother's and led her to the bed to sit down. "I am," she said.

A deep groan escaped Nattie's lips. "That's why you're going to Canada," she said and wrung her hands.

"But I'm not." Becca sucked in her breath and kept talking. She told Nattie how everything had fallen apart with Adam. He'd found someone else. "It's over," she said. "After the flotilla, I'm going back to New York."

Natalie searched Becca's face. "You wouldn't do anything to hurt the baby?"

Becca didn't like the sound of that. "It's different now," she explained. "Women do it every day." She smoothed the black jersey over her middle. "It's a new world, Nattie."

Natalie took Becca's hand and squeezed it hard. "Stay home," she begged. "We'll keep the baby here."

Becca wanted to laugh, but it came out a snarl, a deep, threatening growl that sounded displaced even to her. "Just like you did for my mother?"

Natalie covered her mouth. "I didn't have a choice," she said through her fingers. "It was Daniel's fault. And Rebecca's." She rocked back and forth to soothe herself.

Becca laughed again, only this time hardier. "Think about it, Nattie. All the dirty girl jokes behind my back. 'That slut Becca—she's got round heels.'" Becca picked up her mother's brush and started gathering her hair into a ponytail. "You don't want that any more than I do." She chose a black satin ribbon from the vanity drawer. "This town still isn't ready for unwed mothers."

Nattie stopped rocking. "What about Victor Ramirez?"

Becca sat down on the vanity stool to tie the ribbon in her hair. "What about him?"

"He's a good man. He saved his brother's life. He saved *your* brother's life!"

Becca eyed her grandmother through the vanity mirror. "What if I don't love him?" As much as Becca wanted to love Victor, after Adam, she needed time to trust someone again.

"He loves you," Nattie said. Her voice quivered an octave above normal. "That's even better."

"What about the baby?" Becca picked up the brush to smooth out the ponytail.

Natalie stared down at the wooden floor and shuffled her feet. "It's too late for that," she said. "You'd have to tell him."

Becca threw up her hands, exasperated. "Well, what a shame!" She slammed the brush down. "Don't you see, Nattie? It's easier for everyone if I have the abortion."

Natalie pushed off the bed and trudged toward the window. She stopped abruptly at the Queen Anne's chair and picked up a picture of Rebecca posed in her queen's robe and crown. Natalie held up the photo.

Becca saw it and rushed to her grandmother's side. "How'd that get in here?" The last time she'd seen that picture, it was in the living room. Becca glared at her grandmother. "Did you leave the diaries out when I left for the hospital?"

Nattie stiffened. "No! I hid them upstairs in my closet."

Just then the front door chimes pealed through the house. Becca skirted to the window. There on the front porch, the chauffeur waited patiently. He'd come to drive them to church. "We have to go," Becca said. The black limousine the funeral home had sent over was waiting for them on the driveway.

Nattie clutched the photo to her bosom. "What about this?"

Thoughts scrambled through Becca's head like a band of unruly toddlers. She didn't want anything to upset her mother—not today. "Just leave it," Becca said, and she searched under the bed skirt for the diaries. She scoured the drawers, the closet, and the vanity. She even searched under the Queen Anne's chair but found nothing. Then Becca set her hands on her hips. "Well, maybe she put them back. Why don't you check your closet when you grab your purse." Then Becca hurried to the door and called down the hall. "Niobe, come do Nattie's hair right now. We can't be late for the funeral!"

By the time the limo dropped Becca and Natalie off in front of St. Andrew's, they could barely make their way through the crowd. Victor had been waiting for them at the bottom of the staircase. He took Natalie's arm and helped Becca guide her up the steps. Her grandmother's feet shuffled heavily beneath her, and Becca worried how Nattie would make it through the day.

Once inside the vestibule, Becca peeked into the church at the pews stuffed with funeralgoers who wore dark suits, veiled hats, and gloves—all amid the summer heat. Mothers and fathers sat with the youngest children on their laps, while the older ones had pulled out the prayer kneelers and settled there. Chairs had been lined up along the outside aisles, where those lucky mourners had claimed a seat. But the rest spilled out like subway riders, leaning against the columns or pews or stained-glass windows. A few even sat on the floor.

Father Heims met Becca and Natalie under the arches by the baptismal. Adorned in his white pulpit robe and purple stole, the plump priest appeared quite regal and calm in spite of the late hour. He recommended they start the service immediately. If they wanted a receiving line, that could be arranged after the ceremony. He scanned the church for other members of the family. "It's just us," Becca said. Quickly, the father summoned an usher to escort the women.

Becca turned to Victor. "Do you want to sit with us?" she asked him. She knew how it would look, Victor Ramirez settling into the Westcott family pew with her and Nattie. But today, the day of her granddad's funeral, Becca didn't care.

Before they started down the aisle, Becca whispered to the usher to get a firm grip on her grandmother. The red runner stretched out long and wide and led straight to the altar, where Daniel's casket sat displayed in front of the communion rail. A bit wobbly on her feet, Nattie began the trek just as the organist initiated the slow processional—Pachelbel's Canon in D. Although it was a classical piece, Becca thought the music unusual for a funeral. Wasn't it normally played at weddings? Once Nattie and the usher cleared the last three pews, Becca slipped her arm through Victor's, and together they set out down the aisle. Two violinists joined the organist, and music filled the church with such a buoyant beauty, three parishioners stood up and turned around to watch as Becca and Victor headed toward the altar. Those first viewers caused a ripple effect, and soon almost everyone in the church had risen from their seats to grab a glimpse of the unlikely couple headed for Daniel Westcott's casket.

Becca felt her cheeks burn as she passed the Meekers, the Williamses, the Jeskes, the Meyers—all the families she'd grown up with. Then they passed Carlos Mendoza and Chief Salazar, who stood with his wife. Becca didn't dare look at Victor. She set her lips and tried to keep the pace, even as they progressed toward the front pew that had been cordoned off for the family. When they finally reached it, Becca slid in next to Nattie. It wasn't until Victor sat down beside her that Becca caught of glimpse of his dark eyes, taking in the gawks and goggles of the congregation staring at them. A small gasp escaped her lips. They'd be front-page news by tomorrow.

As soon as the three of them settled in the pew, the organist struck up a lavish rendition of "How Great Thou Art." Anyone who was not already standing sprang to their feet and began belting out the lyrics. The entire church vibrated with song. With everyone's eyes behind her now, Becca inhaled the fresh scent of white carnations, red tea roses, jasmine, and gardenias. The florals lined the communion rail and bordered the steps leading to the altar, which was elegantly draped with white orchids. The fragrant flowers filled the church with new life, even as Daniel's closed casket dwelled heavy and black at the edge of the stairs. One massive bouquet of snowy roses overlaid the foot of his coffin.

When the hymn ended, Father Heims stepped up to the pulpit and began the ceremony with a prayer. Becca bowed her head and glanced down at the empty pew next to her grandmother. Where had everyone gone? As a child, worshiping in this same church, Becca recalled how the Westcott family had filled the entire bench—Daniel, Nattie, her mother, father, brother, and even Rebecca had joined them when Becca was young. Now three of them had passed, three remained, and somehow her mother lingered precariously between the worlds. Victor groped for her hand, and

Becca let him gather it into his. His fingers felt reassuringly warm wrapped around hers. Nestled as they were within the pew, Becca took comfort in knowing no one could see their hands entwined—not even Nattie.

After the prayer, Father Heims launched into a lengthy eulogy, commending Daniel on his community service, his loyalty to family, and his devotion to God. Halfway through, Nattie's head began to bob. Becca nudged her to keep her awake, but it was like trying to arouse a tree trunk. Presently, Nattie began to snore. Not the quiet puffing or a gentle blow through half- parted lips, but an earth-shattering, hog-truffling roar that set the parishioners whispering among themselves. Victor plucked the handkerchief from his top pocket and passed it to Becca. She frowned at him. What was she supposed to do with that, stuff it in Nattie's mouth?

Father Heims kept right on talking, as if immune to any disturbance that could befall him. Becca pinched her grandmother twice, but it only caused her to jerk disruptively. And then, as if in rebuttal, Nattie resumed the snoring with a terrible intensity. There was nothing to do except pray that the father would end the eulogy soon and allow the organist to snap Nattie out of her slumber. Becca was begging for the favor when a little girl, no older than five, slipped off her mother's lap and toddled down the empty pew, her red ringlets bouncing as she approached them. She stopped about a foot away from Nattie and stared open-mouthed at the grunting old woman. Becca could see the girl's mother seated on one of the outer-aisle chairs, waving at her daughter to come back. But the child stood mesmerized. Finally, she gazed up at Becca with starry-eyed wonder and asked in that high-pitched, piercing voice that only little girls possess, "What's she doing?"

The child's ear-splitting trill resonated high above the pastor's hum and took about five seconds to register throughout the congregation. The twittering started harmlessly at first, until the little girl repeated the question, only this time twice as loud. Then the congregation burst into peals of laughter that rolled and frolicked up and down the aisles like jesters on a mission. Father Heims said something about "from the mouths of babes," and let out a good-natured guffaw himself.

After the excitement died down, the father concluded the service with the Lord's Prayer, and the organist began the recessional hymn, "Amazing Grace." After the song, Father Heims, followed by two altar boys, began his walk down the aisle. On his way to the narthex, he stopped at Becca's pew and asked if they wanted to form a receiving line now. But before Becca could answer, Nattie bolted from the bench and marched straight up to Daniel's coffin. She stood there staring at the casket, clutching her purse with both hands.

"I don't think so," Becca said, keeping one eye on Nattie. "I'll greet the guests myself and extend an invitation to the house. But it won't be formal."

Father Heims's kind eyes smiled down on her. "Whatever you choose, my dear." With that he beckoned an usher to escort her from the pew and to follow him down the aisle. Becca asked Victor to please stay and keep a close watch on Nattie. From the looks of it, she was capable of anything.

Once in the vestibule, Becca stood by the baptismal. She thanked the people as they streamed through the church, which had grown stifling with so many overdressed bodies squeezed together. Some left eagerly without acknowledging Becca, while others clutched pieces of her clothing, touched her hair, her hands, her face, and wailed on about poor King Daniel.

Evan stood three people behind when Becca spotted him in line. She caught his attention and smiled at him. She hadn't thanked him yet for saving Kurt's life. Right in front of Evan, Buddy Myers kept turning around and making nasty faces at Evan. When Buddy finally reached her, Becca whispered to him, "Why are you being so snarky?"

Buddy leaned in close and told Becca that Evan had brought back Hank Poppy's boat drenched in blood just hours before they found Daniel's body. Becca realized very few people knew the truth of what happened that night on Egmont Key. "It wasn't Daniel's blood," she said under her breath.

"Yeah, well, some people think it was."

"Chief Salazar needs time to clear it up," Becca said, waving Buddy on. "But for now, just keep quiet."

Buddy rolled his eyes and laughed. "Too late for that, B-B-B-Becca." He turned and gave Evan a dirty look. "Better warn him," he said loudly.

Becca set her hands on her hips. "Looks like you've accomplished that single-handedly, Buddy Boy," she said.

When Buddy took off, Becca threw her arms around Evan and hugged him long and hard. She wanted to show her gratitude for him in the presence of all the Gaspar pirates who were still hanging around the vestibule. "Don't worry," she said to Evan as loudly as she could, "Salazar will make a statement soon. You'll be totally cleared." Over Evan's shoulder, Becca spotted a young woman skirting around the fold-out chairs, as if she were hiding. She wore a long, gauzy dress, not a shade paler than her skin, and her hair was so silvery, Becca wondered how a teenager had acquired such aged hair. Becca tried to keep an eye on her because there was something strange and familiar about her at the same time. But the people kept coming. Lois Fairchild had all but cornered Becca. She was promising to come over and read Scriptures to Natalie, when Becca felt a tug on her dress. She turned around and saw the girl face to face. But before Becca could open her mouth, the girl slipped a small piece of paper into her hand and vanished immediately. It happened so fast, if Becca hadn't tucked the note into her newfound cleavage and felt it lodged there, she would've sworn she'd imagined the entire incident.

After the last guest left the church, Becca raced down the aisle and found Natalie sitting in one of the fold-out chairs at the head of Daniel's casket. Victor leaned over the front pew, his hands folded, resting on the ante rail. "What's she doing?" Becca asked and slid in next to Victor.

Victor leaned in close to Becca and whispered, "She's talking to him."

From the outside aisle, Father Heims wiggled into the pew and sat down next to Becca. "It's common," he said. "Be patient with her." So Becca leaned back to wait.

Natalie talked for a long time—shivery little hisses that echoed through the empty church. Once Becca tried to coax her to leave, but Nattie turned on her. "This is none of your business," she said, her eyes flashing. Then Nattie continued the singsong whisper like a chant, until the sun passed over the west side of the church and cast long shadows over the pews. Some of the flowers had begun to wilt, and the late-afternoon heat settled in, hazy over the town.

After a while, Victor stood up. "Let me try," he offered. Becca agreed, not because she would begrudge her grandmother's last words to Daniel, but she worried about the guests who had been waiting at the Westcott home for more than an hour now.

Victor slipped from the pew. But before he could reach her, Natalie stood up and started talking fast and loud, shifting her weight from one foot to the other as if standing on hot pavement. "We should've found him," she hollered. "That stinking pirate!" Nattie whirled around as if to be sure the church was empty. Then she kept shouting. "And I just might find him without you. What do you think about that?" She pounded on the coffin. "Answer me!"

Before Becca realized that Natalie was struggling to lift the lid on Daniel's casket, Niobe came tromping down the aisle. "Miss Becca! It's your mama. She's in trouble!" Niobe pressed her hands together to keep them from shaking.

Becca gripped her shoulders. "Tell me!"

Natalie let the lid on the coffin slam shut. She wobbled up to Niobe, who fell straight into Nattie's arms. Niobe started to sob. "It's Miss Julia! She's burning up the house."

Natalie pushed Niobe back, looked her square in the face. "What?"

"She's burning something," Niobe blubbered. "Locked in her room. And smoke's pouring out from under the door. Out the windows." Niobe wiped her nose with the edge of her apron.

"What about the guests?" Becca asked.

"They're all out back, eating and drinking like there's no tomorrow."

"They don't know about the fire?"

"Not yet." Niobe shuffled her feet on the red runner. "Mr. Kurt sent me here to fetch you. "He says no police. Or firemen. Just get home."

Becca shuddered. "Kurt's out of bed?"

"He's standing at Miss Julia's door. Knocking on it gentle-like." Niobe stared down at her shoes and then hid her eyes behind her hands. "He's saying, 'Mama, you gotta let me in now. You hear? You gotta let me in.'"

CHAPTER 25 ✳ Eine Kleine Nachtmusik

I wandered today to the hill, Dear Maggie,
To watch the scene below:
The creek and the creaking old mill, Maggie,
As we used to long ago.

So sweet, so catching.

Julia hummed, gathered the silk robe in her hands, and lifted it above her ankles to climb the back stairs to the attic. The creaking stairs. Like the old creaking mill. Shhh! Not loud. Not one, two, three. The fourth step up, still near the bottom, with the black knotty hole, puckered like a walnut, big enough to swallow the cat's-eye marble.

Hide the hole with your big toe now.

Gone, gone.

Julia touched the wall, the tined plaster prickly beneath her fingers, and paintless like the unfinished steps. Two steps from the top she stopped; the ninth step. Worn smooth beneath her bare feet. She turned, faced the thread of light that lined the door at the bottom of the stairs, and sat down. The tenth stair was her sitting step, while the others spread out beneath her in exacting proportions. Three, three, and three. She'd disassembled them like that, in trios, for different stages, different loves in her life.

She spread her hands at her sides, gripping the stair's edge. Even as she leaned over, she could not glimpse the first step from here, the one she called music. But its influence was beyond vision, potent in its ability to rejuvenate her. She hummed Brahms's Waltz in A-Flat.

> Dum da da da dum
> Dah da da da dah dum
> Dah dada dah da dum

Oh, the power of music to transform Julia! This was why it was the first step, chosen to underlie all the others. How reasonable, then, that she'd named the next two stairs "song and dance." But do you imagine that was an easy choice? No, and not for a young soprano, mastering G and E scales, and struggling with *fouette' saute' en tournant*, pirouettes, and *tour jetés*. For years she'd linked the three disciplines together, imagining them as unique expressions of the same order. Wasn't it music that inspired the voice to sing, the body to move? Wasn't a voice music?

It wasn't until she had to give one up that the distinction became clear. Julia was thirteen, dancing the *pas de deux* in Swan Lake, when she felt something snap the back of her left ankle. Entranced in movement, she tried to continue the dance. But she'd collapsed on stage, a burning ache coiling her foot, winding up her calf. Her father, seeing her fall, jumped from his seat and climbed onto the stage. He swooped her into his arms and rushed her to the hospital, where an emergency surgery revealed an Achilles tendon severed at the ankle and retracted to the knee like a rubber band shot through the dark.

Julia would never again dance Giselle. Never feel her body arch and soar through the air in a *grand jeté*. But it was in that knowledge she realized that dance was a part of music, but not music, and should her voice snap like her body, the music would go on and on. So at thirteen she separated music, song, and dance and gave them the three first steps. And how could she have known by that gift, endowing the lost love its own space, its separate stair, that she was setting a pattern that would follow her through life, haunting her, and begging repetition?

A shadow passed beneath the door at the bottom of the stairs. Through the wall, she heard Niobe knocking on her bathroom door. "You getting washed up?" she asked. Julia had left the water trickling in the sink. "Miss Becca wants to take you to church. To your daddy's funeral." Niobe paused, as if she was listening at the door. "That's if you want," she said. "You take your time. I'll be back."

The fourth step was Bobby Hunt. She'd met him at fourteen, after her ankle had healed and the doctor said she could waltz and do the Charleston. "Become the belle of her debutante ball," he'd said. As long as she did not jump.

Bobby was sixteen, a sweet boy with a round face, the color of a peach. He would call for her, holding miniature mums behind his back that Julia suspected he'd picked from the Flynn's garden next door. They would sit on the front porch—Bobby, too shy to hold her hand but entranced with her long, slim fingers that smoothed her skirt or fidgeted with the gold locket her mother had clasped around her neck. He came to her often, a loyal pup, his eyes begging an attention that baffled her until one evening, just before her sixteenth birthday, he walked with her around the back of the house to see the azaleas budding early that year. Standing in the shadow of the gazebo, he grabbed her hands, pressed them to his chest that had grown hard and angled like his jaw. His eyes darted toward the house and then back to hers, as if he knew he must hurry, challenged by an elusive foe he could not pinpoint, but an adversary who threatened and pursued him just the same. "I … I love you, Julia," he whispered into her hair. He pulled her close to his body, which writhed with an urgency, an unbounded insistence that felt decisive and compelling. Julia let him kiss her. She let him force his mouth against hers until his tongue broke the seal of her lips and her body fell fluid against his, filling in his hard angles with her breasts, her hips, and her thighs.

The creaking old mill is still, Dear Maggie
Da da da da dee dum

As sprays by the white breakers flung, my Maggie
Since you and I were young

A thump resounded in the attic behind her. Julia turned. "Daddy?" she whispered. But she would not go up now. What if they had found his body floating in the bay? Stuffed him into a casket? "No," Julia said, hugging her knees. "Wait."

From where she sat, she could just see the edge of the fourth step and the knotty black hole, puckered unevenly round. She was to meet Bobby the day after Gasparilla—after school at the yacht club, because he was home on break from West Point. He would have asked her then, for the flush between them, for the way his hands trembled with desire for her; he would have asked her to marry him. Julia turned on the stairs and peered into the attic. "Did you know that, Daddy?" she whispered.

She laughed, remembering how her mother hovered over her that Gasparilla night as she lay, knees bent to her chest.

"You'll be fine," her mother had said. "We'll find him. String him up."

Find him? Find him?

And what did her mother think she was doing, curled up like a shrimp in her bed?

Hurting? Did anyone think Julia was weak?

Oh God, no! And no. She was thinking about meeting Bobby the next day and the red woolen skirt with the matching cardigan. Or should she choose something more sophisticated? Something more appropriate for an officer's fiancée?

Niobe's voice sounded muffled through the wall. "She's getting washed up." Julia heard the rustle of feet and saw the shadows flicker beneath the door at the bottom of the stairs. "She might go," Niobe said. "But you got to be patient, Miss Becca."

One jagged crack ripped horizontally through the fifth step. Richard. Her Richard. Julia clutched her uncombed hair, feeling it, coarse and brittle through her fingers.

She had not meant to break him. What kind of a woman would do that?

It was true she did not love him, at least not the way she had loved Bobby, but then, Bobby was gone. She had maintained her relationship with him through those days at St. Agnes, the home for unwed mothers, discreetly known as a young woman's "finishing school," in Hamden, Connecticut. Just a year, she had told Bobby over the phone. "Humor them," she'd said about her parents. "They have some crazy notion about the newest styles of etiquette." She laughed lightheartedly into the phone. "To be worthy of you, my dearest." Then she'd hung up the receiver, raced down the hall, past her room, to the line of toilets exposed in the bathroom like a mockery of propriety. She leaned over the middle one and retched.

Could anyone play "Eine Kleine Nachtmusik" for Julia?

She'd not had the baby yet; she was in the middle of her eighth month, waddling the halls of St. Agnes with her stomach poked out and horrifying. But she had taken such care, rubbing her bulging middle with cocoa butter, keeping her feet hiked up on the sofa ends like the older women who insisted that was the only way to avoid varicose veins. And in her eighth month she only had one mark, a shivery, purple blaze that started small and insignificant at her thigh and then shot up around her belly, ending just before her navel. One crude stripe like the lash of a whip. But it would fade, the nurse promised. Turn into a silvery white vein, almost unnoticeable.

Like one gray hair?

Exactly.

But what had it mattered? She received the call on September 17, in the evening after the nurses closed all the windows because the first Canadian front had blown in, and set some of the girls laughing about the old sweaters they'd pulled from their drawers that now barely covered their backs. Julia stood in the hall, holding the phone pinched against one ear, while she cupped the other to muffle the howls of the girls.

"Hurt?" she'd asked.

A jeep accident, Bobby's mother had told her. He was thrown from the driver's seat when a semi, carrying a truckload of cattle, hit the jeep broadside. "He's paralyzed," his mother said. His neck was broken.

Julia slid to the floor, her back straining against the plaster wall, while her belly stretched out like an overinflated balloon. Shocked? She was.

But did anyone think it was strange that an unbridled joy zipped through Julia? She could bathe him, feed him, dress him, wheel him in a chair through the park. And then, would he care about the one crude stripe that slashed her belly? Oh God, no! For he'd been broken too. And it wasn't his fault.

Does anyone think the rape was Julia's fault? Of course not. And in time she planned to tell him—about the pirate, climbing the trellis to her bedroom window, just like she'd told her mother it happened. And then Bobby would understand why she could not come to him as he lay in that hospital bed, unable to talk or lift a hand to write, but waiting, waiting for her to come, until he slipped into a coma and died five days later.

The stairwell to the attic thickened with heat. Julia squirmed on the tenth step, just midway above the fifth where the horizontal crack split the stair in half.

Dear Richard. Didn't she tell you not to come? Don't bring the flowers. Or sit on the porch. And if you wanted to help, then you should have told her when she returned home from St. Agnes with nothing except the fading cruel stripe, why the sun continued to wake her in the morning?

Tchaikovsky, please. "Sleeping Beauty."
Dah da da da de dum
De da da da da da dee

If grief could be transferred, Julia had succeeded. It slid from her like an unwanted birth, painfully at first, then in a streak, a quick, numbing flash that rushed through her body.

But when grief is as palpable as flesh, where does it go?

Julia peered behind her at the darkened entrance to the attic. "Where?" she asked. But remembering Richard with his deep-set eyes and delicate hands that infallibly held a pipe or a newspaper or Julia's hand, she knew even before she married him that he would become the receptacle, the bearer of extremities.

She turned back to the stairs and the horizontal crack that just caught the edge of light creeping through the narrow window at the top of the steps. Julia did not doubt that Richard had, without speaking of it or acknowledging it in anyway, absorbed her grief. But exactly how it passed between them she didn't know. She wondered if it was their shadowy union in the four-poster bed that Julia allowed periodically because she sensed his need. Or it could've been from the one union that produced their daughter. But if Julia had to guess now, after all these years, she would say the grief had passed through sleep. Through the rhythms of night breathing, the exchange of air over time, and Richard's vigilance of holding her in the dark, rocking her, and whispering *shhh* into her hair until it seeped into her brain. "It's all right, darling," he would say. "It's only a dream."

But did anyone think Julia gave up?

She did not indulge sleep or brandy or the pills the doctor gave her to rest. She bathed every morning, dressed, pinned her own hair, ate her breakfast, and strolled Becca down the Bayshore in the four-wheeled carriage her father had given her. When loneliness crept in through the minor chords of "The Pathetique" she played on the piano, and Richard failed to move them out of the Westcott Mansion because he'd lost his job at the electric company, she did not stop practicing her music or singing lullabies to Becca.

But she wanted to know—what is left when a grief is gone except the haunting emptiness of what might have been?

This was why the sixth stair, curiously bleached and brighter than the others, crowned Bobby's and Richard's. This was the sleekest stair, the color of butter and perfectly blank like the last pages of Rebecca's diary she found early one morning nestled in the cushions of her Queen Anne chair. She'd never named this love, but he'd become her joy just the same. Although no one else could see him, she had, sitting in the shade of the gazebo, a head taller than Bobby. He possessed the blackest, wavy hair and a short mustache that he caressed with the tips of his forefinger and thumb. She'd call to him from the library window. He would climb the stairs to her room and sit on the floor across from her while she sat in the chair facing the bay. And there she'd tell him about her Achilles tendon that had snapped dancing the *pas de deux* or the engagement ring she'd boxed up at St. Agnes and returned to Bobby's mother. She'd tell him how some nights she'd dreamt about soaring the stage in one sustained *grand jeté*, and she showed him the silver stripe that shimmered from her navel to the crest of her thigh.

Who thought Julia spent too much time staring out the window?

She chuckled now on the tenth step, thinking how cleverly she'd concealed the man with the blackest hair, deep within the recesses of her mind. Then quickly she muffled the laughter that threatened her hiding place on the stairs. Was that Niobe calling her again?

"Miss Julia! Miss Julia! Miss Julia!"

She drew the lapels of her robe taut across her chest. She had not been wasteful or excessive or squandering time peering out the window; she'd simply been testing the man with the blackest hair. She told him how her mother believed her when Julia said the pirate had climbed the trellis to her bedroom, even though she kept her bedroom window locked. She told him about the deal she'd made with her father that Gasparilla night she heard Becca scream and found him in Becca's room, moving toward her bed. Julia told him how her father had made the same move toward her, dressed in pirate garb and standing drunk in the middle of her bedroom the year Julia turned sixteen.

"No, Daddy," she'd said, when he crawled into her bed and pressed his vested chest against her back.

He squeezed her hands above her head. "You're too sweet," he said. "I just want to hug you."

"But you're hurting me, Daddy. Please."

"Please?" he said. "Is that what you tell that fresh-faced kid who walks you around the back of the house? You tell him *please*. You tell me no."

"No, Daddy, no," Julia said. "It's not like that. Please stop."

"But you're mine," he said. His fingers crept, groping beneath her nightie, caressing her bottom, and then fell like moist snakes between her legs. "Don't you know that?" he whispered to the back of her head because her face was pressed into the pillow. "Don't you know you're mine?"

She squeezed her eyes tight and saw coiling reds swirling like a ballerina's tutu. She squeezed tighter, and the skirts multiplied, turned blue, then purple, and then shot through the pinched dark like lightning, white and clear, and searingly hot. Then her father was gone.

The man with the blackest hair just leaned his head against the window ledge and listened. "So what could I do?" Julia said. "When I caught him in Becca's room?" She twisted her hands in her lap. "I told my father I would meet him. That he should put a penny under the rim of my dinner plate the nights he wanted me to come to him."

"You invited him," said the man with the blackest hair. "And then you protected him."

"I protected my daughter," Julia said.

She looked past the man seated on the floor, out the window to the bay. She had told him everything. But did the knowledge mar him? Gray his hair? Wither his face? No. And for years he slipped in and out of her room, just as she slipped up and down the back stairs to the attic, the two of them as graceful as dancers, and he, stroking his black mustache, thoughtfully saying to her, "What else? What else could you have done?"

Light from the narrow window sifted in through the half-blinds and spilled across the sixth step. It had remained beautifully golden, sleek, and intact. Just as Julia longed for and had dreamt of the lost step of her youth, she loved this pervading vision of the man with the blackest hair more than Bobby or Richard. And why? Because he knew everything, accepted everything, and sloughed it off, not callously or cruelly, but as naturally as molting skin. There was no secret that bewildered him, no crime that offended him, and no shame that ravaged him. Julia could not hurt him.

She stretched her arms above her head and felt how the heat had gathered above her, hovering thick, as tangible as smoke. She studied the last three steps that fell just beyond her, closest to her. Her children. She could not touch the seventh step from here. And this first child—the one she'd never seen or held, even after he'd cracked her pelvic bone in his determination to be born—had become no more to her than the whistle of a night bird, the howling wind, the gamy smell of the bay, or the morning's musty rise. And although she'd called him home, just as she'd called Becca and Kurt, he had diverted her and became that which she sensed existed but was invisible, unknown to her.

But the eighth step, swirled with exquisite auburn markings, was only a short reach for her hands. She bent to touch it, to run her fingers lightly over the extraordinary quality of the lineaments. Her daughter, her miracle. And Richard's. It was the one gift that came to her wholly unblemished and pure, and how could she have done anything else after that Gasparilla night she found her father, a mass of painted scars and drunk, moving toward Becca's bed?

How many times had Julia climbed these stairs, stopping on this eighth one to remind herself why—after she'd threatened to tell Richard and her mother too, if her father did not stop approaching her, catching her by the wrist, and begging her to lie with him again—why, finally she'd decided to meet him in the attic. And why she'd passed through the door at the bottom of the stairs and climbed each one, month after month, to lay her body down on the clotted mattress that was covered only with a stained ivory tablecloth.

> They say we are aged and gray, Maggie,
> As sprays by the white breakers flung;
> But to me you're as fair as you were, Dear Maggie,
> When you and I were young.

Julia smoothed her fingers over the auburn markings of the eighth stair. The day Becca had left for Georgetown, Julia had wept. But in another sense, Becca's leaving freed her. "It's over," she told the man with the blackest hair. "And it's so simple," she said. "I will not go down to dinner again." After all, she was almost fifty—she had been widowed for fourteen years and considered unbalanced by most of the town—so why should she dress for dinner and present herself every evening? "I'll take a tray in my room," she told Eula.

Sitting now on the tenth stair, she laughed, remembering the first time she found the penny under the drinking cup in her bathroom. Then, finding them night after night slipped under her bedroom door, she pictured her father lying on the mattress in the attic, waiting for the sound of her feet on the steps. She imagined how the stairs would creak and set his ears tingling, his arms aching in want of her. "You're mine," he would say to the dank, empty air. When he finally came to her bedroom months after Becca was gone and told her he only wanted to sit with her, maybe sing a tune to her, and if she didn't mind, he would like to hold her hand, she turned to the man with blackest hair, who sat leaning against the window frame, and said, "That's him. Do you see him now? Do you?"

Who thinks those innocent visits disturbed Julia? Why should they? Didn't she accomplish exactly what she'd set out to do? She had in the most meticulous manner brought up her daughter to think for herself, fight for herself, and demand her own life. And how? First, Julia thought, by not being able to save Becca from a fall down the stairs or her painful stuttering—she had learned to rescue herself. Secondly, by Julia laying down her body all those nights on the filthy mattress, covered only with the stained ivory tablecloth, she had spared Becca the razing shame, the twisted, pounding knot that gripped Julia's stomach every time Daniel told her he loved her. Yes, all that. Wasn't that something? Julia caressed the beautiful markings of the eighth step. To her, it was everything. That Becca had grown up strong and lovely and that she had fled—precisely that! Fled to college and then to New York City against her grandfather's wishes.

Wouldn't Julia love to flee also? To run off with the man with the blackest hair, just as Silva eloped with Charles Westcott? Julia gazed up at the thread of light lining the threshold at the bottom of the stairs. But she could not. Not since her Achilles tendon snapped, dancing the *pas de deux* in *Swan Lake*, and her father swept her up like a broken bird, never again to soar the stage in one sustained *grand jeté*.

But Becca had jumped. Escaped. And when she returned, she'd known instinctively it was safe to come home. Julia stood up and turned toward the attic's darkened entry.

What if Daniel did drown in the bay?

His body burned to ash.

Then what reason would there be for Becca to ever leave home again?

The sun had passed through the narrow window, leaving the stairwell dim and the edges of the steps obscured. Julia's legs burned numb, tingled with the time spent sitting with her knees drawn up, waiting for the halls to clear, for Niobe to return to the kitchen. She tried to climb the next step, but the stinging in her ankles and knees stopped her. She wondered just how insentient must one learn to feel, to feel nothing at all?

Looking down at her feet, her head grew light, woozy with the shift of blood from her brain or the heat or the knowledge that she was standing on the ninth step, the last step of her final trio. Her last child. And it stunned her now that through the years it was on this step that she had rested her feet as she sat peering down on her life. That her son, this last child, had been just beneath her—had endured her weight, even as she refused to rock him, nurse him, or hold him. Now Kurt lay upstairs in his room, bandages around his chest from the bullet wound he'd sustained trying to save his grandfather. Julia winced. What would Kurt have done if he'd known the truth? She tapped one foot on the ninth step, thinking. For this child there must be retribution and then reconciliation. Julia stood up, bolstered by the vow that she would finally gather this last child to her and protect him beneath her wing. She faced the doorway that led to the attic.

Julia gathered her robe in her right hand and gripped the rail with the other. She forced her legs to carry her up the last two steps into the attic. Blinking in that failed light, she stumbled through a pile of lampshades, a hat rack, a mildewed suitcase, and a nurse's kit. She knocked over a faded red bike and then sidestepped a rusted tackle box and slipped behind the french armoire where the double mattress lay sprawled on the floor.

"Daddy?" she said, squinting in the near dark.

The sound of the word bounced off the wood frame and hung vibrating in that aphotic space until it scattered, dissipated through the cluttered spaces and crevices of untouched mold and perfect webs. Julia whirled around, waiting for the sound to return, to gather its mastery, to claim that which had always belonged to it. But the attic rang silent. Listening close, so close to the lull, Julia heard the beat of a sousaphone, pulsing low and euphonic. The music swelled in range and depth until she also heard the trumpets, the saxophones, clarinets, trombones, french horns, and flutes, trembling with the opening measures of "Semper Fidelis." Yes, she heard the instruments clearly, as if they were playing behind the attic wall, as if they could play there—just for her.

Da da de da da dah
Dah da da de dum

Julia bent over the mattress and bundled Rebecca's diaries into the ivory tablecloth. She'd hidden them up here after Niobe had come sniffing after some books for Becca. Julia giggled. No one found them up here, clever girl! She clutched them to her chest, thinking she had other plans for them now. Without glancing back, she ran past the armoire, leapt over the fallen bicycle, and headed toward the landing of the stairwell. Once there, she shut the attic door behind her and listened for Niobe or Becca to pass in the hall below her.

When the light beneath the door at the bottom of the stairs remained steady and she heard nothing but the trio section of "Semper Fidelis," quieter now and in a different key, she stepped down the top two stairs. Then quickly, in one agile sweep, she glided over the auburn markings of the eighth step, the golden sleekness of the sixth, the cracked stair, and the knotty black hole. On the first step, she stopped and pressed her ear against the hall door. Nothing.

She imagined Becca had given up and left for the funeral without her. Julia squeezed the diaries. She could slip out the door, slide along the wall to her room, and never be seen. She gripped the doorknob just as the cymbals of the band crashed into a deafening finale. Run! Run! With her eyes pinched tight, she swung the door open and flew down the hall to her bedroom.

Behind the locked door, her room was still except for the lace curtains swelling with the breeze coming in off the bay. She dropped the diaries onto the Queen Anne chair and walked to the window. The sun had already hit the quarter mark in the sky and slipped beyond the live oak, so the bay shone clear, sparkling like a live gem. Julia gazed off toward Ballast Point, toward the yacht club where the *Sea Booty* had been returned. At least, that's what she'd heard.

A pounding on the door startled her. "Mother?" The voice was low, trembling. "Are you in there?"

Julia stepped back from the window, and moving toward the door, she tripped over the ivory tablecloth hanging down from the chair. She ripped it out from beneath the diaries and searched the room. Where could she hide this? She darted toward the closet, holding the stained damask cloth outstretched and away from her body. She flung open the closet door, crouched down to bury the rag beneath a pile of shoeboxes, but stopped. Slowly she straightened. She backed out of the closet and closed the door.

"Mother? It's Kurt." The doorknob rattled. "Answer me."

Julia pinched a corner of the tablecloth and dragged it across the floor to the stone fireplace. She held it for a while and examined its yellowed splotches, its frayed, filthy edges and swirl of designs that once covered the dining room table. Years ago the cloth had a mate, identical in color and patterns, and while one was being used on the table, the other covered the buffet. "I don't like mixing them," Rebecca said when the one disappeared. "It's not proper." So Rebecca gave the extra tablecloth to Daniel to take to the attic.

Julia wadded the cloth in a bundle and pitched it onto the soot-filled grate in the fireplace.

She grabbed the cylindrical box of wooden matches from the mantel and bent to light the ivory cloth. She lit it in five places—one for Bobby, one for Richard. She lit it for Becca, for Kurt, and for the child she'd never seen. In seconds, the cloth roared into flames, licked the sides of the fireplace, and blazed the room in light. As the ivory cloth disintegrated, foul smoke spewed from the fireplace, curled up the walls, and seeped into the room.

"Miss Julia!" Niobe's voice was shrill. "You open this door right now. Or we're gonna break it down."

Niobe and Kurt shook the bedroom door as Julia struggled to open the flue. But it stuck, welded closed. The fetid smoke, riddled with tainted mold, caught in her throat and seared her eyes. She groped away from the fireplace, around the bed and toward the window.

"Mother, it's Kurt." The pounding rattled the door. "Mother, you have to let me in. You hear? You have to let me in now."

Julia stopped at the Queen Anne chair and lifted the second volume of Rebecca's diary. She glanced back at the fire that was still raging. She could throw the diary into the flames. Throw the first volume too. "I could," she screamed. "I could burn this whole stinking place. Fry every drape, every rug, destroy every stick of furniture with one match. I could. I will." She stumbled through the room, clutching the diary, ready to fling it into the flames. She heard her name called. "Julia." The voice was close, so far from the pounding door, it startled her. She turned to see the man with the blackest hair, sitting on her bed, solemnly stroking his mustache.

"What are you doing here?" she asked.

"I live here. Remember?"

Julia's head ached, thrummed with the fumes. She blinked to see him clearer, for either smoke clouded her vision or he was fading. She could almost see through him to the pillows on the unmade bed to the breakfast tray that Niobe had not taken away. And although he grew lucent, he was beautifully kept and peaceful. She held up the diary. "I'm burning," she said.

"You don't have to."

She dropped the diary to her side and waved the smoke and floating ash away from her face. "But what else can I do?"

"Do as I do," he said, caressing his mustache.

"You! You come and go as you please. You're free. Not bound to anything or anyone."

"And who gave me that freedom?"

"I don't know," she said, squinting to see him clearer.

"You did," he said, his voice fading as quickly as his form.

"Me? Me?" She clutched at the sheets. "But where are you going?" She slumped down on the bed, on the linens flecked now with ash. "You can't leave me."

Before he disappeared altogether, he said, "No, I can never leave you. I am you."

Julia sat alone on the bed, listening for the sound of the band or the pounding on her bedroom door. *Isn't anyone ever going to play anything again?* She squeezed the diary and imagined flames devouring the pages. She could burn them, every one of them. She could. But instead she opened the cover, let her fingers flip the pages, rifle through the fallacious, half-told story of her youth. A sham. A mockery.

Did she want the truth of her life spilled over the pages of this book?

No. She had worn the queen's gown of turquoise satin, ridden the float, and waved to the crowd cheering her from the Bayshore. She had married Richard and lain next to him night after sleepless night without once desiring his touch. And when Kurt was conceived years after Richard had stopped wanting her, what haunted her the most was the child's flame-red hair and freckled skin, so like her aunt Corrine's that the sight of him was a constant reminder of how he was conceived.

But hadn't Richard known? Each time she caught him gazing at her when he thought she was sleeping or found the penny clutched in her hand on a night she was to meet Daniel in the attic. She thought now Richard had known Kurt was not his son. But she also understood then that Richard would not follow her those evenings she slipped out of bed, feigning a headache, saying she needed to walk, to ease the sting that split her head. The night his heart gave up, after the cancer in his lung had failed to kill him, Julia knew she had destroyed him as surely as if she had plunged a knife into his chest.

Julia closed the diary. There were some things she could not be held accountable for, like the snap of her Achilles tendon or the cattle truck that hit Bobby's jeep or the silver stripe that shimmered from her navel to the top of her thigh. Some things, God help her, she did because she did not know what else to do. She hugged the diary to her chest and knew she would not burn it. Wasn't it better that the story of the pirate climbing the trellis to her bedroom remained unchanged? For what did the truth matter now?

Hearing the doorknob rattle again and the chink of a blade against metal, Julia sat up straight, but she did not move from the bed. While the door quivered under an immense pressure, she felt a strange radiance, a glint, not coming from the sun outside her window but fluttering inside. It rose within her, golden and beautifully intact, and like the splendor of the sixth stair, there was no secret or crime that offended it, no shame that could ravage it. When Kurt unhinged the door and stood before her, she knew it was her son, her last child she was seeing for the first time.

CHAPTER 26 ✳ A Smoking Gun

WHEN DANIEL'S OLD CADILLAC REFUSED to start, they decided to leave
it in front of St. Andrew's, which had long since emptied out from the
funeral. Victor helped Natalie, Niobe, and Becca pile into the back seat of
the limousine. Just before he closed the door, he promised Becca he would
meet them at the house. Father Heims stood on the landing and crossed
himself. "Peace be with you!" he called out as the limousine pulled away
and took off for the Westcott Mansion.

The late-afternoon sun hovered on the horizon and cast a hazy, orange
glow over the town. The chauffeur sped down Ashley Street, crossed the
Brorein Street Bridge, and turned onto the Bayshore. A frisky breeze had
kicked up from the bay, and in spite of day's heat, the early evening was
rolling in balmy. By the time they reached the Wilson's house, Becca could
see the funeral guests spread out on the front lawn shouting and pointing
up at the smoke that spewed from her mother's bedroom window. Someone
had called the fire department.

Once the chauffeur pulled up beneath the portico, Becca leapt from
the limo and raced up the stairs to Julia's room. On the first landing she
met two firemen, dressed all in black, who assured her the flames had been
put out. One of the firefighters said the lady was burning something in
the fireplace and the flue got stuck. "Lots of smoke," he said, "but nothing
burned except this." He held up what was left of a singed tablecloth.

Becca plucked the dirty remnant from the fireman's hand. She
examined the soiled ivory damask and realized it looked identical to

the tablecloth that had come wrapped around the diaries. Her mother had probably found that too! Becca excused herself and pushed past the firemen and their bulky hose that they dragged behind them. On the second landing she overheard the men as they scuttled down the stairs. "Big party here today," one of them said.

"Actually, it's a funeral," the other one answered.

"Oh, right, Daniel Westcott's funeral. The pirate king." Becca stopped on the stairs to listen. "Nobody knows who killed him, right?" One of the firefighters tugged on the hose that slipped around Becca's legs like a giant snake. "All they found was his body floating in the bay and some stranger with a yacht full of blood."

Becca raced back down the steps and grabbed the first fireman she could reach. "Where'd you hear that?"

The startled young man pulled back. "It's all over town, ma'am. The newspaper reported the dead body, but everyone says there's a big cover-up going on. With the stranger."

Becca gasped. "That's just not true."

The second fireman cocked his head. "Well, I don't know. That bloody yacht story never hit the paper." He trudged through the foyer. "One thing for sure: something fishy's going on 'round here."

By this time, Victor and Niobe were helping Natalie in the front door. Becca met them at the bottom of the stairs and told them the fire was out. Julia was safe. Then she pulled Victor aside. In a half-whisper she asked him to call Chief Salazar. "I need to talk to him. Rumors are flying all over town. They're saying Evan murdered my grandfather."

"The chief might be here." Victor said. "My uncle said they were coming." Victor gripped Becca's arm gently. "Go see your mother, and I'll find him."

Becca turned to go back up the stairs, and this time she didn't stop. She slipped by Niobe and Natalie on the second landing and ran toward her mother's room. Heavy smoke gathered in the east hall and drifted upward like a cluster of cumulus clouds. The fumes caught Becca's throat, and she covered her mouth to keep from coughing. When she reached her mother's room, she found the bedroom door had been ripped from the hinges and had fallen across the corridor. The crash had carved a hole in the wall the size of a trap door. Becca stood on the threshold and peeked in. Amid the floating specks of soot that swirled around the room, her mother sat on the bed next to Kurt, who thumbed through the first volume of Rebecca's diaries.

"There they are!" Natalie said when she'd caught up. She peered over Becca's shoulder. Becca assumed Nattie meant the diaries, but it was equally astonishing to see her mother and Kurt sitting side by side as if something other than the door had fallen between them.

Becca stepped into the room. "What happened?"

Julia smiled up at her. "I was burning something, and the flue got stuck." Becca noticed that her mother's smile was not maddened but unusually cool and self-possessed.

Becca held up the singed tablecloth.

"Yes, that's it," Kurt said. He pulled the edge of his white T-shirt that kept riding up around the bandage that wrapped his chest. "But we didn't need the firemen. I got the door off the hinges and caught Mother before she threw the diary in too."

Becca frowned. "You could've been hurt, messing with that door."

Kurt shrugged. "Better than the house in flames."

Behind them, Niobe had wiggled the bedroom door from its hole and was sealing the gash with newspaper and packing tape. She kept muttering about the attic mice and how the gap was a perfect invitation. "They'd make themselves right at home here. Scuttling about like they owned the place."

Becca turned from Niobe and eyed her mother. "You wanted to burn the diaries?"

Julia nodded. "But I don't now. It's over."

"What's over?" Becca felt Nattie lean into her, her weight heavy against her as if she were holding Nattie up while they waited for Julia's answer.

"Everything's over," she said and grinned again.

A shiver raced down Becca's spine. *Everything* was too broad an answer for the strange expression that smeared her mother's face like a child's vanilla ice-cream cone. Becca didn't trust her. "Would you like to get dressed and greet the guests downstairs?"

Julia glanced down at her nightie as if surprised to see she hadn't bothered to dress at all today. "No, I'd like to sit here with my son," she said, tying the strings on her nightgown. "Is that all right?"

Natalie answered that it was perfectly fine. She and Becca would greet the guests—at least the ones who'd braved the fire.

Halfway down the stairs, Becca heard Victor talking to Chief Salazar and Carlos Mendoza. When they reached the foyer, Becca extended her hand to Salazar and thanked him for coming.

The chief looked distinguished in his black suit and pinstriped tie. He carried a small satchel over his left shoulder. Becca wondered if he always carried a gun. "You've had quite another day, haven't you?" Salazar said to Becca and Natalie.

"Quite," Natalie answered.

Carlos had taken his jacket off, but his dress shirt was still crisp and his necktie intact. He took Natalie's hands into his own and kissed each one tenderly. "I'm so sorry, Mrs. Westcott," he said. "You've suffered more than any lady should ever have to." Natalie visibly melted beneath the shower of Carlos's attention.

Becca seized this opportunity to ask Mr. Mendoza if he would escort Nattie through the backyard and help her welcome the guests.

"It would be my greatest honor," Carlos said and bowed elegantly. As Natalie accepted Carlos's arm, Becca promised she'd be out to join them soon. Once the couple disappeared down the back hall, Becca led Salazar and Victor into the living room.

"Please have a seat," she offered. Salazar sat across from Becca and Victor, who settled in on the loveseat. Becca squirmed, knowing she was out of her league questioning the chief about his investigation of Daniel's death.

But Salazar took the lead. "I know you're anxious about clearing up this mystery, but we can't move too quickly." He leaned in close. "Cuda has a loyal band of cohorts who will lie, cheat, steal, and kill for his release." The chief went on to say these merry bandits turn up every day at the precinct, demanding Cuda be set free. "The facts are, we've nailed him for the drugs, but we can't prove he murdered your grandfather."

"What about his cohorts?" Victor asked. "Offering them a lesser sentence if they talk."

Salazar took a deep breath. "Maybe one out of the three would give us the evidence we need to convict, but the more time passes, the less chance of that."

Becca rubbed her hands along the black jersey that covered her knees. "I just want it over," she blurted out. "Some people are blaming Evan Stone for the murder, when all he did was save my brother's life and risk his own." She pressed her hands together. "Even the firefighters said the rumor's all over town."

Salazar dipped his head, which betrayed more salt than pepper in the last few weeks. He assured Becca it was Cuda's bandits who were fueling the rumors. "They would love to pin Daniel's death on Evan." Anyone to take the spotlight off Cuda, he added. The chief passed a weary hand through his hair. "The fact that Daniel's dead and Cuda's been caught and precious few know how it happened is a formula for turmoil." He leaned forward in his chair and confided his biggest concern—that Cuda would be tried for smuggling but would get away with Daniel's murder.

"So Cuda killed Daniel?" Becca asked.

"Not necessarily Cuda himself." Salazar said Cuda had confessed to giving Daniel a nominal fee when the pirate king offered to lend him the *Sea Booty* for the drug run.

Becca squirmed on the loveseat. She thought about the two thousand dollars Nattie had found in her underwear drawer. "So, my granddad was party to the drug run?"

Salazar nodded. "To some degree. But most likely he had a bigger stake in the deal than just offering the *Sea Booty*. He probably had an investment that Cuda or his investors wanted to control, and therefore they had Daniel murdered." Salazar leaned back in his chair. "Dead men don't lie, they don't squeal, and they don't collect money. Daniel's death is a win-win for Cuda and his gang."

Becca felt her heart sink. She knew Daniel's involvement with the smugglers would destroy her grandmother and tarnish the Westcott name forever. "So this needs to come out?" Her cheeks burned even asking the question.

"Not necessarily," Salazar said. "Remember, this is all speculation. We have no proof of anything except Cuda's confession that he paid Daniel to use the *Sea Booty*."

"But he'll still go to jail, right?" Becca asked.

"Unless he's convicted of Daniel's murder, it'll be a slap on the hand for Cuda. He'll be out in a matter of months."

Becca gazed up at Victor. "So now what?"

Salazar pulled the satchel off his shoulder. "I didn't want to bring this up today, but Victor told me you were anxious to clear Evan once and for all."

Becca clutched her knees and leaned over the coffee table. "I am," she said.

"Good." The chief opened the satchel and pulled out a gun sealed in a plastic bag. "This is the revolver that was found on the Bertram, the one Cuda's bandits are blaming for Daniel's death."

Victor told Becca it was the revolver Kurt pulled on them the night off Egmont Key. "They think it's from Daniel's collection."

"There are three sets of prints on it," Salazar said. "Kurt's, the Spider guy's, and one unknown set."

"Daniel's," Becca said.

The chief shook his head. "We checked. Your grandfather was fingerprinted the night of your debutante ball. No match there."

"So someone else had the gun that night?" Becca asked. "Evan?"

"Unfortunately, there's a print from Evan's left hand on the barrel," Salazar said. "Considering he's right handed, normally we could rule it out. But in this case Cuda's bandits would demand a trial." The chief opened the plastic bag and skillfully removed the revolver with his handkerchief. "There's another set of prints that appear to be under Kurt's and Spider's, which means someone had this gun before the stakeout." Salazar rotated the revolver in his hand. "*We* know Daniel wasn't killed that night on Poppy's boat. But he could've been shot before, and that theory lines up with the disintegration of his body. The time spent in the water."

Becca jumped up. "And it was Kurt's blood all over the boat, not Daniel's!"

Salazar groaned. "Right. And the Spider's. But I ordered the boat to be cleaned, thinking it was the best move at the time." He ran his hand over his mouth. "We've scoured every inch of that yacht for a trace of their blood, but the detailer didn't leave a speck."

Becca sat back in the loveseat. "Now what?"

Salazar turned the revolver in his hand, examining it. "I want to talk to Kurt. Find out where he got the gun."

With that Becca leapt up and headed toward the staircase to find her brother. On the first landing, she heard Niobe marching down the back hall. Becca stopped and turned around. "How's Nattie doing?"

Niobe set her hands on her hips. "Mr. Carlos is parading her 'round like some prize filly, and she's lappin' it up."

Becca smiled. "How's the food holding out?"

"Oowee! We have ourselves some leftovers," Niobe said, pressing her palms together. "People are fixing to leave now. Guess they're full up."

By the time Becca found Kurt and convinced him to come downstairs, Victor was on his feet, pacing the living room. Chief Salazar got up to greet the boy, but Kurt kept his eyes peeled on the rug. "Tiger's real broken up he shot you," the chief said.

Kurt kept his eyes down and rocked back and forth on his bare feet. "It was my fault," he said. "My fault Spider's dead."

Victor stopped pacing. All three of them stared at the boy in his pajama bottoms and white T-shirt stretched taut over his bandaged chest. Although he appeared the same with his red hair hanging down in strings, something in him had shifted. Becca blinked a few times. Not once had she heard her brother apologize for anything.

Salazar picked up on the change immediately and seized his chance. "We really need your help," he said. He held up the revolver. "Was this the gun you had the night you were shot?"

Kurt nodded. A visible shiver ran through his body.

"Where'd you get it?"

An eerie silence fell across the room. The air conditioner clicked on and spewed stale smoke through the vents. "I found it in my room," Kurt said.

Becca frowned and grabbed her brother's arm. "This isn't a joke. Tell the truth," she demanded.

"But I did," Kurt insisted. "It was sitting on top of my dresser the day of the search." He gazed up at Salazar, his eyes clear. "That's when I got the idea to hide on the boat." He hung his head. "I didn't wanna be left behind."

Becca glanced at Salazar, who then looked at Victor and shrugged. It sounded like Kurt was telling the truth.

Just then Carlos and Natalie came through the front door. Nattie was waving wearily to the last guests, who had followed her up the stairs. She closed the door as graciously as she could and leaned against it to catch her breath. Carlos said he would make her some tea. He took her arm, but they stopped in the foyer when they saw the group that had gathered in the living room. Natalie rushed up to Becca. "You never came out," she said accusingly.

Becca sucked in her breath. But Salazar came to the rescue. "I'm to blame," he said. "I needed some information from your grandson. About his gun." The chief held up the revolver.

Natalie edged in to get a closer look. "That's the gun? The one that shot him?"

"No," Salazar answered. "The one that possibly shot Daniel."

Natalie stared at the revolver and then started to swoon. "It can't be," she said, holding her head. Carlos tried to steady her, but it was too late. Nattie passed out in his arms.

Victor and Chief Salazar lifted her to the couch and laid her down while Becca fanned her grandmother with a magazine. "It's all been too much for her," she said. Victor took her pulse and said it was strong, but they called the doctor anyway.

The gibbous moon hung midnight high by the time Becca and Victor made it to the backyard to put up the leftovers. A steady breeze blew in blustery from the bay, and the night air felt almost cool against Becca's skin. After the doctor arrived and gave Nattie a sedative, Victor carried her up the stairs, and Niobe put her to bed. Becca and Kurt thanked Chief Salazar for coming, and he promised Evan would be cleared as soon as possible. When the chief left with Carlos, he told them to get a good night's sleep. There wasn't any more to be done tonight, he'd said.

Becca wrapped leftover slices of ham in plastic while Victor emptied ice from the coolers. The white lights that had been strung from the live oaks still twinkled in the trees like a colony of lightning bugs. Becca had sent Niobe and Eula off to bed in the small guest room beyond the kitchen. It was too late to drive home, and clearly they were both exhausted, especially Eula, who'd spent the entire evening on her feet, serving punch to the guests.

When Victor finished with the coolers, he strode up behind Becca and wrapped his arms around her. He pressed his lips against her hair. "It'll all work out," he whispered. Then he spun her around and kissed her. Becca could have stood that way forever, captivated by the heat of Victor's body melting into hers, the sweet warmth of his tongue, and his arm pressed against the small of her back, cradling her as if nothing could hurt her again.

When the kiss ended, Becca took Victor's hand and led him to the white folding chairs that they'd set up yesterday. She asked him to sit down and then pulled up a chair to face him. She didn't know how to ease into what she had to say, so she just told him. "I'm pregnant."

He sat looking at her for a long time, as if the words she said couldn't possibly be true. Then he dropped his gaze and pressed his hands into his knees. "Adam?" he asked.

Becca nodded. There, her secret was out. She gazed down at the muted-post horn that was partially covered by her watch. Relief flooded her. She thought it strange how she'd been able to tell Victor about the baby, when she could never tell Adam.

Victor squeezed her hand and then stood up slowly like his bones hurt. He gazed into the night sky as if searching the stars for answers. "I'm sorry," he said finally. He grabbed his jacket from a chair back, flung it over his shoulder, and walked away. He didn't bother to go through the kitchen and out the front door. He just disappeared around the side of the house.

Becca leaned back. She listened for the sound of his car as it revved in the driveway. She imagined the Camaro backing out and heading down the Bayshore. She didn't expect anything else. But still, it surprised her when the tears came, filled her eyes, and spilled down her face, into the crevice between her breasts. She sat like that for a long time, until she felt something sticky clinging to her chest. She reached inside her dress and pulled out the note the girl had slipped her in the receiving line at church. Wrinkled and wet, the note was barely legible. She held it up to one the flood lights under the live oak to decipher the smudged handwriting. *Come see me*, it said. *1510 Powhatan.*

CHAPTER 27 ✵ Flower Boxes

Eᴍᴍᴇʟɪɴᴇ ᴀᴡᴀᴋᴇɴᴇᴅ ᴛᴏ ᴛʜᴇ ᴘʟᴜɴᴋ-ᴘʟᴜɴᴋ of a bare foot thrumming the splintered slats of the porch. She blinked. From where she sat on the old rocker with the legs sanded flat, she could see the crown of the waxing moon poking up above the wild cactus. The streetlight pulsed brightly, then wavered and shot bold shadows that faded quickly across the lawn, and then swelled black again as if breathing the night. She looked to the swing, to her granddaughter sprawled across the paint-chipped boards. One leg was drawn up under the gauzy dress, while the other hung down on the porch. From the daze on her granddaughter's face and the way her bare foot tapped insistently, Emmeline knew Morgan had grown impatient watching the moon cross the sky and listening to the snarled moans of an old woman's sleep.

"It's near daybreak," Morgan said, pushing the porch with her foot to set the swing moving.

Emmeline strained against the arms of the rocker to sit up in the chair. Her calves felt numb, as if the blood had pooled there, snagged thick with clots. She kneaded the tops of her thighs to urge the old veins to pump life back into her lower legs. The sky had not visibly begun to lighten, but the stars had vanished, and the moon had shed its earlier luster.

Morgan sat up in the swing. "Do you think Becca will come?"

Emmeline gripped the arms of the rocker. Her head whirled with the question that Morgan had squandered the night waiting to ask. All the other questions, *Does Julia know?* or *Was the rescue of the Indian child a gift to Silva and not a debt to be repaid?* were only preparatory, leading up to the one question that had repelled sleep and spurred her granddaughter's eyes to grow glittery and round like a crazed cat's.

"There's still time," Emmeline said, feeling the words thick on her tongue. For she believed, having received the diaries, that in time, Becca would seek out the Indian family who took in Julia's child born out of wedlock. "She will come."

Morgan jumped up from the swing and flitted across the porch to the railing that overlooked the cactus. She clasped her hands behind her back, where Emmeline saw the nubby fingers clenched as if to keep them from flying up, splayed against the air. "She'll know then," Morgan said and stared out over the weeded lawn.

Emmeline pressed her elbows into the arms of the rocker. She struggled to bear the weight beneath her, but she couldn't move. In the time she'd dozed off, her legs must have hardened, melded to the porch like the wooden flowerboxes Nilo had built on either side of the stairs. And Morgan, who'd been stretched out for hours in the rusted swing, had leapt, catlike across the porch and fretted that Becca knew about the baby—Julia's baby, who was brought to this house thirty-six years ago. "If she's read the diaries, she knows," Emmeline said.

Morgan turned, her face as bright as a neon sign flashing with the streetlight. "She knows about the baby," she said. "About the pirate and how Rebecca brought the baby here to you. But she doesn't know he's Evan Stone."

Emmeline crossed the ends of her afghan over her chest. Morgan's pinched face puzzled her more than her hardened feet that refused to move. "So?" Emmeline said.

Morgan flung her head back, letting her hair fall in thin streams across her shoulders. Then she pushed off the railing as if to gain momentum. She began a slow, measured pace across the porch. "So what if Becca doesn't want to know?" Morgan said, her hands rising like the panic in her voice. "I mean, what if there's some reason that she should never know?"

Emmeline leaned forward in the rocker, stunned, not so much with her granddaughter's pacing or her trembling hands as she gripped the sides of her dress, but rather that Morgan knew something and had for some time hidden it. "Never know?" Emmeline asked. Then she pondered that there was some element in the Westcott blood that lured them, captivated them, and then bound them to keeping secrets. For Morgan had never once, from the time she was a young girl, thought to tell Evan of his natural birth. She had accepted his fate as dictated by Rebecca and the diaries as if it were decreed from God, while Emmeline would lie awake night after night wondering if Julia ever missed the child who was taken from her.

"What if there's a reason," Morgan said, moving across the porch, "that Becca should not know?" She turned to Emmeline. "Then what?"

"What reason?" Emmeline asked. When Morgan dropped her head, Emmeline could only imagine that Morgan worried the burden would be too much for Becca to bear, and she feared one day that Becca would tell Evan. Emmeline glanced down at her feet bound in leather sandals. She clasped her hand to her mouth when she saw the black toes, the purple striations scaling her ankles. She pulled up her burgundy skirt, only to find that her shins and calves had turned blackish-blue.

"What if," Morgan said, "Becca's in love with him?"

Emmeline let the skirt fall around her ankles, and just as she was grateful the she'd sawed off the rounded legs of her chair and ceased the rocking, an odd calm welled within her that her feet were now riveted to the porch as securely as Nilo's flowerboxes. She opened her mouth to speak, to tell Morgan the notion was unthinkable, impossible, but her tongue had thickened into a solid mass against her teeth.

Morgan stopped, glared at Emmeline. "She could be," she said. And when Morgan began again to pace, a flurry of words spilled from her lips and spun across the porch, so Emmeline had to strain to pick up snippets of a bus ride, a downtown church, Becca, and Evan, and a closed casket draped with flowers. As Emmeline leaned forward to grasp the story, Morgan slowed her trek across the porch and eased the words.

"I hid," she said, "behind some chairs. And when Becca was in the receiving line, I saw her hug Evan." Morgan peered at Emmeline and shook her head. "I know the difference," she said. "It wasn't a friendly hug or a brotherly gesture." Morgan kicked a crack in the splintered porch. "You know what I mean. She loves him!"

Despite the heaviness in her legs that crept over her knees and into her thighs, Emmeline felt the sides of her mouth twitch into a smile. She knew Morgan's ideas of love between lovers sprung first from fairytales and then from the literary heroes—Heathcliff, Mr. Darcy, Rochester. Emmeline fought the smile that threatened to break into laughter that Morgan had conjured a dark love between the unnatural siblings.

"It isn't a joke," Morgan said. "I saw them. And now I'm wondering if it isn't best Becca never knows."

Emmeline gripped the arms of the rocker. It was the blood! Bound to secrecy! All those Westcotts have hidden lust, and pirates, and babies and mothers, and then wrote it all down. Then they hid the diaries! Now another masquerade was about to take place. Wasn't there anyone who could stop this? Emmeline shook her head, grateful that her tongue had swollen and jelled in her mouth, for what did she know? A woman who took in a child and lost her husband in return. For had she not accepted the money, would Nilo have swerved off the road and been spared his life? Or was the blood money a blessing and not a curse in the end, because it saved her and the five children she needed to feed? Who was she to know, but an old woman whose legs had turned into a flowerbox.

"So maybe she won't come," Morgan said.

Emmeline shrugged as carefree as the bird's first whistle, for the new day had rendered her not only immovable but speechless.

"You think she won't come, Gramma?" When Emmeline's hand slipped from her lap, Morgan said louder, "Gramma?"

Emmeline felt the flutter of her granddaughter's dress against her arm, felt her hands lift her old fingers. Morgan leaned close to Emmeline's face. "You look so … so strange. Are you all right?" Emmeline squeezed her granddaughter's hand.

Morgan whispered, "She will come." Then Morgan told her about the note she'd slipped Becca in the receiving line, the three words, *Come see me*, and the address. "And when she comes," Morgan said, "she'll know that Evan is the baby from the diary. Julia's baby."

Emmeline felt her other hand slide off her lap. She struggled to wedge her tongue between her teeth. *What if Becca already knew?* she wanted to say. *What if she showed the diaries to Evan and they both knew?* A low, guttural moan escaped Emmeline's chest, and she understood just as her hands had fallen from her lap like the petals of a withered flower, and her grandfather, Samuel Westcott, promised her life would be a special gift to someone because she was born on the day Silva Westcott died, Emmeline knew she'd made the necessary choices. She'd said all the words she needed to say.

"Gramma? Gramma?" Morgan said, tapping Emmeline's hand.

The sun rose in the east, splashing light over the weeded lawn that glistened with dew. The wild cactus, with its mesh of needled arms, appeared vibrant in the new light, cloyingly green and hardy in spite of the drought. Emmeline squinted, and her heart quickened with the shape of a young woman dressed in blue, walking up the graveled driveway. Emmeline blinked to get her granddaughter's attention. *Look! Look!*

But Morgan was bent over Emmeline, touching her face, her lips, and tugging her hand. "Gramma," she cried. "Gramma!"

CHAPTER 28 ✳ Under a Spell

Becca sat up in the twin bed facing the window that overlooked the giant bird feeder in the backyard. She was in Kurt's room. Outside a blue jay lunged at the jenny wrens, chasing them from the feeder. First Becca noticed the clock on the bedside table; then she studied Kurt, who was still sleeping, his face buried so deeply in the pillow that his hair sprang from it like some wild and luxuriant foliage.

Becca threw back the sheets and grabbed her robe from the end of the bed. She swung the cotton kimono around her shoulders and accidentally knocked over a water glass that fell to the floor. Kurt didn't budge; he lay sprawled out, half covered with a summer quilt. The old mahogany clock rattled, and Becca squinted to see the little hand pointing to the ten. She tiptoed across the oak floor, inched the door open, and slipped out.

In the hall, the air was still thick and tinged with smoke. She stepped down the west corridor past Natalie's room and then the library. When she rounded the corner to the east hall, she peeked in the bathroom and noticed the fresh towels hanging untouched.

Was everyone still sleeping?

Becca headed to her mother's bedroom. She didn't open the door or touch the glass knob that dangled like a head fallen from a broken neck. Instead she ran her fingers along the hinges that had been stripped of bolts and ripped apart. Then she pressed her ear against the bedroom door and listened.

Instinctively she covered her other ear to drown out the buzz of the air conditioner and the musty, smoke-tinged air that hovered around her. In the emptiness of the hall, she imagined how a deafening fatigue had claimed the house and everyone in it. Becca shook her head. Had it claimed her too? All she could hear with her ear pressed against the door was the tick-tick of the old mahogany clock, rattling as it did all night on the bedside table in Kurt's room. She stepped back and realized the door had been rehung, the hinges realigned and bolted. The hall took on the semblance of order except for the drooping glass knob that appeared innocent in the morning light.

Becca stepped lightly down the hall toward her own bedroom. The door was slightly ajar, so she peeked in at the girl who lay stretched out on her back beneath the canopy. Her silvery hair splayed across the pillow, and her skin looked as papery as a white onion's. The morning sun gleamed through the lace curtains and cast an odd shimmer across the girl's face. How could she still be sleeping? Becca blinked to clear the image of the girl on the front porch tugging on the old woman's arm that dangled over the side of a stunted rocker like the glass knob on her mother's bedroom door. "She's here," the girl had said, looking at Becca. Then she went on tapping the woman's face. "Wake up, Gramma. Wake up!"

Becca stood outside the bedroom door and watched Morgan sleep. When Becca had found the house on the corner of Seminole and Powhatan, she'd asked the cabbie to wait for her. As she climbed the steps to the bungalow, Becca had the eeriest feeling that she'd been there before. Once Morgan recognized her, she dropped her grandmother's arm and stood staring at Becca. "Did you get them?" she asked finally. The intensity of her voice startled Becca.

"Get what?"

"The diaries," Morgan said.

"You?"

"And my Gramma."

"But how'd *you* get them?" Becca asked.

Frantically Morgan turned away and clasped the woman's arm again. "She's here, Gramma. Wake up!" The girl's voice grew low and monotone. Becca slipped past the stunted rocker and headed toward the house to call for help.

When she opened the screen door, Becca was met with a familiar stench that she recognized at once and had touched. She knew the scent of this house, set as it was in too hot a climate, too humid and susceptible to the untold number of molds that had been infused within the bound navy leather and had spread to the pages of the diaries. Then it hit her. This bungalow, the old woman, and the girl were exactly what she'd envisioned when she'd read the diaries. Now Becca moved as if in a dream into the front room that was strewn with hand-woven rugs, chairs with embroidered seat covers, and a myriad of colored-glass candy dishes on small decorative tables. She spotted the phone.

After Becca called the police, she scanned the white plaster walls that were scattered with photographs of babies in bright yarn caps, a boy in overalls hugging a dog, a dark-haired girl in a powder-blue tutu, the same girl in an Easter dress, a young man in a mortar board and tassel, another man in a black tux with his bride—and there she stopped. In the corner of the adjacent wall, almost within reach, she spotted a picture of a Seminole Indian who had iron-gray braids that fell over his shoulders. He wore a red kerchief tied around his neck like a bow tie. Becca leaned in closer to decipher the elegant handwriting on the bottom of the photograph. It read: To Emma, from her loving Poppa, Samuel Westcott. Westcott! She plucked the picture from the wall, flipped it over to find a date, another signature, or a note, but it was blank, covered only with brown paper. Returning the portrait to its place on the wall, Becca realized that the diaries had been given to this Indian family, the same one that had been entrusted to raise Julia's child.

She glanced at the front door and heard the sirens winding closer. Then she turned back to scrutinize the children's photos. In search of a boy, Becca skipped over the ballerinas, the girls in their Easter dresses, and settled on the young graduate in his cap and gown. She studied his deep-set eyes, full lips, the sandy-colored hair curling from beneath his cap. She knew him! No sooner had she reached for the photo than the girl from the porch barged through the front door. "What're you doing?"

Becca stood staring mutely at the girl. Before she could answer, the paramedics bounded up the stairs of the bungalow and pounded on the door. The girl raced outside while one of the medics took the old woman's pulse. He shook his head. "She's gone," he said.

When the paramedics strapped the woman's bluish body to the stretcher and carried it across the lawn to the ambulance, the girl in the gauzy dress never released her grandmother's arm or stopped looking at Becca. Only after they slid the body into the ambulance did the girl let go and allow them to shut the doors.

"You want to ride with us?" a paramedic asked her. As soon as the words spilled from the man's mouth, the girl fixed her eyes on Becca as if she were a vision, a trick of her imagination that could vaporize at once. "No," Morgan said. "I'll stay with her."

Becca leaned against the door jamb, watching the girl sleep, when a touch on her shoulder startled her. She whirled around to see her mother.

Still in her nightie, Julia peeked through the half-opened door and gazed at the girl, lying propped on the pillows. "Who is she?" her mother asked.

"Evan's niece," Becca whispered.

"She's beautiful."

Curiously, the girl did look lovely against the rose satin sheets. Her skin, although still pale, no longer appeared withered or dry, and her hair had taken on a lustrous sheen, less silvery and more golden in the sunlight that streaked through the room.

"What's she doing here?" Julia asked, her eyes wide and oddly alive.

Becca took her mother's arm. As she led Julia back to her room, Becca told her how the girl's grandmother had died suddenly on the porch. "She came home with me," Becca said, "because we couldn't find Evan."

"But where are her parents?" Julia asked. She asked the question sanely, as if she'd always asked explicit, coherent questions.

"Dead. An automobile accident when she was an infant."

"How sad."

Becca agreed how tragic it was to lose one's parents. "At any age," she said. Then she told her mother how she'd driven the girl home in the grandmother's rusted Chevrolet. "Once she was in the car, she fell instantly to sleep," Becca said. "Been sleeping ever since."

"Exhausted," Julia said.

"Yes, that's it." For an instant, the humming in Becca's head stopped. Her thoughts raced clear, ordering themselves like trained soldiers.

And why? Because she was lying. About the sleep? No. But the fact that Morgan had not fallen asleep immediately. Becca had fired one question after another at her before she fell into the deathlike slumber. Was Samuel Westcott your great-grandfather? *No, my great-great-grandfather.* Did you see the diaries? *Oh, yes.* Did you read them? *Yes.* Did you know about the baby, who certainly wasn't a baby by the time you were born? *Of course.* What's his name? And here the girl with the papery skin said she was too tired. Too tired to think, to move her lips again. "What's your name?" Becca blurted out as she sped down the Bayshore toward the Westcott Mansion.

"Morgan," the girl said.

Becca had pulled off the side of the road. She shook the girl's bony shoulders, which had slumped onto the armrest. "Morgan, tell me. Was the baby's name Evan?" Becca shook the girl again. "Evan Stone?" she asked. "Was it Evan?" But she'd collapsed, plunged into the crushing slumber. Becca stared at Morgan's face, still tense in sleep. A slight shiver passed through the girl's body, and Becca felt it resonate through her hands. There was something strange about the girl, something fragile and forbidden. For a moment Becca thought she had some sort of disorder, perhaps a mental instability. But then she realized the girl had just experienced her grandmother's death. She could be in shock. Becca released her shoulders and eased her gently onto the passenger seat. She knew she would have to be careful with Morgan, watchful as she passed the next few hours. Little did Becca know then that it would be late the next morning, almost twenty-four hours after she and Niobe had carried the girl from the car, up the stairs, and settled her into Becca's bed.

Standing outside her mother's bedroom, still holding Julia's arm, Becca wondered if it was the sleep she resented. No, not in the sense that the girl truly needed the rest, just as Julia needed it and Kurt too. Instead it was the knowledge that something had ended for them, something as tangible as her mother's clear questions this morning, Morgan's strange emerging beauty, or the bliss that had Kurt flung out like a starfish on his bed. Becca smoothed the bathrobe over her bulging tummy. Nothing had ended for her yet except the fragile, budding romance with Victor that she'd squashed two nights ago.

Becca fidgeted with the glass knob on Julia's door. She was waiting for the girl to wake up, just as she'd waited yesterday afternoon, through the evening and into this morning. Somehow she didn't trust Morgan's evasiveness any more than she trusted this eerie peace that had settled on the house like a yellow blanket of oak pollen. Becca was about to guide her mother into the room when she heard a floorboard creak beneath her bare feet. In one quick glance, she spotted a shimmery blonde head peeking out from behind her bedroom door. "Morgan?" she called.

The girl stepped into the hall. Her head was bent, and she moved awkwardly, tugging on the nightgown that kept sliding off her shoulders. An ivory damask tablecloth was flung over her left arm.

"This is my mother," Becca said when she joined them.

"Yes, Miss Julia." Morgan offered her hand.

But Julia's eyes slipped from Morgan's face to the tablecloth that draped the girl's arm.

"Is this yours?" Julia asked, pointing to the cloth.

Morgan looked quizzically at Becca. The tablecloth was identical to the one that Julia had burned in her fireplace yesterday. Could there be two? Becca had assumed the ivory damask belonged to Emmeline, but perhaps it was Rebecca who had wrapped the diaries in the tablecloth and brought them to the house on Powhatan. Becca felt her knees pitch. She didn't want to do anything to upset her mother. But Morgan clung to the tablecloth like a beloved blanket. "Yes, it's hers," Becca said. "A keepsake from her grandmother."

"May I?" Julia asked. Reluctantly Morgan handed the ivory damask to Julia. She held it up, unfolded it once, then twice, and then smoothed her hand over the design. Her green eyes grew round and glittery. As she raised the cloth to touch her face, a stench of mold rose in the hall. Becca's head began to swoon. Surely her mother would know, having touched and read the diaries, that the odor spewing from the tablecloth was identical to the one suffused within the yellowed pages of the journals. But Julia seemed oblivious to the connection. "It's so clean," she said, her eyes flashing at Morgan. "Totally spotless." She handed the tablecloth back to Morgan. "It's a lovely gift."

After Becca settled her mother into the Queen Anne's chair, she led Morgan down the hall, past the sunlit bath. When she reached her bedroom, she asked Morgan to sit on the bed. Becca pulled up the vanity stool and faced her. Then she asked the girl in slow, measured words if the child Rebecca and Daniel brought to the house on Powhatan and Seminole was, in fact, Evan Stone.

Morgan leaned her head against the bedpost. "He is," she said. "But you can't tell him." Becca watched as Morgan wound the end of the tablecloth around her fingers until they turned blue. *A blackish-blue like the sky outside the window,* Becca thought. A muggy breeze hit the lace curtains and sent them swelling into the room.

Becca folded her hands carefully in her lap. She eyed Morgan, looking for signs of imbalance. She worried the slightest misstep could frighten her, clam her up, or even worse, send her running from the house. "Maybe Evan already knows," Becca offered. "He grew up with the diaries too."

Morgan sat straight up on the bed. "Oh no, he was away at school when Rebecca and Daniel brought the diaries to my gramma." She tucked her knees beneath her bottom and leaned back on her heels. "*I* grew up with the diaries," she said. "Evan doesn't know they exist."

Becca watched as Morgan unwound the ivory cloth. She shook her hand to rush the blood to her fingers. "But why don't you want Evan to know?" Becca asked.

"Why should he know?" Morgan's eyes narrowed into slits. "That he's the product of some pirate who climbed the trellis to your mother's bedroom window? And that my gramma, who he thought bore him, and loved him all these years, was actually paid to raise him? Does he need to know that too?" The girl's cheeks flushed. She jumped from the bed and clasped Becca's wrist with her cold fingers. "Isn't it enough that you know Evan's your brother?"

Becca felt the girl's grasp tighten on her arm. She leaned in close. Becca breathed in the musky scent of Morgan's skin, ripe with sweat. For a moment Becca was stunned how this feisty teenager could be the same girl who'd collapsed in the car and lay prostrate for almost twenty-four hours with nothing except a bit of water Niobe managed to ease between her lips. Becca wiggled out of her grip and stood up. "What if it were you?" she asked and crossed her arms akimbo. "Wouldn't you want to know the truth?"

Morgan clutched the ivory tablecloth protectively to her chest. She stood rigid. "No, I wouldn't."

Becca walked to the closet and picked out a sundress. She gathered some underclothes from her dresser and grabbed her hairbrush. Then she turned to Morgan. "There are fresh towels in the bathroom," she said. "And Niobe will bring up your dress. She's washed and pressed it for you." Becca headed toward the door. "When you've dressed, come downstairs for breakfast."

Morgan stopped her in the doorway. "You won't tell him," she ordered Becca, expecting her to comply.

"Not now," Becca said.

Once in the hall, Becca headed for Rebecca's room to dress. She'd just passed the library when she heard the opening measures of "Fur Elise" waft through the house. She dropped the clothes and headed toward the staircase. Halfway there she spotted Natalie, still in her nightgown, scurrying out of her own room. "It's Daniel," Nattie said, her hair falling loose around her shoulders.

"Not Daniel," Becca said and scowled. "It's Mother." For an instant they stood staring at one another. Then they rushed down the west wing of the house toward the staircase. When they reached the landing, the haunting tempo moved with such a simple elegance, the music surprised Becca. It wasn't Julia. Together they slipped quietly down the steps. Once on the lower landing, they bent to catch a glimpse of the pianist. Natalie gripped Becca's arm. "It's him," she whispered.

Becca turned to her grandmother. "Let me," she said. "Go back upstairs. And promise me you'll keep Morgan up there too."

Natalie turned to go up the stairs, her fingers covering her mouth. "How am I supposed to do that?"

"Get the diaries," Becca said. "Have her read them to you."

Becca stopped at the entrance of the living room. She watched Evan at the piano, his back to her and his head bent in concentration. His sandy hair curled down the back of his neck. As his left hand took flight in the rolling arpeggio, the music spun through the house. Evan's shoulders rolled with emotion—for what? The music? Becca leaned against the archway and pulled her bathrobe tightly around her. Perhaps he was playing out grief over his mother's death. She blinked a few times, struggling to come to grips with the fact that Evan was her half-brother. Julia was his real mother. For a moment, Becca wished the song wouldn't end, that she could go on standing there while Evan played Beethoven's love song more expressively than Daniel, more beautifully than Julia. But then the room went silent.

Evan swiveled on the piano bench. He gazed up at the portraits of Charles and Silva Westcott, Rebecca, Nathan, and Daniel. By the shock on his face, Becca realized he knew this house, this family was his birthright. But how?

Evan caught her staring at him, and instantly the room and its familiarity melted into nothingness around her. Becca noted the day-old growth of whiskers shadowing Evan's chin. His eyes were swollen, red-rimmed along the edges, and his face appeared drawn and pale. "Niobe let me in, and I just gravitated to your beautiful piano," he apologized.

"Lucky for us," Becca said and squeezed his hand. "I'm sorry about your mother."

Evan gazed down at the floor for a long time. Then he studied Becca. "The paramedics told me at the hospital that Morgan came home with you." He searched her eyes. "Is she terribly upset?"

Becca thought about the girl's fierce eyes, how she'd clung to the tablecloth. "Yes, I think so."

"My mother …" Evan stopped for a moment. "She was all Morgan ever had." And Becca understood that Emmeline was all he ever had too. Not only had she been his mother and father, but she was the one who'd held him, fed him, and loved him when his real family had not.

Becca gazed down at her hands and told him again how sorry she was. But her words passed over him. He stared past her to the portraits on the wall as if trying to draw answers from their silence.

"Listen," he said, "I'm going away for a few days." He ran his hand over the stubble on his face. "I can't take Morgan with me." Then he told Becca how he'd been getting anonymous threats over the phone at work. "I found a dead cat hanging from the oak tree in my front yard."

Becca's hand flew to cover her mouth. "The pirates?"

Evan shrugged. "It's the youngsters. Not Poppy or Jack Myers." He crossed his arms over his chest. "I'm an easy target for them."

Becca tapped her foot on the rug. "Buddy?" When Evan nodded, Becca told him Chief Salazar was working on it. "You'll be cleared soon," she said.

Evan shook his head wearily. "I'm not worried," he said. "It'll blow over in time." Then his eyes locked on Becca. "But there is something you need to know." The smoky air from the upstairs hall whirled through the vents, spewing yesterday's memory throughout the house. Becca braced herself. Evan leaned in close, and in a barely audible voice, he said, "I know all about the diaries. And exactly what's in them."

Becca stepped back while the room swirled around her. She listened as Evan confessed how he'd found them tucked beneath Emmeline's rocking chair when Morgan was just a child. "They never knew I'd read them, and I never let on." He pressed the tips of his fingers together. "But the diaries confirmed everything. I knew I was different from the beginning." He explained that while his brothers loved to fish, they had little interest in books or music or art. "I was either buried in a book, a drawing, or banging on our neighbor's piano. I just didn't fit in."

Becca smiled. Evan's rendition of "Fur Elise" was better than anything she'd ever played. She thought his delivery was greater than Julia's; maybe even better than Daniel's. "So you're my half-brother," she said.

Evan gazed out the living room window to the live oak, lush with summer rain. The leaves quivered in the wind. "Apparently so."

Becca took his hand into her own and squeezed it. "Welcome home," she said.

Evan turned around to study the family portraits decorating the walls. "I need some time to settle."

Becca nodded. She understood the adjustment would take a while. "Take as long as you want. We'll keep Morgan here."

Evan let out a chuckle. "She belongs here."

Becca started to walk Evan to the front door. "What about Emmeline's funeral?"

"Tell Morgan I'll be there." Then he turned to Becca.

She held up her hand. "I know," she said. "You don't want me to tell her anything else."

Evan smiled. "Right, that should come from me."

In the foyer, Becca gripped the banister to go up the stairs. Her legs felt numb, heavy as she began the long trek. On the first landing, she heard Nattie humming an old Irish tune she used to sing to Daniel. When Becca rounded the curve, she saw Niobe guiding her grandmother, watching every step she took. "It's time to fix the elevator," Natalie said. "These stairs are treacherous."

Becca waited for them to catch up to her. "I'll call someone today."

"Nonsense," Nattie said. "It's the stairs I can't handle, not a phone call." Her eyes sparked, and she flounced her full skirt with the pertness of a young girl. Her hair was pinned back in an elegant twist, and makeup smoothed her face with such artistry that her complexion shone radiant in the muted light that spilled through the two-story windows. "Besides, Eula can't take the stairs anymore either."

"Where is Eula?" Becca asked.

"Still sleeping," Niobe said. "Downstairs buried like an old turnip."

"But it's almost noon!" Suddenly Becca realized she alone had spent the night tossing and fretful, while the rest of the house had fallen under a spell—a healing, blessed spell that excluded her and left her vigilant.

"What about our young guest?" Becca asked.

"I brought up her dress," Niobe said. "She's in the bathroom getting washed up now." Niobe cocked her head and nodded up the staircase without taking her eyes off Nattie. "I found your clothes in the hall and put them in Rebecca's room. I reckon you'll want to get dressed."

At the top of the stairs, Becca headed down the west hall, past the library to her great-grandmother's bedroom. The old chamber was dark and gloomy. Becca flung open the heavy brocade curtains and unlatched the window to let the air rush into the room. A fetid breeze blew in off the bay, but its moisture dispelled the smoke that had seeped beneath the door and had been trapped inside. In the backyard a jenny wren dove at the feeder with a strip of a palm frond swinging from her beak. She dropped it in a pile at the edge of the feeder. Becca watched as the bird poked at the leaves, at the bits of dried fronds quickly and efficiently like a small machine. Then Becca found her clothes on the bed and wiggled into them quickly before anyone could catch her naked again.

When she finished dressing, Becca sat down at the vanity. She felt calm there, sitting on Rebecca's stool, looking at her own reflection in the mirror. She thought of Victor, his raven eyes, the slope of his chin. He had no idea what had happened since the night of the funeral. She wondered if Evan would tell him the truth of his birth. Becca started to brush the tangles from her hair when she heard a faint knock on the door. Before she could answer, Morgan let herself in and closed the door behind her.

The girl hugged Rebecca's diaries against the gauzy dress that had been bleached and starched and hung crisply on her delicate frame. Morgan had washed and brushed her hair until it gleamed silver-gold against her cheeks. Without saying a word, she laid the diaries side by side on the bed. She ran a hand over each one gently, lovingly, as if they were children. Then, as if in a trance, she turned to Becca. "Does Julia know?"

Becca leaned back on the stool, shaken by the queer expression on Morgan's face. "Know what?"

Morgan rested a hand on the second volume. "Who raped her?"

Becca blinked, startled that Morgan, knowing the diaries as she did, would ask such a question. "Of course," Becca said. "The pirate."

"Yes, but did she know him?" Morgan's eyes grew wide, lucent in the dim light. She stared at Becca and shook her head. "Not like that," the girl said. "Not like one knows the day of the week. Or the colors of spring. But like rain coming. By smell."

Becca leaned back again, caught the edge of the vanity to steady herself. *By smell.* The words stampeded her brain. She stared at the bed, at the diaries laid out like two small bodies. She pictured her grandpa Dan staggering into her room, his face a mass of scars and beads hanging from his belt. "Yo ho, sweetheart!" he'd greeted her. And Becca had screamed because the pirate's hair had been too black, and he smelled dank like a root cellar. She gripped the edge of the stool.

"Like rain coming," Morgan said. "She knew him."

In that instant, Becca felt the room shift. Finally the god of all gods had called *halt!* and leveled the house that had been set at a tilt ever since she could remember. Because Becca recognized the voice, she did not flinch, just as her mother had recognized the pirate thirty-seven years ago and did not scream.

Morgan crossed the room and thrust the second volume into Becca arms. "Julia knows," she said, "and always did."

Becca watched Morgan slip out the door, leaving her alone with the diaries. She left the journal on the vanity and slowly crossed the room, turning on the Tiffany lamp that hung over the desk. When she lowered her body into the Chippendale chair, the image of the pirate she'd always imagined in her mother's bedroom mingled with the bawdy laughter of her grandpa Dan. She clutched the arms of the chair. She rocked back and forth and cried out, immediately covering her mouth to stifle the scream.

When she quieted, Becca gazed around the empty room. The thought of her mother left curled up and bleeding and bearing the seed of her own father, inflamed Becca with a disgust so hideous and malignant that she sat rocking in the chair, holding her middle as it burned white ash to dust and threatened to destroy her, even as the flames in her mother's fireplace threatened to destroy the entire house.

The room had grown dim except for the fractured glow of the Tiffany lamp. Becca stopped rocking and sat perfectly still as the dark knowledge seeped into her bones. She had no idea where she would go now or what she would do. Every path she'd taken had been blocked by some force greater than her own. She covered her face and realized there was nothing left. A scattering of black-and-white spots floated before her eyes. She blinked repeatedly, but the darkness rolled in. As she moved through the void, a vast emptiness embraced her, and Becca understood she'd arrived within the dark womb of all creation.

But this time she didn't cry out, didn't flinch. She just let the void lead her, floating, weightless until, across the room, a gust of wind flung the window wide open. Rain blew in and splattered the brocade curtains. As the torrents splashed against the oak floor, she felt a peculiar flutter, almost a tickle moving deep inside her. Becca held her breath and imagined her child swimming in its dark pool, untouched and innocent. In that moment, gratitude welled up within her. The quickening had stirred something deep inside her, and she knew it was too late to end her baby's life.

CHAPTER 29 ✳ Blue Heat

JULIA PRESSED THE FIRST VOLUME of Rebecca's diary to her chest and
read.

> Come back.
> Before you get to the king tree, come back.
> Before you get to the peach tree, come back.

She loved the old chants of the Seminole medicine men, imagined
their high-pitched flutes and feathered fans as they waved them over their
dying elderly. She laid her head back against the satiny quilt of the Queen
Anne chair. She didn't know what a king tree was, but she imagined it as a
mammoth tree with fine white blossoms. Maybe a dogwood. A magnolia.

Other Indian lullabies, rounds, and ditties from the diary floated
through her head.

> You day-sun circling around
> You daylight circling around
> You night-sun circling around
> You, you, you ...

She let the rhythms run freely through her brain, the tempo so soothing,
hypnotic. The chants alone did not captivate her but instead, what it was
she searched for within them. Something like the locked pattern of a

mother's voice to her babe, a woman easing another into childbirth, or the wrinkled soul finally perished and laid to the ground—to what? Rot?

Something, something. Julia searched.

She'd been waiting a long time. Not so long as a life, a chant would tell her. But as long as *her* life. Every day. And her mind kept spinning, kept searching the lullaby or the words within a diary for the answer that would filter through and fall like manna into her hands. She pulled the second volume of Rebecca's diary out from under the skirted chair and held them both in her lap.

She does believe. She does.

> You daylight circling around,
> You night-sun circling around,
> You, poor body, circling around,
> You, you, you …

She did not want to admit she was weary. Did anyone think Julia was weak? No, no, and no.

But her head felt bloated, heavy with the blue heat that comes before the rain. She had pointed it out to Niobe, the two of them standing at the window while the thunderheads gathered in the east. "There," she said. "Do you see it? It's a dark bean blue."

"Like a sapphire, Miss Julia?"

"No, darker. And dull."

"A river stone?"

"Yes, but blue, blue."

"Like a robin's egg?"

"For God's sakes, Niobe. Aren't you listening to me?"

When the blue heat comes, she closes the windows, pulls the blinds. Sometimes she crawls into bed, draws the pillow over her face. But today she sits waiting for it. She will not back down. Because she believes the weariness would break like sunlight through blue heat if she could just see, just know, that the child she conceived at sixteen knew her.

Before, she thinks.

Before.

You, poor body, circling around,
You, wrinkled age, circling around,
You, spotted with gray, circling around
You, you, you ...

Come back.
Before you get to the king tree, come back.
Before you get to the peach tree, come back.
Before you get to the orange tree, come back ...

CHAPTER 30 ✳ Lost in the Belly
of the House

With a hand pressed against the foyer wall, Natalie could feel the entire house shake as the man from Eden's Lift Company banged away at the elevator that was stuck between the floors. He'd come through the house earlier, dragging a ladder, ropes, toolboxes, rubber tubing, and strand wire, and plopped them down in a heap next to the elevator door.

"I'll have her humming in a wink," he'd said and curled his upper lip just like he did when Natalie greeted him at the front door. There he'd thrust his hand out. "Gus Gustafson from Eden's," he said. "You got one hanging, do you?" He'd waddled through the marbled foyer, following Natalie into the hall. "Let's take a look-see."

He flicked on a flashlight that was chained to his belt and shined the beam into the shaft. "Probably the traveling cable," he'd said. He was bent low at the hips, so his bulging middle drooped over his knees. "Could be broke. But I can't tell from here." His lip shot up. Big, chunky teeth glistened in the light. "Could be the pit needs cleaning. I'll have to climb up and check her out."

That was half an hour ago. The banging started just after Kurt, Morgan, and Becca had left for the girl's grandmother's funeral. "You're sure you won't go?" Becca had asked, searching the hall closet for an umbrella. She wore the same black dress she'd worn to Daniel's funeral. Natalie thought it looked suspiciously like a bathing suit cover-up.

"Oh, no. You go on," she said. "I'll stay here and keep an eye on Mr. Gustafson." Natalie shooed them out the front door. She'd been to enough funerals. Besides, she didn't know Evan's mother, didn't know anything about the woman except she'd died sitting on the front porch rocker. Imagine! The woman's feet turning black beneath her skirt. And only sixty-five, a year older than herself. Who ever thought porch sitting could be so treacherous?

Natalie trudged back into foyer, where the house continued to vibrate with a clanging that shook the walls. She marched down the hall to the elevator door, which opened in a swish. She poked her head inside. "Mr. Gustafson," she called. The shaft was dark except for a glint of light shining from his belt. When her eyes adjusted, she spotted him wedged between the elevator and the shaft. "Mr. Gustafson!"

"Yep," he hollered and flashed his light in Natalie's face.

"Is everything all right?"

"The cable's busted." He pointed his flashlight upward. "And the support bracket's bent. Just straightening it out."

Natalie squinted, but the only thing she could make out was Mr. Gustafson's bulging middle lodged between the elevator car and the shaft.

"A new cable and some grease and she'll be purring again," he called. This time Natalie caught a glimpse of his teeth glaring down at her.

Natalie left the elevator door half open. She would check on him later after she'd climbed the stairs to Kurt's room. Ever since Daniel's funeral and the day Julia threatened to burn the house down, Kurt had been acting peculiarly; not solitary or with his usual sour attitude. Instead he was oddly gregarious. Yesterday, right after the doctor said his chest wound had healed, he'd gone looking for a job! Then he found one, down at Streb's Meat Market, working for old man Harney, carving up pigs and sides of beef into chops, steaks, and tenderloins. Well, it wasn't law school, as Natalie had hoped, but neither was he hanging around Kennedy Boulevard at the blood bank, picking up a few dollars to hustle a six-pack of beer or God knows what else he hustled on those corners.

Natalie clasped the banister and took the first steps slowly. The staircase quivered, and Natalie imagined Mr. Gustafson like the pimento of an olive, stuffed between the shaft and the elevator car. But with any luck, by the time she'd found the diaries in Kurt's room and read what she imagined Becca, Julia, and Kurt had already read, the new cable would be installed, and this trip up the stairs would be her last.

Once in the east hall, Natalie peeked into Julia's room. She sat in the Queen Anne chair facing the bay. "Reading?" Natalie asked.

Julia held up a paperback book. "Kurt gave it to me. It's odd, but good." She turned to Natalie. "What's all the noise?"

"It's the elevator man. Fixing the cable." With that, Natalie closed Julia's door and hurried around the corner, down the west hall to Kurt's room.

She flung the door wide open. Natalie peeked in at perfectly made beds and pillows fluffed so pertly that for an instant, Natalie thought Niobe had been up to straighten the room. But that was impossible. Niobe would be downtown by now, sitting in Dr. Moyer's office with Eula. Earlier this morning, she'd shown Natalie the string of raised flowerettes that crawled up the insides of Eula's arms.

"Do they itch?" Natalie had asked, running her fingers over the bumps.

"No'm," Eula said. "But they tingle a little."

Natalie had made the appointment and called for a cab that was honking on the drive within ten minutes. "What about breakfast?" Niobe said, guiding Eula down the front steps.

"Go on," Natalie said, waving them down the stairs.

Kurt had fried the bacon while Becca squeezed the oranges for juice and Natalie scrambled the eggs. Then Kurt fixed Julia's tray. He slipped outside to the back garden and clipped a white rose from a scraggily bush that had perked overnight from the rain. Filling the rosebud vase with water, he asked Becca if she wanted him to take her to the funeral.

Becca glanced at Natalie, who shrugged because she couldn't imagine why Kurt wanted to attend a funeral for an old woman he never knew.

"What about your job?" Becca asked.

"I haven't started yet," he said and hoisted Julia's breakfast tray on his shoulder. Then he left the kitchen, climbing the stairs to Julia's room. After he'd set the tray on his mother's desk, he must've gone to his own room, dressed for the funeral, and made his bed. Natalie smoothed the coverlet. *Where did he learn to make a bed like this?*

The windows overlooking the backyard were open, and rain drizzled in on the sill. On the desk, sitting next to a new stack of books, Natalie spotted the two volumes of Rebecca's diaries, lying out as pretty as you please! She picked up the second volume and ran her fingers over the leather's buttery texture. When the diaries went missing from her closet, she'd written Daniel a note and asked him to find the diaries and bring them to her. Knowing that she wanted them, how could he have given them to Julia? She pulled out the desk chair and sat down. Forgive him? Why should she? Because he was dead? Well, whose fault was that anyway? Not hers. And she said it out loud: "Not mine."

The banging in the center of the house had stopped. Natalie placed one hand on the diary and listened. Could the elevator be fixed already? Outside the rain thickened. It blew past the curtains and onto the wooden floor. Natalie eased out of the desk chair and closed the windows. Rain battered the glass. Quickly Natalie sat down at the desk and flipped through the diary to the page that Becca had read the night of the stakeout.

> *… and there was in the hall, a terrible racket of screams, and crying and fighting going on. I rushed from my room to see Natalie flailing wild arms and fists against Daniel's chest. "Could have been!" Natalie screamed. "She's in there curled*

up and bleeding. And you say, Could have been!" Natalie
kept beating at his chest.

"Go find him then," she said. "Go find the filthy pirate
and string him up!"

Natalie read the words again—her words. That night coming out
of Julia's room, looking for Daniel, she'd seen him stumbling from the
bathroom with his pants unzipped. He grinned at her. "Yo ho ho!" he said
and twirled the beads that hung from his waist. And yes, she'd told him
Julia was curled up and bleeding in her bed, and she did beat his chest,
but what Rebecca failed to record was that Daniel kept grinning, kept
howling his pirate chant because he was too drunk to comprehend what
had happened that night in his daughter's room.

Natalie squeezed the diary until her knuckles blanched. Her breathing
rattled as if the moist air filled her lungs. She felt like she was drowning.
Then she shook off her right shoe and examined her foot. The toes were
bright pink but not purple, and thank God, not even close to black. She
leaned back in the chair and drew in one long breath. Why should she
forgive Daniel? But the kicker was—and she knew this, even as she knew it
the day she told Daniel Julia was pregnant—that until now, she'd forgiven
him everything. His gambling, drinking, late nights out, shady business
deals, and even those Havana women who draped silk scarves over their
naked shoulders. She pressed her palm to her chest.

Why? Because she'd thought it was love.

But looking back on those nights he'd crawled into their bed and
awakened her with his mouth on her breast, teasing her with his tongue
as it slid down her belly, past her navel to the soft folds between her legs,
maybe it wasn't love at all. Maybe she'd been possessed with him, dizzied
with the compelling desire to keep him bound to her, keep him coming
back in spite of where he had been, because no matter how many women,
or how much gin he consumed, she could find a way to excuse him.

Was that love? Maybe.

Natalie puzzled how curiously the behaviors of love mirror obsession. For wasn't she the doting wife? The forgiving one? And faithful? Yes, all of those. But had she acted out of love or pure fear of losing what she could not bear to lose? Then, because she was sixty-four years old and had experienced most things, including the treachery of porch sitting, she wondered if it made any difference. Either way she would have become Daniel's wife.

Natalie turned the pages of the diary and gazed down at her feet. Now that Daniel was gone (except for the few ashes she'd pinched into her jeweled pill box) and Salazar had not asked her to come down to the precinct for fingerprinting, the buzzing in her brain had stopped, flown off like a wild bird spirited into night. Natalie was clear-headed now simply because Daniel was dead.

So why should she ever forgive him again?

The house was unusually quiet. Natalie pictured Mr. Gustafson wedged between the elevator car and shaft, perhaps threading the new cable into place. The rain beat rhythmically against the windows. Natalie leaned forward in the desk chair and flipped through the pages of the diary. After Daniel's funeral, when Natalie climbed the stairs to Julia's room and saw Kurt on the bed holding the diaries, she thought Julia was the one who'd found them in Natalie's closet. But was that like Julia? Well, no, but then whoever thought she could turn against her own son—or threaten to burn the house down? Wasn't Julia capable of almost anything? So after everyone went downstairs and Kurt rehung the door, Natalie stepped inside her daughter's bedroom and flipped the lock behind her.

Still in her dressing gown, Julia stood by the window gazing out at the bay.

"It's over," Natalie said.

Julia did not turn but sighed wearily, her hand clutching the wooden frame of the window. "He's gone?" Julia asked.

Natalie leaned against the Queen Anne chair. She'd expected some show of grief—muffled screams, whimpering, or dry, coughing sobs. But when Julia turned to Natalie, her face was as tranquil as bay water after the wind died.

"Good," Julia said.

Is that what she said? Or had Natalie imagined the word slipping off Julia's tongue and echoing through the room? For wasn't "good" an odd thing to say about a father's death? Especially about a father who'd loved her so completely, so dearly that Natalie knew for certain the last thing on Daniel's mind before his body hit the bay was Julia.

Did that disturb Natalie?

No, not in the sense that after Julia's horror with the Gasparilla pirate, Daniel felt a responsibility toward Julia and showered her with jewelry, flowers, and Japanese silks—for those gifts were hardly compensation for Daniel's inability to track down the pirate and bring him to justice. But concerning the time Daniel spent with Julia up in her room, reading to her, singing to her, coercing her to come down to the back garden and see for herself the gardenias in bloom—that vigilance had more than once shaken Natalie. In the face of all that, what Natalie feared most was not losing Daniel to his gambling, drinking, or womanizing, but the fact that she'd lost him to their own daughter.

This was why, after Julia answered "Good," to Daniel's dead body lying rotten in a closed casket, Natalie asked her how she'd found the diaries.

"They were here," Julia said, pointing to the Queen Anne chair. "One morning when I got up."

"Recently?"

"Maybe a week ago," Julia said. "Maybe less."

Natalie knew then, by that simple act of bringing the diaries to their daughter, that Daniel's loyalties belonged first to Julia.

And that Natalie could not forgive.

She leaned over the desk to examine the pages Becca had read the night of the stakeout. Natalie thumbed through the entries concerning the Ferrettis, the Connecticut family who was supposed to adopt Julia's son. She ran her finger down to the date, November 13, where she reread: *The baby cannot be adopted out. Julia's mental health hinges precariously. She refuses to come out of her room, refuses friends, and will not even see her father …*

Natalie twisted her hands in her lap. They should never have taken the baby away from Julia! Couldn't they see that? But Daniel couldn't face the ridicule, the shame. "What would the town say?" he'd asked.

Natalie lifted her fingers from the page and continued reading about the dream Rebecca had the night before Daniel decided to find the descendants of the Samuel Westcott family.

Natalie glanced up at the window, at the rain pounding the glass. She wondered if Mr. Gustafson could be finished. Natalie read on in a rush.

November 19

> *Daniel has found the descendants of the Samuel Westcott family living in a bungalow in Seminole Heights.*

November 21

> *Sister Cecilia will drive the child and his nurse to the station tomorrow. In two days Daniel and I will pick him up and send the nurse back to Connecticut. We will drive out to the house on Powhatan and Seminole and offer the woman (a granddaughter of Samuel's, I think) a substantial allowance to care for the child. Julia is not improved. If she continues to worsen, we may have to bring the baby to her. Would that work? How can we know? But how can we watch her sink deeper into the quagmire without doing anything to help her? Perhaps we were wrong to separate her from the child. But*

*then, maybe it's just post-delivery blues, intensified because
of Julia's young age and the brutal conception.*

November 24

> *The woman took the child. I thought to tell Natalie, but
> Daniel insisted against it. Why burden her further? And I
> suppose he's right, for Natalie is hopeful today. Let her be,
> Daniel said. And maybe Julia will pop out of this just fine.
> Then he said—How much can a mother take? And thank
> God Samuel Westcott's granddaughter is a good woman. I
> don't think she did it for the money. Daniel and I agree she
> did it out of appreciation. For where would she be if Silva
> hadn't rescued her grandfather? But she's not to tell a soul.
> And today Julia's slightly improved. She dressed this morning
> for the first time in weeks. And for now, we will tell no one.*

Natalie dog-eared the page before closing the diary. That's what she
wanted to read, and if there was more, she no longer wanted to know.
She pushed out of the desk chair and stood up. Her head swooned at the
thought of Julia's son living in a house on Powhatan and Seminole, just a
few miles from them. Before Natalie left the room, she tore a small portion
of paper off a notepad and jotted down the address. She folded the paper
and slipped it into the warm crevice between her breasts.

In the hall Natalie checked her feet. Her toes were swollen in the low
pumps, but they shone pink—the right color for feet. She stopped in front
of Julia's room, where the glass knob dangled like a daisy on a broken stem.
Feeling the knob limp in her hand, she imagined Julia knew—just like
Becca and probably Kurt. But in Julia's state, what was comprehensible?

At the end of the hall, Natalie knocked on the elevator door. "Mr.
Gustafson, are you finished?" She tugged on the door, but it stuck. She
knocked again and then resigned herself to using the stairs. By the time
she reached the second landing, she hoped to see Mr. Gustafson waiting

for her in the foyer, expecting to be paid. But when she stepped off the staircase onto the marble floor, the house went silent. She hurried to the elevator door that had been left ajar and poked her head inside.

"Mr. Gustafson," she called. The elevator shaft was lightless and dingy, and the acrid odor of detergent grabbed her throat. "Hey!" she called again.

When Mr. Gustafson didn't answer, Natalie left the elevator open and rushed out the front door onto the porch. A steady rain fell now, a summer soaker. The Eden Elevator truck was still parked on the driveway, but there was no sign of Mr. Gustafson. Just as Natalie turned to go back into the house, she saw Victor Ramirez across the Bayshore, pacing into the wind toward Howard Avenue. With his head thrust down and his hands shoved into his pockets, he took about twenty steps, turned, and walked back. Natalie slipped behind a column to watch him. Then suddenly, without looking, he crossed the boulevard, causing a melon truck to swerve into another lane. Once in front of the house, he ran up the stairs, his black hair straggly from the rain. His white shirt was drenched, and the way it clung to his chest, Natalie thought she could see the vertical scar that split his body in half. She said his name, but he didn't hear her. He stood, his eyes transfixed on the front door as if contemplating whether or not to ring the bell.

"Victor," Natalie said again.

This time he spun around and blinked at her. His eyes were puffy like Kurt's after a long night out.

"Mrs. Westcott." He stumbled over a wicker chair, knocking the cushion onto the porch.

"Sorry," he said, bending to pick it up. "I'm so sorry."

Natalie eyed him. "What're you doing here?"

Victor's dark eyes beamed right through her. "I wanted to talk to Becca."

When Natalie said she wasn't home, he turned to leave. "No, wait," she pleaded and grabbed hold of his arm. "May I give her a message?"

Victor gazed down at his feet. "I behaved badly," he said. "I came to apologize."

"Well, come in and wait," Natalie said. "She'll be home soon."

"Oh no." He turned to leave. "I'm sure she doesn't want to see me." With that he took off down the stairs. He pulled his collar up around his neck and dodged the four lanes of cars to get back to the walkway. Then he picked up his pace and headed toward downtown, leaving Natalie alone on the porch. She didn't know what had happened between Becca and Victor, but she could guess.

Natalie wiped her feet on the Oriental rug and crossed the foyer to the elevator. Looking into the blackened shaft, she remembered Mr. Gustafson saying something about a cleaning a pit. Could he have fallen into it? She was about to call for him again when she heard Niobe and Eula coming through the front door. They stood in the foyer, running their hands down their arms and legs, shedding water like garments.

"It's a frog strangler out there," Niobe said, slipping out of her shoes. Natalie could not help but notice Niobe's feet, a fine ebony poised against the red and gold rug. They looked strong and slender but just as black as Natalie pictured the old woman's on the porch. Well, what does that mean? Only that Niobe had no need to fear something that was as natural to her as the color of grass.

Natalie stepped into the powder room and grabbed two towels from the cabinet. She handed them to Niobe. "What did the doctor say?"

Niobe wiped the water dripping from Eula's braid onto her neck. "He says she's got some nervous condition he'd never seen before." Niobe pulled a folded piece of paper from her uniform pocket. "He gave us this."

Natalie took the prescription while Niobe fluffed the towel through her hair. "How's the elevator coming?" she asked.

"Almost finished," Natalie said. She hurried the two of them past the elevator into the kitchen. She told them the elevator man was cleaning the pit, that he'd already fixed the traveling cable. "Tea?" she asked them.

Natalie was relieved when Niobe took the kettle and didn't ask another question about Mr. Gustafson, because she didn't want to lie, but neither did she want to inflame Eula's condition by telling her, as far as she knew, the belly of the house had swallowed Mr. Gustafson whole.

Was that absurd? Of course. But then, wasn't it equally bizarre that a woman could die while porch sitting? Or a son could grow up in the same town as his mother and grandmother and never know them? Or in the time Daniel's body was submerged in the bay that another Daniel came home to what, weed the lawn? Fetch the pickled watermelon? Give his daughter her grandmother's old diaries? Natalie dragged a stool from the counter and guided Eula to sit down. She wondered after this summer if there would ever be any event, any chance happening so ludicrous that she could not accept it.

Natalie trudged down the hall to check the elevator shaft once more. She poked her head into the gloomy tube. "Mr. Gustafson," she called. And when her voice echoed back to her, she felt some relief realizing if he'd fallen, she would have found him there at her feet. She shuffled into the living room knowing she would have to call Eden's Lift Company. But what would she say? Yes, he was right there. She'd seen him. Socked in between the elevator car and shaft, banging on the traveling cable, and then poof. Gone! Swallowed up by the belly of the house.

Natalie opened the top desk drawer and rifled through the envelopes, paper clips, a deck of cards, and rubber bands, looking for the piece of scratch paper where she'd jotted down Eden's phone number. For an instant a pounding rattled the house. Natalie stopped her search and listened. The banging faded, and Natalie realized it was her own head pounding, swelling with the humidity and the pelting rain soaking the house. But her brain didn't buzz, didn't hum like the night she stopped Daniel on the stairs and pointed the gun at his heart. In fact, bending over the desk drawer in search of Eden's telephone number, Natalie realized that even the dignified anger that had grown steadily inside her since Daniel's funeral had begun to subside. And why? Because the house had swallowed Mr. Gustafson? Or was it what Daniel had said to Rebecca in the diary?

Let her be, he'd said.

And how much can a mother take?

By not telling her and not giving her the diaries, Daniel had wanted to protect her, just like he wanted to protect her from Rebecca's cruel bribe the day they stood in this same living room forty-four years ago. Could she hold that against him? Natalie continued rummaging through the desk. She was sure another woman could and would have held Daniel accountable for each act of unkindness, unfaithfulness, untruthfulness, for each drunken night, each dollar fooled away, each woman he'd hustled— and perhaps she should've condemned him too, but because she knew without a doubt how he loved her, standing up to Rebecca as he did, and how he'd cried, sincerely regretting the crimes he'd committed, Natalie understood there was a part of Daniel that had been buried deep and unknowable, even to himself.

Natalie closed the top drawer and opened another. Now that Daniel was gone and there was no fury to gather or comfort to gain, how could fear be driving her? No, she would rather believe it was love, an enduring, persistent love. Because she was sixty-four years old and had heard the thoughts of others, seen ghosts rise from the bay and elevator men swallowed up by the belly of the house, why couldn't she call it love? More than anything, as she searched the desk drawers, she felt a certain gratitude that Daniel never committed an act she couldn't forgive. For how could she have endured that?

The phone rang. Even though she stood next to the desk, she let it ring without answering it. Then she heard footsteps across the marble foyer. "Miss Natalie," Niobe said and stopped at the entrance to the living room, "it's for Mr. Gustafson. His boss is calling."

In spite of her practiced speech, Natalie could not talk to Mr. Gustafson's boss. She pressed her hands together. Could it be her fault the elevator man was lost in the belly of the house? Initially she didn't think so, but now that someone was looking for him, and the fact it was her house that had swallowed him, she felt culpable. "Tell him Mr. Gustafson's busy," Natalie said, "cleaning the pit."

Niobe strolled across the living room, her eyes riveted on Natalie. She picked up the phone. "He'll call you back," she said. Then she touched Natalie's shoulder. "You all right, Miss Natalie? You look spooked."

Natalie would not have told her, would not have burdened Niobe or Eula, or even Becca and Kurt, because she believed in carrying her own burdens. But with Mr. Gustafson's truck parked out front and his boss calling, how long could she hide the fact that the elevator man had disappeared?

"He's missing," Natalie said.

Niobe's eyes widened. "Mr. Gustafson?"

"One minute he's banging on the cable, shaking the whole house—then poof he's gone." Natalie stared at her watch. "Been missing over an hour."

Niobe swept up the envelopes from the desk and rubbed the cherry wood with the corner of her apron. "Don't go worrying yourself over no elevator man who should know how to get down out of a house if he can climb up in it." Niobe shook her head. "Like we don't have enough troubles around here without ..."

Just then a crash sounded from the foyer. As Natalie raced through the living room, she pictured Mr. Gustafson falling through the ceiling, spit out like an overripe plum onto the marble floor with the chandelier shattered in bits of glass around him. But when she reached the staircase with Niobe just behind her, she found Eula clutching a feather duster and Rebecca's jade vase in shards at her feet. There, picking up pieces of the gemstone, was Mr. Gustafson!

"I thought she saw me coming with my ladder and box," he said, his big teeth flashing. "She looked right at me." He set the green fragments on the foyer table. "But then going for the front door, she walked right into the tail of my ladder. It jumped her so, she knocked into the table and upset the vase."

Niobe rushed past Natalie. "You all right?" she asked, patting Eula's face. But Eula stood rigid, her mouth open and slightly awry as if her feet were fastened to the spot on the marble.

"I'm terribly sorry," Mr. Gustafson said. "Looks like I scared the bejeesus out of her."

Niobe grabbed Eula's hands and tried to rub the life back into them while Natalie spotted the insides of Eula's arms. "Look!" Natalie said. And standing in the middle of Rebecca's broken vase, Natalie, Niobe, and the elevator man watched as the raised flowerettes disappeared first on Eula's wrists, then vanished up her forearms, all the way to her shoulders.

Niobe stared at Mr. Gustafson. "It was the devil."

When Niobe led Eula through the foyer toward the back hall into the kitchen, Natalie knew it was not the devil Mr. Gustafson had scared out of Eula. She knew the house had become too quiet, too serene for Eula, who had grown accustomed to Daniel's drunken treks up the stairs or Julia's precarious threats. Eula had learned to accept hush-hush babies and babies who were not wanted; she was adept at supplying a lap, a bottle, a chest of polished silver in a time's pinch, a starched shirt, or a row of beads that had fallen from a Gasparilla gown. She knew how to answer the door and keep Sophia Myers entranced with compliments on her snakeskin shoes or the color of her hair, without ever letting on that Julia was upstairs delirious again or that Daniel, shuffling up the walkway at 10 a.m., had been out all night. Eula had become a consort, an acolyte in the rituals of the Westcott home, and this morning her unlikely encounter with Mr. Gustafson's ladder was just the kind of jolt she needed to shock the creeping rash from her body. As Natalie climbed the stairs to find her purse to pay Mr. Gustafson, she knew it was not the devil, as Niobe thought, but now that the house had become serene, Eula had acquired a nervous allergy to its peace.

In the time it took Natalie to reach her bedroom and write the check to Eden's Lift Company, Niobe had swept up the broken vase and settled Eula in the guest room downstairs. Mr. Gustafson waited in the foyer, having lugged his ladder, wires, and tools to his truck. When he spotted Natalie descending the staircase, he begged her to try the elevator.

"She's a running beauty," he said. "A real hummer now."

"I know that," Natalie answered. For she'd watched Mr. Gustafson climb into the elevator car and ride to the second floor and back three times without getting stuck. It made sense that he'd slithered his way through the shaft to the top of the elevator car and lowered himself inside, because after he'd replaced the traveling cable, the elevator still didn't run.

"The contact on the door was rusty," he'd said, his upper lip rolled like a sausage. "And you can't run an elevator if the door won't shut."

"I'll ride it later," Natalie said, handing him the check.

Mr. Gustafson stared hard at the floor, ignoring the payment in Natalie's hand. She knew how he felt. Imagine spending three hours preparing a meal and having a guest say "It looks wonderful. I'll eat it later." But the thought of stepping into that tomblike space knowing the traveling cable could burst or the pit become mucked or God forbid the door wouldn't shut tight, and then she'd be the one trapped inside the belly of the house set her teeth on edge.

"I have a condition," Natalie said, and Mr. Gustafson perked up. "A buzzing sort of thing in my head that might worsen if I ride the elevator today."

A smile split Mr. Gustafson's face. He pulled a business card from the pocket of his overalls. "You ride it later," he said. "And call me." He took the check from Natalie, shook her hand and squeezed it until it hurt. "Then you can tell me if it isn't the smoothest, most hummingest ride you've ever had."

The rain had slowed but not stopped. Mr. Gustafson bounded down the front steps, his rotund middle jouncing from side to side. It wasn't until he jumped in his truck and pulled out of the driveway that Natalie remembered he was supposed to call his boss. The least of his worries—and hers, Natalie said to herself and closed the front door. The grandfather clock chimed twice. She shook her head, puzzled. What kind of a funeral lasts four hours?

Natalie shuffled wearily into the living room and lowered her body into the canary-yellow armchair, promising herself she would not fret. Instead she would count her blessings that although her feet were swollen, they were not purple. In spite of what she told Mr. Gustafson, her head did not buzz; a little white lie.

Natalie pressed her hand against her chest and felt the edges of the torn paper prick her skin. She did not drag it out, for she knew what it said. Somehow she felt it belonged there, hidden in the dark folds of her flesh. Julia's first child was here in town. The idea staggered her. She counted back the years. The child would be a grown man now. Oddly she'd never pictured her first grandchild beyond the age of five or six. But a hundred times, she'd imagined Julia's son a plump-faced boy with tawny hair and sparkly, round eyes, chasing a cocker spaniel puppy through a fenced backyard with clumps of snow still clinging to the ground. On Christmas morning, she'd pictured him dressed in red, footed pajamas standing on the staircase in awe of his presents beneath the tree, because she always believed the Ferrettis were good, gracious people who wanted a child so desperately they'd waited years to adopt just this one.

Now that child would be thirty-six come November. For all she knew, she'd seen him dropping a penny in the gumball machine at the grocery store or singing in the church choir or chasing a pirate in the Gasparilla parade to collect beads, perhaps now for his own children.

Natalie pressed her feet hard against the floor, feeling the wood solid beneath her. She was surprised but not entirely overwhelmed, because now that the elevator was no longer stuck between the floors, she'd gained new footing. Not the fleeting kind of peace that came at the end of a day's work well done, but the unremitting calm that seeped in slowly, year after year. A gift? Not really. But more simply she imagined that's what remained when one ceased to worry—when one let go, gave up. Out of laziness? Oh no, but the fired knowledge that whatever came, whatever was given would be met with a certain graciousness, an acquired amount of acceptance that this one, Natalie, had cultivated for sixty-four years. And that she should be the one to utilize the white lie to shield a child or protect a man's pride and forgive him as many wrongs as he could possibly surrender. Even that—not knowing for certain in her heart of hearts if she acted out of love or pure fear, that she could still lay her body down night after night in the hope that just the act would make it true—was reason enough that this Natalie was touched by the fairest tip of an angel's wing.

Did she know that?

She knew only, as she leaned her head against the pillowed back of the armchair, that Becca, Kurt, and Morgan had come home from the funeral, because she heard them talking first in the hall and then the foyer.

"The elevator's been fixed?" Kurt asked, gliding into the living room.

"A new traveling cable and new contacts for the door," Natalie said. She sat up in the chair. "She's humming."

Kurt smiled. "Humming?"

Becca slid by Kurt and bent to kiss her grandmother. "You look so tired, Nattie. Did you get lunch?"

Natalie glanced at her watch. It was already past three, but she had no intention of telling Becca she'd skipped lunch, any more than she would tell her about the elevator man, Eula's allergy, or Rebecca's broken vase.

"I'm fine," Natalie said, and she said it convincingly, because she wanted to hear about the funeral. "The poor woman."

"She looked beautiful today." Becca squeezed Natalie's hand. "She really did."

"But it was such a long funeral, wasn't it?"

"We went back to the house," Kurt said.

"The neighbors brought over a ham, a turkey breast, and some salads—you know," Becca said. "Cakes and cookies." She wrapped her arm around Morgan, who appeared waxy and sullen in her black dress.

Natalie eyed the girl. She knew they were keeping her for a while until Evan could be cleared—hopefully not with her own fingerprints on that gun. But Natalie wouldn't think about that now. She studied Becca. "Did you eat on the porch?"

"For heaven's sake, Nattie, some of us did."

"Not the ones who knew, I bet," she said, sinking into the cushions.

"It's a small house," Kurt said "Well, not terribly small. But not everyone could fit inside." Kurt slipped out of his jacket. "It's in the Heights."

"Oh?" Natalie said.

"In Seminole Heights," Kurt said. "On the corner of Powhatan and Seminole."

Natalie gripped the arms of the chair. "Where?" she asked. "Where did you say it was?

Powhatan and Seminole?"

Becca clasped Natalie's hand. "You know the house, Nattie? Do you?"

CHAPTER 31 ✳ Ashes to Sea

On the morning of July 8, the sun rose high above the water, and an eager wind teased the half-hoisted mainsails of sloops and yawls preparing for the flotilla to scatter Daniel's ashes across Hillsborough Bay. The entire Krewe of Gaspar had turned out for the event, some dressed in their pirate regalia. As preparations were made, the unbridled excitement that swept through the Tampa Yacht Club was more aligned to a merry excursion than the solemn crossing to spill the last of their Gasparilla King into the bay. What galvanized their passion was the pronouncement in the Saturday morning *Tribune* that the investigation of Daniel's demise had been closed. Chief Salazar stated that the coroner could not determine the cause of death. In light of that, there was not enough evidence to arrest and try, much less convict a suspect on such circumstantial grounds.

Waiting on the dock, Buddy Myers, his father Jack, Mr. Jeske, and Hank Poppy read the article once and tossed the newspaper into the trash. "That's rubbish," Mr. Jeske jeered. Flies flew up from the garbage can, which stank with rotting fish guts.

"Downright trickery," agreed Jack Myers, nursing a milk punch. The men were waiting for Poppy's crew to finish stocking the Bertram for the flotilla. Hank Poppy slugged back a straight scotch and called Salazar a lily-livered pussy.

What most pirates failed to see in the newspaper that morning was another smaller article, tucked away in the Metro section. The notorious smuggler known as Cuda, who was captured near Hurricane Hole with six thousand pounds of marijuana, had been sentenced to eighteen months in prison, with possible parole for good behavior. But even those pirates who read the article didn't connect the smugglers with Daniel's death. Only Salazar, Carlos Mendoza, Victor, and Captain Mortensen suspected Cuda's hand in the untimely death of Tampa's oldest pirate king.

In the Westcott home over breakfast that morning, Kurt, Becca, and Morgan were cheering and high-fiving each other. Chief Salazar's announcement had come just in time for Evan to join the flotilla. Becca took Nattie's hands and danced with her around the kitchen counter. Even Julia had promised to attend the ceremony, provided she could ride with Kurt on the *Sea Booty*. Morgan squealed and joined Becca and Nattie in the dance. She wanted to go on the *Sea Booty* too! Natalie tripped over her feet trying to keep up with the girls, who tugged on her like a pair of excited puppies. Two days ago, when Nattie came to Becca asking about Julia's infant who was taken to the house on Seminole and Powhatan, Becca told her that child was Evan Stone. Natalie's eyes lit up. "Evan, really! He's a fine young man!" she said and clasped her hands together. "That's why he can play the piano like a master."

By the time the Westcotts arrived at the yacht club, waiters dressed all in white met them just inside the front doors. They carried trays of mimosas, Bloody Marys, and champagne. Becca and her mother led the family through the long entry hall, while Kurt followed with Natalie and Morgan. Becca scanned the room, awed at the number of guests who had come. She was grateful that Nattie had warned them to dress up in spite of the fact they'd be boarding boats and yachts soon.

Julia appeared regal in a pair of chartreuse silk pants and a multicolored blouse painted with peacock feathers. Niobe had brushed Julia's hair until it gleamed and then tied her locks back in a wide bow that graced the nape of her neck. Every head turned to watch Julia Westcott glide through the dining room. When she passed the buffet table laden with silver servers that would be filled with shrimp creole, bacon-wrapped scallops, and yellow rice for the luncheon following the ceremonial cruise, Becca could hear the fleeting whispers as Julia passed by—*It's been years! She looks stunning. Not sick at all.*

Nattie tapped Becca from behind. "Daniel would love this," she said, her eyes wide. She sidled up next to Becca, her head swiveling to take in the elaborate place settings, complete with tropical flowers set in miniature pirate ships that centered every table. A sense of relief flooded Becca that Nattie appeared serene this morning. Yesterday, their attorney called and said Daniel had an insurance policy that would pay Natalie one million dollars. Nattie had hung up the phone, speechless. After a while, she said something about fixing up the house, how it was left up to her now. Becca watched as her grandmother scanned the dining room. She carried a wicker basket that Niobe had found in the garden house. Eula had lined the basket with white linen, and together she and Niobe had poured the grainy ash into the wicker from a thick, plastic bag the funeral home had sent over. Then they covered the contents with a silk scarf.

Once outside the double french doors that led to the open patio, Nattie was immediately surrounded by her old friends. They were all decked out in long, flowing skirts, as was Natalie. Becca recognized Sophia Myers, Georgia Meeker, and Helen Bates, but a couple of faces escaped Becca's memory. Nattie hugged the wicker basket to her chest and chatted on with the best of them.

Just as she passed the cocktail tables, Becca spotted Buddy in a cherry-red golf shirt and a pair of khaki pants, weaving his way through the crowd. When he caught up to them, he slapped Kurt on the back and then took Julia's hand and kissed it gallantly. *Such an Eddie Haskell!* Becca thought.

"And who's this young lady?" Buddy asked about Morgan. His eyes flashed at Kurt. Becca groaned inwardly. She didn't trust Buddy's reaction to the fact Morgan was Evan's niece. She suspected Buddy was one of the culprits behind the shenanigans being played on Evan. Becca placed a calm hand on Kurt's arm.

Kurt got the message. "She's a friend of mine," he said. Morgan leaned into him as if she could hide beneath the cover of his arm. Becca had found an orange sundress in her closet that fit Morgan perfectly. With her pale hair and skin, she looked curiously sweet, like a Dreamsicle.

"You old dog!" Buddy laughed. "Robbing the cradle, aren't ya?"

Morgan slumped lower, and Kurt hugged her in close. Becca understood that the chattering people, flitting around in jewels and pirate garb and drinking champagne at ten in the morning were a steep contrast from 1510 Powhatan.

Buddy flung his arms out wide. "We have room for all of you on the *Rod Father.*" He bounced at the knees and pointed down the docks to the forty-two-foot Trojan Sea Voyager. Buddy's father had named the new yacht after the mobster movie that had just hit town a few months ago. The timing had been impeccable. "She's fueled up and polished—ready to lead the flotilla," Buddy said.

Kurt eyed Becca, and Morgan held on tighter.

Then Julia stepped forward. "We'll be riding on the *Sea Booty,*" she said, as majestically as if she'd announced they'd be mounting the royal float on Gasparilla Day. "My father would be pleased to know I'll be on his boat." Julia stared out over the water and then back at Kurt. "Our King Daniel would be proud of how we've taken over the helm of this family, right, son?"

Kurt grinned from ear to ear. "Right, Mom."

With that, Julia floated across the patio toward the docks with Kurt and Morgan at her heels.

Buddy peered after them. "Wow, your mom's a stunner. Where's she been hiding all these years?"

Becca blinked back the tears that stung her eyes. *In her room,* Becca thought. But now, as she watched her mother mingling with her subjects once more, Becca realized Julia was a wild bird, free to live her own life exactly as she pleased. The sight of her mother and Kurt sharing this day was more than Becca ever hoped possible. Knowing what her mother had endured, Becca felt utter awe and respect as Queen Julia greeted the pirates and ladies alike with an elegance found only in royalty. As Julia stepped onto the docks, Becca wondered how much her mother had deduced from the diaries. Surely she knew Evan was her son. Or did she?

Just then Natalie joined them. "Good morning, Mrs. Westcott," Buddy said in his sweetie voice. "I'm happy you're here. We should get going." He smiled and offered to carry Natalie's basket, but Nattie ignored him, hugging the basket to her chest.

"It's Daniel," Becca said.

Buddy stepped back. "Oh, of course."

A bawdy breeze kicked up from the bay and blew the teal chiffon of Becca's skirt tight against her knees. Nattie had found this dress in Julia's closet. The full skirt, complete with two side pockets, hid everything Becca wanted to conceal. She sucked in the salty air. "My grandfather would say it's a wind biting day with fury enough to dare the sails." Becca could hear Daniel's blustery laugh, the merry clap of his hand across a knee, the glug-glug of a rum bottle emptying as he threw back his head. She gazed out over the bay, where a gull glided close to the water in search of food. She would never hold her grandfather in the same esteem that she had as a child. But knowing how her mother had braved this day so courageously, Becca would do her part to honor her granddad.

"And no rain," Buddy added. "Do you want to board now?"

Becca nodded to Buddy and glanced down the docks to the motor yachts buzzing with music and laughter. Tunes floated through the air— everything from "Moon River" to "Riders on the Storm." In the first slip, Becca spotted the Wilsons' boat captain climbing the main mast *of A Lil' Nauti* in a pair of frayed shorts and a half pint of rum sticking out of his back pocket. On deck, Betty Wilson was serving mimosas to the

Williamses, while one slip down on the *For Play*, Helen Bates handed out fresh daisies to everyone who passed. The wind gusted up again and blew the silk scarf off the top of Natalie's basket. The grainy contents scattered into the air.

"Not yet," Natalie cried. She crouched down to protect the ashes with her body.

Buddy ran back to the tables to pick up a couple of napkins and two spoons. He spread the napkins over the top of the basket and weighted them with the silverware. "That should fix it," he said proudly.

Natalie straightened up and adjusted her hat that the wind had set askew. She tucked the basket into the crook of her arm and continued her walk down the pier in front of Becca and Buddy, as if taking the lead in a ceremonial procession.

"It's a fine morning," said Hank Poppy as they passed the *Blew Bayou*.

"Lovely," Natalie answered.

In the next slip down, Dell Williams leaned over the stern of their cabin cruiser. She beckoned Natalie to the yacht. Once Nattie was close, Dell laid a small bouquet of white carnations into the flower basket. Then from the opposite side of the dock, aboard Dr. Bates's *Knot So Fast,* Georgia Meeker held up a bunch of daisies. As Natalie crossed the dock with her head erect and her sure step, Becca marveled at how quickly her grandmother had regained composure. While Georgia Meeker arranged the daisies in Natalie's basket, Becca felt a hand grip her shoulder. She spun around. There was her best friend, Margie.

"I brought you these," she whispered and pushed Buddy aside. She pressed a string of rosary beads into Becca's hand. "Shh," she said and pointed to Natalie. "I was going to give them to you at the funeral, but I didn't want to start a war."

Becca hugged Margie. When Becca's father died, Margie had given her a set of beads and taught her how to pray the Our Father, the Glory Be, and the Hail Mary around the rosary. At her father's funeral she was doing just that when Nattie spotted her. "Where'd you get those?" Becca had claimed them as her own, but Nattie's eyes narrowed and grew black. "They're not yours," she'd hissed, "because *you* are not a Catholic." Then with one swift yank, Nattie ripped the rosary from Becca's hands and they broke, scattering beads all over the floor.

Margie smiled. "I'm on the Saunderses' boat." She turned and waved to a young man who waited for her three slips down on the deck of the *Prize Package*. Then she leaned in close to Becca. "Are you leaving soon?"

Becca shrugged.

Margie peered down at Becca's middle. "What about Adam?" she said under her breath.

"It's over."

Margie's eyes howled, and she gripped Becca's shoulders. "Are you okay?"

"I am," Becca said and smiled reassuringly. Margie promised she'd come over tomorrow. They'd figure everything out then. Becca slid the beads into her skirt pocket. As she watched Margie pass through the crowd, she puzzled how the day felt oddly familiar with the sun's heat weighted against her skin and the smell of sulfur rising from the port.

Becca shielded her eyes from the brightness and squinted down the docks while Nattie continued her walk toward the *Rod Father*. Under the glare of the pirates' eyes and the July sun, Becca felt suddenly absurd and fleeting, in that her grandfather's fate had come to no more than finding a dead fish floating on the water. What did this mean, this life? Or death? Or even the glass rosary hidden in her pocket that was worth no more than a string of pirate beads? Becca felt the rosary cool beneath her fingers. She squeezed a large bead and remembered her father's funeral and how she'd said a prayer on each bead to speed him from purgatory. Was that silly? Maybe, but it'd been comforting to fill her mind with the words, the rhythms of the Hail Mary, the Apostle's Creed, and the conviction that she was doing something to help her father. She squeezed the metal crucifix. At the time, the prayers were better than thinking of her father's body rotting in the satin-lined coffin, or today, imagining her grandfather a fish, washing up on shore to be burned and then thrown back to sea.

Buddy kept a firm grip on Becca's arm and led her down the docks, just a few feet behind Natalie. "She's doing so well," Buddy said, as if the sight of Natalie greeting each guest surprised him. But Becca knew Nattie's procession this morning, and the ceremony of scattering Daniel's ashes on the bay was exactly the kind of distraction her grandmother needed to stave off the grief of Daniel's death.

Two slips down, Buddy's father, Jack, sprayed off the running board of the *Rod Father* with a hose. "Hey!" he called. Buddy waved back. But it wasn't until they passed the Stokeses' cigarette boat that Becca spotted Evan Stone in a pair of blue jeans, leaning against the lamppost at the end of the dock and smoking a cigarette. His white shirt shimmered against the navy water, and he wore a red bandanna tied around his neck.

"What's he doing here?" Buddy hissed.

"I'm sure he's come to pay his respects," Becca said.

"But why?" Buddy asked. "He's got nothing to do with us!"

Becca glared at Buddy. But of course, he knew nothing! Only that Evan had shown up with Hank Poppy's boat drenched in blood on the same day Daniel's body was found in the bay.

"I just want to talk to him," Becca said.

She slid past Nattie who was thanking Edna Saunders for the scones and clotted cream she'd sent over after the funeral. Becca kept walking until she was close enough to touch Evan's arm. He flicked his cigarette into the water. "How's Morgan?" he asked.

Becca pointed midway down the dock. "She's on the *Sea Booty* with my mother and Kurt."

Evan smiled. "She'll love that. I'm ..." He stopped, and Becca saw his body tighten. His eyes grew as dark as the water behind him.

"What?" Becca asked. She spun around and was blinded by a throng of faces that had lined the pier to watch them. An odd silence fell over the docks. The crowd blurred. Becca stood riveted, feeling the tension spin through air as palpable as the wind rushing her skin.

Then, in the midst of the crowd, striding down the pier in a light-blue suit, was Victor. His face appeared calm, but his dark eyes glistened with an intensity that made Becca's knees weak. When he reached them, he handed Becca one red rose.

"It's beautiful," she said, smelling its fragrance. A small envelope was attached to the stem. "I would invite you to join us, but ..."

Victor raised his hand to stop her. "We'll be on my uncle's sailboat," he said. "It's leaving from Davis Island at eleven." He glanced at his watch and then over the bay. "We need to head out." With that, he threw an arm around Evan's shoulders, and together they took off. They didn't hurry or lag. They kept their eyes riveted straight ahead and strolled down the pier. Evan matched his stride to Victor's long, steady gait as best he could, and together they passed the onlookers who gawked at the mismatched pair. As the men swept by, the crowd filled in behind them, jabbering like a flock of gulls over fast-moving prey.

From the deck of the *Rod Father*, Jack Meyers helped Nattie board the Trojan Sea Voyager, while Buddy stood behind her to catch anything that might fall. Then they guided Becca on board. She'd tucked Victor's rose into her other skirt pocket and ran her fingers over the small white envelope. "I wish your mother would've joined us," Jack said. He plopped on a fishing cap to shield his bald head from the sun's glare.

Becca peered down the dock in search of the *Sea Booty*, four slips away. She searched for her mother, but all she could see was Kurt propped at the helm on the fly bridge, ready to go. Becca turned to Jack. "She wanted to ride on my granddad's boat," she said. "It's been a long time."

Jack agreed, and together they settled in on the long cushion that lined the stern of the Trojan Sea Voyager.

"Such a beautiful boat," Becca said, noticing the mahogany planking, teak decks, and trim.

Jack beamed. He'd come from a long lineage of Gaspar royalty. His father, grandfather, and great-grandfathers had all been kings, and his grandmother had been crowned Queen Gasparilla, after the krewe's hiatus following the Great Depression. His daughter would be up for queen next year, and given Jack's popularity, everyone considered it a shoo-in she'd win the crown. After Jack was crowned Gasparilla King last year, he'd bought this new yacht to take his court to the Bahamas on the annual king's trip. He leaned in close to Becca. "This boat was actually fashioned after the yacht used in *Sea Hunt*," he said. "Do you ever watch *Sea Hunt*?"

"Sometimes," Becca said, eyeing him cautiously. She knew Buddy had been pumping his father with rumors about Evan. She shifted her weight uneasily on the cushion and wished they'd get this cruise going. Then she watched her grandmother.

Buddy had settled Nattie in one of the captain's chairs up front. Her feet dangled six inches above the floor, and she resembled a plucky child, anxious for the ride to begin. Sophia Myers sat in the captain's chair next to her. Nattie twirled in the chair. "Let's go!" she shouted.

Jack laughed and got up fast. "Right! We're leading this parade." With that, Jack ordered the captain to start the engines. Then he untied the lines at the stern while Buddy jumped onto the bow and released the lines from the moorings. As the captain backed out of the slip, Jack returned and sat down next to Becca. He picked up his drink and cocked his head toward Natalie. "She could press charges if she wanted to," he said, "with those wounds."

Becca withdrew her hand from the skirt pocket, leaving Victor's note intact. She glared into Jack's eyes. "The coroner doesn't know what caused the wounds."

Jack glared right back. "But what about the cement block tied to his ankle? That screams foul play."

Becca leaned back against the cushion. She knew this Gaspar Don would need a prospect he couldn't refuse. "It's not over," she said and set her arms akimbo. "Salazar has another suspect."

Jack's eyebrows shot up. "For real?"

"Absolutely." Becca peered behind them and watched as the Bateses' forty-five-foot yawl caught the southeast wind with its jib sail. The boat sliced neatly through the water like a fine blade. "It may take some time, but Salazar won't give up," she said. "The truth will be known."

A big grin flashed across Jack's face. "Buddy! Get this young woman a drink." He pointed to the cooler next to Natalie's chair. "We'll toast to that!"

As the motor yacht swung out onto the bay, the engines tapered to a hum. Buddy grabbed Becca a Coke from the cooler, and together the three of them toasted to Salazar, to Daniel, and finally, to justice.

Once they were well out into Hillsborough Bay, a low bray wailed across the water. Becca stood up to see Carlos Mendoza's sixty-foot schooner careening toward them. All five sails were raised. The Mendoza family crest, the American flag, and the new krewe banner flew in blues, reds, and greens. They all shimmered against the cloudless sky. Mario Sanchez's ketch skimmed directly behind the schooner, while a parade of sloops and small motorboats flitted in succession. Becca twirled around to watch the Bateses' yawl, the Saunderses' ketch, and the fine array of sails sweeping the sky like white handkerchiefs puffed against the wind. From where she stood, Becca could see the *Sea Booty*. Her mother and Morgan waved to her from the deck. And behind them came Captain Mortensen in the *Lady Luck*, Hank Poppy in the Bertram, Mr. Jeske in *Meals on Reels*, and the Wilsons in *A Lil' Nauti*. The whole bay pranced with color, music, and motion beneath the bright-blue sky. The flotilla looked just like Gasparilla Day without the pirate ship.

As the boats soared through Hillsborough Bay toward an undefined center, Jack called to his captain to cut the engines halfway between the Tampa Yacht Club and Davis Island.

The engines sputtered, churning water behind the Sea Voyager. The captain maneuvered the *Rod Father* into the center of boats that formed a circle around them. Buddy threw an anchor, while Jack blew into a portable PA to test its power.

One by one the motorboats shut off, leaving only the sound of wind tossing the sails and waves slapping against the boats. From the stern, Becca could see the Mendoza schooner anchored just to the right of them. She spotted Victor talking to Carlos Mendoza. His arm was flung around Victor's shoulders, as if giving him advice. Becca leaned over the back seat and waved to catch his attention, but the roll of the boat unbalanced her. She fell against the rail.

"Whoa, Missy!" Jack said. "No sea legs on you." He laughed. "You'd better sit down." Then he turned on the portable PA that looked a lot like a megaphone. He began welcoming the members of the Gaspar Krewe and the Knights of SantY'ago who had come to pay their final respects to King Daniel. Becca sat on the cushion, her hands thrust into her skirt pockets.

"Daniel was a fine man," Jack bellowed through the megaphone. He turned in a slow, tight circle to reach every listener. "I knew him for thirty-seven years. I sailed with him, fished with him, and crowned him Gasparilla King." Jack's voice boomed over the water. "And I know he's with us today, watching as we gather in this circle." Buddy helped Nattie off the captain's chair and led her to the side of the boat while Jack continued. "And I'm calling for a moment of silence, of prayerful thought, while Natalie, his lovely wife, scatters his ashes over these waters Daniel loved so much."

Natalie started throwing the carnations and daisies from the basket. She tossed the roses, two and three at a time, while everyone applauded. Then Georgia Meeker, aboard the *Knots So Fast* flung daisies into the water, which began a wave from one boat to the next, creating a circle of flowers around the *Rod Father*.

When Nattie finished, she folded back the napkin and stared into the basket. Then she whirled around. "Becca!" she called.

Becca stood up and gripped the railing. She followed it to the middle of the yacht, while the sun flared overhead, suddenly hot. When she reached Natalie, her grandmother handed her the wicker basket. "You do it," Nattie whispered.

Becca dipped into the ashes and tossed a handful over the side, where the wind caught it and blew it back in her face. The ashes fell, alternately smooth and then gritty beneath her feet.

"Lower," Jack said. "Drop them straight down."

Becca grabbed another handful, felt it sift through her fingers. She thought of the ash beneath her feet, the washed-out sockets, the scraped nose and swollen lips, the unidentified wounds in the belly, all spilling into the bay and floating on the water until the waves swallowed them.

Jack edged up next to her. "Here," he said. He positioned the basket on his arm. "You tip it."

Becca gripped the edge of the basket and tilted it forward. The gritty ash poured sand-smooth into the water, while the finer substance floated through the air in smoky gusts like gunpowder from a pirate's pistol. When half the contents were emptied, Becca stepped back and let Nattie tip the remainder of the ashes into the bay.

While flowers drifted away from the boats, an eerie pall fell over the group. Everyone watched as gray puffs hovered above their circle and lifted slowly, southeasterly, until they dissipated into the cloudless sky. For a moment it was silent except for the water lapping up against the boats. Becca started to go back to her seat when a voice broke through the air. She leaned out over the water, and halfway up the mainmast of the *Lobo Marino*, she recognized Carlos Mendoza belting out the first stanza of "The Battle Hymn of the Republic." His explosive voice boomed in a deep, sonorous tone, and soon everyone joined in. The air grew thick with music. Voices filled the spaces between the boats, where puffs of smoke had begun to vanish. The patriotic lyrics washed over the crowd. *Glory, glory, hallelujah!* Pirates and ladies alike gripped hands. They offered smiles, hugs, tears. When the song was over, they stood looking at one another, grateful for the reprieve, for the instant their hearts rose with their voices.

Somewhere an engine started, then another. The Mendozas' schooner pulled in its anchor and circled around the *Rod Father.* Becca stepped back from the edge of the boat. She pulled the rose from her pocket and detached the note. With shaking fingers, she opened the envelope. *This life will ebb and flow in the tide of a day, but here within your hand lies my future in its palm.* Becca glanced up at the schooner, at Victor leaning over the edge, expectant. She pressed the note to her breast and nodded up to him.

Victor circled his fist in the air, and the schooner scudded off toward Davis Island. Becca watched it go. Waiting for the last of the boats to set off for the yacht club, she pressed her bulging middle against the railing. She peered down at the bay, brilliant in the late-morning sun. A veil of ashes mingled with the glittering water. Suddenly it was clear to her that this extraordinary passage—from life to death to life—was the force that held up the world into which all separation dissolved. The rumble of engines revved, and Becca braced herself against the jolt of the Trojan Sea Voyager as it motored back to the yacht club.

CHAPTER 32 ✳ Harmony in
the Flowers

AFTER DANIEL'S LAST CRUISE ACROSS the bay, most of the townspeople
settled back into their summer routines. They shelled the beaches of Indian
Rocks, fished along the causeway, and picnicked beneath the granddaddy
oaks in their backyards. But a few young pirates from the Krewe of Gaspar
held fast to the notion that Evan Stone had dealt their king his last card.
They stalked him.

Chief Salazar paid personal visits to the offenders, threatening to arrest
them, to fine them, or both. He also convinced the Westcott family that
keeping Daniel's involvement with the smugglers a secret would preserve
the family's reputation. He reminded them that what they actually knew
about Daniel's willingness to allow the *Sea Booty* to carry the smugglers'
load was entirely based on Cuda's testimony. Better to let the ash settle
to the sea's bottom, he'd said. Then Salazar promised that given enough
time, even the most irascible pranksters would relinquish their hooks from
Evan's flesh and move on.

But until that time, Evan kept a low profile. He stayed away from the
Westcott Mansion, knowing his presence would only bring them more
trouble. In spite of the harassment, he managed to keep pace with the
drawings on the Sun Coast Building for Victor, who eventually closed
that deal and began construction. When Salazar's prediction began to
materialize, Becca, Victor, and Natalie thought it ironic that the hecklers'
attention turned dramatically from Daniel's demise to the fact that his

granddaughter was seen in town, clearly in a motherly way. For the record, through that summer's end and into September, the Westcott family remained on tenterhooks until emotions simmered down. Everyone, that is, except for Julia. Anyone who passed by the Westcott Mansion late at night and saw the light on in her bedroom at odd hours—one, two, three o'clock in the morning—guessed she struggled with inconsolable grief. Ever since the day the fire broke out, whenever the townspeople drove by the house, they thought about Julia. But leaning against the window frame, watching the headlights whiz down the Bayshore, she wasn't thinking about them.

"Julia? Aren't you sleeping?"

Julia turned to see Natalie poking her head around the bedroom door. "Soon," she said.

"But it's after two."

"Is it?" She settled back in the Queen Anne chair and looked out the window to the lights on Davis Island.

"They're all in," Natalie said. "Even Kurt. He got home half an hour ago."

"Good, that's good."

"To bed then?"

"Yes, yes. I'll go to bed."

Natalie closed the door, and Julia stood up to turn off the light on her bedside table. It was easier to see in the dark. She walked to the window and opened it. The air was balmy, fetid with the smell of seaweed exposed at low tide. She leaned against the casement to wait. She hummed "The Mama Song."

> So, Mother-my-Love, let me take your dear hand,
> We'll walk in a sweet posie-garden,
> Where moonlight and starlight are streaming

> And flowers and birds are filling the air
> With the fragrance and music of dreaming.

When did Julia know? Not at the dinner party. No, not then. And not the day of Daniel's funeral, when she burned the filthy rag in her fireplace. It was after that. After the Indian chants clicked through her brain like a ratchet wheel and the pieces fell into place. In that moment she connected the infant who came by train from Connecticut to the name written in backward on the Westcott family tree. She knew Evan Stone was her last child to come home. The first shall be last. Her mind raced. On a train. Her son. Evan was her son. He came on a train from Connecticut. She peered out over the Bayshore, where an occasional car passed by.

She sat up nights now, looking out across the boulevard to the stone balustrade that separated the walkway from the water. He'd come in the night and lean against the stone rail. Of course, Evan Stone! Evan, her son. He came by train when he was supposed to stay in Connecticut like all the other babies at St. Agnes.

She knew it was he who leaned against the balustrade, because he wore a red kerchief tied around his neck or the white jacket he wore to the dinner party. Natalie said he wore the jacket to Daniel's funeral. No one wears white to funerals. But Evan did. Her son, Evan, wore white.

She'd asked Natalie, "Where's the young man who used to come to the house?"

"Victor?" Natalie said.

"No, the other one."

"I'm sure I don't know."

"And Becca?"

"No."

Only Julia knows.

Evan. He comes late at night, when the moon has already crossed the sky, and the only sound is that of a night bird whistling low in the trees. Julia saw him first by mistake. She sat up in bed, her head swollen from the blue heat. She poured herself a glass of water from the pitcher on the bedside table. She needed her pills. She got up to look for them on her dresser, on the vanity, on the chiffonier. Earlier she'd forgotten to close the blinds, and the lights from the street glared in through the window. *Close them, close them.* So she walked to the window to draw the curtains, and there on the Bayshore, leaning against the balustrade, was a man in a white jacket that appeared luminous beneath the streetlight. The man in white. She'd not known then. But her mind was ever turning. When the ratchet wheel clicked into place, she knew it all instantly.

Evan. On a train from Connecticut to the bungalow on Powhatan and Seminole. The child, Evan, is her son.

He does not come every night, but she waits for him anyway. Sometimes he carries a roll of papers tucked beneath his arm. Sometimes he wears the red kerchief tied around his neck. He leans against the stone rail and looks toward the house. She stands by the window and not near the chair, because with the window open and her head just outside, she imagines they are breathing the same air.

She and her son.

Sometimes when he's out there, she turns on the Tiffany lamp that sits on her bedside table. She can barely see him then. She moves toward the window, the light behind her like a flare. She raises her arms, presses her palms against the casements. She stands there, not seeing him—her son. But she knows he's there, and she knows he sees her.